CAPRICORN CHUCK'S CRUEL WORLD

CAPRICORN CHUCK'S
CRUEL WORLD

STEVE PENDELTON

Charleston, SC
www.PalmettoPublishing.com

Capricorn Chuck's Cruel World

Copyright © 2022 Steven Sevivas

First Edition

Paperback: 978-1-63837-574-6

Hardcover: 978-1-63837-573-9

eBook: 978-1-63837-575-3

For Rupert,
whose loyalty and love is unconditional

To my father, Gus,
who would often talk about writing a novel of his own.
Enjoy, Dad!

DISCLAIMER

Capricorn Chuck's Cruel World is a work of fiction. Any resemblance to actual events or persons, living or dead, is entirely coincidental. Space and time have been rearranged to suit the convenience of the book.

CONTENTS

CHAPTER 1
CAPRICORN MAN
DECEMBER 2001

IT WAS DECEMBER 25, 2001, a wintry afternoon at the Pocomtuc prison facility in Western Massachusetts. Inside the ZX cell block, Officer Rick Guardian was getting ready to make his hourly round to ensure all inmates complied with institutional rules. This particular unruly housing block had 102 inmates and had been a serious ongoing issue for some time. There were numerous fights, drugs, and assaults on staff, and Officer Guardian was having a hard time adjusting.

Ever since he began as an officer in 1997, he had been in trouble with Captain Gavin, including several suspensions for dereliction of duty. Finally, after several warnings from the captain, Rick was put in one of the toughest blocks in the prison – perhaps even in the state – in hopes that he would smarten up or toughen up.

Rick was at the officer's podium, ceaselessly talking, while chaos in the unit ensued. It was nothing new when Rick was on duty.

In the block, only half the cells were supposed to be open between 1:00 p.m. and 2:30 p.m., and the other half of the inmates would be allowed out from 2:30 p.m. to 4:00 p.m. due to how dangerous it could be to have everyone out at the same time. Normally, the atmosphere grew even louder than usual at this time of day because inmates were shouting at the officers to open and close their doors. When Rick was working, the inmates knew he would often let them get away with things that other officers wouldn't, like letting inmates out of their cells to hang out with their buddies from the opposite side of the block, even though he knew he shouldn't. He figured the inmates would take it easy on him if he let them break a few security rules.

Rick's partner for the day, Henry Milinozzo, was just filling in. Everyone called him Milly for short. Even though he had only been an officer for less than a year, he recognized the block was running unusually wild per the allowance of Rick. While all the yelling and screaming was going on, Officer Milinozzo was doing his best to watch the tier for any fights, and Rick was unloading some of his abnormal personal family matters on him.

"You know I have an older brother that's at the medium prison down the hill?" Rick asked Henry.

"No, I didn't know that," Henry responded distractedly, trying his best to keep his attention on the inmates. "Is he a CO or a Sergeant?"

"No, he's an inmate!" Rick said animatedly.

Henry wasn't sure if Rick was pulling his leg.

"An inmate?"

"Oh yeah. He robbed a bank and a couple of drug stores. You know, that kind of stuff."

Henry was in shock, especially because he barely knew Rick. He was uncomfortable with the conversation and also knew they hadn't made a round in the block for a while, which they were supposed to have done every hour.

"Oh Rick, do we need a round?" Henry asked, hoping to divert his attention from the subject at hand.

Rick looked at the log book he had next to him.

"Oh shucks, yeah we're late. The last one we did was over 2 hours ago."

"What, are you kidding me? It's been that long?"

Rick jumped up out of his chair. "Oh, don't worry. It's no big deal, I'll get it."

Rick walked down one side of the tier, looking inside the cells as he passed by them. He was making his way down the tier and inmates kept approaching him, asking silly, nonsensical questions and telling him he was a brilliant officer. Officer Milinozzo was watching him from the podium and couldn't help feeling that something strange was going on in the block. Something was amiss. The inmates seemed to be purposely distracting Officer Guardian. Maybe the inmates on the block actually liked Rick Guardian, but wasn't likely. He looked and acted a lot like a younger version of Don Knotts.

Rick reached the shower stall area and looked inside the ones that were not covered with towels. He turned the corner and was slowly walking back down the other side of the tier looking inside those cells. When he reached cell number 27, the door was wide open but there was a heavy woolen blanket hanging from the top of the doorway covering the entire opening.

As Rick approached the doorway, officers in the neighboring LJ block were watching the ZX block via a live camera feed. The officer in charge, Juan Vidal, could see on his cameras that something was definitely wrong, so he picked up the phone to call next door.

"Hey, what the fuck is going on over there? Your inmates are running around like crazy and you guys have cell doors open on the opposite side," Juan said to Henry.

"Believe me, not my idea. Rick said it was okay, and he's out on the tier now making a round," Henry replied.

Officer Vidal trusted his instincts and knew Rick was a total boob.

"I'm sending the extra roving officer, Dave Loomis, over there now just in case."

"OK, thank you, Juan," Henry said, relieved.

Rick was still stopped at the doorway of cell 27, hesitant to move the blanket. The inmates nearby scattered into various open cells. A convict named Lindsey Higgins lived in cell 27. He was in for the murder of at least five men in an opposing street gang. Higgins was a white man about 40 years of age, five foot seven, and weighed in at 135 pounds. He was balding, but had a big wooly beard and was covered in tattoos from head to toe.

Rick stood in front of the doorway, cleared his throat, and softly said, "Lindsey, you in there? Everything okay?"

There was no immediate response. Then Rick saw blood pooling from the cell floor out onto the tier. He stumbled back a few steps, his knees shaking like they were going to buckle.

With effort, he called the inmate again. "Lindsey?"

Inmate Higgins ripped the blanket down from the doorway and with his right hand, he held the head of inmate Father Frank Schaffner like he was proudly holding up a lantern. Directly behind inmate Higgins was Father Schaffner's headless body. Schaffner was a Catholic priest from the '70s and a notorious child rapist.

Higgins laughed loud enough for the entire block to hear him. In his left hand, he had an 18-inch piece of sawed-off metal from his bed bunk, also covered in blood, that he had used to cut the ex-priest's head off. He lowered the arm holding the bloodied head, swung it back, and threw the head out of his cell in Rick's direction. Schaffner's severed head went flying, hitting Rick directly in his pelvis. He staggered back again, and fell to the floor, sitting up with the head between his legs.

The priest's mouth and eyes were still wide open, looking up at Rick in horror. Officer Guardian started screaming at the top of his lungs like the world was ending while at the same time sliding back from the head and kicking it away from his body. Schaffner's head rolled down the tier about 10 feet, and Rick began screaming into his microphone.

"HELP! HELP! HELLLLLP!"

Officer Dave Loomis came running into the block like Flash Gordon, shouting at Officer Milinozzo to close all cell doors immediately. Dave then hit the emergency all-call button on his radio.

More than a month had passed since the incident had happened in Cell Block ZX. It had been locked down and all the inmates considered to be involved were transferred to more secured out-of-state prison facilities. Captain Gavin was ordered by his superiors to reopen it again, but before doing so, he had to find some officers that could clean it up.

Officers Jed Ferrari and Chuck Barreto were called into the Captain's office shortly after starting their seven to three shift. Both entered the office wondering if they were in trouble for something.

"Boys, I've got a new assignment for you," Captain Gavin said to them. "I need you to report to Unit ZX tomorrow morning. As you are aware, it's a disaster in there. I'd like you to work together and take it back for me. The Superintendent and the Captains will back you guys one-hundred percent. Anything you need, we will provide – within reason – to assist you."

The men looked at each other, then back at the Captain, and nodded.

"OK, men, that's all then. See you in ZX tomorrow," the Captain dismissed them.

Chuck and Jed left his office and glanced at each other with apprehension.

During the meeting in the Captain's office, a female lieutenant had been sitting in the corner listening to the exchange.

After they were out of earshot, she said to Gavin, "Are you absolutely sure about Barreto?"

"I'm sure. He's a tough bastard," he replied.

"OK," she sighed. "Hope you're right."

Captain Gavin knew he screwed up big time with Officer Guardian. It was his hope that these two had different distinct styles, but would offer each other a balance. Officer Ferrari was tough, tirelessly adhering to the rules. He would not waiver, no matter how hard the job was. Barreto on the other hand was impulsive and worked in the moment, taking his fair amount of chances on the job. Gavin thought it would work for the task at hand. For better or worse, they'd find out.

Jed arrived home that day and called his coworker, Tim, to ask if he knew anything about Chuck other than the rumors he had heard and to tell him about the new assignment they had been given.

Tim answered his phone immediately. "Hey Jed, what's happening?"

"You will not believe this shit," said Jed.

"What?"

"The Captain is pulling me from my unit and having me reassigned to Unit ZX with Barreto."

"What? That's insane. You can't do that. Barreto is tapped out. Ragged, a real burn-out. He lost his father last year in the 911 attack, and supposedly long before he came to even work for the Department, his girlfriend was murdered."

Tim just loved the gossip.

"I know that, Timmy, thanks!" Jed said sarcastically. "I gotta do what I'm told, but I really don't need this shit right now with the messy divorce I'm dealing with. I can't believe this crap, Tim."

"Before the thing with his father, I did hear he was one hell of an officer. You gotta go to the Captain privately and tell him your situation," Tim replied.

"I'll see how it goes tomorrow first," Jed replied, reluctance in his voice.

"OK, good luck with that. Kid is nuts," Tim concluded.

Jed hung up the phone, feeling dejected.

Chuck had also gone home to an empty house. He turned on his 32-inch television and broke out some Jack Daniels and Diet Coke, pouring it over ice. *I need something to relax after today's news*, he thought to himself. Chuck had heard that Ferarri was a stickler for rules and a pain in the ass, essentially not easy to work with. After stoking the fireplace, he became engrossed in *The Towering Inferno,* an old classic film starring Paul Newman and Faye Dunaway. He played with the ice in his glass, seemingly mesmerized by the cubes. Suddenly, there was a knock on his front door.

Standing on his doorstep was Uncle Armond. Chuck lived on the larger side of the two-family house he owned. It was on an old country road off a wide, slow-moving river with the backside of the house abutting the woods.

"Haven't seen you around much. I was just seeing how you're doing. And I thought I'd bring Rupert back to you," said Uncle Armond.

Rupert, Chuck's dog, spent a lot of time with his uncle who helped watch, feed, and walk him while Chuck was off working or on other excursions.

"Yeah, bring the boy home. I'm good, Arm, just keeping busy. Working and stuff," he said.

Armond extended a container towards him. "I bought an enormous amount of meatloaf from the grocery store. I can't eat it all. I'm stuffed already."

"Oh, thank you, Unc. I'll bring this back when I finish," Chuck said, slightly shaking the container.

"No problem, Meathead. I'll be right back with Sir Rupert."

Chuck went back inside, put the container of food in the fridge, and then let Rupert in the house when he heard his collar jingling outside the door. The dog jumped up onto the couch and sat next to Chuck, who returned to sipping his drink. He muted the television and started playing music on his stereo while he watched the picture. He was feeling lousy and reckless, a combination he had become all too familiar with. He pulled out some old yellow legal pads to jot down some ideas for a book he was attempting to write, something his late father, Gus, always talked about doing.

Chuck was compelled to write a fictional story loosely based on life experiences, a perspective on both monotonous and challenging moments. He thought he should get it down, get it straight for the telling, or would it all be forgotten like teardrops falling and lost in the rain. The main character was loosely based on himself, and as the whiskey went down smooth, his pen began to write.

My name is Steve Burnett. Born in January 1969, they call me the Capricorn Man. How does one man have so much luck, yet so much scandal and tragedy, in one lifetime? Is it all luck, pre-ordained, or does a man make his own destiny? Could it be a combination of all? The stuff of dreams! Who really knows?

As he wrote, the movie playing on television changed and happened to be an all-time favorite of Shandi's. It just made him miss her all the more as he poured extra whiskey in the glass and drank faster until finally, he passed out.

Chuck woke up abruptly on his couch. "Shit, I'm late. Gotta get to work!" The morning had come fast.

It would be his first day working in the ZX Unit and he was already off to a poor start, most likely from the drink. He jumped in the shower, got dressed, and quickly jumped in his Jeep, speeding down the slippery roads and hoping to make it somewhat on time.

It was a cold, icy winter morning. His hair was still long and overgrown, and his face was covered in a week-and-a-half of stubble. He had other priorities on his mind. He hurriedly threw on a long winter coat.

Chuck was halfway to work when a tractor-trailer caught up to him and was riding right on his rear bumper while flashing his high beams. The roads were too icy to warrant this level of impatience, and Chuck had no threshold for nonsense like this these days. Against his better judgment, he sped up and left the trucker in the dust.

At the end of the road was a large gas station that had separate pumps for diesel. Chuck realized he had nothing to eat for the day due to his hasty departure. He pulled into the station, parked, and looked through his pockets for some cash or his ATM card. Uncannily enough, the truck driver pulled in, got out, fueled the truck, and went inside the convenience store. Chuck went inside, too.

The man went over to the refrigerator for a soda and walked towards the cash register. Chuck purposely walked faster towards the man and bumped into the trucker's right shoulder with his left from behind.

Chuck put his left hand on top of the man's shoulder. "Excuse me, sir. You should watch where you're going. You never know who you're going to bump into!"

The trucker looked at Chuck, saying nothing.

When Chuck got to work, he was mercifully only a few minutes late. Jed was already there working on inmate schedules and doing security inspections for the new unit. They said hello to one another and made small talk, both unsure of how it was going to work out.

Jed was very good at taking the lead and discussing strategies while making you feel relevant and part of the process. Right off, Chuck felt at ease and looked forward to throwing himself into the tasks ahead of them, thankful for anything to do that would keep his tortured mind off of his problems outside of work.

Jed had formulated a strategy for the morning. He would run all the cell doors and computer work from the officers' station, while Chuck made all the unit rounds on foot. At eleven, they would switch it up. They had a hard day ahead of them and likely even harder weeks to come. There would be a lot of moaning and groaning from the inmates in their new unit as growing pains occurred.

As the morning progressed, Chuck and Jed found out how much their work ethic was actually in tune. The men had two different styles but worked extremely well as a team. It was almost as if they had served in the same military unit- something Chuck knew well. They always had eyes on each other and the unit, especially given the known hostility. Both were fearless, though Jed used a little more caution than Chuck.

At eleven-thirty, Jed posted up outside the unit and waited. All the inmates would leave their cells shortly to adjourn to the large main dining area to eat lunch. Chuck was in the unit by himself where he would get a phone call from another officer who was monitoring the dining hall. That officer would give Chuck the go-ahead to unlock the inmates' cells for lunch, which gave them only a brief taste of minute freedom. When the inmates got done eating, they would go back to the unit to be locked back into their assigned cells.

Chuck's desk phone rang for them to go. He opened up all the cell doors using a touch screen on their secured computer system and cell-block doors opened one at a time, starting on the first floor. The unit also had a second floor, referred to as a second tier. There were seventy-five cells and they had about 100 inmates in total.

The inmates walked out of their cells, out of the unit, and down the long hallway to the prison dining hall. When the cell doors first opened up, it got loud. The inmates began talking and whooping with delight to be out of their cells.

Jed stood just outside the hallway of their unit – close enough for him to be able to still see Chuck – while all the inmates left. As a safety norm, the officer that remained would close all the cell doors and then walk the entire unit for a security round. There had been previous incidents when inmates had jumped out of their cells to attack officers when left alone to make their rounds.

Chuck didn't care.

He left all their doors wide open while he did his round, so if he had an issue with something inside a cell, he could handle it right then and there. It was also to let the inmates know and understand if they had a problem with him personally, he was open for confrontation with no backup, just him alone. It took Jed a little aback when he saw Chuck conducting the round his way, but he kind of liked it.

Chuck was walking downstairs after finishing up his security round up top when he walked by an inmate inside his cell who hadn't gone to lunch, still lying down on top of a bunk.

"Close my fucking cell door, nigga!" he shouted at Chuck.

Chuck backed up to the opened cell door, looked at the convict, and said, "What?"

"Close my fucking door, nigga!" the inmate yelled louder.

"You fucking close it yourself."

"What?"

"You heard me. Close it yourself," Chuck said and walked back to his desk.

Jed was laughing hysterically at this. He had never seen an exchange like it and was ready to respond if needed. As the seconds ticked by, Jed thought, *Wow, this just might work out.* Then the inmate came out of his cell and walked over to the officer's desk, clearly pissed off at Chuck.

"You gonna close my fucking door?" he said.

"I said no. You close it," Chuck responded.

There was no way the inmate could actually close the door. He'd have to go behind the officers' station to do so, and that was forbidden. If the inmate attempted it, the officer had every right to take any action necessary to prevent it, but he knew the game Chuck was playing. It was his move. The inmate looked around, clearly contemplating an act of violence. He stared at the clipboard on the officer's desk.

"Go ahead, pick it up. You want to. Pick it up and throw it at me," Chuck challenged.

It dumbfounded the inmate. He walked away, went over to the billboard area for inmate postings of different programs and rules. He then walked back inside his cell without saying another word.

Events like this went on for weeks, the inmates not liking Jed and Chuck's style of following institution rules so strictly. In those early days, an inmate named Chevy approached the officer's desk with his cellmate. He was holding a plastic soda bottle. Inside it was not soda, but instead mashed, fermented fruits. It was called "homebrew". While crudely made, it could make you drunk. There was no eating or drinking anything outside of the cells or dining hall, nevermind homemade alcohol.

The inmate was already very drunk when he came up to their station. He staggered and slurred his words as he talked to Jed and Chuck.

"Yo, CO, why are you such an asshole?" he said to Jed, laughing.

"Yeah, farthead. Why are you an asshole?" his roommate laughed along with him.

"You both drinking homebrew?" Jed asked.

"Yeah, so what? What's the big deal? You gotta have a problem with that, too? Like you do everything else?" they bantered.

"You guys have to hand over that bottle you're drinking right now. Then go to your cell and lock in for the rest of the day 'til you're sober."

While Jed talked with them, Chuck picked up the phone and called the Sergeant outside their unit.

"Sarge, it's Chuck. Send everyone you got. We're having an issue here."

"Okay, on our way," the Sergeant responded as the exchange became more heated.

"No fucking way, Officer Douche. We're not causing any problems. We're staying out and we will finish this deli-shish brew!" he slurred, laughing hysterically.

"Closing all cell doors, bring it in," Chuck shouted to the rest of the inmates who remained outside their cells. He then started closing the cell doors in the unit. The inmates surprisingly all ran inside their cells, except for the two drunk ones at the officers' desk.

By this time a small army of officers had arrived in the unit. Chevy's cellmate noticed and ran inside his cell, but Chevy did not. Instead, he ran upstairs to the second tier and jumped around manically, yelling and screaming. The officers that had responded pursued him. Chevy jumped off the second floor and landed back on the first floor. He then ran after Jed, and they both squared up, ready to exchange punches. Before that happened, Officer Dave Loomis tackled Chevy from behind. Down he went and a pile of officers put handcuffs and leg restraints on him. He was placed on a medical stretcher and they brought him to the Hole, a twenty-four-hour lockdown area.

After all the commotion was over and everyone left, Jed looked at Chuck smiling and said, "Great Caesar's ghost! That was hands-down, by-the-book, perfect!"

. . .

When Chuck woke up the next morning in bed from a bad dream, he looked over to his left and was devastated at the vacancy. Chuck was perspiring with his heart pounding but he wasn't as hungover as the morning before. He had to get up and moving for work so he threw on his uniform, made coffee, and jumped in his Jeep for the ride to work. Once he got inside Block ZX, he and Jed made more coffee and planned out the day's strategies to try to get the unit running like a well-oiled machine.

Jed first inspected the broom closet and found there was a missing hand brush, called a foxtail. All equipment had to be accounted for on every shift. Someone on the night shift must have forgotten to inspect the janitor's closet before going home, unfortunately a common occurrence.

"Who has the foxtail?" Jed shouted out loud for every inmate in the block to hear him.

No answer. He repeated himself.

Someone shouted, "Fuck you!"

All the inmates, still locked in their cells, laughed out loud at Jed. Jed said to himself, "Okay, that's the way they want to play it, will do."

He started at cell number one, conducting visual inspections. If he saw contraband in them – like homebrew, speakers, clotheslines hanging up – he took it from them. When he got ten cells down on the bottom floor of the unit, someone came clean and gave up the foxtail.

"I found the foxtail," said the inmate that lived in cell number twenty, and he actually apologized to the inmates that had lost their stuff for not speaking up sooner.

Okay, Chuck thought to himself, *it's gonna be another great day. We'll see how it goes from here.*

The inmates seemed to be quiet for the rest of the morning, but you could still feel a lot of tension and resistance. They were used to getting their way by breaking department rules, so they were not liking Chuck and Jed's management system.

From the central control room, the direction came for all inmates in the prison to stand up on their feet for a count. Jed and Chuck locked all the inmates back in their cells, then Chuck turned the lights on in every cell by using a control button on the computer system. Most inmates never had to stand up for the count before, but Jed made them stand. They did not like it, but had no choice but to get used to it. If they refused, he had them removed from the block and taken to the Hole. Eventually, they got the hint.

Chuck was beginning to think maybe he had purpose again, working with this guy. Something he had forgotten about since the disappearance of his father back in September. Jed was strict and by-the-book, but fair.

After their count was finished and verified by the central control room, Jed and Chuck had about forty-five minutes of quiet time to themselves before the inmates would be released to go to the dining hall to eat.

CHAPTER 2
SHANDI
JUNE - NOVEMBER 1986

CHUCK AND HIS high school buddies were going to be performing at a large indoor roller-skating rink in the area with their garage rock band. They were setting up their instruments and equipment on a stage that they performed on once, sometimes twice, a month. The boys were very efficient when it came to getting ready for the show.

Chuck was wearing an old, white leather bomber jacket with N.A.S.A. and American flag patches, which had been sewn on by his mother when he was younger. It was part of his musical alter-ego ensemble; he enjoyed wearing it when playing in front of an audience. People would always comment on how cool it was or how much they liked it. Chuck had a fascination with wanting to fly ever since he could remember. Any time there was something on television about an airplane or space shuttle, it glued him to the TV. After a few songs, he would take it off and hang it on his guitar stand on the stage.

Underneath, he always wore a tight-fitting, black v-neck paired with intentionally torn jeans and work boots. Following every show, he would change into his usual heavy flannel or corduroy shirt over the t-shirt and put his famed bomber jacket in the car, hanging it over the driver's seat until they did another gig.

Chuck had been playing guitar since he was in the sixth grade. He was very talented and loved playing loudly. His favorite guitar was a Guild with double Macintosh pickups. When he had first started playing, he would walk over to the guitar store after school and look at the Guilds hanging up on the wall, dreaming about owning one. Sometimes his dad would accompany him.

"Chucky, those are too expensive," he'd always say, until one day he came home with one in the back of his truck, wrapped in an old, dirty blanket. After showing it to Chuck, his dad took the guitar and sanded it down to the natural wood color. Then he painted a thick, clear coat of polyurethane onto it. That guitar *shone* and the wood grain was mesmerizing.

Chuck had suspected that his father had "unknowingly" bought the guitar stolen, which is why he sanded the engraved serial number off of it before painting it, but he only cared that he had his dream guitar. It played and sounded like a dream. He just barely touched the strings and it made the most beautiful sounds.

Stirring from his reverie about where it all started, Chuck walked over to Shandi's cash register to talk with her. She worked passing out skates or sometimes running the register and concessions. He thought she was beautiful. She had the deepest blue eyes he'd ever seen and long, flowing black hair.

"Hey Chuck. You boys were outstanding last week," said Shandi.

Chuck laughed nervously. "Yeah, thanks. Maybe you wanna help us out and sing a song or two tonight? Somebody told us you have a good voice."

"Yeah, I don't know about that. Maybe I will, we'll see," she replied. They bantered back and forth with each other for a bit until customers started coming inside.

"See ya later," Chuck said and walked back over with his bandmates for sound checks.

Shortly after, the band began to play. Some kids gathered around them to listen, while others skated round and round the waxed but worn wooden rink.

The band started out jamming with Van Halen, "Little Guitars", followed by "Detroit Rock City" by KISS. The crowd around the stage went crazy. Chuck reveled in the moment, loving to play the lead riffs to the songs.

As his fingers moved deftly over the strings, Chuck noticed a kid over at the counter area Shandi was working at, talking with her. His name was Leroy Stick. Leroy and his younger brother, Jonathan, were both on the rough side and known for being troublemakers. They had gone to the same high school as Chuck in the small town of Woodrow in the western part of Massachusetts, and Chuck and his younger brother, Gary, used to see Leroy at their local gym after school sometimes. Some years later, Chuck heard from a friend that the brothers had both done a year in county prison for robbing a Burger King while wearing ski masks.

Leroy was a big kid. He could have been a football player, but he also seemed a little socially awkward. He went to great lengths to present himself as being a tough guy and a bully. The kids that hung out with him did so out of fear. Chuck and Gary avoided Leroy and the gang he hung out with; the lot of them were nothing but trouble.

Chuck, still trying to focus on playing guitar, saw Leroy begin to point aggressively at Shandi, who appeared to be frightened. Leroy had on a dingy Army jacket with his last name on the upper left pocket that he wore everywhere, even though he'd never been in the Army. He kept a constant eye on them, just in case; he had a feeling. Chuck always thought if he had to tussle with him, he'd have his work cut out, but he would never back down from a physical confrontation. He would roll the dice, no matter the outcome.

As the band went into a third song, he watched Shandi angrily walk away from Leroy and the area she was working, ending up in front of the stage. There were no customers at her counter. She shook off her irritation and smiled, waving at Chuck and the boys.

Once the song they were playing ended, Chuck leaned over to Bob, their lead singer and rhythm guitar player, and whispered something in his ear.

Bob then said into his microphone, gesturing towards Shandi, "We have this spectacular lady we all know and love. Maybe she could come up here and help us out?"

"Come on, Shandi!" the small crowd cheered for her to get on stage.

She blushed and slowly stepped up onto the stage.

"OK, guys," she said. "Can you play A1, B1, B7, and B5 minor, and watch for the changes?"

Bob and Chuck smiled at each other and said, "Hell yeah!"

They began to play and Shandi said to them, "Just a tad faster guys."

Wow, what a sound! Chuck thought to himself.

Shandi began moving her body with the smooth sounds coming from the amplifiers and the matching beats on the drums by their bandmate, Harry. Then Shandi started singing.

Chuck and the rest of the band could not believe their ears. She had one of the most incredible voices they had ever heard. She sang with confidence and raspy, sexy tones to *Sensible Shoes* by David Lee Roth.

"I got a fast car, go cruisin' down the highway/ A corvette stingray, I do it my way/ Got a good job, making lots of money/ I look good and I'm funny, so why am I lonesome honey?/ The gypsy said the problem with you/ You need some sensible shoes," she belted.

Chuck then broke out into a lead on the strings on the neck of his guitar, and Shandi shocked everyone when she pulled out a harmonica from the tight back pocket of her jeans. She put it to her mouth and started blowing into the instrument, complimenting Chuck's playing. The growing crowd was jumping up and down, cheering and clapping. Kids who were still skating out on the rink came off and gathered around the dimly lit stage, the huge disco strobe light making it look as though stars danced across the room.

Leroy was way in the back, just watching. His eyes looked as if they could burn holes through a cement wall. He was clenching his fists, appearing to grow angrier by the second. Before Shandi went up on stage to sing with the boys, apparently she had broken up with Leroy. That's what they had been arguing about. They had been out on several dates in the previous weeks. She felt he was extremely possessive and wanted to end it before things got complicated. It seemed Shandi may have been right; he appeared to be overly upset about such a short relationship.

While Shandi continued singing, she moved closer to Chuck, swaying provocatively, her mouth manipulating the harmonica. It increased Chuck's attraction to her, and he felt even more drawn to her than ever before. They finished the song, and the crowd of kids cheered wildly.

"How about one more, Shandi? How about it, y'all? Wanna hear one more with the gorgeous Shandi?" Bob said into his microphone.

The crowd erupted in encouragement.

She whispered the name of a Pat Benatar song in Chuck's ear while gently touching his back and then his hair. Chuck started the song and the boys followed in behind.

Shandi began to sing. "You're a real tough cookie with a long history..."

Chuck and his bandmates again exchanged impressed glances. He thought she had the voice of an angel. He noticed Leroy walk off disgusted, disappearing mid-song, and was glad for it. After it ended, the crowd again applauded with enthusiasm.

"Thank you, boys, thank you, everyone, but I gotta get back to work. Duty calls," Shandi said into her microphone. She gently stepped off the stage and walked back to her station.

"Wow. I'm not sure if we can carry on without you now, but let's try it. Thank you, Shandi," Bob said.

The band played again for three more songs then stopped for a brief break. The rink disc jockey, who had an office in the rink's corner, took over playing music for the kids skating. Some of the boys in the band went outside for a cigarette but Chuck didn't smoke. He instead went to the men's bathroom, which appeared to be empty when he walked in. He finished zipping the fly on his pants at the urinal, and turned around to find Leroy standing directly behind him.

Before Chuck realized what was happening, Leroy swung his right fist, landing it squarely between Chuck's eyes. Chuck saw stars and felt a sharp pain, along with the sudden smell of blood. He staggered back against the urinal, somehow remaining on his feet. His father had always told him he had a hard head. In more ways than one, it turned out to be the truth.

Chuck shook it off within a split second. Even though he was still somewhat stunned, he knew he had to strike back quickly. Chuck swung his own right hand hard and upwards, striking the underside of Leroy's sizable jawbone. The momentum of it nearly caused Leroy to fall backward and away from Chuck.

Having gained energy from the successful hit, Chuck jumped up in the air sideways and gave Leroy a kick, landing his right foot on Leroy's left hip. Leroy flew backward into the stall door and it broke, hanging on by one hinge and leaving him in a heap on the floor inside the stall. Chuck was startled by what he had done. He couldn't tell if Leroy was OK or even conscious.

Unsure of what to do next, Chuck got the hell out of the bathroom and went to find Bob. He located him outside and relayed what had happened.

"Bob, that dickhead, Leroy, went psycho in the bathroom when I was trying to take a fucking piss. I don't know what I did to him. He punched me in the face so I fucked him up. I think he might still be passed out on the floor in there," Chuck said.

Bob looked amused. "Wait here. I'll go back in to see what's going on with the asshole."

He went inside and ran into Leroy's brother, Jonathan. Bob told him what happened, and they both ran into the men's room together to find Leroy by the sink, splashing cold water on his face.

"Lee, what happened? You OK?" Jonathan asked.

"Yeah, I'm fine. Once I get my hands on your boy, Bobby..." he replied nastily.

"Yeah, shit-for-fucking-brains, you're not going to cause any more problems here tonight. You started this, not Chuck!" Bob yelled back. "You try anything else tonight and you'll be dealing with us all, you fuck. Why don't you and your brother take the train out of here while the getting is good?"

"Oh, big man, you gonna make us?" said Leroy.

"Fucking right, I will," Bob said and walked out to find Chuck walking back into the rink.

"Asshole is all set, Chuck," Bob said.

"What happened?"

"It's all good. Won't be any more problems with him tonight."

"Boy, I hope not. Thanks, Bobby."

Bob gave Chuck a thump on the back. "Nice job. He had it coming."

Before they could even get back to the stage to play another block of songs to end the night, the whole place was buzzing with gossip about what Chuck did to Leroy. Kids were running around the rink and rushing towards the stage saying things like, "Did you hear what Chuck did to Stick?"

Most people did not like the brothers and couldn't understand why Shandi had been seeing Leroy. Several of her girlfriends had already told her what took place. It was hard to tell by her facial expressions how she felt about it, but eyes kept flickering between Shandi, Chuck, and Leroy, who had just come out of the bathroom with his brother.

"What do we do now, Lee?" Jonathan asked.

"Let's get the heck out of here. I'll take care of that little prick when he's not expecting it. Real soon." The brothers then left the building, vanishing from sight so quickly it was as if they were never there.

The band started performing again, and this time no one skated while they played, everyone gathering around the stage instead. Shandi walked over to them and handed a small piece of paper up to Chuck while he was playing. He put it in his pocket quickly without looking at it but wondered what it was. After a few minutes, Chuck could not take the suspense, so he walked behind Harry's drum set while he was still playing and pulled the piece of paper out of his pocket to read it.

Chuck, if you can, meet me behind the rink at the old Parkway Drive-In Theater tonight.

The theater was just through the woods behind the skating rink. It had been closed down and abandoned for a few years now. He remembered his parents talking about going there with him before he was even able to walk. It was a happening theater at one time, packed with cars during the fifties, sixties, and seventies. Baby Chuck would be in the back seat enthralled with watching a Planet of the Apes marathon while his young parents were enthralled with each other.

Now, it was desolate. The big screen was still standing, but it was torn and weathered. The projector and concession building were also intact, but the windows were boarded up. Overgrown weeds covered all surfaces, and the poles for the speakers in each parking space were standing but rusted and tarnished. Some were bent over.

Since the beginning of high school, Chuck, his friends, and many other kids would go there to hang out and party. There was an old, dirt road behind the rink that only some of them had known to go down to get inside the abandoned drive-in discreetly. Getting in undetected was no problem, but getting out quickly without being seen was a problem. The police would randomly cruise into the drive-in to break up the festivities and sometimes arrest kids for underage drinking.

Chuck and his friend, Andy, once got caught by the police drinking beer there and were driven to the police station. Chuck knew most of the local police officers because they would stop by his father's auto body shop during the day to have coffee with him. They put a scare into Andy and Chuck by putting them both in a jail cell. Then they called their parents to pick them up, and Chuck's father said to leave him in custody for the night.

In the morning, Chuck was released and walked home. There were no charges from the police on either of the boys. He would like to say he learned his lesson that night, but truthfully, they just got better at not getting caught.

After the show, Chuck and his bandmates finished loading up their equipment and instruments into their 1974 Chevy van as the rink closed down for the night. Bob and Chuck had plans to hang out afterward like they did every weekend, but Chuck told Bob he was going to meet up with Shandi instead. Bob was a little jealous, but he absolutely would do the same in a heartbeat if it was him instead.

"I'll talk to you later on the CB, Bobby," Chuck said as they split up.

All the guys in the band had CB radios in their vehicles to communicate with each other. They each had a unique handle and used the same radio frequency. Chuck's handle was Capricorn One, which stood for his zodiac sign and the month he was born. It was also a nod to his father who had nicknamed him Capricorn Chuck.

Bob took the van and Chuck pulled out of the rink parking lot slowly in his 1972 Dodge Charger. The vehicle looked brand new, its metallic, midnight-blue paint glistening like glass.

Chuck had saved all his money working summers and after school to buy the car. One Sunday, Chuck and his father took the old tow truck and went to a nearby junkyard. His old man knew the owner and he let them walk around whenever his dad wanted to buy vehicles to restore and sell for profit. As they walked through the yard, his dad would point out options. His finger always landed on practical, family types of vehicles, which made teenage Chuck grimace.

Chuck felt discouraged until he saw the nose of a vehicle sticking out of an enormous pile of scrap cars. As Chuck got closer, he realized it was a Dodge Charger: a dream. He hoped it would still be intact and affordable. The owner told them it still purred like a kitten but needed a little mechanical and body work. Chuck's dad had the owner get one of his workers to get the surrounding scrap away from the Charger using a crane.

"How's six hundred dollars sound, Gus?" the owner said to his father.

Oh my God, Chuck thought to himself. He had saved up exactly $650. An hour later, they had the Charger hooked up to his father's truck, and they were towing it back to his dad's shop.

He spent every free second working to get the Charger road-worthy. His father did all the welding and patching up of holes and rust, while Chuck worked for weeks, with the help of his friends, prepping for its ultimate paint job.

On that glorious summer Sunday, the Charger went into the shop's painting room. Chuck and his friends spent all morning masking up the chrome, headlights, taillights, and windows. The room had layers of paint built up on the walls from the many previous vehicles that had entered. It looked like a complex work of art to Chuck, all the different molded, clumped up colors like abstract rainbows everywhere.

His father went into the sealed room wearing his gas mask to prevent fumes from entering his lungs and Chuck was so damn excited. He watched as best he could through the clouded windows. In between coats of paint, his dad would come out of the room for twenty or thirty minutes and take a break with Chuck and his friends.

"Rome wasn't built in a day," Gus said to them. After twenty coats on the Charger, she was done. "Let's go home, son. It'll be dry tomorrow and we can take off the tape and paper then."

Before they left the shop, Chuck went into the paint room to take a brief look and was amazed by the transformation. He had seen it happen many times before with customers' vehicles, but this time was different because it was his.

Chuck woke up hours before his father the next day. He couldn't wait to get back to the shop to work on his car. After they arrived and he removed all the tape and paper, he began putting a compound lotion onto the brand new paint job and used a buffer machine to shine up the paint even more. The Charger shone so that you could easily see your reflection.

The car meant so much to Chuck even now as he slowly pulled into the desolate drive-in to meet up with Shandi. His heart was pounding with nervousness and the excitement of the evening. He found a spot in front of the big screen and parked. You could see the enchanting moon shining off the Charger's hood.

Shandi pulled in and parked alongside his car in a red 1980 Ford Mustang. She got out of her car first and stretched her arms up into the sky.

"Boy, what a gorgeous night!" she said. "You got any beer, Chucky?"

"Yeah, of course," he replied and pulled out a twelve-pack of Coors Light from his back seat.

"Is it okay if we sit on the hood of your beastly car? I got a blanket we could put over it," she said as she gave him a lovely smile.

"Absolutely," Chuck said. "Sounds great."

She pulled out a large, brown and white horse blanket from inside her car and Chuck helped her spread it on the hood. They sat a few inches apart and started sipping on their beers, making small talk. While they talked, Chuck's radio played quietly in the background.

"Sorry about that dickhead, Leroy. I've only been on a few dates with him. He was getting weird real quick, so I tried breaking it off right away, and that just seemed to spark his jealousy," Shandi apologized.

"No, that's OK, no big deal."

"I know, but that was crazy. He's a big guy. Where'd you learn to fight? Everyone told me what you did."

"Not sure. It just came to me. No biggie," Chuck said, now slightly embarrassed. Her mention of his actions made Chuck nervous and want to change the subject. He still couldn't believe he was sitting alone next to the most stunning girl he'd ever seen.

"What about you? That singing voice? Wow! And the harmonica-where did you learn that?"

"Just messing around in my bedroom at night," she shrugged.

"You should come sing in our band regularly. Bob does pretty well on his own, but I don't think he would mind at all. I could ask the band, if you're interested."

"Well… let me think about it, okay?"

He nodded.

They continued talking and drinking, both unsure if the other felt the same powerful chemistry and attraction, both fueled by the adrenaline rush of the events earlier in the night.

The song "Stairway to Heaven" came on the Charger's radio.

Shandi jumped off the hood of the car. "Oh, come on, we gotta dance under the moonlight to this."

"OK, I can't argue with that."

As they began dancing closely, Chuck thought to himself, *Can this night get any better?* As if answering his thoughts, Shandi started singing in Chuck's right ear, gently and softly.

"There's a feeling I get when I look to the west/ And my spirit is crying for leaving/ In my thoughts, I have seen rings of smoke through the trees/ And the voices of those who stand looking/ That's you," she sang.

In that moment, he felt he had never heard anything so sweet and beautiful, a voice straight from the heavens.

The song ended on the radio. He wished it didn't, but it did.

They went back over to the nose of his car and sat on the edge. "Sweet Home Alabama" by Lynyrd Skynyrd came on and it felt like fate. They looked into each other's eyes, leaned in, and began passionately kissing as if it were the most natural thing in the world.

Shandi couldn't wait to put her delicate fingers into his thick, dark locks. She always thought Chuck was dreamy and undeniably sweet. They were hungry for one another, hungry like they hadn't eaten in years. Their bodies tingled as they rolled across the Charger's massive hood.

Shandi also had to admit to herself, she was hands-down, undeniably in like with this guy. She was still a virgin, but she felt out of control when it came to Chuck.

Shandi pulled herself away from him, flushed and flustered. "Whew, oh boy!"

Then she grabbed him again by his thick, button-up shirt, pulling him back to her wet, voluptuous lips. She whispered in his ear, "Let's go inside the car."

He opened the driver's door and she quickly threw the blanket over the long front bench seat inside it. Shandi slid into the front seat, pulling Chuck in after her. He gently moved his hands lower, running them over her body, all the while thinking she was the most beautiful creature he'd ever seen. He couldn't help periodically pulling back to look into her deep, penetrating ocean-blue eyes. They touched and kissed, and the song on the car radio changed to "This Is Love" by White Snake.

Shandi reached up underneath Chuck's clothes, touching his hardened muscles, and her hormones went into overdrive. She then quickly removed his shirts and then unbuttoned and unzipped his jeans. Chuck, following her lead, did the same to her. When he got to her bra, he had some difficulty with the clasp, so she reached behind for him and took it off herself.

The moonlight spilled through the windows despite them being fogged. The rock ballad continued to play. Their lovemaking went on for a long time. Afterward, they remained tightly wrapped, holding each other, not wanting to let go. The horse blanket partially covered them as they laughed and kissed, wishing the night would never end.

After high school, Chuck and Shandi's relationship blossomed quickly and they were actually thinking of marriage. They bought their first home together in town, just across from a small river in the woods. Chuck's mother, Rita, was a realtor and Shandi's parents helped them with the down-payment. Chuck, Gus, and Shandi's dad worked on weekends to build a front porch and an enormous deck on the back of the house. Inside, Chuck built a bar area with a pellet stove next to it and a small music studio in the basement.

The band was growing more successful. Shandi had only been the lead singer in the band for a short time, but they were already playing in some pretty big venues.

On one particular occasion, their band was getting ready to play at a huge Halloween party in the Wolford City Sheraton's grand ballroom. The band was super excited for the upcoming night and practiced as much as they could by playing at smaller venues.

Bob, Harry, and Dan met at Chuck and Shandi's country home to get dressed up in their Halloween costumes for the gig. They had agreed as a band to dress up as Star Wars characters. Shandi came out of the upstairs bedroom and strolled down the stairs as Princess Leia. All the boys' jaws dropped. She wore the classic white dress with a golden belt around her tiny waistline, her thick hair twisted into donut-like buns on the sides of her head.

Chuck was beside her, handsomely dressed as the space pirate, Han Solo. Bob was the debonair Luke Skywalker, and Harry donned a very authentic-looking Chewbacca costume. Dan completed the ensemble as a killer droid C-3PO.

Chuck's brother Gary, his sister Stacey, and Gary's girlfriend Lilly were also going to the Halloween show. It was the biggest event in the area, advertising the famous station, Rock 102, in Wolford City. Their band had received some free publicity from the station for their involvement with the event, and they were looking forward to the opportunities that might follow a successful night.

They loaded the van with equipment, and Chuck and Shandi got in the 1972 Charger to leave. As they all were driving in separate vehicles, the bandmates kept in contact using their CB radios, laughing and having fun doing so.

Shandi took the mic from Chuck, pressed the receiver button down, and said to Bob, who was driving a 78 Monte Carlo, "Aren't you a little too short to be a Stormtrooper?"

Bob laughed into the receiver. "You mean the uniform? No, I'm Luke Skywalker. I'm here to rescue you!"

"I don't need rescuing. I'm with this hunky-ass space pirate sitting next to me!" She laughed and turned to look at Chuck, still speaking into the CB. "What's your name, big guy?"

"Solo," Chuck responded, blushing. She kissed him on the cheek.

Shortly after, their caravan pulled into the rear of the Sheraton building, descended down a ramp into the basement, and pulled up to a loading dock that had elevators nearby. The band had passes indicating their status, which they showed to the parking attendant before they were allowed inside the garage. Another hotel staff member helped Shandi and the boys load all the musical equipment on several flatbed carts. Minutes later, they set all their equipment up for the show and started doing sound checks to make sure they were ready to rock out. There was a sizeable curtain directly in front of the stage that would fall for effect once they hit their first musical chords and started to perform.

In addition to the main ballroom, there were two other smaller ballrooms in the hotel being used that night for events related to the party. One room was for karaoke lovers and costume contests. Five monetary prizes would be given to costume contest winners by Rock 102.

As the band still had an hour after their preparations were complete before it all kicked off, they went to an obscured window to observe people pouring into the hotel. They all wanted to stay out of sight until the show started so no one would be able to get a look at their costumes before the curtain dropped.

They watched what looked like hundreds of people entering, dressed up in all manner of Halloween costumes. You could feel the excitement in the air. It was going to be a magical night. As they continued watching the crowd in amazement, Dan pulled out the small schnapps and whisky bottles he had snuck in, and they had some drinks to calm their nerves.

One of the hotel managers came into their room and said, "Five minutes, people. Are you all ready?"

"Yes sir," they answered.

Gary was with them backstage to help with some of the special effects they had planned for the evening, while Lilly and Stacey were out in the audience. Gary was dressed up as Batman, resembling Michael Keaton's version, while Lilly was Batgirl, wearing all black spandex, and Stacey made a sleek Catwoman.

"You ready, Batman?" Chuck said to Gary.

"Same time, same bat channel!" Gary said, and they laughed.

The band went through a doorway and up some stairs, which took them backstage. The stagefront was covered by a large black curtain so no one waiting in the ballroom could see them. They could hear the crowd, most definitely the largest crowd they had ever performed for. Every one of them was nervous but excited, Gary included.

Gary was always a little jealous of Chuck's ambition and cavalier ways, but he also admired him. He often tried to compete with Chuck; whatever Chuck achieved or accomplished, Gary attempted to do something similar yet grander. Chuck always tried to help Gary, even though he knew what Gary was up to. Gary worked hard to make sure the band – especially his big brother – looked great by being an attentive special effects technician. He took much pride in his part of the work.

"OK, it's go-time, lady and gents. Let's do this !" urged Bob.

They grabbed their instruments and got into position. Gary ignited their smoke machines and lights, which seemed to come out of every direction in the dark ballroom. He played some prerecorded music, which was pumped through the amplifiers, to get the crowd excited. He pressed "Play" on the machine and The Star Wars theme music blasted. The crowd went crazy, screaming, and Gary turned on the disco strobe lights.

After the theme played for a few moments, Bob spoke loudly into his microphone. "Shandi, I'm bored. What plaything can you offer me today?"

"An obscure body in the S-K System, your majesty. The inhabitants refer to it as the planet Earth," she returned.

"How peaceful it looks," Bob laughed evilly.

"Most impactful, your majesty. Will you destroy this Earth?"

Gary played thunderous effects while Bob and Shandi continued their lines.

"Later. I like to play with things a while before annihilation," he laughed again devilishly.

Bob, Chuck, and Dan began to play the theme song live on their guitars. The curtain in front of the band fell dramatically to the floor and more smoke and strobe lights exploded. They began to play "Flash Gordon" by Queen and the crowd grew louder.

"Flash, aahhh," Shandi rasped. "Savior of the universe/ Flash, aahhh, he'll save every one of us/ Flash, aahhh, he's a miracle/ Flash, aahhh, king of the impossible/ He's for every one of us..."

The band played while the vast crowd was noisy and overexcited.

"Oh man, this is totally working!" Bob said to Chuck. Chuck smiled back at his longtime friend. They smoothly transitioned into "The Joker" by The Steve Miller Band. Chuck and Bob hit the chords on their guitars like it was second nature. The energy in the ballroom was palpable.

Shandi sang, putting her own spin on the song. "Some people call me the space cowgirl, yeah/ Some people call me the gangster of love/ Some people call me Clarice/ Cause I speak of the pompitous of love/ People talk about me, baby/ Say I'm doing you wrong, doing you wrong/ Well, don't worry baby... "

While singing and dancing on stage, Shandi noticed one particular individual with a male build. He was standing alone in the humongous crowd wearing a Michael Myers mask from the movie *Halloween* paired with a dark green jacket. He was just staring at her and lacked the enthusiasm for the music that his fellow concert-goers expressed. She was a little unnerved by it. Maybe it was just the mask from that movie that always scared her. She shook it off and continued performing.

The band then broke off from the space-themed songs and played some more popular Halloween tunes, starting with "Thriller" by Michael Jackson. It was a perfect song for a costume party. Shandi did a great little zombie dance and egged the crowd on to follow along and mimic her moves. It was something to see.

When Shandi looked back into the crowd, the man with the Myers mask was gone and she thought maybe she had imagined it. She shook it off and refocused by thinking about the lyrics and staying in sync with the guitars and drums to achieve the best performance possible.

Next on the setlist were classic rock songs, which was what they were known for as a band. Chuck and Bob led them into the song "Dancing in the Streets". Chuck played the leads in the style and sound of Eddie Van Halen, and Shandi came in with vocals, making the crowd melt and fall in love with her.

"Calling out around the world," she sang, "Are you ready for a brand new beat?/ Summer's here and the time is right/ For dancin' in the streets/ They're dancing in Chicago/ Down in New Orleans/ Up in our own little WOLFORD City... "

When the crowd heard her say their city instead of New York City, they clapped and screamed with glee. The band went into another classic song, "White Room".

"In the white room, with black curtains near the station/ Black roof country, no gold pavements, tired starlings/ Silver horses ran down moonbeams in your dark eyes/ Dawn light smiles on you leaving, my contentment..."

Harry was destroying it on his drums like a warrior in command of his domain. Bob, Dan, and Chuck were so in tune with Harry and Shandi's voice, it was like a graceful dance. They played to bring the enormous ballroom down, so to speak, for another hour. Then Shandi announced that they were going on break and Rock 102 would DJ the room until they got back.

Chuck, Shandi, and Gary met up with Stacey and Lilly, while the boys moseyed off in their own direction. Gary and Lilly had signed up for a karaoke song in the other ballroom, so they all went in there to watch. While they were waiting for their turn, Shandi told Chuck about the person she saw earlier, dressed in the scary Michael Myers mask.

"I'll keep an eye out, babe, okay?" Chuck said as he looked around. He didn't see anyone like that at the moment, but there were hundreds of people.

A guy dressed up as the singer Robert Palmer in a black suit with four young ladies all in black tight dresses and holding fake white guitars got up and sang "Addicted to Love". His lady sidekicks pretended to play their guitars while dancing sensually back and forth and the spectators loved it.

"Everyone give Robert Palmer and his sexy guitar players a hand," said the DJ. The crowd applauded.

"Now I'd like to have Gary and Lilly come on up for a little summer loving." Seeing the costumes they had on, he added, "Oh, wait a minute. I mean Batman and Batgirl."

The song "Summer Lovin'" from *Grease* began to play and Gary took off his bat-mask so he could sing better.

"Summer lovin', had me a blast," Gary began loudly and off-key.

"Summer lovin', happened so fast," Lilly followed, making up for where Gary lacked.

"I met a girl, crazy for me," Gary screeched.

"I met a boy, cute as can be."

"Summer days drifting away, to uh-oh, those summer nights," they sang in unison.

When they sang together, Gary was so badly out of tune that he drowned out Lilly's more pleasant voice, but the crowd loved it anyway. The entire room of people laughed hysterically at Gary in good humor. That did not deter him. Gary pushed forward, and Lilly started cracking up on stage next to him. Shandi and Stacey laughed along wildly, too.

Then, without warning, an inebriated girl dressed up as a cavewoman and holding a big plastic club, ran up onto the stage and wrapped her arms and legs tightly around Gary, humping him. You could see Lilly become infuriated. She and the DJ, who was dressed in a Superman costume, attempted to get the drunken girl off of Gary. The whole situation spurred the laughter of the crowd. Finally, the girl got off Gary and staggered away into another ballroom. The song ended while the scuffle took place, and Gary and Lilly exited the stage to a round of applause.

Gary's face was beet-red in humiliation. Chuck patted Gary on the back, laughing.

"Come on, bro. We gotta head back to finish the show. That was freaking awesome."

"Did I do good until that hideous girl jumped on me?" asked Gary.

"Oh yeah, you were a superstar up there."

"Really?"

"Absolutely."

They all headed backstage in the main ballroom to play the second half of the show. As they gathered together, one of the hotel managers came in with another man, dressed in a suit and tie. The manager introduced the mystery man to the band.

"Hey guys, this is Kenny Saxon. He's been looking for you all," he said.

"Hello everyone," Kenny followed. "I work for a producer, Bill Arkin. He sent me here tonight to see what you guys got. I am very impressed. Here is Bill's card with his phone number. We would like you to call us tomorrow to set up a meeting. Do you have any original material of your own?"

"We have a few songs we've all been working on, sir," Bob replied.

"Okay, great. I hope to hear from you folks soon. Have a great rest of your evening. From what I've seen, that's sure to happen."

The band thanked him and watched the man leave with their jaws dropped.

"Wow," Bob said. "This could be our big break."

"I think Bill Arkin is a huge record producer of KISS and other bands," said Dan.

"Get the fuck out of here," Chuck said in disbelief.

"No, I really think he is."

"We'll find out soon enough," said Bob.

"Okay, fellas. We still have a show to finish. Let's get set up," Shandi said, bringing them back to the reality of the moment.

The DJ then announced the band's return. "Ladies and gentleman, Shandi and the Boys are back in action!"

Speaking of KISS, they kicked the second act with "Detroit Rock City".

Shandi, as usual, knocked the audience's socks off with the first note. "I feel uptight on a Saturday night/ Nine o'clock, the radio's the only light/ I hear my song and it pulls me through/ Comes on strong and tells me what to do."

Harry smashed on the drums again while the boys struck the strings on their guitars in perfect sync. Chuck went off into some stunning lead riffs. The whole place was cheering loudly at what they were hearing. The band played like never before, fueled by a known record producer's interest in them. As the song ended with mammoth applause, Shandi announced Chuck was stepping up to the microphone to sing a song.

Chuck swung his guitar around his backside, wearing it like a Samurai sword and Shandi grabbed her saxophone. They started playing and Shandi blew into her saxophone, playing smooth and solid wonderful notes. Her instrument gave out passionate vibrations to the swarm. It was a slow song and people in the crowd grabbed a partner for a delicate dance.

"Little girl, tonight baby don't feel blue/ Look at those pretty lights along the avenue/ You're out there on your own/ Spending all your time alone/ So come on girl, tonight I want to be with you," Chuck sang.

Shandi went into another sweet solo on the sax before Chuck continued. After the song ended, Shandi took back the mic and said, "Let's give it up for my fiancé!"

The audience went bananas again. They couldn't believe how well he sang, having not heard him all night until that point.

"Okay, let's keep this slow grind going. I like it," said Shandi.

The boys played "Since I Don't Have You" like it was their own new hit while Shandi took back the reins on the mic.

"I don't have plans and schemes/ And I don't have hopes and dreams/ I, I, don't have anything/ Since I don't have you," she crooned.

As she was singing, she noticed the anonymous man in the mask, standing alone off to the side by an exit door. Once again, it appeared that the character focused his attention solely on her.

She inconspicuously moved towards Chuck, nudged him, and whispered in his ear, "He's over there by the exit door, babe."

Chuck glanced over to the area, and he saw the vague shape of someone's back as he exited. It was too fast and dark for him to see much else. He shrugged and smiled at Shandi while continuing to play the guitar.

The band went on to play an assortment of seventies and eighties hits. At the end of the show, Shandi informed the excited crowd that the winners of the costume contest were to be announced. One of the judges brought up some envelopes for her.

"Okay folks, let's announce our winners of the night," she said. "Our fifth place winner: Crockett from the television show *Miami Vice*. Come on up Jimmy!" The crowd applauded as Jimmy came up onto the stage. He looked like Don Johnson's twin brother. "Congratulations, Detective

Crockett. Here's a fifty-dollar gift certificate to the City Cinema!" said Shandi. He shook her hand and left the stage.

"And coming in fourth place, this man needs no introduction. The one and only,
Frankenstein!"

The crowd applauded again, loudly. This guy had gigantic platform boots that must have made him eight feet tall. Frankenstein moved slowly with his arms straight out, mimicking the monster in the movie. She handed him a $150 gift card for a local sports restaurant.

"OK! Coming in third is our own stagehand. Don't know what we'd do without him- The Batman," Shandi announced and Gary came out from behind the stage. "Here's a one-year membership to the gym at Central City, although I don't think he needs it," she said as everyone laughed.

"Our second place winner is – Happy Birthday, Mr. President! – Marilyn Monroe!" There was no sign of her, so Shandi shouted out, "Anyone see Marilyn Monroe? Anyone?"

A moment went by and the winner trotted through the sizable crowd, wearing a gorgeous pink dress and white heels. Everyone cheered.

"There you are, beautiful. Come on up, Miss Monroe. I'm a little jealous of this prize. Two tickets to the KISS concert next month!"

Miss Monroe accepted her prize, visibly thrilled.

"And our first place winner… let's give it up for Elvira! Come on up!" Men whistled loudly as she slinked up onto the stage, and Shandi handed her a prize of $500.

The girl dressed as Elvira leaned into Shandi's mic and said, "I've seen The People's Court, and I'm entitled to one phone call and a strip search!" The crowd cheered, clapped and whistled at her as she brought the house down.

After Elvira graciously left the stage, Shandi said, "Okay, everyone, how about one more song before we go home?"

The applause erupted in encouragement.

"I'll take that as a yes! Okay, guys, let's rock!" said Shandi, and she began to sing. "I need a lover that won't drive me crazy/ I need a lover that won't drive me crazy/ I need a lover that won't drive me crazy/ I need a lover that won't drive me crazy/ Someone to thrill me, and then go away/ I need a lover that won't drive me crazy/ Someone that knows the meaning of ah/ Hey, hit the highway."

After the song ended, Shandi said, "Thank you all for a wonderful evening. Drive safely tonight. And, oh, by the way, next weekend me and the boys are playing at Checkers. Thank you all very much."

The band went backstage, hugging one another with joy over the evening and the possible record deal they could have on the horizon. The hotel manager was also back there, thanking them and asking them to come back the next month to play – virtually begging them – and they agreed. He had some of his staff help them load their equipment back into their vehicles, and the band decided to meet later the next morning to call the producer.

The boys drove off in their trucks. Gary and Lilly and Stacey had booked rooms in addition to Chuck and Shandi. The five of them took the elevator up to Chuck and Shandi's room for a few more drinks before calling it a night. After Gary, Lilly, and Stacey left, Chuck and Shandi looked at each other and knew their night was far from over.

They began to kiss passionately and undress each other, like it was their first night together. It never got old with the two of them. They were still crazy about each other.

Afterwards, alone in their room under the covers, Shandi laid her head on Chuck's chest, wide awake.

"Chuck, I'm so excited right now, I can't hardly sleep. How 'bout you?"

"Hell no, I can't!" He smiled at her and kissed her until it led to something more once again.

A week later the band went out to Connecticut, roughly a half-hour drive from Chuck and Shandi's place, to meet with Mr. Bill Arkin himself to discuss a potential first record deal. Everyone piled in Chuck's Charger for the ride to Bill's. Bob, Dan, and Harry all sat in the back seat, trying to help navigate, while Shandi sat up front next to Chuck.

It was a beautiful day in November, not too cold, and the foliage was still picturesque for the time of year. They noticed the area grow more affluent as they neared their destination. The Charger slowly drove past a large golden fence with letters "BA" standing out prominently on the gate.

"I think you just went past it, babe," Shandi said.

"Oh, yeah, I think you're right," Chuck replied. He stopped the car, backed up, then read the number on the wide mailbox. "Yep, that's it, gotta be."

There was an intercom system on the side of the enormous gate. Chuck pulled the car in front of it with his window rolled down and pushed the button, waiting for some sort of response. He had never seen anything like this.

"Hello, please state your name and business. Press the button when you speak," came a voice through the speaker.

Chuck pressed it and said, "Yes, we have an appointment with Mr. Arkin. We're the band, Shandi and the Boys."

"Okay, yes, he's expecting you. I'll buzz you guys in. Just one moment."

There was a loud clanking noise and the golden gate slowly opened inwards. Chuck drove down a driveway that was long enough to call it a winding road. Tall, emerald green Arborvitae lined the path on one side, and there was a small brook running along it on the other.

Finally, they saw an opening with a large oval parking area in front of an incredibly grand white house. The place was surrounded by lush shrubs and greenery. A large scale of ivy rose from the foundation to the top of the roofline. The shutters were highlighted in bright red paint and the walkways were beautifully paved. The large, dutch-colonial front door stood prominently in the center.

A middle-aged man with a decent head of hair and a bushy mustache came out of the house to greet them.

"Just park anywhere, guys," he said. He wore plaid pants with a pink sweater, brown platform boots, and large Elvis-inspired sunglasses.

Chuck parked and they all slowly got out.

"Wow, nice car. 383 engine?" Mr. Arkin asked Chuck

"Ah, a 440, Mr. Arkin," Chuck responded.

"Bill, son, please. Call me Bill. What a beauty she is. Did you do any work to her yourself?"

"Well, yes sir, with the help of my father and friends."

"That's fantastic. Well, welcome to my home, lady and gents. I am very glad to meet everyone. I am a fan from what I've heard, and I think we might be able to do something together. Let's all go inside and have a chat, see if we can work something out."

They thanked him as he opened the door and showed them the way down a long hallway. The floor was covered with a colorful, shaggy carpet and the walls were filled with gold and silver albums framed in glass cases. There were also pictures with him and well-known rockstars. They saw KISS, Billy Idol, Donna Summer, Piper, Spider, and Tobey Beau to name a few. It left them in awe that this was their current reality.

Bill led them all into a vast room that looked like the White House's Oval Office.

"Please, everyone, find a seat and make yourselves comfortable," said Bill. "Would any of you like a drink? Coffee, tea, a nice alcoholic beverage? Anything at all?"

They all uttered nervous variations of, "No, sir, thank you."

"OK then. Let me get one for myself." Bill poured himself a Scotch on the rocks. "So folks, my attorneys have prepared a standard contract. Let me be clear on this. You can look it over today... tomorrow. If you want your own attorney to look everything over, that's perfectly fine too, and then I'll get back to you in a few weeks to see what you think.

So, let's get into some details. I want to send you to a recording studio in Ayer, Massachusetts on the weekends, and maybe a few nights after your day-jobs on weekdays. When we, or if we – work together – I can get your schedules and reserve the time in the studio for your sessions. If you have vacation time coming, we can use it for more studio time. I will put you up at a hotel close by on weekends or vacations paid for by my company, food included. Travel expenses also included.

Each of you will receive $100,000 when the album is completed. I can give everyone $10,000 to start. There are also bonuses for every hit song played on the radio. Once the album is completed, if it's a successful album, there will be potential for a nationwide tour. If you folks want to continue, we all then sign bigger contracts for more money, albums, and tours in the future. Those are the basics in layman's terms. Do you guys have questions for me? Do you want to go home and talk about it? Or can I leave the room so you all can discuss the contract now?"

"Mr. Arkin?" said Bob.

"Bill, please."

"Bill, we have new songs written, but we know nothing about recording," he said, uncertainness evident in his voice.

"No worries. At the studio, we have producers and technicians that will guide you and be at your disposal during the creative process."

"Bill, I think we'll take you up on the few private minutes to discuss it right here in the room alone," said Chuck, and everyone else nodded.

"OK then, I'll step out and let you discuss it. Just give me a shout when you're done." Bill got up and left the room, closing the door behind him.

None of them wanted to go home to think it over. They all were excited and ready to sign.

"So, are we all good guys? This could be our big break!" said Bob.

"Yeah, let's do this!" they agreed collectively.

Bob opened the door and said, "Mr. Arkin? Bill, that is. We're all set."

Bill walked back into the room.

"We love the offer, the deal. We're all ready to sign now," Bob continued.

"That's fantastic. I have a great feeling about all of this, I really do. This is going to be something special," said Bill. He pulled out five separate, identical contracts from his desk drawer and dispersed them. "Each contract has a name on it. Find yours and sign away. You'll have a year to fulfill the contract, as far as the recording goes. If not, you won't receive the rest of the money."

"We won't have a problem doing that, sir," said Bob.

"I know. I have confidence in you all. When you come to the studio on your first day, I will have your first check ready in hand. I was hoping everyone could make it next weekend. If so, I'll have the rooms ready at the Holiday Inn if that's good for everyone."

They all nodded excitedly.

Bill passed out pens and they signed, attempting to keep a calm facade. He gave them each a copy of the contract and shook hands individually, congratulating them. He then detailed directions to the studio and hotel in Ayer.

"You only need to bring your guitars and drums, if you want. The rest – amps, mixers, and the like – we have. So just bring yourselves, your clothes, and the songs you've written so far, and we will see everyone next weekend."

They agreed, thanking him, and slowly followed Bill out of the house. He waved as they turned around and drove back down the long driveway. They contained their excitement until they felt they were far enough away to not be heard, and then everyone in the car started screaming and hollering with joy.

They could not believe the good fortune that was upon them. They mused about quitting their day jobs to commit more time to recording. The money upfront would give them that opportunity, but Chuck and Shandi knew they would need to be more cautious at first. They had a new mortgage and a wedding to pay for, but they shared in the group's euphoria.

Bob and Dan leaned out of the car windows, sitting on the ledge of the doors, hair blowing.

Shandi turned the radio all the way up and everyone sang the words together:

"I've paid my dues/
Time after time/
I've done my sentence/
But committed no crime/
And bad mistakes/
I've made a few/
I've had my share of sand/
Kicked in my face/
But I've come through/
And we mean to go on and on and on and on/
We are the champions, my friends/
And we'll keep on fighting 'til the end!"

CHAPTER 3

MEDICATION TIME
APRIL 2002

AFTER THE 11:00 AM counting of inmates, Chuck decided to take a short nap in their back office. He nodded off hard, so Jed woke him up as he seemed to be in the middle of some sort of dream.

"Chuck, the inmates gotta come out for their meds," he said.

Chuck opened his eyes, a strand of drool coming down his chin. "Oh, okay, I'm ready. Wow, what a nice, toe-straightening break."

Jed was becoming accustomed to these nonsensical, dry quips and jibes that his partner made now and then.

Chuck jumped up out of his chair and walked out to the officers' station. Knowing what time it was, some inmates began to yell for the officers to open up their cell doors, impatient for their turn. Jed and Chuck ignored their wild shouting; some inmates did not like that. They shut the inmate phones off over by the recreation area as well. If they did not do that, some inmates would attempt to run over to the phones to use them, even though they were not let out for that reason, creating an opportunity for additional conflict between officer and inmate.

To prevent any potential issues or problems, Jed and Chuck only let a few inmates out of their cells at a time to get their medication, locking them back in immediately after. They started on the bottom tier and worked their way up to the second, walking each group of inmates to where the nurse handed them their medication one at a time. The nurse was locked in a secure room along with a big cart that held the presorted medication. The room had a caged window that opened slightly for her to pass medication through. A third assigned officer stood outside her window to make sure the inmates actually swallowed the meds they were given, and to make sure the nurse was provided an extra measure of security.

Dave Loomis was the third officer that day, floating between their unit and the unit next door to them. Loomis was helping both blocks with the inmates getting their medication and other miscellaneous tasks needed for an orderly operation. He went out to the nurse's station to watch the inmates while Chuck began letting them out of their cells as the shouting and banging continued.

They need to learn. If I ignore them and stand my ground, sooner or later, I'll break them, Chuck thought to himself.

Chuck was doing pretty well with his restraint until one inmate behind the very last door at the end of the second tier decided to kick his door belligerently, disrupting the entire unit. Every cell door had alarms built in. When the inmate kicked his door, it set off the alarm on Chuck's computer, causing it to need to be reset. The inmate continued kicking the door, and it incited other inmates to cheer him on.

Chuck could feel his temper blazing like in past moments in his life when he lost control and reacted without thinking. Over time, he had become able to reasonably manage his emotions; it was as if a guardian angel was watching over him, helping to calm him when he felt the uncontrollable rage rising. Usually.

Chuck reached into his pocket, grabbed a rubber band, and put his long hair up in a ponytail to keep it out of his face. It was the asshole with the lead foot's turn to come out of his cell for medication. Most officers would keep him locked in and have the nurse bring the meds up to his cell door at that point because of the hostility, but Chuck wasn't most officers. He opened the inmate's door and began walking towards the stairwell.

He left the desk, telling Jed, "I'll be right back!"

Chuck ran full speed up the stairwell, taking two, three steps at a time, and met the disruptive inmate at the top landing. He was pissed and full of adrenaline, and poked his two index fingers hard into the asshole's chest.

"Don't ever kick that goddamn door again, you got me?" he shouted at him.

"Yeah, yeah, I got it. I just didn't want you guys to forget me."

"How could I forget you?"

He could see the inmate change his tune once he was physically confronted, and he was going to relax now that Chuck put him on the spot in front of all his convict buddies.

Chuck walked back to his desk, murmuring to Jed, "Goddamn cell warriors!"

Jed started laughing. The rest of the day went more smoothly and they felt as though they were finally seeing their hard work pay off, that the unit was turning around.

They joked with their fellow officers to make the day go faster. One officer, Bennet, brought in a can of fart spray, and when the inmates were walking to the dining hall, schoolrooms, library, gym, or outside yard, he would spray it and wait for a reaction. Little things like this could make the day much more enjoyable. It cooled Chuck down after the issue with the door-kicking.

He was getting comfortable working in sync with Jed to bring order back to a place that had not seen it for some time. He was getting into a rhythm, taking pride in their work. The mission was bringing both men to a better place, even though they had troubles outside of work.

Chuck decided to open his locker in the locker room, which he hadn't used since his father's disappearance. He changed in there and put his gym clothes on. Weight lifting was something he enjoyed doing, though Chuck was not a big, muscle-head kind of guy. He was slender and fit for his age.

He jumped in his Jeep after changing, turned on his favorite classic rock station, and began driving. The song brought back the memory of the meeting he and the band had with Mr. Arkin, and Chuck thought back to the weekend at the recording studio where they had laid down their very first tracks.

CHAPTER 4

RECORDING ROCK AND POETRY

THE PLACE THEY were recording their first album was like something out of a dream. The studio was located in a town founded in New England in 1649. It had beautiful seventeenth-century colonial architecture covered in vines and historic homes of brick.

The studio building itself looked like the old Grand Movie Theater, renovated for modern use. Above the building hung a large billboard that still said "The Sound of Rock-and-Roll" on it. The entrance had retained the middle booth where you once would buy your movie tickets to get in the theater, only there were now pictures of different musical bands that had recorded at the studio on the walls.

Chuck's band was set up in the studio's largest available room, with some smaller adjoining rooms connected to it. The control room contained a sizable audio workstation, and all glassed-in were three technicians who worked their magic: a recording engineer, who set up and operated the equipment and was responsible for creating and producing music; a sound engineer, in charge of operating the technical equipment; and a residential engineer, who helped musicians with original ideas. There was also a separate glassed-in, soundproof booth for the lead singer.

The main floor was for the rest of the band and their equipment. They filled the place with technical machines, monitors, headphones, microphones, snake cables, power supplies, headphone amps, amplifiers, compressors, and consoles. The floors were made of high-gloss hardwood with rubber matting for the equipment and instruments to sit atop. The ceilings were adorned in classic, decorative plaster painted off-white.

Chuck, Shandi, and the boys were simply astonished by every detail they encountered.

The three engineers and producer that Bill had working with the band were all easy-going guys. The record and sound engineers, Kevin and Tom, were brothers with long brown hair and beards. They looked close in age, maybe even twins. Kenny, the assistant producer to Bill, was a very energetic guy. He was tall and completely balding at the front. And the residential engineer, Dominic Learner, was a very tall and broad African-American man with heavy facial scruff and a head of thick, black hair.

Shandi was in her booth nervously humming a song getting her vocals warmed up while Chuck, Bob and Dan tuned their guitars. Harry was lightly tapping on his drums and cymbals. They were anxious and ready to roll.

When they began, the engineers did their thing in the control room, while Bob, Chuck, and Dan were on the main floor playing their hearts out and Shandi was in the booth. She held a square headphone against her right ear and cheek and sang into the microphone, sounding like angels from heaven were descending upon them all. It was a song the band wrote and they were putting it down on tracks for the first time. It was simply extraordinary.

The song was coming together effortlessly. Shandi always killed it on vocals, but this was exceptional, even for her. Her long, dark hair flowed as she bobbed her head to the rhythm and swayed side-to-side wearing a tight acid-washed jean skirt. She tapped her tiny feet in a pair of opened-toed, cork sandals. Even the guys in the control room appeared impressed even though they had seen numerous talents walk through their doors. Chuck felt like he fell a little more in love with Shandi every time he watched her work.

The producer and technicians were all thinking, *This is pure gold*. If the rest of the track recordings went like this… every song would be a hit.

They couldn't wait for Bill to come in and see the success of his discovery first-hand.

Kenny spoke through the intercom after the band ran through the song and said, "OK everyone, let's do it again. That was fucking fantastic!"

The boys started playing, and then Shandi's raspy tones emerged from the depths of her soul.

She sang, "I'm fair in searching for a reply to my questions for dreams to become genuine/ It's just I feel my love needs more harmony/ I'm brief of luck and out of time, I'm beginning to lose my intellect/ I'm losing touch with reality, I never have wished upon a star/ I never thought that dreams may or would be true to me/ but in the midst of all my doubts/Presently I feel I am late and behind time/ I have combed the skies to find my pot of gold/ And that's why, darling"

As Shandi reached a high octave, the hairs on the back of everyone's necks stood straight up.

Shandi continued. "Someday I'm gonna to see my rainbow/ Sometime in the near future I'm reaching tall for the sky."

As she sang, Chuck thought back to when Shandi wrote the song, shortly after they had been dating and she joined the band. They had rehearsed it time and time again at Chuck and Shandi's house, but it never sounded this epic in their little basement studio.

They ended the song and Shandi said, "How was it that time? Another go or what?"

Kenny spoke through the intercom, "No, no, no. That's going to be great for now. We'll come back to it later if we need more of that one. Let's try that second song you wrote, *Nowhere Slowly.* Shandi, actually, come on out from inside the booth for a second, please."

She walked out of the booth and onto the floor with her bandmates.

"Okay people, we have a surprise for this number. Come in, ladies," Kenny said. In walked four young ladies all dressed in tight jeans or skirts. "I'd like you all to meet Sasha, Kira, Rebecca, and Stephanie. I hired them for an hour or so as backup singers on this song with Shandi. I'd like to try using a piano, too."

Kevin wheeled in a medium-sized piano from one of the side rooms. The girls introduced themselves to the band while Kevin prepared the piano.

"I love this song, but I want to try picking up the tempo just a little faster than you guys have written it. Harry, you're going to have to really whale on those drums. I hope your arms are ready for a serious workout."

"I won't let you down, sir," said Harry.

"That's what I love to hear, man. Okay everyone, places. Let's do this!"

Shandi went back inside the booth while the backup singers walked to the microphone stands Kevin had set up for them. Kenny went back to his station in the control room and commanded with excitement and much enthusiasm, "OK people, from the top. On the count of three... one, two, three!"

Harry smashed on his drums, the microphones creating a cacophonous echo. The backup singers began humming in sync as Shandi danced in the booth again, getting herself ready to sing. As they played the incredible intro, Bill Arkin walked into the control room from a back entrance to join Kenny and the other engineers.

Bill said to his men, "Wow, they sound even better than I could have imagined."

"I know, Bill, it's freaking incredible," said Kenny.

Shandi looked up and saw Bill in the control room and became a little nervous as she started to sing.

"Sleeping in your bed on a Saturday evening/ There's no heat, yet your sweatin' buckets/ But your brain understands/ And it's sending it out to all the nerves in your body/ Dreams abound in your life..."

"You've got to be fucking kidding me! This is gonna go platinum," said Bill.

"I know," Kenny said, smiling.

"There's nowhere to put them/ You'd better let some of them go/ As if your body's starting to rust/ Put it to work and rev it up/ It's hard to imagine how I ever did it."

The backup singers went into a heavy choir, swaying back and forth in place. Kevin played the piano like he had bolts of lightning coming from his fingertips. Chuck and the boys were all grinning from ear to ear. The band knew they had captured something very special, and they felt so lucky that Bill had discovered them. They ended the track to applause from everyone inside the control room.

"We got enough time for another go. How about it?" asked Kenny. There was resounding agreement from the band and the singers.

After they finished the song again, Bill went out on the floor and thanked all the backup singers before they left for the day. Some of the ladies asked if they could stick around to watch the rest of the session.

"You folks feel up to doing another track you've been working on?" Bill asked Shandi and the boys.

"Yes sir, we do!"

"Ahh, it's getting late and I know how Kenny and the fellas are about staying overtime." Bill looked into the control room at Kenny, Tom, Dominic, and Kevin. "Right boys?"

They exchanged smirks. Kenny said, "Well, what the hell, Bill. We love hearing Shandi sing!"

Bill laughed aloud, "Well, alright then. Let's hear this beauty!"

Bill returned to the control room and Shandi got ready again in the booth.

"OK," Kenny said. "Everyone, from the top. One, two, three!"

The band played forty-five seconds of introduction to the melody and then Shandi began.

"The night was long and sleepless/ Tears and the morning sun have replaced it/ We have run out of ways to say sorry/ Despite all the love we've shared/ Our words now touch what is/ Pain took the place of love/ As soon as you open the door/ There's no way to close it/What can I do if love must go."

Bill said to Kenny, "If the rest of the album continues like this, it will go Gold. These guys will be huge!"

"If love must go, how can I face the world," Shandi crooned, "I built around you? You took me up on/ Golden wings, let me feel the gentle things that love/ Could be/ Ooooh, the world was you and me/ What will I do? I've used my love on you and me/ What will I do?"

After they finished, Bill sounded off on the intercom.

"Okay everyone, that was remarkable. That's a wrap for today. Before everyone leaves, I have some news to share with you. I'll be down in a minute," he said.

Chuck, Shandi, and the boys all looked at each other in wonder as to what it could be that Bill had to say. A few moments later, they gathered on the main floor while Kenny and his techs packed up to go home for the night.

"OK folks, here it is," said Bill. "How would you like to take a trip to New York City in the month of May to perform on the television show, *Don Kirshner's Rock Concert*?"

"What? Are you kidding me?" the band exclaimed. They all knew the show very well.

"No, I'm not, and I would like you to play your song, "My Rainbow". I think it will end up being an enormous hit. In fact, I'm going to release that song to the radio stations ahead of the album's release. I have a great feeling about that track."

"Mr. Arkin, thank you so much!" said Chuck, the others also voicing their gratitude.

"No need to thank me, people. Just keep this up and I'll see everyone here tomorrow. I will fill you in on more details for the New York show then."

• • •

Later that evening when Chuck and Shandi got home, they broke out Jack Daniels 'and Coke. Chuck got the fireplace going.

"Just one or two small drinkie-poos. The little man should be all set for a few hours, babe," said Shandi.

She had just got in from walking their new male pug puppy, and she was rearing to do a little celebrating with her man. Shandi named the little tyke Rupert. He was a tiny, light-brown-colored pup with a crinkly black face and nose. He was full of energy and took right to Shandi and Chuck.

"Okay, how about the Sam Cooke album, *Ain't That Good News*?"

"Absolutely, babe. 'A Change Is Gonna Come'."

Chuck pulled it out of their collection of vinyl albums on the fireplace mantle. When pulling the record from the sleeve, a piece of pink note paper fell out onto the floor. Chuck picked it up, opened it, and saw Shandi's handwriting.

It said, "Though lovers be lost, death shall not;/ And death shall have no dominion."

He recognized it as a piece of a Dylan Thomas poem. She had poetry like this all over the house, but this particular one stuck out to Chuck. He put it back in the sleeve gently. Shandi had been studying and reading a lot of poetry. She had many unique books, but was especially dedicated to this poet. Chuck was always curious about her passion for poetry.

The record spun on the turntable in the entertainment center. They sipped on whiskey and danced the night away slowly. Rupert jumped up onto the bay window, watching them with love in his eyes. Shandi sang softly in Chuck's ear. He loved it when she did that; he felt like they were in a protective love bubble.

As they were dancing, she said to him, "Maybe if we make it big, babe... maybe we could buy all that land at the end of our street and build a small horse ranch. Work it during the day, and dance our nights away together forever."

"We will, babe. We will."

CHAPTER 5

GUS

CHUCK S FLIP PHONE rang while he was driving home from work, daydreaming of his past. It was Gary, who was now living in Virginia with Lilly.

"Hey what's up, broheim?" Chuck answered.

"Oh, not much. I called to tell you something."

"Yeah… ?"

"Have you heard from mom?" Gary asked.

"No, why?"

"Well, she should call you pretty soon, so you have to promise not to tell her I called you first."

"Okay, got it, I promise. Tell me what's going on."

"Next month she is having us – you, me, and Stacey — meet at her lawyer's office for the reading of Dad's will. She was very vague and said she wanted it to be a surprise."

"Wow, I wonder what it is. Are you coming up here?"

"Yep, I'll be there. Can I stay next door with Uncle Armond or your spare room?"

"Oh yeah, of course you can stay with me, brother. I'll even pick you up at the airport."

They carried on for a little while laughing and joking before Chuck hung up and pulled into his driveway. He went next door to his uncle's to get Rupert and tell him the good news about Gary coming home to visit. After hanging out with Armond for a while, Chuck took Rupert for a walk, and then they went back to his place to feed the little man. Chuck lit the fireplace and wondered when his mother would call.

As he stared into the firelight, he couldn't help thinking about his mentor that he sorely missed every single day- his father, Gus.

He had immigrated from Chazes, Portugal when he was a child in the early 1940s with his father Augusto Sr., mother Mary, and infant brother Charlie. Augusto was a notorious bootlegger, which was how he made most of the money to get his family passage to America on the famous ship, the SS *Serpa Pinto*. His parents, Mary and Augusto, had had an arranged marriage in Portugal. It was said amongst family members in private that Gus Senior may have never really loved her and only used her to get to America.

The ship docked in New York City. Augusto Barreto and his family eventually migrated to Massachusetts to join other family and friends they had there. At some point in Gus Junior's young life, his father left, taking Charlie with him, and they were never to be seen or heard from again. He had, however, left Mary with a lot of money and also land he owned in Portugal. Chuck's grandfather was rarely discussed amongst the family because of the heartache he caused, but Chuck always assumed his father must have inherited some of his grandfather's swagger.

Gus was dazzling and ambitious from a young age and took much pride in helping his mother growing up. The girls were very attracted to Gus in school because of his charm, good looks, and athletic ability. In his junior year, he met Chuck's mother, Rita, and they fell madly in love. When they graduated high school, Gus, Rita's older brother Richard, and two of his friends joined the Army and shipped out to Vietnam shortly after bootcamp. Before leaving, Gus married Rita, who was still living at home with her parents and younger brother, Armond.

What happened when they were at war was always very unclear and the stories told were vague. Upon his return, Gus mostly talked of only positive memories of his time in the military, but Chuck knew Gus had been in Cambodia and Laos for a time during their tour of duty and saw action. He and the other guys never discussed killing enemy soldiers. Miraculously they all survived, though Gus was badly injured and given a medical discharge.

When they got home, Gus bought an auto body shop and it flourished into an immense success. When he was of age and received his inheritance from his mother, it included 300 acres of land in Chazes, Portugal. He flew to Portugal and sold most of it, keeping a small portion for his growing family.

With the money he made from that sale, he bought 150 acres of industrial land in the sleepy town of Woodrow. It featured a somewhat rugged landscape: wooded areas crossed with trails, small river beds, and a large prominent mountain that separated the city from the town they lived in. Gus also purchased a small beach house in Rhode Island for Rita who loved the ocean. When Chuck, Gary, and Stacey were growing up, Gus and Rita would take them there for long summer vacations, creating fond memories for them all.

Chuck woke up the next morning, having fallen asleep while lost in memories of his father, and still hadn't heard from his mother. He was feeling unusually energetic and took Rupert out for a walk, dropping him off with his uncle before he left for work. He sipped on coffee and blared KISS tunes on the way there.

When Chuck, Jed, and Dave Loomis got inside the block, they had their usual coffee together. Dave was becoming a regular fixture working in the unit with Jed and Chuck. He was tall, thin and had a complexion like ivory. They enjoyed his dry, monotone approach to corrections. That morning, they discussed a plan for keeping large groups of inmates from hanging out on the second tier.

When a fight broke out between inmates on the second tier, it could get dangerous for everyone involved, including responding officers. It was also a department rule that no inmates were allowed up there unless they had an assigned cell in that location. Chuck and Jed devised a plan to allow up only one inmate at a time. Chuck and Jed made a homemade pass and laminated it. An inmate would have to come to the officers' station and ask for it to gain access to the top tier. If another inmate wanted to go up, he would have to wait for the inmate using the pass to come down.

At first, Jed and Chuck were not sure if it would work, but strangely enough it was utilized extremely well and the inmates started policing themselves. They seemed to like the system. They also knew that if issues began to occur, no one would be permitted up there except the inmates that lived on the second tier.

The block was running smoother by the day. Jed and Chuck were relentless with their dedication and consistency. Around noon, there was a call on both the radio and prison intercom that an officer was in need of assistance. Those kinds of calls were dire. When you heard the call sign, that meant an officer was in trouble and to move like no one's business to help your brother officer, no exceptions.

Chuck and Jed ran out of the block at full speed, leaving Dave in charge. He locked all inmates in their cells, as was standard for the emergency code. When Jed, Chuck, and other officers arrived at the scene, it looked like two or three inmates had jumped on one officer working there. The officer was bleeding from the forehead. As the violent inmates that assaulted the officer were being placed in handcuffs, a lieutenant on the scene ordered Chuck and Jed to grab the main troublemaker and bring him to the Hole. The Lieutenant gave Chuck a look, and Chuck knew what it meant.

On their way to the Hole, Chuck and Jed dragged the inmate over to a quiet corner and Chuck began punching the inmate in the back of the head until he started crying. He wasn't before, but he was sorry now.

Jed threw a few hard shots too, and then said to Chuck, "Okay, bro, he's had enough."

"You're lucky my partner's with me, you sorry a-hole."

"I'm sorry, Rockstar," said the inmate. "I don't want no smoke."

Even some inmates, aware of his first career, called Chuck that nickname.

"Yeah, yeah. You shut up now!" said Chuck.

Jed invited Chuck over to his house after work for a few drinks, along with two other fellow officers. They all followed Jed to his place in their separate vehicles. As they pulled into the driveway, they saw a gorgeous house that Chuck referred to as a mini version of the Wayne Manor from the Batman movies- another dry quip. It was actually only a comfortable Victorian, about 3500 square feet. He assumed it had to be an inheritance, but he didn't pry into others' business unless they opened up the conversation first.

Jed graciously showed the guys around his home and then made them drinks before getting them some spare swimming trunks from his bedroom. They spent a few hours horsing around in Jed's in-ground swimming pool, drinking and joking about the incident earlier at work.

After Dave and the other officer went home, Jed made some daiquiris. He and Chuck floated around on the pool chairs, talking about one of Jed's favorite topics- politics. Jed was telling Chuck about candidate Chip Karrington, his ideals, and an upcoming campaign rally. Jed knew Chip personally and asked Chuck if he wanted to go with him to the event. Chuck was extremely reluctant to attend a political event due to his unfamiliarity with politics and feeling out of place in that type of atmosphere, but his partner assured him it would be a great time. Jed would introduce him to some interesting people and it would be another opportunity to hang out, drink, and eat. Chuck finally gave in and accepted. Jed told him he wouldn't regret it and meeting Chip Karrington would be invigorating.

Chuck half-smiled at that idea. He was also surprised to learn that Jed himself had recently taken and passed the bar exam after many years of dedicated night school. Like Chuck, he was also full of surprises.

When they called it a night, it was late and Jed insisted that Chuck not drive home, but Chuck insisted he had stopped drinking earlier and assured him he was good to go.

That was a little white lie.

Chuck still had a decent buzz, but he had the next day off and just wanted to hit his own bed. While he was navigating his way home, the booze in his system, the solitary drive, and the song "This Is Love" by White Snake led him to think about Shandi again. When he pulled into the driveway, he saw Uncle Armond was still awake, so he stopped in for a quick visit and to retrieve Rupert.

Chuck was in a good mood, so he and Armond had a few Jack and Cokes and talked about the television show that his uncle was watching. Armond eventually told Chuck to go home, get some rest, and come back for the now-sleeping Rupert in the morning. Chuck crashed hard onto his king-size bed, only bothering to kick off his shoes. The alcohol drove him quickly into a R.E.M. state, and he began dreaming about the last time he ever saw Shandi.

CHAPTER 6
KELLY ANN TEXEIRA
APRIL 2002

A VERY ATTRACTIVE woman in her mid-thirties who owned the real-estate company, The Silver Bell, was about to have a meeting with the local State Representative, Chip Karrington. Kelly Ann Texeira was originally a southerner who moved from Texas seven years ago to start her own business. She was slender with long, thick red hair and a freckled, southern-belle face. Kelly was very aggressive and carried herself with an abundance of confidence. She knew what she wanted in life and never quit until she got it; she never took no for an answer.

Kelly knew and dealt with many lawyers, politicians, business executives, contractors, inspectors, and land developers. In the short time she had lived in the area, she opened two offices: one was in town in a plaza off the main road by Gussy's Pitts, which was owned by Chuck's mother Rita, and the other was in Wolford City inside the Skytower. She advertised on billboards on main roads and highways, her classic face smiling down at you as you drove by.

At one time, Rita had worked for Kelly part-time as an agent just to keep herself busy. Rita enjoyed selling homes and the world of real estate but didn't want the responsibility of running her own agency. She liked the freedom to pick and choose her work hours.

Chuck's sister, Stacey, who had become a well-paid accountant, got to know Kelly pretty well through Rita. They had many mutual friends and would end up at the same get-togethers or work parties. Kelly often told Stacey how she loved working with her mother, highlighting her intelligence.

There was a knock on Kelly's office door.

"Come in," said Kelly.

Chip entered her office and closed the door behind him. He gave her a devilish look and then they began making out.

"We have to stop meeting like this, sexy lady," said Chip.

"I know, handsome. What would your wifey think?" Kelly winked at him.

"She's never going to find out."

"We need you, sir, in the Senate. So we have to be extra careful."

Chip Karrington was campaigning for a Senate seat, and Kelly, along with many others, had invested in his campaign because of special agendas and interests that needed influence in D.C.

"I have a campaign rally next week, as you know. Will you be there?"

"Yes, of course, my sexy future senator. Some of my agents and staff will also be available to help out, voluntarily."

"You're the best, thank you. I have another favor to ask."

"You keep asking for favors, but when do I see a return?"

"Don't worry, Kelly. You will, tenfold."

"I better," she said and kissed him again.

"So I have a huge donor," Chip continued. "You know I only like to have smaller contributors, but it's been hard getting anywhere, as you can imagine. These larger donations could help get me across the finish line in the election. It's a big land developer by the name of The LoneStar Group. I've never actually met or spoken to the guy in charge. Maybe there is no one individual; maybe it's all co-owned. I don't know. Anyway, I did speak with one of their attorneys, Silus Sin Kobol, and they are offering a large sum of money. Have you ever heard of them?"

"Oh, yeah. They're an expansive group, involved with building condos, casinos... the list goes on, throughout the U.S."

"Well, here's my issue. Rita Barreto, she used to work for you?"

Kelly nodded.

"She currently owns around 150 acres of land, called Gussy's Pitts, in the Woodrow Valley."

"Yes, she sure does."

"This group wants to make her an extremely generous offer. If accepted, it would make her a very wealthy woman. They want to develop all that empty land."

"Yes, I know all about that property. When she worked here, I asked her about it. She told me it wasn't for sale. She said that she may have her own plans to do something with it."

"Hmmm. Is there any way you could talk with her again to change her mind?"

"I can try."

"Okay, thank you. I have to go, I'm running late for a meeting."

After Chip left, Kelly thought to herself, *How will I pull this one off? I know how tough Rita can be.*

Rita had been so adamant about not selling it for some reason. But where there's a will, there's a way, and no one had a greater will than Kelly.

CHAPTER 7
THE BOYSCOUT CAMP
MAY 1988

CHUCK JUST GOT out of work. He was thinking a lot these days about putting in his notice to focus more on the new album. The band was halfway done recording, and in two days they'd be leaving for New York to perform on *The Kirshner Show*.

He was on his way to the gym to meet Shandi like he normally did. They worked out together on most days and it proved to be one of his favorite routines. Shandi was athletic in the gym and he appreciated the competition. They knew just about everyone there; the two of them shone together. You could see how in love they were, and people wanted to be around them when they entered a room. They could be working out on a hammer squat machine and people would flock to them to have a quick chat. Chuck felt it was all Shandi; she had a beautiful aura that made her magnetic.

As they worked out, their routine in sync, they discussed details of their upcoming event in New York, tentative tour dates across the country, and their hit song on the radio that was rapidly climbing the charts. Music consumed their thoughts, and any free time they had outside of recording was spent finalizing little details for the show and beyond.

After their workout, Chuck had to head over to his parents' house because Gus wanted him to stop by. Shandi was going straight home to take Rupert out for a walk. When Chuck got home, they had plans for a quick dinner before the boys came over for a band meeting to go over things for New York. Outside the gym, Chuck gave Shandi a kiss and they went their separate ways.

"I'll see you soon, babe. I won't be all that long," said Chuck.

"I love you, Chuck Taylor Barreto!"

Chuck smiled as he watched Shandi get in her car. He couldn't help checking her out in the skin-tight spandex she had on. *Boy, how lucky did I get?* Chuck thought to himself.

When Chuck arrived at his parents' home, they congratulated him on the band's success and handed him his grandmother's wedding ring from Rita's side. Grandma Lussier had passed on years ago, and they offered their son her ring when Chuck told his parents that he was going to ask for Shandi's hand in marriage when they were in New York. After the show, Chuck was going to take Shandi to the Empire State Building and pop the question when they got to the top. The whole band and Shandi's parents also secretly knew about Chuck's plans and were ecstatic for them. Gus was especially so happy for his son that he could not wipe the ear-to-ear smile off his face.

Chuck left his parents' house and was driving down his own beautiful street when "My Rainbow" came on the radio. The disc jockey enthusiastically announced that the song was by Shandi and the Boys. It played through his beefed-up speakers.

Wow! This is our song, playing right now on my car radio, he thought, and then the Charger pulled into their driveway.

He saw Shandi's car was parked. Chuck looked over to the front door and saw Rupert sitting by himself, crying loudly with his leash still attached. He knew right away something was wrong. Shandi would never leave Rupert outside unattended.

When Chuck got out of his car, Rupert ran towards him, jumping up on his legs, barking. He felt a strange panic like he had never known.

"Where's Shandi, boy?" Chuck asked the dog.

Rupert barked repeatedly.

"Come on, boy." Chuck brought Rupert into the house and took off his leash and noticed a few drops of fresh blood on it. He quickly felt Rupert's body for any kind of injuries. There were none.

He began calling Shandi's name as he checked every room in the house. He ran out into the backyard, looking everywhere, including the shed. No Shandi.

His head was spinning and he could feel his blood pressure rising.

"Shandi! Shandi! Shandi!" Chuck shouted more loudly each time. A neighbor heard him and came to see what was going on.

"Chuck, everything alright?" he said.

"No, it's not, Tom," Chuck responded, his face red. "I'm a little screwed up right now. Shandi was walking Rupert and he came home without her. Did you see anything?"

"No I didn't, Chuck. You should calm down, son. I'm sure she'll be home soon. There has to be an explanation."

"Boy, I hope so, Tom. It's just that she dotes on our dog and she would never let him get loose while she was walking him."

As Tom tried to help calm Chuck down, a police cruiser drove down the street slowly. Chuck ran over to it, recognizing the officer. It was Niel Reeves, his former high school classmate.

Niel rolled down his window. "Hey, Chuck, how are you? Everything okay?"

"Hi Niel, no, not really. What brings you to our street?" Chuck asked. A police cruiser wasn't a common sight.

"A caller reported a loud bang somewhere near here. Said it sounded like a gunshot maybe."

Chuck felt himself stagger and held himself up using the roof of the police cruiser.

"Chuck, what's wrong? Did you guys hear anything?"

Tom shook his head. Niel got out of his car and Chuck told him what had happened when he arrived home. Now that there was some sort of bang in the neighborhood, he instinctually felt that it involved Shandi; intuition told him Shandi was in some sort of danger. Chuck told Niel about the blood on his dog's collar.

"Chuck, relax. I'm sure this is a coincidence. We will find Shandi. I'm sure she's fine."

Chuck tried to believe in Niel and Tom's assurances, but the more the moments ticked by, the more his adrenaline pumped, filling him with dread and despair. Niel decided against typical protocol to try and calm Chuck down some by calling a missing person into the station.

"I'm going to call this in, Chuck, and get some more help out here. Just as a precaution."

"Thanks, Niel. Appreciate it," Chuck choked out.

While Niel was talking to dispatch, Chuck ran inside the house to see if anyone else knew where Shandi was. He called both of their parents, his siblings, and uncle, but no one had heard from her or knew where she was.

Within an hour and a half, police cruisers, family, and friends showed up in droves. It was like a military operation. An assigned supervisor started delegating with impressive speed. Stacey was tasked with writing down a list of extended family and friends who she then began calling. A notetaker began putting together a timeline of the day's events. Photos from their house and her parents were given randomly to those who would be conducting the on-foot search. Chuck gave the supervisor and Niel a full description of the attire she had been wearing.

The Chief of Police, George, arrived on the scene. He wanted to be able to tell Chuck and Shandi's parents not to worry, but that would go against his practice. Instead, he told them he would do everything possible to find her. A group of volunteers was assigned to go door-to-door, armed with notepads and pens to write down any pertinent information about whether neighbors had seen or heard anything out of the ordinary. The rest of the volunteers were paired up and given walkie-talkies, flashlights, and whistles. Chief George and his officers assigned specific areas to volunteers to search in the neighborhood, through the woods, and along the lake.

Two bases were created for people to report back to, either via radio or on foot. The first one was set up with two cruisers and a table at the top of the street leading to the main road, and the second was at Chuck and Shandi's house. Two men were posted at each to keep track of places that were already covered and re-assign people to unsearched territory when needed. Some people ran out and bought water and snacks and put them at the two bases. Hundreds of people were involved. With Shandi being so well-loved, word had spread unbelievably quickly. It was an operation to be admired, if only Shandi's well-being wasn't at stake.

THE BOYSCOUT CAMP

Soon after the search began, Chuck was deep in the woods with Bob and Gary, screaming louder than anyone. His voice was so thunderous it was somewhat alarming to others but understandable. He was determined to find Shandi no matter what.

Hours went by. It was now pitch-black outside, but no volunteer was quitting. People were worried for Shandi and desperately wanted to help find her. With some neighbors having reported that they, like the caller, had heard what sounded like a gunshot, the situation felt dire. Some said that maybe it was a hunter or some kids with fireworks, but that wasn't the norm for the area either.

Around 3:20 in the morning, someone started frantically blowing his whistle. Almost in conjunction with the whistle sounding off, another person began yelling repeatedly.

"Help! Help! Somebody, help!"

Gary, Bob, and Chuck faintly heard the commotion, as they were somewhat far away from the area of the whistle and screams.

Gary turned up the volume on the walkie-talkie. "Anyone there? Please, we found something. We're at the old Boy Scouts' Camp!"

"Something's up at the Scouts' camp," Gary relayed to Bob and Chuck.

The camp had been used for meetings and such. The place looked like something out of a Friday the 13th movie. It had a small party area and some old wooden docks off the lake. The depth of the water could get over 25 feet depending on the season.

Chuck knew the area. He drove by it every day to and from work. Sometimes he saw cars parked over in the small, dirt parking lot, which was most likely when the Scout leaders and kids were meeting.

He took off like a bolt of lightning through the woods. Gary and Bob tried to keep up with Chuck, but he was too fast. Chuck emerged from the woods and blazed down the street heel-to-heel for roughly a half-mile until he saw the main camp building. He ran to the building, then pivoted back into the woods past the cement structure, down a long hill with a path leading to the lake.

Chuck heard Shandi's mother screaming and crying uncontrollably. He then saw Shandi's father holding his wife back from approaching the dock. About twenty people, including police officers, watched as Chuck came barreling down the hill. Niel had officers cut him off before he got to the dock.

"Please hold Chuck back. This is a crime scene," Niel said.

This only spurred Chuck forward. The officers attempted to hold him back, but he just threw them out of the way like paper dolls. It was their job to preserve the area, but they also saw Chuck's rage and knew it would just make things worse to try to interfere with his emotional actions.

"Chuck, come on, please! Chuck, no!" Niel yelled, knowing it was a moot point to try to stop him now. He said, giving in, "OK, stay out of his way please."

Shandi was still half in the water and half on the river bed. Her skin was purple, clothes were torn, and she was covered in blood. He ran into the water, picked her up in his arms, and gently put her back down on the wooden dock. Chuck screamed so loud you could probably hear him for miles.

"Shandi, wake up. Wake up! God fucking damn it, baby, wake up! Wake up!" He started blowing air into her mouth and giving chest compressions, continuing to howl like an animal. After a few minutes of Chuck trying to revive her, Niel and the others decided to try to get him to stop. Eventually family and friends were able to pull Chuck from her lifeless body so the police could do their job. It was revealed that Shandi's cause of death had been a gunshot to the stomach.

CHUCK WOKE UP out of a dead sleep on his couch, screaming. "She's not dead! Shandi, wake up! Wake up, noooo!"

He fell off the couch, confused and covered in sweat. His eyes were tearing up. Chuck realized again that Shandi had been murdered and picked himself up off the floor, shaking from the recurrent nightmare about her death. He went into the kitchen to splash water on his face and guzzle down some water to replenish himself from the dehydration of drinking the night before.

Armond knocked on the front door and said, "Chuck, everything okay?"

He staggered to the door and opened it up for his uncle. "Yeah, I'm fine. I think I was dreaming or something."

"Oh, okay, just checking."

"Come on inside for some coffee, Unc."

Armond followed him through the door. "Rupert is sound asleep on my couch."

"OK, thanks, Arm."

"You got it, Meathead."

Chuck laughed. It always cheered him up when his uncle called him that. Chuck had taken a page from his uncle's book in giving people nicknames. He would give people he liked fascinating ones, but people he didn't like got weird, fucked-up ones.

Chuck made the coffee and put four sugars and lots of cream in Armond's, just the way he liked it. Then he turned on the television for background noise and they talked about various things while they sat on the couch sipping their coffee. Chuck told Armond he had a bit of a hangover but not too bad, and that a couple of his Army buddies were coming over to the house to hang out downstairs at the bar to watch football later. He invited Armond too, but he declined, saying he had to catch up on some of his favorite shows.

After his uncle went home, Chuck took a shower and got dressed in basketball shorts and a t-shirt to go for a run. He went to Armond's to get Rupert, quickly fed him, and off they went. The dog kept up with Chuck for a while, but when Rupert began panting, they walked the rest of the way.

On their way back to the house, Chuck called Stacey to tell her about the campaign rally for Chip Karrington. She was in Chip's grade in school so she knew him well. Chuck had met Chip a few times briefly at his sister's house when she had barbecues on occasion. She told him that she and some of her friends might also be at the rally, and then razzed her big brother about going to his first political event before they hung up.

When Chuck and Rupert got home, he took another shower, got dressed, cleaned up the house a little, and got some drinks ready for his guests. Chuck figured he could cover the food by ordering takeout.

Mitch pulled in the driveway first in an old Gremlin wagon; Mike followed in a big SUV.

Chuck greeted them loudly, "Hey, little Mitch, Mikey G. Come in, fellas. How are you doing?"

"Good, never better. Great to see you, Rockstar!" they responded.

Rupert ran over to sniff their legs and Mike petted him until he settled down. He was the size of a giant, carrying a humongous cooler in his right hand filled with beer and homemade sandwiches. That's how Mike was when he went to a get-together. He always brought lots of food and alcohol, even if there was already going to be plenty at the event.

"No Jem, huh guys?" Chuck asked, referring to another member of their squad.

"No, he said he was busy with his fam today."

"OK guys, let's go downstairs to the bar. I already got the football game on for ya, Mitch."

Mitch loved watching football. Chuck and Mike could not care less about it, but they liked the company. Whenever Chuck and Mike hung out, in or out of the military, they loved discussing old classic movies and eighties rock music. At some point in time, they were hoping to see a KISS concert together if the band ever came around the area. And even though it wasn't really Mitch's scene, he'd be there too.

They sat down on the stools at Chuck's bar, which was decorated with movie and rock memorabilia and pictures of him with his platoon in Panama. There were also pictures of his Charger and his father, but there were none of Shandi and his bandmates.

There was another room directly behind them. The door to that room was closed for good, as far as Chuck was concerned. It held Chuck's old guitars, amps, and equipment from his musical days, now collecting dust. Chuck had not picked up his guitar – or anything else in that room – since before Shandi was murdered.

Mike and Mitch suspected something was up with it since they had never seen the inside, but they never did ask. Mitch was naturally quiet. Chuck would have to get him talking sometimes. Chuck and Mike carried the conversation, as usual, by talking about some of their favorite classic war movies. Mikey loved the old movie *A Bridge Too Far*, so he began spewing quotes from it to Chuck.

"What's the best way to take a bridge, sir?"

"Both ends at once, General!" Chuck responded. They both start laughing loudly.

"What made you join the Army, Rockstar?" Mitch asked, out of the blue.

Chuck had never told anyone why before. But these guys saved his life and he theirs, so what the hell. It was time.

CHAPTER 9

BE ALL THAT YOU CAN BE

AUGUST 1988

THE TURNOUT FOR Shandi's funeral was huge. Practically the entire town was there. Hundreds of people from all different aspects of their lives were in attendance. The parking lot at the local church had been filled to capacity, leaving people forced to park on surrounding streets.

Shandi's dad spoke of her to the captivated hall of people for a while, and then Chuck went up to say a eulogy. After speaking a few lines, he got too emotional. Stacey saw and ran up to the podium to finish the speech for him. Gus grabbed Chuck and sat him down on the bench next to him, Stacey continuing also with difficulty, as she had become good friends with Shandi herself. All the people in the church unsuccessfully fought back tears.

Weeks had passed since the funeral and her murder, and there was no word or evidence found of who had done it. Shandi's parents, Patrick and Julie Monroe, were persistent, calling or going to the station every day for updates. Each call or visit was a major disappointment. Chuck also stopped by every single day to talk with the detective in charge of the case. He was an older man, skinny, with long gray hair like the actor, Sam Elliot.

His name was Scott Austin. He was staunch in his dedication, trying to find out anything about Shandi's death.

The FBI also had allowed a special agent to get involved. Chief George made some phone calls and pulled some strings for it to happen. His name was Jack Bufford. Agent Bufford kept in periodic contact with Chuck, relaying messages to him and Shandi's parents.

Along with the habit he developed to visit the station, he also began sipping on his daily dose of whiskey. If Chuck drank before going there, he would limit his intake until after he left the station. Afterwards, the sky was the limit.

He had quit his job at the factory shortly after Shandi's death and was living off the money he got paid for the half-album they recorded with Bill. There was also some money coming in from royalties on their hit song, which had become even more popular after Shandi died.

After getting nowhere with the investigation and his frustration increasing, Chuck needed distractions to keep him busy. He began obsessively fixing things around the house. At one point, Chuck was consumed with sanding off all the old stains on the back deck. It was twenty feet by twenty feet, and he sanded it all by hand with sandpaper attached to a rubber block. His bandmates and brother kept stopping over, trying to stop Chuck from embarking on his destructive path or offer their help, but he just kept sanding and drinking while they talked and said nothing to them until they got the hint and left.

Gus came over to try to get through to him. Chuck would do something evasive, like grab Rupert and say, "I gotta walk the dog, Dad, I'll talk to you later," to avoid conversation. He would leave his father standing at the house alone and walk off, pulling a bottle out of his pocket when he was far enough out of sight. Nothing could deter Chuck from the dangerous way he decided to cope.

When his father was gone each time, he went back to sanding the deck, day after day, until the actual wood felt like glass under your fingers. Every single square inch.

Rupert hung outside with Chuck on the deck all day, watching him work, and later in the day they would often go for walks. On one evening, as Chuck and Rupert got closer to the Boy Scout Camp, Rupert pulled Chuck along harder, trying to lead him down to the dock. Once they were on the property, Rupert cried and howled as if he was in agony because he knew what happened to Shandi in that campground. Rupert was the last living creature to see Shandi alive and to see the killer.

Chuck stood at the dock with Rupert, thinking and getting angrier. Something finally snapped in his head, and he staggered back to the house with Rupert. He brought the dog inside, took his leash off, and grabbed the keys to the Charger.

Chuck was very, very drunk.

"You stay here, boy. I'll be right back," he said to Rupert. Rupert barked at Chuck in response.

Chuck got into the Charger with a glance at Shandi's car, which had sat unmoved since her death. He turned the key in the ignition and the block engine roared to life with a fury. He backed out of his driveway, burning rubber, taking off with the radio at full blast. Chuck had reached an internal boiling point. He felt helpless and could do nothing about Shandi's death or his misery without her; he didn't know what he was doing anymore. Chuck drove for miles, somehow keeping his car at the speed limit.

Before he even realized he had driven so far, he was passing Gussy's Pitts, his father's 150 acres, vacant except for the large commercial building Gus had built. He rented out offices in the building to doctors, lawyers, therapists, and other business owners. The extensive building was rather noticeable off the main road, sitting by itself in front of all that vast land.

Chuck stepped hard on his brakes and spun the big car around, kicking up dirt into the entrance of Gussy's Pitts. The car felt like it was going slightly airborne off the soft dunes and bumpy dirt road trails, bringing him back to his younger days.

When Chuck was a kid, still in grade school, he would ride a dirtbike on his dad's land for recreation. He knew every trail in there. Luckily most of the trails were wide enough for the fast and furious vehicle. As he was driving, the layout came back pretty quickly. The Charger continued spinning up dirt as the song "Purple Haze" blared out of the speakers. He did something he normally never did – buckled up his seat belt – and stepped on the accelerator even harder.

Chuck was hitting some significant dirt mounds and the beastly car was getting airborne on some of them. He felt a high when the vehicle was floating in the air. He was able to stay in control, and to his amazement, the car had not taken on any serious damage as far as he knew. He spun the car around and sped her down narrow trails surrounded by trees. As the

Jimi Hendrix song played on the radio, Chuck felt euphoric and pissed off all at once. The car scraped tree trunks as he whizzed by them. His prized vehicle was now picking up some pretty nasty scratches and dents on the fender and door panels.

Chuck didn't care; he was beyond giving a fuck at this point. He was out of his mind.

He saw a decent-sized hill ahead of him, so he decided to try to drive up it. *Hell yeah*, Chuck thought, and put the pedal to the floor.

The Charger raced to the top, the engine straining as if it was about to blow up. He made it to the top, then stopped the car, idling. He looked down, took a small breath, and floored it. The car reached the bottom of the other side, and the Charger's undercarriage hit rocks so hard that metal sparks flew.

Chuck continued on after that gutsy maneuver, driving through shallow riverbeds, the car engine almost stalling out. Once he got clear of the water, the Charger flew into open, grassy fields. Chuck saw an enormous boulder at the bottom of a vast mountain. The boulder was half the size of his Charger and the mountain it was in front of was named Indian's Leap. This great wonder of the little town of Woodrow separated Wolford City from entry into the surrounding towns, with the exception of the main city bridge.

The legend of the landmark went that a tribe of Indians called the Wigwams kidnapped a young female settler during King Philip's War. The Indians were being pursued by settlers, and they jumped off the other side of this mountain, escaping into the vast, endless wilderness. That wilderness was now all torn down by modern man, and in its place was the big city below, filled with corruption and plight. Indians Leap essentially stopped city life from getting into Woodrow.

Chuck sped forward towards the boulder, not looking at the speedometer, but hit the brakes lightly before the impact. The Charger smashed the boulder head-on, the front end of his vehicle crushed like a tin can. Chuck lurched forward on impact and walloped his chest on the steering wheel. Glass shattered everywhere, cutting open the top of Chuck's forehead. Blood ran down his face. The car was smoking and the engine stalled out.

Fuck, Chuck thought to himself, *that felt good.*

No more Jimi Hendrix played on the radio. Smoke and steam continued to pour from the smashed radiator. The Charger was totaled. He got out of the car and thanked God he and his father had built and welded a thick metal, barred-frame roll cage inside the vehicle. It came in handy.

Chuck knew Gus would be upset with him, but in the moment it wasn't important. He was a little sore, his t-shirt and right pant leg were torn from shards of glass and stained with blood that dripped from his face. Even the crash hadn't sobered him up; he was still buzzed.

Chuck walked forward on the warm breezy night until he reached the foot of Indian's Leap. Getting to the top was a nice workout, but getting down the other side was a different story. It was a straight drop peppered with cliffs and ledges. In the distance were all the tiny lights of the big city. Chuck lowered himself down carefully onto the first ledge. He wondered if he would be trying this if he were sober. At this point in his life, probably. As he maneuvered each precipice, not really worrying if he slipped and fell to his death, Chuck started talking to himself out loud. It helped him focus better as he talked.

"I doubt Indians leapt off this sucker and lived to tell about it. That's why they call it a legend. I bet they all died, and no one wanted to climb down to find out," he laughed to himself.

He kept talking nonsense and laughing at his own jokes aloud for what seemed forever, until his feet hovered over a river bed. He jumped from the cliff about five feet, landing in the water a few inches deep. He walked until he reached an old, rusted chain-link fence just before the main road in the city. Chuck grabbed it and jumped over while cars whizzed by, not even noticing him.

Chuck continued walking a few miles through the busy streets, past restaurants, bars, clubs, gas stations, and stores. Chuck thought about going to a bar for a drink.

"Nah, not right now," he said to himself.

He thought about whether he should get something to eat or call someone for a ride home.

"Nah," he said. He kept walking.

The last thing he wanted was to go back home and think about Shandi. Chuck knew he would never really be able to rest until the one responsible was found, so he kept walking forward, past a popular sports bar. He saw a big sign with a light over it to the side of the bar. It had a big picture of Uncle Sam wearing an American flag top hat, pointing his finger right at Chuck. Underneath Sam, the sign said, "I WANT YOU FOR THE U.S.

ARMY!" He walked toward the attractive sign. Through the glass pane, Chuck saw two men in uniform who must be recruiters.

He stared inside at the men in green for a few minutes before saying to himself, "Yes, I've had enough."

Chuck opened the door and a little bell rang. Both men stood up from behind their desks dressed in Class C's. One man was very young and the other was older with high and tight gray hair. They noticed the blood on Chuck's head and clothes, but pretended not to see it.

The older recruiter, Greg, thought to himself, *Look at this sorry-looking kid. The Army is just what he needs.*

"Hello," Greg said to Chuck. "You thinking of joining the U.S. Army?"

"Yes, maybe," said Chuck.

"My name is Greg, and this is Private Max. What's your name, son?"

"Chuck Barreto."

"Have a seat, Chuck Barreto."

Chuck sat on the opposite side of the desk.

"Okay, how many tours are you looking to do? Or are you interested in Reserves?"

"Ah, just one tour for now, I think. How many years is that?"

"Two years, young man."

"What will I do if I join?"

"I'll show you a list of jobs and you can apply for all the ones you're interested in, if you sign up. When your application gets processed and you pass the physical, you get assigned what's available. Depending on what's happening, you may leave the United States for active duty, or sometimes you do your entire tour of duty here in the States."

"Okay," Chuck answered, unsure.

They went through the rest of the process thoroughly. They discussed all of the medical, physical, and written tests he'd be doing, where he would go to take them, and when he'd be officially sworn in. He thought about it for a second then agreed.

"Where do I sign?" Chuck said.

Greg gave him the official form and he signed away. He then showed him a long list of jobs they had available. Chuck chose infantry; halfway down the list he saw an entry for helicopter pilot. Chuck said to himself, *Definitely*, and marked it down as well.

Then he looked at Greg and said, "Can I use your phone for a ride home? My car broke down a little ways from here."

"Sure, Chuck, but Max can give you a ride home."

"Ah, no thanks. I'll give my uncle a call."

"It's really no problem, but okay, if you insist," Greg said and slid the phone over to him.

Chuck told his uncle he needed a ride, and Armond said he'd be at his location within an hour. Armond was in his mid forties and his mother's younger brother. He was known in the family as the rebel without a cause. A little chunky with long brown hair and a big beard, Armond considered himself a hippie.

Chuck said goodbye to the recruiters, thanking them, and went to sit on a bench outside. Armond pulled up in his old, black Monte Carlo with the passenger window rolled down.

Armond shouted, "Let's go, Meathead."

Chuck jumped off the bench. "Okay, Unc."

"Where are we going?" Uncle Armond asked after they had driven out of the city.

"Drop me off at my parents. I'm going to borrow the old man's tow truck to get my car," said Chuck.

"What happened to your car?"

"I was driving around in the Pitts and she overheated on me."

"Really? What's that cut on your head and the blood on your torn shirt and pants?"

"I ran into a lot of pricker bushes walking out of there."

"Right, what were you doing outside a recruiter's office?"

"You won't believe it. I joined."

"What?"

"Yep, I'm in the military now, just like my father was. And Grandpa," Chuck said, referring to Armond's father, Armond Senior, who was also in the Army when he was a young man.

"Hey Unc, would you be interested in moving into my in-law apartment rent-free while I'm in boot camp? If you would just take care of Rupert for me, and look after my side of the house. I can hire someone for the yard upkeep and leave money for dog food."

The apartment attached to Chuck's house had been vacant for some time. He had not bothered trying to rent it out since Shandi's passing.

Uncle Armond couldn't pass up the deal. He didn't make an enormous amount of money working at the Child World store as an assistant manager. Plus, Armond loved the area Chuck lived in. It was quiet, the lake, woods, and the scenery beautiful, so he gladly accepted.

Chuck said goodnight to his uncle and thanked him for the ride. Then he got out of his uncle's car and went into his parents' house to get his father's keys to the tow truck. Rita was still up watching television while his dad was sound asleep in bed.

"Hey Mom," Chuck said.

"Hey, you. What a nice surprise. Come in the living room."

"I can't right now, Ma. I gotta borrow dad's truck, my car broke down."

"You need your father's help?"

"No, I got it. I'll go get my car, drop it off at my house, then bring the tow truck back after."

"Okay, when you get back, you can sleep over and your dad can give you a ride back in the morning."

"Yeah, that works. I'll see you if you're still up when I get back."

Chuck left to get his car, not telling her anything about joining the Army. Chuck figured he would tell them in the morning.

He had borrowed an old shirt that his uncle had in his car and threw it on over the torn one so his mother didn't notice the blood. It was dark in the house when Chuck came in, so Rita didn't notice his beat-up appearance. He walked out with his head hung low, knowing once his parents found out about him joining the military and destroying his car, they'd be disappointed in him.

CHAPTER 10

THESE LOVELY DAYS

THAT S PRETTY MUCH the story of why I joined the military, and as they say, the rest is Kismet," Chuck said to Mitch and Mike.

"So you obviously never got to be a helicopter pilot."

"Nope, they had infantry available."

"Thank God for that. We might not be sitting with you right now if you did get it."

Chuck changed the subject.

"Remember us on the shooting range for the first time?"

"Yep, I do."

There had been a group of twenty men on the shooting range lying down with AR-15's. Chuck felt pretty comfortable with his weapon. In fact, better than that. He was hitting every bullseye with little instruction at all. Soldiers standing around him, including the Drill Sergeant, took notice. Some of the other recruits were having difficulty getting the hang of it. Mitch had been in that group, not doing too well and getting yelled at by the Sergeant. Getting screamed at made Mitch even more nervous.

"Private Barreto, switch places with Sanchez, double time," yelled the Sergeant.

The two Privates exchanged spots, which moved Chuck next to Mitch. That's how the two met formally for the first time.

"Private Barreto, you are to help Private Genpowski get his weapon working at least half as good as you. Are we clear, Private?"

"Sir, yes sir," said Chuck. He said hello to Mitch, happy to try to teach him what he knew and how he got the weapon to work for him.

Despite Chuck's recent temperament, he used to have a calming way about him that put you at ease. It was exactly what Mitch needed to understand the mechanisms of his weapon. After training on the range, they were ready to move on to physical training, but the Sergeant instructed Chuck and Mitch to stay on the range for another thirty minutes.

"Sir, yes sir, Drill Sergeant," they both responded.

Chuck worked quickly and brilliantly, helping Mitch to maneuver the weapon by having him take breaths before squeezing the trigger. Mitch was hitting the target and getting excited about it.

"Thanks, Chuck," Mitch said.

"Ah, no problem. We got each other's back."

"Yeah, I heard you were pretty good with a sidearm, too."

Chuck smiled.

When the Sergeant came back to them, he had Mitch go through the drill with the weapon. After Mitch performed well enough to pass, the instructor said, "Jesus, Privates! We still got more work to do, but this will do for right now. Double-time it to the PT course."

"Wish I could have been there to see Mitchell that day," Mike said, breaking the reverie.

"Yeah, it was a good day. We got through it."

The three of them had a good night hanging out, joking around, talking about their boot camp days and the fun they all had when they were stationed down in Panama. Once Mike started getting his drink on and was feeling good, he had Chuck play some eighties rock music. The first song was "Panama" from Van Halen. Mike sang the lyrics as the song played and sounded pretty good.

"Jump back, what's that sound?/ Here she comes, full blastin' down the avenue/ Model citizen, zero discipline/ Don't you know she's coming home with me."

In the middle of the song, Chuck changed the station, and Mike grunted. "Hey, what's up with that, Chucky?"

Chuck gave Mike a look. It was too much of a reminder for him of what happened down there. They never talked about their last mission together. They would discuss everything but that incident in Panama.

It was getting late and Mitch headed home. Chuck and Mike hung out a while longer. Mike slept in his spare bedroom for the night so he wouldn't be driving home under the influence.

Chuck got up early the next day to take care of Rupert and left a short note for Mike saying if he was still around when he got home later on, they could go out and fire off some rounds in the woods in a clearing with paper targets. He then headed off to work. Mike had a key to lock up the house.

Chuck was in such deep thought, he didn't even notice the song playing on the radio before he turned off the ignition.

"When I wake up in the morning, love/ And the sunlight hurts my eyes/ And something without warning, love/ Bears heavy on my mind," Bill Withers sang.

Chuck smiled sarcastically and said out loud to himself, "Wow, what a lovely day I'm gonna have."

Jed pulled up next to Chuck's Jeep and got out to greet him. As they walked in together, Jed said, "Hey, how was your weekend?"

"Not too bad."

"I wanted to talk to you about that Karrington rally. Maybe we could carpool to the event?"

"Yeah that sounds cool. We can talk more about it in the block."

"OK, I'll see you there."

Jed always came fully uniformed and went straight to the block after punching his time card. After Chuck clocked in, he would go to the locker room and joke around with his co-workers while changing. After Chuck changed, he walked through the lobby to enter the prison through a se-cured trap, and he noticed Jed was still there off to the side. He was talking with two internal investigators and had a look on his face that Chuck had become very familiar with. So much for the lovely day.

When Jed saw Chuck, he waved him over to talk to the two investiga-tors, Ned Lender and Warren Leaver. They weren't very well-liked amongst the officers because of their job description. They got paid to investigate officers for any alleged wrongdoings, such as when an inmate made allegations against an officer. Chuck could never wrap his brain around why another officer would take that type of job. He figured only rats would do that type of work, investigating their own.. The way he saw it, the investigators could take everything you worked for, all based on nonsense. Inmates hated the word "no" more than anything. They hated following rules, and when diligent, hard workers tried getting them to obey, certain convicts would go to the extremes of making up lies to get rid of any officers enforcing them.

"Hey, Chuck. Just gotta ask you fellas a few questions before you go inside," Leaver said greasily.

Chuck nodded and looked at Jed, rolling his eyes.

"You remember that officer-needs-assistance you responded to last week when Officer Jarred got assaulted, and you and Chuck escorted inmate Harris up to the Hole?" Leaver questioned.

"Yeah," Jed responded.

"The inmate is claiming that you and Chuck assaulted him in the stairwell on the way up. Believe me, I'm on your side, but I have to ask this stuff," said Lender.

Jed acted insulted by the question and replied heatedly, "That never happened, Warren. I do my job!"

"Okay, okay, calm down, Jed. I know you guys are total professionals. I'm sorry I had to ask."

"Now, Chuck, after you finished punching inmate Harris, did you grab the back of his head and whisper in his ear, 'I heard you're a diaper sniper'?" asked Leaver slimily, low so that only Chuck could hear.

"First off, Leavey," said Chuck, " I never punched that upstanding convict. I'd never do that to an inmate. And what the hell is a diaper sniper?"

Having been simultaneously occupied by conversation with Jed, Officer Leaver looked confused.

"Are we all set?" asked Jed.

"Yeah, that's all. Thanks, guys. Sorry about all this. Have a good and safe day," said Officer Lender.

Chuck and Jed quietly walked to their block, dying to talk about what just happened. On their way, they became giddy and gave one another rabbit punches to their arms. They relieved the officer who worked the overnight shift on their block. After he left, Jed jumped up and down, dancing with laughter while Chuck made fresh coffee in the office with a huge smirk on his face.

"What's a diaper sniper?" asked Jed, laughing hysterically, even though he knew full well it was a term for a child molester.

"I know, can you believe that schlub? Accusing me of calling the guy a name like that! Plus, you can't trust those guys. Always trying to jam people up."

"Leaver quoted you, verbatim," said Jed as he continued to laugh.

"Yeah, I know. What the hell. That inmate Harris is a fucking rat, too."

They laughed some more, then began a smooth day on the block. Again, they could acknowledge their hard work was paying off. Things had done a one-eighty in the unit since they first started there. Chuck and Jed were receiving compliments from Captains, Sergeants, the Superintendent, Deputies, and even a few inmates.

It was early in the afternoon and the inmates had had their lunch already. They were locked in their cells until 1:00. Jed and Chuck had a few of them out of their cells, cleaning up the tiers and flats before they all came out for afternoon recreation. This period was a quiet time while those selected inmates, hired by the block officers, cleaned everything from floors to showers to windows. The State paid them one dollar per day, or they had the option to earn time off their sentence. If they chose money, it would be credited to their commissary account and could be used toward buying items in the prison store called "the canteen".

Jed and Chuck enjoyed this part of the afternoon, watching their working inmates, also called runners, shine up the block while they both sipped on another cup of freshly made coffee. Their block had some of the best head runners in the whole prison. The two inmates loved to clean and would even stay out to do other runners' jobs. It was like they lived to clean and took great pride in doing it.

Their names were Dick Kranski and Randy Blumenthal, and both men were doing life for murder in the first degree. It was rumored that they were in a homosexual relationship. They never left one another's side unless they were locked in their cells for the night. Randy was very flamboyant and open about being gay. Dick would always deny it, but people didn't believe him or care one way or another.

Randy lived on the top tier in a cell over the officers' desk. Chuck and Jed were talking about the upcoming campaign rally when Randy came out of his cell, very quietly. He looked down with big puppy eyes, and Chuck saw a stream of blood running from his forehead down to the tip of his nose. A drop of blood fell off his nose, all the way to the first floor.

Chuck looked around the block and saw no one outside of their cells except for a third runner. His name was Manuel Sohrab. He was working at the very end of the flats by the showers, mopping up the floors with his head low.

"Randy, what the hell happened to you?" Chuck asked.

Blumenthal pointed directly at inmate Sohrab. "The Jew got me!"

Chuck told Randy to lock in his cell and yelled down to Manuel to do the same. He knew he was in trouble. He walked dejectedly inside his cell.

Inmate Sohrab was also in for murder; his crime was well-known. They had broadcast it on prime-time crime shows and the inmates in the block would joke about it. He was originally from Iran and had rich parents who were putting him through college in the U.S. Manuel, when residing in a dorm, was jealous of two gay men living together. Maybe it had something to do with his religious beliefs, or maybe he had been attracted to one of them. One night, he broke into their room and fatally shot them both.

Chuck and Jed called their Unit Sergeant. Assisting officers arrived to handcuff Manuel. Then they escorted him to the Hole and Blumenthal was taken to the inmate hospital. Chuck and Jed didn't see Sohrab originally run into Randy's cell to attack him. Randy's buddy, Dick, caught on right away and tried to intervene, leaving Manuel time to punch Randy only once. Dick grabbed Daniel to get him off Randy and when he did, Manuel bit him in his right hand. Dick then threw Manul across the cell. Inmate Sohrab was afraid of being caught, so he ran out afterwards and went back to mopping as if nothing had happened. Dick had gone back to his cell, also afraid of getting into trouble. After it was all over, Chuck and Jed got a good laugh out of the entire day before they went home.

CHAPTER 11

PANAMA
JULY 1989 - MARCH 1990

CHUCK AND HIS unit had been in Panama for a few weeks with twenty-six thousand other American troops on an operation called "Just Cause". They were stationed there to take out the dictator and his army called the PDF, Panamanian Defense Forces. The dictator went by the name of General Manuel Noriega. The General amassed a personal fortune through drug trafficking operations. Before his problems with the U.S., he worked for the Central Intelligence Agency. He was at one time a U.S. ally, but by the late eighties he had fallen out of favor with the United States and President Bush.

It was surreal for Chuck to be in another country as he had never even left his state before now. He and Shandi always talked about their dreams to travel when they made it big, but that never had a chance to happen.

Chuck felt like she was somewhere close by, maybe watching over him, like another layer of battle armor. He couldn't put his finger on it, but he always felt her presence. There were times, moments after her passing, that he thought maybe he saw her walking in a crowd nearby.

A young female soldier was unloading a military plane when they all arrived in Panama, dressed in her Army Class Bs. She had her back turned to him, and Chuck couldn't see her face while she was taking equipment off the plane. From where he was standing, her body shape and her hair looked a lot like Shandi. Chuck walked towards the woman to see, without thinking about what he was tasked to be doing. The woman turned around and Chuck saw her face.

"Hey there, soldier boy. Want to give me a hand instead of checking out my ass?" the woman said to him.

"Sure," realizing she looked nothing like Shandi after all.

After a week of setting up temporary quarters and doing military drills in this new country, Chuck's unit got assigned a mission. There were seven of them altogether. Mike Geller, the Sergeant in charge, became a loyal friend. Mike loved classic films like Chuck. He named their team the Magnificent Seven from one of his favorite movies. The rest of the group was Mitch Genpowski, who Chuck had first met on the shooting range, Jemel Landau, Kirk Donaldson, Will Ulysses, and Burt Langley. They were all mostly from out west, except for Jemel who had grown up relatively close to Chuck.

Their unit had been rucking in the jungle for a day and a half and were about eight miles away from their destination. They were in an area called Rio Hato and headed for an Army barracks in the Canal Zone. They were on point looking for drug traffickers, looting, irregularities... anything out of sorts. Mike would report into their command center every hour. The guys knew, or thought they knew, there was no way they would find the criminal Manuel Noriega, let alone capture him. That was the ultimate agenda to end the mission, but it would be highly unlikely,

The men walked up a large hill, moving into seemingly endless thick trees and brush. Mike was extraordinary with his compass and maps. If he didn't know where he was headed, you'd never know it from his display of physical and mental confidence. The men were glad to have him on their side. Everyone felt assured they would make it to the barracks with no issues. Because of the thickness of the woods, they abruptly reached the top of the hill they were ascending without seeing it coming. They heard strange noises that didn't come from any of them. It sounded like something hitting hollow metal on metal.

Mike reached the top first and motioned to them to stay quiet and drop to the ground on their bellies quickly, then signaled everyone to crawl up to the very top, slowly and quietly. The men edged up like turtles. When they looked down over a cliff, they saw a vertical drop about a hundred feet. At the very bottom of it was an old dirt road that passed through the hillside. Along the road below were old telephone poles and wires. Most of them looked to be in awful shape. They also saw a rusted utility truck with equipment in the back of it. The words on the driver's door were not legible from their vantage point. There was a man high on a ladder against one of the poles; that was where the noise had originated. The unknown man working on the pole did not appear to know he was being watched by Mike's Magnificent Seven.

"Rockstar, stay here and watch this guy. I'm going back down the hill to call this situation into Command for instructions," Mike whispered to Chuck. He nodded.

Mike descended the hill enough to remain unheard, while the rest of the men kept observing the mysterious man working on the telephone pole. He was talking with someone via walkie-talkie in Spanish, which none of them understood.

A short time passed, then Mike returned and got back in his position. "It's curfew hours. They have instructed us to take him out."

They looked at Mike blankly. None of them had ever killed another living being.

"Get your ARs in position and line him up in your sights. We'll all fire on him together. On my mark," Mike said.

Without hesitation, they all got into position with their weapons and line of sight on the man, ready to go. Then Mike said, "On three. One, two, three!"

Crack, crack, crack! You could hear the echoes of their weapons in the trees and see the smoke. The unknown man instantly fell off his ladder and hit the ground, making a hard *thump*. His body did not move. The guys couldn't believe they just killed someone.

Mike looked down at the lifeless man with his binoculars. "No movement, guys. I think he's deader than a doornail!"

"OK, what do we do now?" Kirk asked. They all waited in silence, still looking down at the man.

"Okay, here's the plan. Chuck, you're pretty damn good with that thing in your arms. You stay up here and give us cover. The rest of us will go down below, confirm the kill, and clear the area. After that's complete, I'll signal you to join us," said Mike. Chuck was honored but apprehensive. He had to be on point.

Mike reported into command again, and he and Will, Mitch, Kirk, Jemel, and Burt slowly worked their way down the steep hill to the dirt road where their kill lay. It was hard for them to keep a firm footing as they slid down the slope. Eventually, the men made it to the road. They approached their target with caution and moved in circular motions, giving one another cover for any type of potential harm or danger.

Mike approached the fatality and touched the man several times with the tip of his weapon barrel. There was no movement from him whatsoever. Mike then rolled him over onto his back and searched for weapons on or near his person. He discovered a handgun in the front of his belt, tucked halfway in his pants.

Meanwhile, Chuck was still up top in the ready position, watching his unit intently. He was exhilarated, his senses heightened.

Mike pulled the dead man's handgun out from his waistline. Mitch and Kirk kept their weapons aimed at the lifeless man. Blood seeped from his body. Mike knelt over the man, securing his weapon, then took his pulse by putting his index finger on the man's neck. Through the silence you could hear the birds chirping in the woods.

"He's dead. Let me call this in and get further instructions," said Mike.

Suddenly, there was a crunching noise coming from the other side of the road. From a hidden gully, five soldiers dressed in enemy guerilla fatigues jumped out onto the road armed with rifles, yelling and shouting in Spanish at Mike and his men. They were Noriega's men, the Panamanian Defense Force. They had the drop on The Magnificent Seven and Mike knew it. He confidently told his men to stand down and not make any sudden movements. They didn't want to die in a foreign country like this. They made no sudden moves. They were hesitant about what to do next, but didn't give up any of their weapons.

The enemy quickly surrounded the unit, forming a circle around them. Chuck wasted no time at all. He had one of the enemy soldiers in his crosshairs. This soldier was standing close to Mitch. Feeling assured in his decision, Chuck pulled the trigger. He quickly moved the tip of the barrel over to the next enemy soldier. Within half a second, he blasted the next man in the side of the head. Mike whipped out the handgun he had confiscated earlier and shot the soldier standing right in front of him twice in the chest. At the same time, Kirk raised his weapon and started firing rounds on another soldier while Jemel went for the last standing soldier by wrapping his enormous arms around him, picking the man clear up off the ground, and attempting to squeeze the breath out of him. Mike grabbed the knife he had holstered to his right leg and slit the soldier's throat with it, while Jemel still had a tight hold on him. Jemel dropped the dead man to the ground.

"Holy fuck, holy fuck, holy fuck!" Will shouted.

"Will, calm down, it's over. It's over, bro," said Burt.

Will stopped, taking deep breaths.

Chuck stood up in absolute amazement and shouted down the hill to his boys, "Yo ladies, stop your grinnin' and drop your linen." He started laughing, then shouted at them, "You okay down there? What the fuck?! That was freaking crazy!"

"Yeah, we're all good, I think," Mike yelled back. "Goddamn, boy, you did a superb fucking job. Get the hell down here, Rockstar, while we secure the area. I'll call this in."

"Roger that," Chuck replied. Suddenly, gunfire began again, only this time it was coming from behind Chuck. Chuck turned quickly with his weapon to return fire when he felt a sharp, hot sting on the right side of his leg. He saw what was coming and thought for a split second, *I'm screwed.*

It looked like he was out-manned and out-gunned. Chuck quickly pivoted back around and dove headfirst down the steep hill, uncontrollably rolling almost to the bottom. Mike and the rest of the unit aimed at the top of the hill and returned gunfire. The boys saw nothing up there, but kept blazing away while taking cover behind the old utility truck.

Mike hoisted Chuck up under his armpits and dragged him behind the truck. They heard no further return fire. Mike quickly assessed the damage on Chuck. He had a gunshot to the side of the upper right leg and it went through. Chuck also unfortunately dislocated his right shoulder from the fall. Mike took off his headband to use it as a splint for Chuck's leg, tying it off tautly.

As Mike worked on him with impressive speed, Chuck passed out.

His subconscious was in another state he could never describe to anyone unless he wanted to be thought of as crazy. In Chuck's mind, he heard a familiar musical sound and was surrounded by a large, white cloudy tunnel. Chuck's Army fatigues were completely white, and he was walking through it. He realized what music was playing- it was the song Shandi wrote for the album that he heard on his car radio the day she died.

Chuck then saw Shandi at the end of the tunnel, wearing white jeans and a white t-shirt as she walked towards him. She was singing the lyrics she wrote.

"I'm not being unfair seeking out for a reply to my quest for my dreams to become genuine/ It's just I feel my love needs more harmony/ I'm brief of luck and out of time, I'm beginning to lose my intellect."

She was even closer to Chuck now, so close he could touch her. He was so damn happy to see her... and then she was gone.

Mike had taken a smelling salts stick from a side pocket, put it under Chuck's nose, and snapped it. Chuck jumped up, grunting and swinging his fists.

"Whoa, whoa, whoa. Welcome back to the world, Rockstar! You were unconscious, and you dislocated your shoulder, brother. We have to pop your shoulder back in its socket, then we will move you. Capiche?" Mike asked.

"Yeah okay, got it, Mike. I'm sorry."

"Nothing to be sorry about, but we have to move quickly. We're all still in danger here. They know where we are. I'm going to move you off the road into this gully next to us, so we can get your shoulder taken care of. Then we can all get the fuck out of here! Okay, let's move." The rest of the boys gave cover while Mike grabbed Chuck and helped him down off the road. He then leaned him up against a tree.

"You ready, Rockstar?"

"No," said Chuck.

Mike grabbed his shoulder with one hand and put the other on Chuck's back. Before Chuck knew what was happening, he felt a quick, sharp crack and a significant amount of pain. Instantly, Chuck's arm went back in its socket.

"Wow, thanks, Mike. Holy cow, that actually feels good."

"Okay, I'm going to have Mitch help you walk out of here because I forgot to tell you that they also shot you in the leg. But the good news is it went right through your quad, clean."

"What?"

"Yeah, I had to deal with your shoulder first. Now I have to make sure I get the rest of us out of here in one piece. You stay down here. I'll be right back." Chuck now knew what the sharp pain that he felt earlier was as he looked down at his leg.

Mike climbed back up on the road behind the truck with the guys. He looked through the passenger window to see if the keys were still in the ignition. They weren't.

"Damn, cover me guys. I'm going to check that asshole's pockets," Mike said.

"You got that, Mikey," Kirk replied.

They were wired, thinking about everything that could possibly be on top of the hill. They were scared that the enemy soldiers were still up there somewhere and would start shooting at them again.

Mike looked through the man's pockets, frantically. "Bingo, got 'em!"

He pulled out a set of keys and ran back to the truck. "Will, Burt- go grab Chuck and put him in the passenger seat. Then you guys jump in the back bed. Have your weapons hot and ready for unfriendlies. Let's do this, boys, double time!"

"I heard that! Don't need to tell me twice!" said Mitch.

Once Chuck was placed in the truck and they all got into position in the back, Mike turned the key in the ignition and hit the gas pedal hard. The truck sounded like it wanted to stall out. Heavy smoke poured from the tailpipe. He shifted the vehicle into drive and floored it, as the old truck made loud, clunky noises.

The enemy soldiers heard the truck from where they were on top of the hill. They ran to the edge shouting at the Magnificent Seven in Spanish and started firing their weapons on the truck.

"Keep your goddamn heads down!" Mike yelled to the unit.

They fired their weapons back as they drove away. Soon after, they all could barely hear or see their enemies. They laughed with gratitude that they made it out of there alive.

Mike turned his head as he drove and said, "Everyone good back there? Has anyone got any holes where they don't belong?"

Jemel jokingly looked over his body and said, "Nope, just the Rockstar!"

Chuck heard his fellow brother's attempted humor. "Thanks, bro!"

"Damn, Rockstar! You're the fucking man! You really saved our asses!" said Will.

"Any of you would've done the same."

"Yeah, I would've tried, but I can't shoot. Not like that!"

Chuck laughed and said, "I didn't know I could either. Got lucky I guess."

"Lucky, my ass. You're a legit sniper, bro!"

After Mike drove the truck for about five miles, he pulled over to the side of the road.

"Hey guys, I have to call this into base. This road here is taking us off course and the truck is getting low on gas," he said.

Mike got out of the vehicle and walked around the back to call in their status. A responding commander told Mike to keep driving. Only a few miles ahead would be an open field on their right side. They were sending a chopper to the site to fly them out. They were relieved about the news. Mike continued driving and they arrived at a field full of tall, green grass. He parked the truck and they heard a helicopter getting louder, headed in their direction.

"Fellas, let it be known that I need a vacation. I'm too young for this shit!" said Jemel. They all laughed.

Once the helicopter landed, they flew back to their primary base. Chuck was immediately taken to a nearby field hospital for a medical evaluation and treatment plan. They deemed Chuck stable, but he would need time to heal and would eventually require physical therapy for his leg. He would also need a minor surgery to repair his rotator cuff. It was decided that Chuck would fly back to the United States right away.

Mike and the rest of the unit remained in Panama for a few more weeks of military jungle training only. Shortly after this, Manuel Noriega was captured by the United States and everyone went back home because Operation Just Cause was over.

They had flown Chuck from the Panamanian hospital to one close to his home. He had a minor rotator cuff surgery on his shoulder. The surgeon scraped it out and stitched the tendon. They started physical therapy on his leg, which was healing rapidly. Chuck's family was in and out visiting him for the two weeks he was there. He was awarded an honorable discharge from the Army.

Chuck was so relieved to be going home from the hospital as he waited for his father to pick him up that he insisted on going out front for some fresh air before his arrival. One of the hospital nurses wheeled Chuck out to the front of the building to wait for Gus. It was hospital policy that he had to be in a wheelchair when leaving. The nurse pushing him was a few years older than him and cute. She innocently flirted with him in the entranceway.

While they were waiting, they talked about the sunny weather and she asked him about his time in the military. He didn't tell her too much about it, keeping the conversation light-hearted. She couldn't believe how cute he was and looked for a wedding band on his finger, but realized he was definitely too young to have one. Their ears perked up as they heard a roar of machinery approaching from the distance.

Chuck smiled and said, "That's my old man coming!"

"What?" asked the nurse.

"Yep, that's his tow truck. I've been listening to that noise since I was a kid."

Gus had refused to buy a new tow truck for his business. He would keep patching the old, rusted truck to hold her together. It was like an old dinosaur that refused to die. When Chuck was a kid and he and his siblings would be out playing in the neighborhood with their friends after school, they would hear that sound and know Gus was coming home from work. They would hear the gears shifting and grinding back and forth and know it was time to go home for dinner.

Finally, Chuck saw his father's truck pulling into the hospital parking lot with its chipped and faded blue paint. Chuck thanked the young lady for helping him and keeping him company.

"No problem. You take care of yourself," she said, wishing at the same time that she dared to ask for his phone number.

Gus pulled his truck up to Chuck, with the passenger window down, and shouted, "You're already hitting on the young ladies, Chucky?"

"Ah, very funny, Dad," Chuck blushed.

"You need some help getting in?"

"Nope, I got it."

Chuck climbed up inside the cab, putting his cane in the back of the truck and closing the clunky passenger door behind him. God, he forgot how much he loved the dirty gas, paint, and leather smell of the inside of the truck. The seats were red and cracked. He missed sitting on them. As a kid he had loved riding in the truck and things hadn't changed a lick; he still did.

Gus immediately started discussing Army life with Chuck, enjoying the subject because of his own days in the military. Gus relished talking about all the pranks he and his fellow men played on each other. He kept the conversation light and fun. His glass was half full, no matter what was going on in life; that could have been part of the secret to his success.

Gus was thrilled that Chuck would get a paycheck from the military for the rest of his life for his misfortune. Back in the sixties when Gus had been injured, that was not available to him or other soldiers. He treasured those young, youthful times when he served just the same, though. He loved talking to his sons about those happy days with his unit.

As they were driving to Chuck's house, he suspected his father was up to something. He didn't know for sure, but his father was overly giddy, like he had a secret he was holding onto. It was a game Gus would play when Chuck and his siblings were little. They would all anxiously open their gifts on Christmas morning and think they made off with a pretty good haul.

Then Gus would say something to each of them like, "Oh, Chucky, can you get the broom out of the closet?"

Chuck would get up to get it, open the kitchen pantry door, and there would be the guitar amplifier he'd wanted with a red bow on it.

Gus would laugh and say something like, "Oh, look what Santa brought you, Chucky." He reveled in surprising people and making them happy.

As they drove, Gus told Chuck a little about some issues that he and his mother were having with Stacey while he was away. They were putting Stacey through college – Business Law – and she was dating an older guy. Gus and Rita didn't approve of him. Rita particularly had a sense that he wasn't a very good person.

Suddenly, a deer sprinted across the street. Chuck said, "Look out, Dad!"

Gus downshifted the old 1970 Ford tow truck. She made a loud, whining noise and the deer made it safely into the woods.

Before Gus could talk any further about Stacey, they pulled onto Chuck's street. Chuck was feeling bittersweet to see his old street again.

The old truck went down a slight hill to Chuck's long, private road. You couldn't see his house until you came around a sharp turn, at which point Chuck saw cars parked everywhere on both sides of the street and some neighbors' yards as well.

"What the hell is going on, Dad?" asked Chuck.

"A few people wanted to drop by to see you. I hope it's alright."

A huge banner hung high over the driveway from one side to the other, tied from pine tree to pine tree. *Welcome Home, Chucky!* it said. Chuck couldn't believe it. There was one space in the middle of the driveway reserved for Gus to park. People were everywhere in the driveway and front yard screaming "Surprise!" at the top of their lungs.

"Holy crap, Dad, you're something else."

Chuck also saw a big red ribbon tied from one end of his house to the other. He wasn't sure what that was about. Chuck was overwhelmed by the scene. His entire family was waiting to hug him as he got out of the truck, starting with his mother.

"Chuck, after everyone says hello, we set up tents in the backyard for a little get-together," said Rita.

Chuck never had so many loved ones in one place at the same time, except maybe for Shandi's funeral.

He slowly made his way down the driveway, thanking his family and friends for coming, and they thanked him for his heroic service in return. At the end was a set of steps that went down to a cobblestone sidewalk, leading to the front of the house. It was about thirty feet long and lined with relatives and friends he hadn't seen in forever. As Chuck made his way through the people and edged closer to the front door of the house, he saw his bandmates and Uncle Armond with Rupert waiting at the end of the line. Rupert came running full blast at Chuck, barking at him wildly and jumping up on his legs.

"Okay, okay, boy. Take it easy. I love you too." Chuck petted him for a few minutes and talked to him, trying to get the little dog to calm down. Everyone laughed over how cute it was and how much Rupert had missed Chuck.

Chuck continued on his way to the front porch. It surprised him to see Shandi's parents among the crowd.

Julie gave Chuck an enveloping hug and said to him, "Welcome home, son."

"Thanks, Ma. I love you guys." Mr. Monroe shook Chuck's hand, emotional as well. They both loved Chuck. He was their living link to their only daughter, who was forever gone. They didn't say much about the case, but they did say that the detectives still had no damn clue who had stolen her life. He was sure Patrick and Julie, at some point, would like to vent with him about it all, and he wanted to talk with them about her, but it wasn't the time or the place at that moment.

Chuck finally made it to the end with Rupert. He stepped up onto the porch, smiling at his bandmates and Uncle Armond. He moved closer to them and Bob, Harry, Dan all grabbed him, giving the war hero a whopping hug.

As Chuck was embraced, Armond smiled and said, "Welcome home, Meathead."

Chuck wanted to cry but held back. "So good to see you guys. You too, Unc. Boy, I missed you."

"We, well not us, but Bill, had this made for you, Chuck. We all have a copy," said Bob as he handed Chuck a slim package wrapped in brown paper with a red bow.

Chuck took it, wondering what it was. Chuck tore the paper off and realized it was an actual album cover, with Shandi sitting tantalizingly on the hood of Chuck's Charger. Chuck and the rest of the guys stood behind her. The title of their album was *No Prisoners Allowed*. At the bottom, it said "Shandi and the Boys" in bright red lettering. He was startled by her photo and tried to play it off so that he would not look as upset and stunned as he felt suddenly seeing her face.

"Oh, wow, what the fuck. Thank you so much, guys."

"Not from us, bro," said Harry. "Bill produced the six songs we recorded. The album is doing pretty well. He wanted to be here, but he's away right now. So he sent this to us to give to you. Pull out the vinyl from the sleeve."

Chuck pulled the record out and taped to the round plastic vinyl were two envelopes. Both envelopes had written on them, "Chuck, have a nice day." He opened up the first envelope, and it was a check for $30,000.

"Are you kidding me?" said Chuck.

"Yeah, a little bonus, bro. Advanced royalties from the hit song sales."

"Open up the other one," said Harry.

"Oh yeah, okay," said Chuck, still shocked. He opened it and pulled out a thick, folded piece of paper. He opened it and had to take a second look before he realized it was the deed to his house. On the deed, a red-inked stamp on the bottom of the document said, "PAID".

Chuck stood motionless and speechless.

The guys, Armond, and everyone around him smiled and applauded.

"Chuck, you okay?" asked Bob, laughing at him.

"I think so, I mean, I can't believe it," said Chuck. "I have no mortgage anymore?"

"Bill said it was the least he could do."

Chuck's mother came up on the porch and said, "Hey Chuck, that was pretty nice of Mr. Arkin. You'll have to call and thank him."

"Absolutely, Ma. I will, first thing tomorrow."

"Well, come inside for a minute. I bought you some new furniture while you were away. I hope you don't mind. Everyone else is going to meet us in the backyard for a little celebration. Is that good?"

"Oh yeah, Ma, that's awesome."

They went inside and Rita showed him a new leather couch and armchair in the living room. Chuck was ecstatic. She pointed out a brand new breakfast bar she had a carpenter build in the kitchen out of all-natural oak. Chuck gave her a big hug and thanked her.

Rita was trembling and her eyes were tearing up. "Did I ever tell you, a few months after you were born, you got extremely sick?"

"No, Ma. I don't think so."

"You had pneumonia. Your father and I rushed you to the hospital and you couldn't come back home with us right away. They kept you for over two months to get you healthy. The doctors didn't think you were going to live, but you proved them wrong. You fought hard. When you finally did come home, your father was so happy he ran around the house with you yelling out 'Little Capricorn Chucky!' over and over again, every day."

"Ma, wow that's a nice story!"

Rita dried her eyes. "Sorry. Well I guess the point is I'm glad you're finally home, let's go out back and join everyone."

"Okay, Ma."

Chuck opened the French doors off of his kitchen that led to the back deck. Outside there were tents set up with tables and chairs, food cooking on grills, and – holy shit – underneath his favorite oak tree was the Charger. She was gleaming and glistening, looking brand new again.

"Ma, what the hell?!" Chuck exclaimed.

Everyone in the backyard screamed, "SURPRISE!"

"Chuck, your father worked on your car almost every night while you were gone until it was finished," said his mother.

Chuck hurried off the deck as quickly as his injured leg would allow out to the blue beast to touch her. Gus came over and gave Chuck a brief hug.

"Now don't ever take off on us again!" Gus said.

"Okay, pops," said Chuck, fighting back tears again.

The party then began in earnest. None of Chuck's unit could make it; they had all shipped to the Gulf as they were still actively enlisted. Chuck wished they were back in the States, safe like him.

There was music playing and everyone was having a good time catching up. Gary told him that he and Lilly would soon move to Virginia for a computer job he got. He also met his sister's unliked boyfriend, Brian Nevel. He wasn't sure what to make of him; he seemed shifty to Chuck too, though he couldn't put his finger on exactly why. Stacey talked about how her college classes were going. As they were talking, Chuck heard a whispered commotion coming from the deck.

Chuck's grandmother, Gus's mother who lived in New York, had arrived along with his cousins- another surprise for Chuck. She shouted out when she saw Chuck. "Chucky! Chucky!"

"Vovo!" Chuck called, using the Portuguese term of endearment. She was being helped along by Gus's younger sister, Chuck's Aunt Joanne. They greeted each other with handshakes and hugs.

"Chucky, thank God you're home," said Vovo. "You must come and visit me, maybe come to stay with me for a while."

"Yeah, of course, Vovo," said Chuck. Chuck asked her if she was going to stay at his place for the weekend, but she told him she was staying with his parents.

The night stretched on and time passed all too quickly. Shandi's parents were the first to tell Chuck it was time for them to head home and that they would like to catch up with him later. Chuck thanked them and assured them he would focus his efforts back on Shandi's case now that he was home.

After midnight, everyone else made their way home, except for Gary and Armond. The three of them went inside to wind down. Rupert sacked out, exhausted from all the excitement. Gary said he would be back sometime the next day to help Chuck clean up the party remnants. Chuck thanked Armond for everything, taking care of the house and Rupert while he was away.

"By the way, the apartment is indefinitely rent-free, Unc." Now that Chuck had no mortgage, he was glad to be able to do something to make his uncle's life easier.

Chuck still couldn't get over the party and the people who had come out to see him. The money. His house being paid off. The new furniture. The return of his beloved car. After all Chuck had been through, things were starting to look up.

Chuck woke up in his king-size bed the following morning with Rupert jumping on top of him, excited that his master was finally home. It was the first time Chuck had slept in his bed since the day before Shandi's death. He felt like he had dreamt about her in the night, but couldn't quite remember.

The sun was shining through the windows, inspiring Chuck to make the most of his day. He put his clothes and sneakers on, made a coffee, and got Rupert leashed up for his morning walk. Chuck and Rupert got all the way down to the end of the street where the mailboxes stood. He was managing pretty well with his cane while holding Rupert's leash and enjoying the beautiful scenery of the lake. Being home, though, Chuck was again feeling the impact of Shandi's absence.

Across the way, Chuck saw a sign that read "Land for Sale - Tombstone Realtor" in a stretch of woods.

"Hmmm," muttered Chuck. That was the land Shandi had pictured them buying someday to start their own little horse ranch. He couldn't believe it hadn't sold yet; he had forgotten all about it.

"Well, let's take a walk through here, my little man," Chuck said to Rupert.

Chuck and Rupert meandered onto the unsold, vacant land, wondering exactly how much property was for sale and for what price. The realtor's sign didn't specify any of that. They walked through the area for a couple of minutes more and then headed back to the house. Chuck took a shower, got dressed for the day, and tried calling FBI Agent Jack Bufford. As usual, there was no answer, so Chuck left a message.

He had a big day ahead of him. Chuck promised to visit his grandmother and then Gary was coming over to the house later on. Chuck went next door to have another coffee with his uncle and again thank him for everything. After he visited with Armond, Chuck grabbed the big check he had received from Bill, then hobbled to his shiny, revamped Charger. He put his cane on the passenger side floor, breathing in the scent of leather as he leaned over the seat.

"Wow, I missed that smell!" he said aloud to himself.

Chuck turned the key and she started up with a lovely roar. He backed her slowly out of the driveway and onto the street. He drove to the local bank where his accounts were held and presented the teller with his check.

"Wow, you don't see that every day," she said.

"No, ma'am," said Chuck.

"You want all of it in your checking account?"

"For now, please."

He got his receipt, thanked the teller, and left. His next stop was the police station. Chuck walked into the lobby and up to the duty station where an older police woman was sitting.

"How can I help you?" she asked from behind the glass window.

"Yes, ma'am, is Detective Scott Austin in today?"

"Yes, he is. Can I have your name?"

"It's Chuck Barreto."

"Oh, you're the Rockstar!"

Chuck cracked a slight smile but said nothing. She walked in the back, out of sight for a few minutes, while Chuck waited. Shortly after, she came back with the detective and buzzed Chuck through a security door.

"Come into my office, Chuck," said Detective Austin as he shook his hand. "Welcome home."

"Thank you, Scott."

They sat down in the office.

"Can I get you anything, Chuck? Coffee? Soda?"

"No thank you, I'm good. I just wanted to check in and see if there's anything new."

"I'm sorry, Chuck. All they have is some clothing fibers that are definitely not Shandi's and the footprints that were found at the scene. Still no witnesses at all, except nearby neighbors hearing that gunshot."

Chuck left the station disappointed as usual. He got back in his car and began cruising and an idea dawned on him. He drove all the way back to his street by the mailboxes, stopped, and got out of the car with a pen and piece of paper. Chuck walked over to the realtor's sign, wrote the phone number down, and drove back to his house. Uncle Armond came over with Rupert when he saw Chuck was home again.

"Forget something, Meathead?"

"Nope, I have an idea."

"Oh. Everything okay?"

"Yep."

Chuck picked up the telephone and dialed the number he had written down. Someone answered almost right away.

"Yes, hello, I'm calling about the land you have for sale at the end of Piney Lane in Woodrow. Do you know how much land it is? And how much money are you asking for it?" There was a pause. "Yes, I'll hold."

A few minutes later, Chuck said, "Yes, I'm inquiring about that property. Wow, just over eleven acres. Really? And it's negotiable? Is there an agent that would be able to meet with me to talk about it?"

Chuck listened for a moment and then continued. "I actually live on the same street as the property you're selling. If you want to meet me here, that would be great. One hour is fantastic!"

Chuck gave the agent his address and hung up the phone. He called his mother to see if she could meet him at his house to talk with the owner of the real estate company, who was on her way to Chuck's house. Rita lectured Chuck about being impulsive and told him not to sign anything. Uncle Armond couldn't believe what Chuck was contemplating either, but he was his father's son, after all.

Rita arrived at Chuck's place before the realtor. She advised him not to rush into a big move like this and to take time to consider it. Rita went over all the pitfalls and hardships that could come with taking this on. Chuck didn't care. Rita secretly admired his ambition. She thought that maybe her son was a chip off the old block, like her and his father.

She had brought a big Tupperware container with her and told Chuck, "That's for later. Your grandmother made it for you."

Uncle Armond left for the meeting, bringing Rupert with him to his apartment. Shortly afterward, the realtor pulled into the driveway. Chuck and Rita went outside to greet her. Rita recognized the woman from former business dealings.

"Hello," Rita said. The realtor recognized her as well.

"Oh, Rita, this is your son?"

They went inside the kitchen and sat down at Chuck's breakfast bar. The realtor, Beth Chandler, took out a leather briefcase, and when the pleasantries were out of the way, she pulled out paperwork. She went over all the details of the land sale with Rita and all it would, or could, entail. Rita was a tough and masterful negotiator, and she knew all the tactics. She would only accept the best deal possible for her son.

The land was ready to build on. The asking price was $28,000. Rita went back and forth with Beth until she conceded at $24,000. She knew it was a great deal, but she didn't want Mrs. Chandler to see that she knew that. Beth told Rita and Chuck that there was a land developer who was also interested, but had not yet made them an offer. Rita then told Beth that her son would do better things with the land than a developer could.

"I think it's best if we wait and think it over," Rita told Beth, but her son was sold, and secretly, so was she. Chuck's mother had good instincts, and her instincts were telling her that even if Chuck did nothing with the land after buying it, he could flip it down the road for a huge profit.

"I understand. The offer stands for a week. I'll draw up the paperwork and Chuck can come in with an attorney to look everything over before signing, if he decides he would like to proceed," said Beth.

"I'll be in touch," said Chuck as he walked her to the door.

When she had gone, Rita smiled at Chuck and said, "I hope you're up for this, Chucky."

"Mom, I have a good feeling about this. I'll be a big landowner like Dad!"

"You will be," she smiled back at him.

Chuck poured them both another robust cup of coffee as Rita pulled out a mouthwatering round cake from the Tupperware she had brought.

"Carrot cake, Chuck. Your favorite. Would you like a piece?"

Chuck started salivating and his eyes widened. He was always envious of people in his family that would devour all kinds of sweets, especially Uncle Armond. Growing up, his parents would eat cakes and pastries from Portuguese bakeries. Chuck had refrained from bad eating habits starting at a young age because he wanted to stay in shape. Now and then he would break down and pig out on junk food. Then the guilt would make him exercise harder and longer to burn the calories off.

With that in mind, Chuck said, "Nah, I'll pass, Ma. I've been laying around too much lately, waiting for my leg to heal. I'm good, really. Thanks."

"Okay, you don't know what you're missing. I'm going to have a nice slice."

Chuck sipped on his coffee and relaxed while talking more about his land purchase and workable plans once the deal was signed.

Rita abruptly changed the subject. She never had problems expressing her thoughts, whether others liked it or not. So Rita decided to tell her son a little hard truth and hoped he wouldn't take it the wrong way.

"You know, Chuck, I'm glad they discharged you from the Army."

"Ma!"

"No, it's true. You and I don't always see eye to eye, but it's just because I put my foot down when l don't agree with you and take some situations a step further than most."

"What does that mean, Ma?"

"You never got good grades in school like your brother and sister, but you were born with other gifts. You're the kindest guy in the world and people love that about you. You get that from your father. But you have another side to you. Maybe only a few have seen it."

"What side?"

"A dark side."

Chuck was enthralled by his mother's open and honest analysis of him.

"If someone crosses you, God help them. You're notorious for knee-jerk reactions. Without hesitation, you will go for a person's jugular. I worried about that side of you for years, but I'm getting wiser in my older years. Now I see that maybe it's a strength in you. A strong will, like when you were born, a survival instinct to combat this cruel world. So Chucky, what I'm saying is... good for you, son." She smiled at him, then said, "Even though this may be all true, for God's sake, Chuck, stay out of trouble. Understand?"

"Yeah, Ma. But if I'm getting you, what you're saying is that I'm capable of being a real son of a bitch, but it's okay for me to be like that?"

"I am, yes, definitely," she smiled again at him.

"You know what, Ma?"

"What?"

"I will have a piece of that cake."

Chuck said to himself as he bit into the delicious piece of pastry, *I'll just hit the gym harder tomorrow to burn this off.* He couldn't wait to take a stroll on his newly purchased land to fully scope it out once the deal was sealed.

Six months had passed since Chuck made his land purchase. He was motivated to turn it into the dream he and Shandi once envisioned. Chuck's father had a good friend he grew up with that was a builder, Tony Palluzi. After Gus came home from Vietnam, he had helped Gus and Rita build their house, as well as other commercial businesses throughout their more youthful years.

Chuck grew up with Tony's son, Chad, who now worked with his father as a partner. Chuck made a deal with him. Chad needed land to store large equipment as the Paluzzi business continued to grow. Chuck offered to let Chad store it on his property, and in return, Chad would spend weekends clearing sections of land for Chuck at a discounted price. It went like one of Gus' favorite sayings: one hand washes the other.

Chuck had another high school friend who owned a tree-cutting company. His name was Mick Bronson. Mick also made a deal with Chuck to cut trees for him at a cheap price in exchange for being able to take the wood to sell.

Chuck worked on his land every day, but after a while he was running low on funds for his new venture. Gus stopped by Chuck's almost every night after work to help him. He was so proud of him, but he also knew eventually Chuck would need to find a job. Military disability wasn't enough to keep going. Now and then, he asked Chuck to come and work with him at the shop. Chuck would tell him he'd think about it.

One night after busting his hump all day, Chuck went back to the house with Rupert, took a shower, and had his uncle over for drinks while they watched an old Clint Eastwood western. As they were getting into the movie, Gary pulled into the driveway.

"Oh look, Unc. My brother just pulled in," said Chuck. Gary got out of his car and walked down the sidewalk and up on the porch. Chuck opened the front door and said, "Hey, brother. You coming over to say goodbye to us?"

Lilly was still sitting in the passenger seat, Chuck noticed. "Lilly's not coming in?"

Gary had a bizarre look on his face.

"Come in, Gary. What's wrong?"

Gary entered the house, saying a quick hello to his uncle before turning gravely to Chuck. "Something fucked up just happened."

"What happened?"

"Lilly and I were at the movie theater, downtown in the city," said Gary intensely. "Well, we were watching the movie when we saw a couple sitting in front of us, making out. The man got up to go to the concession. It was dark, obviously, but when he came back with popcorn, me and Lilly realized it was Stacey's boyfriend, Brian. So I said to him, 'Hey Brian, what's going on?' He got nervous when he saw us and said hello back. Then we saw the girl with him wasn't our sister."

"I see," said Chuck, scowling. "What happened next?"

"After the movie ended, me and Lilly followed them out to the parking lot. I shouted at him and called him a fucking asshole. He turned on me, walked up in my face, and poked his finger in my chest, telling me to mind my own fucking business and keep my mouth shut or else. The prick then walked to his car with the girl and drove off."

"Is that all of it?"

"Yeah. I didn't know what else to do, so I came here."

"You know where this punk lives?"

"Yeah..."

"Okay, let's pay him a visit."

"Chuck, wait," Armond interjected. "I don't think that's a good idea. Plus, you've been drinking."

"Just gonna have a word or two with him, that's all. No worries, Unc."

"Yeah, right!" Armond said doubtfully.

"Let's go, Gary."

Chuck got in the backseat of Gary's car and said hello to Lilly. They drove off, headed to Brian Nevel's house. Friction between Stacey and her parents had recently grown worse over her dating this guy, and now Chuck knew why. Stacey was going straight to the top in life, and he was not about to let this guy do anything that might get in the way.

No one in the car said a word on the way to Nevel's house. It was one long, quiet ride. Gary had only been over there once before. It was a typical suburban area with homes lining the streets closely together. Gary realized he had passed Brian's driveway and backed up until he was in it. The driveway went all the way to the back of the house. Gary drove right to the end where they saw Brian standing, talking on a big cordless phone.

Chuck didn't waste any time. He instantly got out of the car and walked quickly towards the scumbag. Brian didn't immediately see Chuck coming. When he did, he didn't seem concerned and kept talking on his phone, like

Chuck was a nobody. Maybe Brian thought he could never owe anyone any type of respect, apology, or excuse for his behavior. Whatever his reason was, Chuck didn't care. He got right to it.

Chuck stepped up onto the small cement patio that Brian was standing on and swung his right fist fast and hard into Brian's smug face. The phone flew out of Brian's hand, hitting the ground and smashing into pieces. Before Brian really knew what was happening, Chuck began to pummel him, not caring where his fists landed. Brian retreated into his house before any further damage was done. Looking through the screen door, Chuck saw a very young girl – who they would later find out was a local stripper – dressed in lacy black lingerie. He turned and started walking back to the car.

Gary and Lilly were standing in front of it, slack-jawed at what they just witnessed. Before Chuck could get into the car, Brian came running back out of the screen door swinging a pair of nunchucks. Chuck snickered and ran towards Brian. As Brian swung at Chuck, he swiftly grabbed the loose end of the weapon and forcefully ripped it out of the already-winded Brian's hand, who then turned around and tried to run back inside the house again. The half-naked mystery girl was standing in the doorway, watching.

She held the door open for Brian as Chuck swung the wooden stick over his back, breaking it. The wooden spindle attached to the chain that hit Brian's backside went flying across the yard. Brian fell to the ground and tried crawling to the house. Chuck began kicking him in the stomach wearing his trusty construction boots. Brian barely made it back to the door.

"Excuse me," Chuck politely said to her.

She stepped back into the house as Brian crawled halfway through the doorway. Chuck took the screen door and began slamming it repeatedly on his midsection. He was almost finished having his fun with Brian when the cops pulled into the driveway next to Gary's car. Two officers got out of the cruiser. Gary and Lilly tried to interfere, relaying their skewed side of the situation to one officer. The other officer told Chuck to get away from the house and stand next to Gary.

The officers went into the house to talk with Brian and the girl.

Chuck heard one officer yelling at Brian to shut the fuck up. A few minutes later, the officers came out and told Gary to take Chuck home. They couldn't believe it- no charges for Chuck? They got in the car and got the hell out of there.

Much later on, Gary found out that Brian Nevel was on probation for dealing drugs and the cops in town did not like him, to say the least. When Stacey found out, she never went back to Brian again. Gary spilled the beans to their parents about what Chuck did, and Rita pretended not to approve of it. Gus was elated and didn't hesitate to outwardly praise Chuck for beating the crap out of Brian.

Gus always knew his firstborn was different than most.

CHAPTER 12
LESS TALK, MORE ACTION:
CHIP'S ALL FOR THAT IN THE U.S. SENATE
JUNE 2002

CHUCK PICKED JED up from his house, driving his Jeep with the top still on so their clothes and hair didn't get messed up. He wore one of his father's old suits, probably made in the seventies. Chuck still cleaned up nicely in it. Jed wore a black tuxedo. They joked around as they drove.

"Maybe you'll meet some nice ladies there," Jed said to Chuck.

"Right!" Chuck said sarcastically.

The rally was being held at the Sheraton in Wolford City, the same one where Chuck's band played years ago at the Halloween party where they had been discovered. Chuck pulled into the parking garage and looked for a spot, thinking about how familiar it still looked all these years later.

People were making their way towards the elevator, dressed up for the event. Chuck knew this was a scene he was not used to or comfortable with. He wasn't graceful at political small talk or accustomed to people that lived that life, but Chuck was curious and wanted to support Jed in his cause.

Jed, on the other hand, was comfortable and cool as a cucumber. This was his thing. He was in his own element in this environment. Chuck always wondered what the hell was Jed doing in being a simple corrections officer, especially after he learned about him having a law degree and passing the Bar. After Jed parked, they walked over to a glass entrance with doors that led to the elevators.

They waited by the elevators with other well-dressed gorgeous men and women. The first three elevators opened and people piled in. Chuck and Jed generously waited for the next one, then stepped in with another group. When the doors closed, people began to introduce themselves. Jed, of course, was very outgoing; Chuck, not so much.

A striking woman with dazzling long, straight brown hair wearing a short, dark green cashmere skirt with golden buckles and a white dress shirt shook Jed and Chuck's hands.

"Hello, I'm Nikita Heston. I am doing all the promotional and television ads for Chip. How about you, gentlemen?"

"I'm good friends with Chip. He's going to be a great Senator," said Jed. Nikita told Jed she hoped to see them later on during the rally.

The elevator doors opened and they all stepped into the lobby. Streamers hung from wall to wall and red, white, and blue balloons were tied to everything that didn't move. Chuck was in total awe of the festive spectacle, especially when he saw bold signs with Chip's picture and the words, "CHIP FOR SENATOR" hung around the great room. Upbeat music played behind loud chants of, "Less talk, more action, Chip Karrington!"

Chuck and Jed hadn't even reached the ballroom yet where the key event was being held. As they ascended the escalator toward the ballroom, the music and festivities grew louder. The whole place looked very different from when Chuck was last there with Shandi and the boys. Everything from the fixtures to the carpets to the furniture had been updated. Throngs of people walked around drinking, laughing, and schmoozing. There was a comedian on the main stage and a group of people were clustered around, laughing.

People that knew Jed began grabbing him to say hello. He could see Chuck was a little nervous and told him he'd drive home. "Chuck, go ahead and have a few drinks. Relax, brother."

Under the circumstances, Chuck gladly accepted his offer. He moseyed on over to the bar as Jed began to chat with acquaintances. There were a couple of local news crews set up for the rally that Chuck noticed while he waited for a Jack and Coke. He couldn't get over all the hats and pins people were wearing with Chip's name on them.

People started to go up on stage to speak about how great Chip is when he saw his sister Stacey walking towards him with a big smile on her face.

"Hey, brother, there you are. I was looking for you!"

"Me? Ah, yeah, you found me. Where are your girlfriends?"

"They're getting some drinks over there," she said as she pointed to one of the bars. "Where's your buddy?"

"He's around somewhere talking to friends."

"Nice. Maybe you guys want to join us for a drink or two later?"

"Sounds good."

Jed suddenly walked over and Chuck introduced him to Stacey before she excused herself.

"If I don't see you later tonight, I'll see you at Mom's attorney's office with Gary this week."

"Roger that, Stace."

Jed then brought Chuck over to reacquaint him with the chief man of the hour, Chip Karrington. Chip was dressed to kill in a debonair black tie and tuxedo. Chip's wife, Mellisa, was extremely friendly, a blonde knock-out who received compliments from everyone. She graciously thanked everyone for coming out. They also introduced Chuck to Chip's campaign manager, another stunner, Alicia Stone. They asked Chuck what he did for a living and thanked him for his support.

A well-dressed man in a blue pinstripe suit walked over to Chip. Chip said to Jed and Chuck, "I'd like you to meet the District Attorney General, Nick Columbo."

Jed shook his hand and the two men started conversing, but Chuck got a weird vibe from him. Maybe it was all in his head, but it was the same feeling he got way back when he met his sister's old boyfriend when he first returned home from Panama. The Attorney General was short and stocky with an arrogant demeanor. Jed always gave folks the benefit of doubt, maybe in this case because he was a fellow Italian. Chuck only knew his gut instincts, and this one wasn't good.

In a corner close by stood a small cluster of men dressed all in black, staring at Chip and his group. They looked like the Earp brothers from an old western.

One man said to another very tall, thin man, "Mr. Kobol, that guy with the dark brown blazer and no tie... he's Rita Barreto's son. The one who owns Gussy's Pitts."

"That guy?" asked Kobol in disbelief.

"Yes, sir."

Kobol turned and said, "Well, maybe we will be getting to know him soon."

Chip made his rounds thanking a few more people, then went up on the stage to give an extraordinary speech. As he talked, Alicia and Nick were having a side conversation about how their candidate had moved up in the polls by twenty points and was within only four points of his incumbent challenger, Byron Lee. This kind of talk was all strange to Chuck and didn't impress him. Chip carried on, talking about jobs, building and infrastructure without harming nature, fewer taxes, and regular folks having a voice, if he were to win.

As Chip continued to speak and Jed and Nick entered into another political discussion, Chuck snuck off to the bar again. Drink in hand, he turned around to walk back over to Jed when he saw a woman in a long, white sparkly gown across the ballroom. The garment had very thin straps, which fell gently over her sculpted shoulders. She had long, platinum-blond hair, pulled tightly back at the neckline. Even from a distance, Chuck could see that her eyes were a striking blue.

Chuck was pretty damn sure he was looking at a blond, reincarnated Shandi, or she had a twin sister. He stood there, frozen in shock for a minute, watching her. Then he thought to himself, *The hell with it. I gotta know!*

He stepped forward towards her when someone tapped him softly on his right shoulder from behind. Chuck heard a feminine southern accent say, "Excuse me, sir."

He turned around to see who it was. A pretty woman with red hair and freckles across her nose and cheeks and a gleaming smile said, "Hello. I'm Kelly Ann Texeira!"

She had on a sleek and slender red dress with matching shiny high heels.

Chuck, taken aback by her, simply said, "Hello."

"Are you Chucky Barreto?"

"Yes," responded Chuck, now curious.

"I thought so," said Kelly Ann. "I know your Mom. She worked for me, and I know Stacey, too. I rent an office from your mom at her building on the main road just outside Gussy's Pitts."

"Oh, yeah of course, ah… The Silver Bell. Nice to meet you." He shook her tiny, graceful, French-manicured right hand. Chuck thought she was definitely in the high-maintenance department. Way out of his league.

"Rita and Stacey talked about you all the time, and wooooo-wee. You're a handsome hunk of a devil."

"Thank you." Chuck blushed.

She tried talking with him about his job, but he desperately wanted to get back to the woman he saw in the white dress. Kelly saw he was a little distracted, so she ended their conversation.

"Maybe we could go out for dinner sometime, just you and I?" she suggested, handing Chuck her business card with her personal cell phone number hand-written on the back next to a smiley face. "Call me anytime."

Kelly sashayed away from Chuck saying, "I'll see you soon, hopefully."

She gave him a sassy smile and vanished into the crowd of people.

Once she disappeared, Chuck turned back around to find the mystery woman he saw across the way, but she was gone. He searched and saw no sign of her anywhere. Chuck walked around the ballroom in a tizzy, continuing to scan areas where she might be found. It seemed she just vanished into thin air.

Damn it, he thought to himself.

Chuck was lingering by the bathrooms, waiting to see if she would come out of there, when Jed then walked up to him.

"Hey, Chuck, where'd you take off to?"

"Ah, I just went to get a beverage and this lady, a realtor, gave me her personal phone number."

"No kidding! See, I told you. Are you going to call her?"

"I'm not sure. We'll see."

"You definitely should. Hey, you will not believe what just happened."

"What?"

"Chip and Nick Columbo are starting a new crime program to help promote his campaign, and they need an assistant to head all that up. They asked me to come on in, to maybe consider taking the job."

"Wow, that's awesome, Jed!" said Chuck, genuinely excited for him.

"I haven't said anything yet, and I don't want to leave you hanging either."

"Are you kidding me? You can't pass an opportunity like this up if they decide to give it to you. Don't worry about me, for God's sake!"

"Well, I'll think it over."

After the energetic evening, they drove home. Jed had to work in the morning and Chuck had to pick up his brother from the airport. Gary was flying in from Virginia for the reading of the will.

On their way home, Chuck couldn't stop thinking about the beautiful woman who looked like Shandi. Had she been imagined or real? Chuck couldn't be sure, so he kept it to himself. When he finally got home, he called Gary to confirm the time of his arrival. Afterward, Chuck settled in by the fireplace with Rupert.

The next day, Chuck was on his way to the airport to pick up Gary for the mystery unveiling ahead of them. He pulled curbside at Gary's terminal. While Chuck waited for his arrival, he still had the beautiful blond that looked identical to Shandi – and also the redhead, Kelly, he met last night – on his mind. He had been contemplating selling his house and moving into the one he had built on his new land.

Chuck thought, *Maybe I'll give the realtor, Kelly, a call after all.*

He then spotted Gary walking out of the airport with his suitcase in one hand, the other waving at Chuck. He got out, walked over to Gary, and patted him on the shoulder. Without skipping a beat, they started ragging on each other.

On the drive back to Chuck's house, Gary filled his brother in about his life in Virginia, his job, and Lilly. They talked about the will-reading. As they drove for a while Chuck filled in Gary about the new land and his house.

"Let me show it to you," Chuck said as he finally pulled onto his street.

"Yeah, sounds awesome. Can't wait to see it."

As Chuck's Jeep barrelled down the old country road, he popped in an Eagles CD – his brother and late father's favorite – not realizing the effect it would have on Gary at that moment.

"Sometimes I wonder where it is love goes/ I don't know if even Heaven knows/ I know you had some dreams that didn't quite come true/ Now I'm not the one, little girl, who's keeping you."

Chuck sang along with the song, seemingly unaffected, but it hit Gary differently. He hadn't been home since their father's funeral and he missed everyone. Gary started sobbing uncontrollably. Chuck ejected the CD right away and pulled over to the side of the road.

Gary pulled himself together and said, "I'm sorry, I'm sorry. All these memories of Dad just flooded in all at once and I couldn't help it."

"It's okay, bro, it's all good. I shouldn't have played that music. I wasn't thinking."

Gary dried his eyes and started laughing. "I'm okay now."

Chuck patted him on the back and resumed driving. As he pulled down the road, he told Gary about his plans.

"I'm saving up right now for a large gate at the entrance and big wide, steel columns on each side of the driveway, which will be hung with lights and lead up to the house. We already did all the electrical for them underground. But right now it's just a dirt road."

"Wow, that's going to look awesome," said Gary.

They entered the dirt driveway and Chuck drove slowly so Gary could appreciate the beautiful drive up to the house.

"Chuck, this is incredible."

"Thanks. You haven't seen anything yet."

They pulled up to the sprawling, white ranch with a turnaround driveway in front.

"Jesus, Chuck, this is crazy. How much to build this?"

"With Chad and his father's help- just under $160,000."

"That's a steal!"

"Yep, I paid in cash. I almost own her free and clear. Just have to pay taxes. Next, I'll build a barn and stables to begin this dream of mine. I have $23,000 put away."

"How much to build the rest?"

"Maybe $100,000 or so."

"Really. What about your other house? Why don't you sell that one and move in here?"

"Funny you mention it- I'm thinking of doing just that. Either mom could sell it or her former boss, who I just met for the first time. She gave me her phone number."

"Personal?"

"Yep, and she is a looker. I think she was flirting with me when I met her."

"What the hell are you waiting for?"

Chuck blushed. "I'll get around to it."

They got out of the Jeep and Chuck said, "Leave your stuff in here. We're going to my old house after."

They walked up onto the farmer's porch and Chuck unlocked the front door. They walked around the house with its fresh white walls and hardwood floors, their footsteps echoing from the lack of furniture to fill the space. But what Chuck was really proud to show his little brother was the basement where he was building his own private gym, and he also was storing all his old music equipment on one side of it. After Chuck gave Gary the full tour, he took him out to the backyard where Chuck had an old golf cart parked under a tarp.

"Let's take a little ride around the property, bro."

They drove around a few acres in the cart. Gary was in awe and full of compliments. They returned to the Jeep and drove to the old house.

The next day, they got up early in the morning to meet Rita and Stacey. Gary and Chuck pulled into the parking lot of the shopping plaza, one of several their father had built with the help of his friend Tony so many years ago. It was in a small town called Belchertown, right next to the town of Woodrow. Rita's attorney had her office there, and she and Stacey were already there, waiting outside.

Chuck and Gary got out of the Charger and greeted their mother and sister. Both Rita and Stacey gave Gary a big hug, welcoming him home. They talked to Gary for a few minutes, Rita and Stacey expressing that they missed him very much, before they adjourned to go inside.

"Hey guys, after we're done here let's go out to a little restaurant I know close by," Gary suggested. They all agreed, then Rita smiled and led the way into the building.

The four of them walked down a short hallway until they reached double glass doors with mighty gold handles. Above the doors in gold sculpted lettering, were the words "Marsha Wilcox at Law". They walked into a lobby area with decorative lighting, brown Berber carpet, and a handful of matching wingback chairs. Rita walked over to a large oak desk where the receptionist sat.

"Hello. I'm Rita Barreto and we're here to see Marsha."

"Oh yes, of course, she's been waiting for everyone. This way, please."

They walked through another set of glass doors. On the right was a huge wooden door that was already open.

"Hello, everyone. Come inside and sit down," said Marsha Wilcox, who was also a long-time friend to Rita and Gus. Rita walked over to her and they hugged. They sat down in the four chairs in front of her desk.

Chuck, Gary, and Stacey looked around her office where pictures of national monuments were hung on the walls. They also noticed different plaques, awards, and degrees. A huge bookcase against the far wall was filled with books and small, porcelain elephants and tigers.

"So, Gary, Chuck, Stacey- I'm sure you're wondering why you're here," Marsha smiled. "I'll get to it then. Well, it was your father's wish to divide up some of his assets between the three of you in the event of his passing. Gussy's Pitts, along with the commercial property located there, will be divided among the three of you, per your father's – and your mother's – wishes. There's currently a management company that is handling the rent for that building. The rent money will be divided evenly into three separate checks and sent to each of you. Your mom can take it from here," Marsha said and turned to Rita.

Gary, Stacey, and Chuck were all stone-faced, not quite knowing how to respond.

"Kids, the land that's on Gussy's Pitts is all commercial land as you know. One hundred and fifty acres, worth enough to set you up for the rest of your lives. Your father bought it originally to preserve it. Many have tried buying it from him, but he turned every single offer down. There's a land developer who has recently been inquiring about it. I kept telling them no, that my husband wanted his children to inherit the land. Once I sign this document here, you'll have many options. Before I do, I want a verbal promise from you all today, right here and now," said Rita.

"What's that, Mom?" asked Stacey.

"That you three do nothing at all with this land for at least six months. Just sit on it for now, no matter what you decide to do with it after."

They nodded in unison.

Rita continued. "After the six months go by and everyone has had time to think, you each can do what you want with your share. The will details the boundaries of the land which has been divided into thirds. Gary has the section at the entrance. Stacey has the section behind that, in the middle. And Chuck has the far end of the land towards Indian's Leap."

She pointed to the sections on a small map lying on the desk as she spoke.

"After, like I said, you guys can develop the land yourselves, sell, or just keep it for your future children and grandchildren. Six months okay?" she reiterated.

They again nodded.

"The rest of your father's business, I am going to keep for now. It provides me with an income to live on, and it would be a lot to take on all at once."

Rita then picked up a pen and signed the commercial building and Gussy's Pitts over to her children. Chuck, Gary, and Stacey also put their John Hancocks on it, sealing the deal. After the signing, Gary and Stacey asked a few common-sense questions to Marsha, but Chuck said nothing, in awe of his new economic status.

I can definitely sell my old house now, and I'll give that realtor, Kelly, a call after my brother goes back to Virginia, he thought to himself.

"I wish your father were here right now to see this; he would have been proud to see his legacy handed down to you all."

"Me too, Mom. Me too," said Gary.

They all got up to hug their mother and thank her. Marsha gave Rita a hug goodbye, and they left the office.

"Where are we going to eat, Mom?" asked Chuck. "I'm starving after all this... and I'm buying!"

CHAPTER 13
FATHER AND SON
JUNE 1994

MOST OF THE land that Chuck purchased had been cleared and cleaned up by June. The place was showing real promise. About three years ago, Chuck had finally taken his father up on his offer to work for him and learn the auto body business. He had needed a steady paycheck again. Even though his mortgage was paid off, he still had to come up with the taxes and other life expenses.

Chuck's father had a small, talented crew at his shop that worked for him. Joe, Carmine, Tony, and John were all immigrants from Portugal. Carmine was the only one who spoke English fluently. He was excellent at his workmanship and so was Tony. They called him Little Tony because he was only about five feet. He was a workaholic and an alcoholic.

Joe, John, and Tony would often joke around in Portuguese, being sexually inappropriate. They would grab each other a lot and then laugh about it. Chuck would think to himself, *They better not touch me like that.*

Joe and John appeared to be jealous that Gus had given Chuck a job. Sometimes they made comments about him being born with a silver spoon. Chuck just ignored them when they talked shit. Maybe they thought Chuck would be in charge of them one day. Gus, to them, was proof that the American dream was real, and they all wanted a taste of it too. Maybe they thought Chuck was going to get handed Gus's empire on a platter.

Gus's other two workers, George and Larry, were born and bred Americans. Larry was mediocre at being a body man. He wasn't in it for the long haul. He had other plans in mind and made no bones about it.

George was the oldest man in the shop, older than Chuck's father. He had a big mountain-man beard, like a member of ZZ Top. George drove an old, green Chevy pickup truck. He took a liking to Chuck, maybe the only worker who did. George felt bad for Chuck in some ways. He thought he was too young and smart to be working there. At times, he would try to give Chuck advice, telling him he should go to college before it was too late and he wound up like him. George would often be late for work due to his drinking. He was a heavy whiskey man, empty bottles lining the floor of his truck.

Chuck worked long and hard every day, trying to be as good as his father was at his craft. He struggled with it but didn't want to give up, convinced he'd get it eventually. He was good at some things, but not so much at others. Chuck had perfected the art of fixing dents, working with a chemical called "Bondo". He wasn't that great at welding, and the actual painting was discouraging. It was nothing like being in the military which had come naturally to him.

The one thing Chuck looked forward to was lunch. He would walk over to the nearby Portuguese pizza shop and buy a large, tuna sub with no tomatoes and bring it back to the shop. In the summer, he would sit outside and eat his sandwich, enjoying every bite while daydreaming about clocking out at three-thirty to go work on his land. Chuck was saving what money he could to build a house there.

One summer day at lunchtime, Chuck had just finished eating and was sipping on a can of Coke when Little Tony thought it would be funny to sneak up behind Chuck and grab his ass. Tony and Joe called it "goosing". It startled Chuck, causing Joe and John to laugh hysterically. Chuck grabbed Tony's head from behind and used his bodyweight to flip him right over onto his back. Tony went flying over Chuck's head and landed flat on his back, the cigarette in his mouth accidentally swallowed. Tony started wildly choking on it until it came out.

Joe was mad at Chuck for sacking Tony and lunged at him. Chuck saw Joe coming, and he swung his right leg up, kicking him hard in the balls.

Joe whiffed it off, then raised his fists to swing at Chuck. Chuck cocked his right arm back to punch Joe in the face, but Carmine had come up behind Chuck to grab him, and Chuck's elbow smashed into the bridge of Carmine's nose. Carmine howled in pain, bent over and holding his face, screaming in Portuguese.

Joe and Chuck stopped fighting when they realized what had happened. Then Joe started blaming Chuck.

Gus heard the commotion and came running out of his office.

"What the fuck, Chuck!" Gus yelled. He always worried about Chuck's temper with his workers. Gus knew Chuck would only put up with so much bullshit.

George chuckled, then walked over to steer Chuck away from Joe and Little Tony. Gus helped Tony up and Carmine ran to the big sink by the paint mixing table to run cold water on his nose. He asked him if he was okay, Carmine angrily motioned to Gus that he was alright. Everyone else then slowly went back to work.

Chuck was dumbfounded; it all happened so fast, he had just reacted. No matter the case, Chuck was sure these clowns deserved what they got, except for Carmine.

Gus was furious with Chuck and took him for a private talk. Gus scolded Chuck in a barely audible whisper. He was never good at disciplining him; he knew when Chuck screwed up it was never on purpose. It came from unadulterated emotion when he reacted impulsively like that.

"Chuck, what the hell is going on? This is a place of employment and I'm the boss here. You're doing really well, but you can't behave like this."

"Dad, I'm sorry, but Tony shouldn't be grabbing people like that. So I handled it."

"Yeah, that's handling it alright! You can't go on like this, solving problems with your fists."

"I thought you liked it," Chuck replied haughtily.

"Don't be a smart ass! Enough is enough- you know what I mean."

"Okay, okay, I get it. Calm down."

"I'll calm down when you calm down."

"Dad, I promise. I will try."

"Chuck, just remember one thing if anything, please! Two wrongs don't make it right."

Chuck had grown up hearing that saying time and time again from his father.

"But I gotta tell you something. Don't get mad," Chuck started.

Gus cocked his head, listening.

"Please don't take this the wrong way. It's not you. I just can't do this job anymore. It's been almost three long years. This is not my thing. After today, I'm done here. I'll apologize to Carmine, Joe, and Tony to make amends. I know Tony and Joe are a couple of morons and mean no harm, but being a body-man is just not my thing."

"What are you going to do for work?"

"I've saved up a bit of money, thanks to you. I'll take a little time off, then I'm going to have Chad start construction on the new house. After we get that started, I'll look for a new job."

"What kind of job?"

"Don't laugh, but I want to join the police department."

"Why do that?"

"You know why."

"Shandi."

"Maybe I could do something for her and, in the process, help others."

"Chuck, you have to stop kicking yourself."

"I'm not, Dad. I just have to do this."

"Okay, but will you be able to stay out of trouble this time?"

"I'll try like hell, Dad."

Gus patted Chuck on the back and walked with him back inside the shop.

CHAPTER 14
THE FATHER BECOMES THE SON AND THE SON THE FATHER
JUNE 2002

CHUCK DROVE GARY back to the airport. They had a lot to think about over the next year. Chuck couldn't wait to get back to work and tell Jed about his inheritance.

"How was the big weekend with your family?" Jed asked when Chuck returned to work.

"I inherited a humongous section of my father's land, Gussy's Pitts, including the legendary Indians Leap."

"Wow, congratulations! I'm ecstatic for you."

"Thanks, Jed. And now I'll feel much better about construction on the barn, stables, and selling my old house. What's going on with you and the job interview?"

"Well, I have a second interview, so that's a good sign I suppose."

Chuck was happy for Jed and knew he'd pull it off, but was still wary about that Colombo character he'd be working under.

When Chuck arrived home from work that day, he got Kelly's card out and called her. A secretary answered the phone, and Chuck asked for Kelly Teixeira. She said Kelly was tied up at the moment, then asked him if he wanted to wait on hold or have her call him back. Chuck opted for Kelly to call him back.

He got Rupert situated, made himself a tuna sandwich, started a load of laundry, and made a drink. He had just sat down on the couch with Rupert and began to channel surf when the phone rang.

"Hello," Chuck answered.

"Hello there yourself, handsome. I was wondering when you'd call me," said Kelly. "You calling for a date?"

Chuck didn't know what to say for a second, but quickly recovered. "Absolutely, I'd like that. And I'm also looking to sell my house. I was wondering if you'd be interested in that, too?"

"How's this? I'll come over this weekend. Saturday, if you're free? I'll take a look at the house, and then I'll take you out for some lunch or dinner."

"That sounds like a date, ma'am."

Kelly laughed. "Please Chuck, darling, call me Kelly."

"Okay... Kelly," Chuck said nervously.

"Okay. How's around three-thirty?"

"It's a date, Kelly."

"Okay, then. I can't wait. See you soon."

They hung up and Chuck felt mighty fine. Things had been going well lately. He couldn't wait to tell his uncle the news that they would most likely be moving over to the new house soon.

Chuck went back to channel surfing when he came upon a film he loved. It was *Superman* starring Christopher Reeve, Glenn Ford, Marlon Brando, and Margot Kidder. It caught Chuck's attention, especially because he hadn't seen the classic movie since before his father passed away.

It was special to Chuck. He remembered back when he was a child and his father had come home from a hard day's work, after the family had dinner, homework was done, and chores were finished, Chuck and his father would often watch old black and white shows being broadcast on the big tube TV with the antenna on the roof for reception. Two shows in particular, *The Lone Ranger* and *The Adventures of Superman*, were their favorites. They both looked forward to those weeknights, to see what new adventures and problems Superman, Clark, Louis, and Jimmy would have to resolve. Chuck could still remember the great introduction to the show.

"Faster than a speeding bullet... More powerful than a locomotive... Able to leap tall buildings in a single bound... Lookup in the sky, it's a bird, no a plane...It's Superman! Yes, it's Superman, strange visitor from another planet who came to Earth with powers and abilities far beyond those of mortal men... Superman who can change the course of mighty rivers...Bend steel with his bare hands... And who disguised as Clark Kent, mild-mannered reporter for a great metropolitan newspaper fights a never-ending battle for truth, justice, and the American way."

Gus and little Chuck were so excited to hear the theme every time; it never got old. In the late seventies, when Chuck was about nine, the movie came out. The opening musical score needed no words or narrator. John Williams had masterfully composed it; the music said it all. The movie, for its time, had big, blockbuster special effects. Movies like that were in their infancy.

Gus took his sons to see it on its opening weekend. Gus was probably more excited than the kids. It was their first film adventure of this kind. Chuck recalled the long lines of people, literally wrapped around the building, everyone excited to get inside. When they finally did, Gus bought huge buckets of popcorn with extra butter. They rushed in to get the closest seats possible to the movie screen. When the movie trailers rolled, they were enthralled, even with the ads before the movie. Each popcorn kernel was like a slice of heaven.

Once the movie began, they couldn't believe their eyes. They were seeing the hero wearing red and blue tights, not black and white, for the first time ever. The film was epic; seeing Reeve flying on the big screen with no strings attached to him was surreal. There was one scene early in the film when a young Clark Kent, still in high school, was running along the side of a speeding locomotive train and outran it. Gus laughed and pointed out how it was a nod to the original television show. He picked up on little things hidden in the movie for the fans.

As he watched the movie with Rupert, the story itself touched Chuck profoundly still today, particularly that Superman had two fathers: his Earth father who had raised him and his biological father, both who ended up dying on Clark before their time. Each of Superman's fathers had a major influence on his moral character and the man he became in life, the way that Gus had been for Chuck. He thought of getting up and making some popcorn but didn't want to miss the upcoming scenes in the film, so he contentedly stayed glued to the screen while petting his little buddy.

Chuck began getting emotional watching one key scene between Clark and a hologram vision of his dead biological father played by Marlon Brando.

His father said, "Listen carefully, my son, for we shall never speak again... Look at me, son. Once before, when you were small, I died while giving you a chance for life, and now even though it will exhaust the final energy left within me–"

"Father, no!" Clark exclaimed.

"Look at me, son. The Kryptonian prophecy will be at last fulfilled, the son becomes the father, the father becomes the son. Farewell, forever son. Remember me."

Clark's father moved closer to him and transferred everything he had left in him back into his son until he was whole again and ready to fight another day.

As Chuck continued watching with Rupert, he started to think, *Am I becoming my old man? Is it possible?*

CHAPTER 15
THE ATTACK
SEPTEMBER 2001

CHUCK HAD BEEN working for the Department of Corrections for five and a half years. He was dedicated and worked hard at being an exemplary officer. The higher-ups at the prison saw how consistent he was and put Chuck in charge of the tougher blocks to keep them running smoothly.

His new house was currently under construction, and Chad and Mick were clearing more acres of land. Things were moving along at a faster pace than Chuck could have anticipated. Each day after leaving the prison, he worked on the interior of the house, installing hardwood flooring with the help of his father.

One night while they were putting down floorboards, Gus said to his son, "Hey Chuck, do you want to go to New York with me tomorrow for a few days to see Vovo? Your Mom is watching over the office for me. It's just a quick visit."

Vovo lived in Mount Vernon, and Chuck had only seen her twice since his return from Panama and felt bad about it. Chuck was anguished. "Ah, Dad this is kind of short notice. I would have to call out sick and get a note. I could if you really want me to."

"No, no don't do that. You're doing well and I'm proud of you. I would have told you sooner but it was a spontaneous idea. We can go together another time soon."

A few days later, Chuck was working in his assigned unit when the inmates began talking about something that was happening on their televisions.

"We're under attack, we're under attack!" they started screaming.

Chuck ran over to one inmate's cell close to the officers' podium to see what they were talking about. His eyes widened. He saw one of the Twin Towers in New York City smoking and on fire.

"What the fuck is going on?" Chuck asked.

"A plane crashed into it!" the inmate responded.

All of a sudden, Chuck saw another large commercial plane fly right into the second Twin Tower.

"What the fuck!" exclaimed Chuck.

He ran back to the podium and called his Sergeant on the desk phone. "Sarge, it's Chuck. I don't know if you heard, but planes have hit both Twin Towers in New York. My father is in the city today with my grandmother and aunt."

"Chuck, you're not screwing with me, are you?"

"I wouldn't do that, not about this," Chuck said, panic in his voice.

"Let me see what I can do. I'll call you right back."

"Okay thanks, Sarge."

A few minutes later, an announcement came over the prison intercom system to lock all inmates in their cells until further notice. Chuck immediately followed the order.

The phone rang on his desk and the Sergeant told Chuck that he could leave. His partner would be enough because the block was locked down. Chuck thanked the Sergeant, then bolted out of his block, down the hallways, out the front doors, and into his Jeep. He grabbed his flip phone out of the middle console and panicked because he had forgotten to charge it. Thank the Lord there was somehow still half the battery left.

He started the vehicle, then searched through his contacts until he found his father. It was the longest ring he'd ever waited for, and all he got was Gus's voicemail.

Chuck left a quick message. "Dad, I just left work. Please call me!"

He raced down the old patched, paved access road and redialed his father's number with the same result. Chuck looked up his grandmother's number next. No answer. Chuck left a message on her answering machine as well.

He called his mother, who was in the office at the auto body shop. The phone seemed to ring louder than usual.

"Chuck, hold on please," Rita answered. "I'm on the other line with your grandmother and aunt. I'll click back over to you in a second."

Chuck felt a little more relieved as he waited for her to come back, but it was almost like a replay of the feeling he had when they couldn't find Shandi.

Rita clicked back over. "Chuck, I can't talk long. I have to call your Aunt Joanne back. She's with your grandmother and father."

"OK, thank God. Dad's alright?"

"I'm sure he is."

"What do you mean? Where is he? He is with them, right?"

"Chuck, I want you to pull over and calm down. I can hear you breathing."

"I'll calm down when you tell me what's going on."

"They're at a restaurant, maybe a block from the towers. Your father left Vovo with your aunt to see if he could help. You know your dad. I'm sure he's fine."

"Okay, Mom, I'm gonna try to call him back. He didn't answer his cell when I called."

"I know, I tried too. He's probably busy helping people, but that's okay. Keep trying and I'll call your aunt back."

"Okay, Mom. Call me back if you hear anything."

"You too."

They hung up. Chuck kept calling his father's cell phone to no avail. Now Gus's phone was going straight to voicemail.

Still driving, Chuck turned on the radio to listen for any new information they might have about what happened. They reported both planes hit the Twin Towers and that it was a potential terrorist attack. Then his radio announced that the Pentagon had been struck, too.

"Fuck this. I'm headed for New York," said Chuck. He estimated it would be a two-and-a-half hour drive if he didn't run into traffic.

Rita then called Chuck back. "Chuck, I'm a little worried. The Pentagon was just hit."

"Yeah, I just heard, Mom. I'm on my way to New York."

She knew better than to argue with him at this point. "Be careful driving. We'll call each other if we hear anything from your dad or Vovo, okay?"

Chuck agreed and they hung up. Rita wanted Chuck to focus on the road, and his phone needed to be charged or he wouldn't be able to contact anyone for much longer.

He knew how to get to his grandmother's pretty quickly, but he wasn't sure if he could get in with the chaos at hand. The radio announcer said the first tower collapsed, and shortly after, the second one. Chuck tried his father and there was no answer. He called his aunt's phone and she picked up.

Joanne was frantic, saying there were thick clouds of dust everywhere. Chuck told her to stay put with Vovo and hunker down in a basement if they could. He told them not to go out on the streets; she agreed.

Rita called Chuck back, but this time she was crying uncontrollably.

"Everything will be fine," Chuck reassured her. "I'm sure dad got out of there. He's a resourceful human being."

He calmed her down, hung up, and continued his unfortunate journey. The cause of what was happening was somewhat confirmed by another plane that crashed in a field in Pennsylvania; it was a terrorist attack on the United States.

Once Chuck got closer to New York City, it became harder to travel. It took him an extra hour and a half to get to his grandmother's house. He had gotten as far as he could go in his vehicle due to road blocks, traffic, and general hysteria. He pulled the vehicle over into a big parking lot. There were no attendants around, so he parked, locked her up, and ran a few blocks while calling for a taxi at the same time. Before anyone answered, Chuck saw a taxi at the end of the street he was running down. He ran up to the cabby and begged the driver for a ride. The man said he'd try to do his best to help him. He got him as close as he could to the restaurant, then Chuck ran on foot the rest of the way.

Eventually, he found his grandmother and aunt and got them out of the building and back to Vovo's house safely. Chuck went back to the vicinity of the Towers, running on adrenaline and looking for his father. Like many others, Gus was never seen again.

The Department of Corrections let him stay out of work while he remained in New York. After weeks of waiting for answers, Chuck went home feeling defeated. He didn't know how much more death in his life he could handle, but he had to be strong for his family. If Gus was still out there somewhere, he was watching Chuck and he didn't want to let his father down.

Chuck's memory of the horrific time had become vague, like when Shandi was found murdered. He couldn't protect her, and now, adding injury to his unhealed wounds, his father was most likely killed because of terrorists. Whenever things started going well for him, Doctor Doom was right around the corner to take away any hope of happiness in his life.

Chuck was getting pretty sick and tired of it all.

Gus's funeral was in late November. Hundreds of people that knew and loved him attended. It was a long day, a longer year. Vovo's heart weighed heavily for Gus having come into the city that day to shop and sightsee close to the Towers. It was more than she could bear, and she passed away a few days after Gus's funeral.

Chuck went back to work but was not the same officer anymore. He drank almost every night and let himself go. He never waited for backup when a fight broke out between inmates. He would jump in like he didn't have a care in the world. Chuck exploded on inmates that looked at him the wrong way. It now scared other officers to work with him and he wasn't a trusted colleague.

Until that fateful day that Captain Gavin decided to team Jed and Chuck together to clean up block ZX.

CHAPTER 16

CHUCK'S DATE

JUNE 2002

CHUCK CHEERED UP and called his sister to tell her the news of selling his house. After he had a short talk with her, Chuck went next door to tell his uncle. Armond was enthusiastic about the news and looking forward to the move over to the larger house. Chuck made a mental note to call Chad and Mick to see if they had any friends that wanted to make a few extra dollars by helping them move.

Chuck went back to work with Jed for the rest of the week. At night, he kept busy by helping Chad and Mick finish up clearing the last of the areas that needed it. The landscaping had come a long way.

The weekend came quickly and Chuck was getting nervous about his upcoming date with Kelly. He laid out a bunch of clothes on the bed, trying to find something suitable. Rupert was in the room with Chuck and wore a confused look. His forehead wrinkled and protruding eyes were questioning as he barked at his master.

Every time Chuck tried something on, he'd say to Rupert, "Well, what about this one, Rupee?"

After changing five different times, he ended up with a casual look: jeans, a black t-shirt, and a neatly ironed flannel shirt with a pair of squared-toed boots. He blew dry his long-flowing locks that almost touched his shoulders to make it look neater than usual.

Chuck faced Rupert and said, "Well?"

Rupert barked at Chuck.

"Sold, little buddy! I'm not sure, but fuck it. I'm owning this!" he said and smiled at his dog, who was looking up at him and wagging his tail.

Chuck went downstairs to make a pot of coffee and wait for his date to arrive. Uncle Armond knocked on the front door.

Chuck shouted, "Come on in, Unc."

"Well, look at the Meathead!" Armond said as he walked in.

"Ha, ha, ha, ha. Hilarious, Arm. You want a cup of coffee?"

"That's why I'm here."

"Sure, sure," Chuck said as he poured him a cup. "Lots of cream and sugar?"

"Til the spoon stands up."

Chuck smiled.

Armond sipped on the coffee and joked with Chuck while he waited. "Wanna borrow some of my old English Leather cologne?"

"Hell no! Unc, no one uses that stuff anymore."

"This man does. It never goes out of style."

"Right, that's why the women are running in and out of your place."

"I'm a bachelor. That's why you don't see any women."

"That makes no sense, Unc," said Chuck, grinning and shaking his head.

The sound of a loud muffler coming down the road paused their conversation, and Rupert jumped from the couch to the big bay window to see who was coming. They saw a blue 1969 Corvette Stingray, a gorgeous car with all chrome trim and mag wheels. It pulled slowly into Chuck's driveway. The roof was a T-top that was already off for the drive on this beautiful, sunny day.

The engine shut off, and the curved driver's door opened up. A slender bare leg came out of the door and set a gentle foot on Chuck's driveway.

"Whoa!" Uncle Armond said with his mouth wide open.

"Wait 'til you hear her accent."

"Get out there, Meathead, to greet her."

"Right," said Chuck and he put his coffee down and ran out the front door.

Kelly was all dolled up. She was wearing a tight-fitting, light blue velour dress that ended just past her knees to accentuate her sexy, sculpted legs. The side of the garment had slits, exposing the captivating skin on her sides. A wide v-shaped neckline exposed her well-defined shoulders and dipped far enough to expose some cleavage. Around her neck she wore large white pearls. She had these fantastic cork, open-toed heels with white leather straps and little gold latches that showed off her perfect, tiny feet.

Kelly was wearing bright red lipstick on her already amazing lips. Blush highlighted her cheeks and she wore exotic purples and grays around her eyes with big lashes that she batted sexily at Chuck when she greeted him. Her thick, red hair was all curled up like a supermodel from the seventies.

Armond was still inside watching, glued to the window alongside Rupert. "Boy, oh boy, Sir Rupert. Your master is one lucky guy."

Rupert barked at Armond in agreement.

Outside, Chuck nervously walked up to Kelly to say hello. She pulled him in gently and gave him a kiss on the cheek, speaking first. "Wow, Chuck. It's really nice out here. I can't wait to see inside! I should have no problem at all selling her for you."

"That's one hell of a car. I'm into the classics myself," said Chuck.

"Really? You have a Vette, too?"

Chuck shook his head. "I have a 72 Charger parked up the road at my other house."

"Nice. You'll have to take me over there for a ride later," said Kelly flirtatiously.

"Yeah, sure," said Chuck, at a loss for words.

"Well, handsome, how about that grand tour?"

"Sure, Kelly, right this way."

She smiled at him.

Chuck helped her down the small set of steps to reach the sidewalk and then they walked up onto the front porch.

"Nice. This is amazing," said Kelly.

"Thank you."

They walked through the front door into the living room. Uncle Armond, Rupert, and Kelly exchanged hellos. Rupert sniffed her leg and ran over to Armond, which was odd because he usually loved all women and children immediately.

Chuck led Kelly through the first-floor rooms and back dining area. Then they went upstairs to Chuck's bedroom and bathroom before ending in the basement.

"Your little man-town paradise?" asked Kelly, eyeing his bar setup.

"Ah, you know, sometimes my old Army buddies come over to hang out."

"Your mother told me you were in the Army for a while, a rockstar, and now a corrections officer? My, my, you get around."

"My mom exaggerates way too much."

"Not from where I'm standing!" Kelly drawled.

Chuck couldn't believe this sophisticated, classy woman wanted to hang out with the likes of him. He didn't understand what her interest in him could be. She was beautiful, intelligent, and worldly; he thought that maybe this was one way his dad was looking out for him. Sometimes unexplained gifts were given to those who had been through tough times. If this was a gift being thrown his way, Chuck accepted it.

Kelly was attracted to his naiveté, his strength and roughness, his handsome looks and physique. She admired his innocence and nervousness. She loved that he found success in life even though he really had no clue about any of it. Chuck was a stud of a man for her to conquer, and when Kelly wanted something, she was determined to get it.

Chuck blushed again. He was pretty sure she was coming on to him, but then again maybe she was just *that* friendly when she stood to gain from the sale of a house.

"What's back here, Chuck, an extra room?" she asked.

Behind them was the closed door of the studio he never went inside.

"I need to see it. Is it a mess? Trust me, there's nothing I haven't seen in this business," she continued.

Chuck was reluctant, but he also didn't want to explain how he really hadn't gone into that room since before Shandi passed. Only once. When he came home from Panama and he got their album from Bill, he had run in quickly and placed it on a shelf.

"Oh, yeah. Well, it's just storage where I keep some music equipment from my band days."

Chuck tried to be nonchalant about it. He opened the door, turned on the light, and gestured for Kelly to step in. It was dusty, everything covered in cobwebs.

"Chuck, you have a lot of equipment in here. I heard about your band. Maybe you could play me a song sometime?"

Kelly didn't want to ask too many questions. She knew about what happened to Shandi from Chuck's mother and didn't want to spoil the date she had planned. Kelly noticed the album sitting on the shelf, Shandi front and center on the cover.

Kelly thought to herself with credence, *She's a gorgeous girl. She's perfect!*

Chuck saw Kelly staring at the album cover and tried to draw her attention away. "I've gotta pack all this stuff up. I'm building a small gym in the basement of my new house and getting rid of most of this."

"You don't look like you need to work out," Kelly replied. "If you don't mind me asking… what are you doing with your new house and the land it's on?"

"No, not at all. After I sell this house, I'm building a barn and stables to start a small horse ranch. It's my retirement plan."

"Oh, very nice. From what I can see you're already doing pretty well for yourself."

"Ah, you know, it's just a dream I have."

"For what it's worth, I think it will come true," she said.

They left the basement and finished their tour with a viewing of the back deck and Uncle Armond's apartment. Kelly again assured Chuck the house would sell like a hotcake, and then they took off to an early dinner in her Corvette.

Chuck opened her door for her and then got in on his side. She started the car and shifted into reverse.

"Wow, five-speed shift stick," said Chuck.

"You betcha. You like Bob Seger?"

"Of course. Who doesn't?"

"Bob it is!" she said as she put the CD on. "I have all his stuff."

The song "Turn the Page" came on, just loud enough so they could still hear each other talk, but with the top off, they still had to contend with the open air.

"Where'd you get this beauty?" Chuck asked.

"I bought it last year. I had a good year in sales."

They drove past Chuck's land.

"You'll have to show me around your new place sometime. I'd love to see it," said Kelly.

"Yeah, after dinner maybe."

"Sure, that would be nice."

They made small talk as she drove towards the city, and Chuck tried not to stare at her sensational legs. It wasn't easy. She was so damn hot. Kelly had no problem looking him up and down, so much so that she was hardly watching the road.

They drove past Gussy's Pitts and Kelly said, "Your mom stops in at my office here every once in a while. She told me about your inheritance. I know a lot of investors who are trying to buy up all that land."

Chuck didn't know quite what to say about that. He tried to remain neutral. "Yeah, with my brother and sister. We haven't decided anything yet."

Kelly changed the subject to Chuck's sister and how they knew one another. "I can't believe with your mother working for me and my friendship with Stacey that I'm just meeting and getting to know you now."

Chuck blushed. "Better late than never."

Kelly told Chuck she had made reservations at a nice Italian restaurant in the city. She talked about her job and asked him some questions about his work at the prison. Chuck left out the more vulgar details; he didn't want to scare her off with some of the crazy shit that went on at work. Before Chuck knew it, Kelly pulled her car into the garage of a big building called "The SkyTower".

"I have an office here also. I just realized... now you're my landlord for the office by Gussy's Pitts," she smiled at him as she parked. "Maybe you can give me a discount on my rent if I do good on your house?"

Chuck didn't know what to say.

"I'm just kidding with you, sweetie," said Kelly. "The restaurant we're going to is within walking distance. By the looks of the size of your arms, we should be okay if we run into any trouble." She batted her eyelashes at him and smiled coyly. "We have a few minutes. Would you like to see my office?"

"Sure," said Chuck in disbelief that she had an office in this building. It was known to be for the rich.

They walked towards the elevator. A parking attendant and security guard sat in a glass booth. Kelly waved at the men.

"Hello, Miss Teixeira," they said.

Kelly and Chuck got on the elevator. She pressed the number five and wrapped her small arm around his. As they ascended, Kelly gently reached up, grabbed the back of Chuck's neck, and pulled him towards her and their lips collided.

Holy shit! Is this really happening? Chuck thought.

The elevator door opened and four men, lawyer types, stood waiting at the entrance. Chuck and Kelly quickly pulled apart, blushing and tingling all over.

"Excuse us," said Chuck as they got off the elevator.

Kelly escorted Chuck to her office down the hall. She held on to him as she showed him around.

"Very nice setup. Nice view too," said Chuck.

"I'm sorry about that on the elevator. I've never done anything like that before. It's just, you're so damn ..."

"It's alright," said Chuck. "I didn't mind at all."

"Then you won't mind this!" She leaned up towards him and their mouths found each other again for several minutes before they came up for oxygen.

"Whew! We better take a break or we'll be late for our dinner reservation," said Kelly. "But I'd love to continue this later with you, handsome."

"Me too," said Chuck.

"Great. I can't wait for you to see this restaurant," she said as they made their way to dinner, her arm interlocked with his, gently scratching her manicured fingernails along his bicep with her other delicate hand.

Kelly was pretty confident she had him- hook, line, and sinker.

They walked for half a block to the restaurant. It was large and lined with windows. A gold sign overhead read "The Villa Rose". About thirty people were waiting outside to get in. Kelly walked past them and up to the host's podium with Chuck in tow. The maitre d' stood waiting with a smile.

"I have a reservation for two under 'Teixeira," Kelly said.

The woman looked down, checking her list. "Oh yes, ma'am, come right in."

The two of them followed her inside. There were huge white leather booths with oversized, seat cushions of assorted colors. The floor, ceiling, and tables were made of glossy oak. Some walls were covered top to bottom with white shelving, displaying hundreds of wine bottles. The lighting inside, of course, was low. Chuck could tell the silverware and glassware was high end as well, and he didn't know if he should actually touch any of it.

The place was packed, the only empty seats being the booth to which the maitre d' accompanied them. Chuck wasn't worried about how much dinner was, for he was doing well financially, but he got the feeling she ate at places like this a lot, and that was totally not Chuck. They picked up their menus, and she talked about life in the city as Chuck read. He had a hard time understanding the language on the menu, but was able to make out the word "chicken" and figured he'd order something like that, pretending he knew what was going on.

"How about if I order us a nice bottle of wine? I won't have too many, I promise. I know I have to drive."

"That sounds great," said Chuck.

The server came over and Kelly ordered the bottle. Shortly after, the cork was popped and they each had a glass in front of them. They ordered their meals, and after the waitress left, they sipped on their wine while Kelly talked about when she first met Chuck's mother. She again asked Chuck questions about his future plans for the ranch. He explained some of it without telling her anything too personal.

While they were talking, a woman who recognized Kelly came up to their table. "Kelly? How are you?"

Kelly got up and hugged her. "I'm great. What are you doing here?"

"I'm here with Chip, Nick Columbo, and his wife. Right over there." Mellisa pointed to their table and called her husband over.

"Chuck, this is Mellisa Karrington," said Kelly.

Chuck stood up. "We met once before at your husband's campaign rally. Nice to see you again, Mrs. Karrington."

Chip and Nick came over to say hello, recognizing Chuck from previously making his acquaintance.

"Hello again. Jed's friend, right?"

"Yes, sir. Chuck Barreto."

"Nick, you remember Mr. Barreto, Jed's friend?" reiterated Chip.

"Yes, of course. How could I forget this guy? " he said sarcastically. "Nice outfit. Wish I could pull that look off in here. You used to be some sort of rockstar, right?"

"No, not really," Chuck said coldly.

"Okay, my mistake," Nick replied with an ugly smirk on his face.

Sensing the tension between them, Kelly changed the subject. "Nick, where's your wife?"

"Gina's over there at our table. She's cutting up my steak for me the way I like it."

"Oh, you can't cut your own food?" Kelly joked.

"Yeah, but she enjoys doing it for me."

Chuck couldn't tell if this wise guy was joking around or not. He looked over at their table, saw the young woman cutting up food, and got that feeling of bad intuition again. He couldn't believe Jed might work for this guy who looked like a real prick with ears to Chuck. He supposed Jed had to do what was in his best interest to further his career. Unfortunately, you sometimes had to deal with special people like this along that journey. Jed was much better at it than Chuck.

"Why don't you two come on over to our table and join us?" suggested Chip.

"We'd love to, but this is kind of a business dinner," said Kelly.

"Oh, that's okay. Another time then. Nick, don't you have an interview with Jed coming up?"

"On Monday, in fact," said Nick.

"Nice. Well, Kelly, Chuck, we'll see you soon. And thank you for your support at the rally."

"You're welcome, Mr. Karrington."

"Call me Chip, Chuck. Any friend of Jed's is a friend of mine."

"Yeah, we'll see you around, slick," said Nick.

They returned to their tables and Kelly said to Chuck, "Don't mind Nick. That's just his demeanor."

"I'm fine. I get guys like that, not a big deal."

Kelly asked Chuck if he wanted her to put a kind word in for Jed. She was good friends with the Karringtons and Columbos. Chuck told her he thought Jed was pretty capable.

"OK, let me know if you change your mind."

After they finished eating, the server came over to clear the table. Chuck whipped out his credit card.

"What are you doing, mister? I don't think so," said Kelly.

"I got it."

"Actually, you're both all set. Mr. McDuffy, the owner, said it's on the house," said the waitress.

"Oh, thank you. Can you tell Mr. McDuffy we said thank you as well?" said Kelly.

"I will do that, ma'am. He wanted me to tell you he was going to come out himself to say hello, but something came up and he had to leave."

Kelly thanked her again and they got up to leave. She waved at everyone sitting at Chip's table on their way out.

Kelly explained to Chuck that she often brought a lot of business clients to the restaurant, which was probably why they received a complimentary meal.

"Hey, I have an idea," Kelly said when they were just outside. "I know this is crazy, but just hear me out. What if we go do a little dancing at a nightclub a few blocks from here? After that, maybe we can have a nightcap at my apartment. You can sleep on my couch, and then in the morning we can go see your new house."

"You have a place around here?" asked Chuck.

"I do. The same building my office is in. Just a few more stories up."

"Ah... yeah, okay. Let's do it."

Chuck hadn't danced in well over a decade, and Kelly looked like she'd be good at it. When they arrived at the club, there was another small line of people outside waiting to get in. The music spilling out onto the sidewalk sounded like modernized disco music. Chuck had a pleasant buzz; he wasn't used to drinking wine.

"You got a special skip to the front of the line here?" asked Chuck.

"No, silly. I've never been here before. Seen it driving by many times and thought it looked like fun."

She rubbed his back while they waited to get in. When they got to the front of the line, Chuck expediently got out cash to pay the cover charge. She let him with no argument.

Kelly moved her sleek body to the music as she led him over to the bar to get drinks. Chuck figured he better be cool, so he got a beer and Kelly a martini. She led Chuck around the luxurious place until they found a cozy corner booth to sit and mingle. Once they sat, Chuck noticed a good number of male heads turning to look at his stunning date.

Chuck got the feeling they wouldn't be doing much sitting unless it involved touching. Chuck and Kelly were not drinking long before she grabbed his hand and pulled him out onto the packed dance floor. She was grinding her body close to his. Chuck tried to keep up, but she had some moves that he couldn't compete with. He thought she might have had some sort of dance lessons when she was younger. Either that or it came much more naturally to her than him. Having been deeply in the music world once upon a time, Chuck was holding his own, and Kelly was getting hot over it. Chuck was a whole different kind of man for her.

After a few songs, Kelly suggested they rest for a few minutes and get another drink. Chuck went to the bar to fetch them, then met her back at their booth. When he slid in comfortably next to her, they couldn't keep their hands off each other. The chemistry was intense.

After steaming up their space for a while, she told Chuck she had to make a trip to the ladies' room for a minute to powder her nose, jokingly telling him not to go anywhere.

He waited happily, reflecting on the day and night so far, wondering how the heck he got there. Chuck didn't want it to end. Kelly returned and grabbed Chuck to hit the dance floor.

"You're smiling, Chuck. I don't see you do that much," Kelly said. She knew why and so did he. Chuck was having fun for once and loving every inch of her, a feeling he forgot about a long time ago.

A slow song came on. Kelly whispered, "Finally. Hold me tight, Chuck."

They held each other close, moving their feet in step and passionately kissing. After the song ended, another slow song followed, which Chuck was thankful for.

Suddenly, through the darkly-lit club and the throng of people, Chuck saw a woman leaning against the end of the bar, wearing a shin-length black cocktail dress with sparkly silver heels shining like diamonds. She had long, platinum-blonde hair pulled back. Chuck looked harder. Was he drunk already? Maybe, but it looked like the same beauty he saw at Chip Karrington's campaign rally. Yes, it was her.

Was it worth blowing this perfect night with Kelly? *Yes*, he thought. *I have to know who she is!*

Kelly could feel something in Chuck change. "You okay?"

"Oh yeah, I'm perfect, Kell."

The song ended and Chuck told Kelly he'd meet her back at their booth after he went to use the bathroom. When Kelly was out of sight, he left the bathroom and bee-lined it over to the bar area where he saw the mystery woman. His heart was pounding, the blood rushing to his head. Chuck frantically looked everywhere and couldn't find her. She was gone. He ran to the front door and looked outside in every direction. Maybe she was having a cigarette if she smoked. Nothing. *Damnit,* he thought.

He flipped his cell phone open and called Armond to let him know he was spending the night in the city. Armond tried joking with Chuck about it, but he was too distracted to care. Chuck showed the man at the door his hand stamp and went back inside.

Chuck went to the bar and asked the bartender, "Excuse me, sir, did you see a woman with blonde hair and a black cocktail dress standing right here a few minutes ago?"

"No, I'm sorry. Can I get you anything?"

"Yeah, a martini and a Jack and Coke," said Chuck, frustrated. He probably shouldn't, but what the hell. He was either seeing things or the woman was still there somewhere.

"I thought you abandoned me," Kelly said when he got back to the booth.

"No, I got us another drink, and I had to call my uncle to let him know I was staying out here."

"Oh, that's sweet."

Chuck decided to forget about the mystery woman. He must be losing his mind. He spent the rest of the night in Kelly's arms, dancing or otherwise.

"Well, while it's getting late, but not too late, why don't we go back to my place for that nightcap?"

Chuck didn't know what to expect once they got there, but he happily agreed. They left to walk back to her place, holding each other on the way. Chuck looked nonchalantly one last time for the woman in the black dress as they crossed the club, but there was still no sign of her. *That's it. I'm done for now,* he thought.

Back at the building they got on the elevator again, only this time, Kelly pressed button number twenty. Chuck wondered just how much money she had. They reached her floor and she showed him to her extravagant, iron-paneled front door. She unlocked it and they went inside.

The studio penthouse had an open floor plan. From his vantage point, he could see the exposed kitchen, dining room, and bedroom. Marble tiles lined the floor. The kitchen had a breakfast bar which separated her dining area and bedroom. The bathroom was in the corner and larger than his bedroom. Chuck's favorite feature was that the television in the living room was in an enclosed glass nook that jutted out from the living space, overlooking the entire city.

"Here's the pull-out couch for you, handsome. It comes with a view," said Kelly.

"Wow, I've never seen anything like this before," said Chuck.

"You should be honored, sir. I've never brought anyone back to my place before."

He wasn't sure if she was telling the truth.

"How about a drink and some music?" she said.

"Sure."

She walked over to an elegantly-styled bar that flaunted a lot of masculine black and gold decor and was lit by modern pendant lighting, while featuring a stereo system built into the wall. Also on the wall was a gas-lit fireplace. Kelly made him another Jack Daniels and a martini for herself, and then she turned on a radio station that played seventies and eighties love songs. The fireplace flames conducted their own gentle dance. Kelly undid the straps on her shoes and slid them off onto the floor.

"Come on over and dance with me, Chucky," she said.

Chuck took his drink from her. They held each other with one arm, while they drank with the other and danced into the night. She was gently kissing him on the neck when a song from Quarterflash came on.

"Frankie, out on the street/ You know you see much better at night/ They call you cat's eyes/ Down on the corner, they call you Mr. Flash/ The god some ladies who never see the light," sang Randy Ross through the speakers.

She was humming the lyrics in Chuck's ear and necking with him. It reminded Chuck a little of when Shandi used to sing softly to him. The only problem was she wasn't Shandi and her humming was off-key. But that was alright. She had other things going for her; she didn't need to hum well.

By the next song they put down their drinks, fully engaged in dancing and kissing, hands wandering to explore each other. Instead of her humming the current song, Chuck took over and sang a little of it to her instead.

"Between the darkness on the street/ And the houses filling up with light/ Between the stillness in my heart/ And the roar of the approaching night/ Somebody's calling after somebody/ Somebody turns the corner out of sight/ Looking for somebody/ Somewhere in the night/ Tender is the night."

"Oh, there it is. This boy's got skills," said Kelly.

Chuck blushed and stopped singing. They kept on dancing for one more song knowing that if they carried on, their clothes would melt off their bodies.

"We better get some sleep if we're going to get back to your place tomorrow," said Kelly. "I'll help you with the couch."

She showed him how to pull it out into a bed. She started kissing him again and said, "Would you mind if I sleep with you under the stars tonight?"

Chuck was nervous, but also excited. "No, not at all."

Kelly took a few steps back from Chuck and unzipped the back of her dress, slowly slipping the glove-fitting garment off her petite body. As the dress fell to the floor, she stepped out from it and came closer to Chuck. She had on nothing underneath except a skimpy pair of pink panties. Chuck's eyes felt like they were bulging out of his skull, and the only word that came to mind was *LORD*!

He took off his shirt, and she moved right up to him and unbuckled his belt, then his pants. Chuck hadn't seen a female body that perfect since Shandi. Not that he slept around much.

Chuck and Kelly made passionate love for hours under the stars and city lights. Kelly was like an alley cat, giving him tiny love bites on his tanned skin, and he gently touched every square inch of her. After it was over, they were both exhausted. She laid on top of him, with her fingers softly nestled in the hair on his chest while they fell asleep, content.

Chuck was sleeping soundly and began dreaming of Shandi. He was looking for her in the woods, yelling manically for her. He could hear her voice, faintly. He moved in its direction and eventually saw her from afar through the trees, dressed in all white.

Chuck abruptly woke up to Kelly gently shaking him. "You okay? It looked like you were having a bad dream."

"Oh, yeah. I'm fine, Kelly. What time is it?"

"Nine."

"What? Oh Christ, I never sleep that late."

"Well, we did drink a lot and, you know, all the other fun, physical activities," she said, making Chuck smile. "I'll make us some coffee."

She got out of bed, still naked, and went over to her bedroom to put sweats and a t-shirt on. Chuck watched her and had to remind himself *this* was not a dream. Kelly was one sexy creature and he loved that accent. They sat at her breakfast bar and she wrapped her legs around his waist while they alternated between exchanging more vigorous kissing and sipping their coffees.

Chuck was coming out of his shell. He gestured around the apartment. "What is all this stuff? Are you rich?"

"No silly. My daddy is. He lives in Texas and every now and then he sends me money."

"Oh, your pops, nice. What's he do?"

"Oil," she laughed. "I moved out here to see if I could make my own palace in the clouds, so to speak. Like him."

"Sounds like you and I have something in common."

"I know your dad was an entrepreneur around here. You will be just as successful. And you're a great guy, I can see that."

"Thanks. I'm sure your father is proud of you."

"I'm trying. Enough of the serious stuff, sugar pie. Shall we get dressed and see your new homestead? Unfortunately, I have to get some work done. I have clients to deal with later today," she said.

Chuck nodded reluctantly. He didn't want the day with her to be cut short.

Kelly drove Chuck to the house. He showed her around and she appeared to be impressed with it and the surrounding land. She told him she'd take a raincheck on a tour of the acres she didn't get to see that day.

Kelly spotted his Charger in the driveway and loved it.

"That was my first car," Chuck said.

"Very nice. Is that a leather jacket hung over the seat?"

"Oh, that. I used to wear it when I played in my band a lifetime ago. It's supposed to be a NASA flight jacket."

Before Kelly left, she asked Chuck if he wanted a ride back to his other house, but he declined as he had a few things to do around the ranch.

She kissed him deeply. "I wish I didn't have to leave, but I will call you later today. Maybe we can do something tomorrow night after work?"

"Yeah, absolutely," said Chuck.

Kelly got in her car and Chuck watched her drive out of sight. She reached the road by the lake, turned, and continued until she reached the main road. Once she was sure to be far enough away from Chuck's house, she pulled her car over to the side of the road and took her cellphone out of her purse. She flipped the phone open, dialed a number, waited, and then spoke into the receiver.

"Yeah it's me. It was perfecto! You were magnificent!" She listened to the reply. "Yeah, like I said, couldn't have gone better. I'll talk to you later."

Kelly hung up the phone, turned her radio on, and sped down the road. She smiled and hummed to the song playing on the radio, feeling as sated as the cat that ate the canary.

Chuck woke up bright and early and more chipper than usual to take Rupert outside before he headed in for work. He noticed he had a text message on his cell phone. He flipped it open. It read, *Call me tonight, handsome man:)*

Kelly! That was a good sign that the date went well. Chuck couldn't wait to get into work to tell Jed all about it. As he got Rupert leashed up and went outside with him, Chuck sang a song.

"When a man loves a woman/ Can't keep his mind on nothin' else/ He'd trade the world/ For the good thing, he's found/ If she is bad, he can't see it."

Chuck felt a new pep in his step as he and Rupert chugged along down the street. When they returned, Uncle Armond was standing outside having his morning cigarette, waiting to razz Chuck about sleeping over at Kelly's place. Before he could get the chance, Chuck waved his uncle off to avoid him, then rushed through his morning rituals so he could get to work.

He went to the locker room to change as usual. Some of his co-workers noticed a glow about him. His buddy Emm, who was a few lockers away, said laughing, "Hey Chuck. What's up, man? You get laid last night or something?"

"Me? No!" Chuck blushed.

"Yeah right, Rockstar!"

As Chuck walked with a swagger down the corridors of the prison to get to his block, it dawned on him. *My God, I'm sleeping with my real estate agent and she's a few years older than me.* Chuck felt pretty good about it.

He reached the main door of the block and noticed a younger, newer officer at his podium and not Jed. Then he realized he had such a great weekend that he had forgotten Jed took the day off for his big interview.

Chuck thought, *Oh well, I'll catch up with Jed tomorrow. We'll both have refreshing news to discuss.* Chuck was sure Jed had the job in the barrel.

The young officer Chuck was working with that day was Ben Dobson. He was eager to learn the job and a little hot-headed at times. Chuck understood that very well. Ben had worked with Jed and Chuck a few times in the past. Jed was good at teaching a newbie, using a very father-like approach. Chuck preferred to just lead by example.

When Chuck walked in, Ben said hello. He had the utmost respect for Chuck, Jed, and other experienced officers. Shortly afterward, Dave Loomis walked in behind Chuck as the extra in the block for the shift. They talked over coffee before the inmates came out of their cells to adjourn for breakfast. After they ate, all inmates on the block were locked back in their cells.

It seemed to be a normal day. Nothing felt out of the ordinary. The nurse called Chuck on his desk phone to let them know she was ready to administer medication. Loomis went out to observe and watch the inmates.

Chuck was not aware that one inmate on the top tier who got meds every day had been giving Ben issues when Chuck and Jed had days off. Ben thought his problems had been resolved with the convict, so he didn't tell Chuck about it. Chuck, as usual, started opening a few doors only on the bottom floor while Richard and Randall were also out of their cells to clean. Chuck got halfway through the bottom and suddenly the inmate who had troubles with Ben began kicking his cell door like a madman.

His name was Diego Perez. Chuck was not a fan of Perez, but the inmate respected Chuck, or so he thought. He was at a loss as to why Perez would be kicking his door. Chuck opened the door, damn curious as to what his problem was. Perez came barreling down the metal stairs, yelling and screaming profanities at Richard and Randall, causing a commotion in the block. As Perez got close to the officers' podium, Ben went around the front of it and got in Diego's face, yelling back at him. They were both swearing at each other. Chuck raised his voice louder than both of them, ordering Perez to go back to his cell immediately and lock in until it was all sorted out.

Inmate Perez stopped yelling when Chuck told him this. Chuck lowered his voice and repeated his orders to the inmate who then walked back to the stairs leading to his cell.

When he got to the foot of the stairs, Perez started shouting and swearing at Ben again, but continued walking. Ben got upset, so he followed Perez and screamed back at him. When Ben reached the foot of the stairs, Perez had made it to the top. He snapped and ran full blast down the stairwell at Ben. When he got to the bottom, Perez grabbed Ben and placed him in a chokehold.

As this was going down, the block Sergeant was coincidentally walking in to bring them their weekly supplies. Chuck and Sergeant Sean Carter acted immediately, running towards Perez and Ben. Sean got to Ben first and tackled them to the floor. Loomis heard the commotion from around the corner and ran into the block to help, hitting his body alarm for a backup response. Now Dave, Chuck, and Sean were all piled on top of Ben, trying to get Perez to let go of him.

One of the straggling inmates, Dunbar Perkins, who Dave had left out in the hallway, was in the same street gang as Perez. It was part of their code – inmate politics – that he had to jump in to help. Dunbar ran over to the pile of men on the floor and repeatedly sucker-punched the officers. He struck Dave hard on the side of the head and knocked him unconscious. The blows he landed on the back of Chuck and Sean's heads seemed to have little effect, but they still couldn't get Perez to let go of Ben.

Dunbar's interference was detrimental to their efforts, so Chuck broke off and went after him. Dunbar was much younger and faster than Chuck, but he held his own. They exchanged wild, fast punches at each other, making no actual contact.

Randall tried to intervene by yelling at Dunbar to stop. When he didn't listen, he bravely walked up to Dunbar and tapped on his shoulder for him to stop. Dunbar turned angrily on Randall and punched him, knocking him on his ass. Chuck seized the opportunity, jumped up in the air, and drop-kicked Dunbar. He fell next to Randall, but quickly jumped back on his feet and tried to go after Chuck again.

Richard saw Randall get knocked down and was pissed. He ran at Dunbar. Chuck saw him and yelled, "Stay out of it, Richard. This punk is mine!"

Richard grabbed Randall by his arms and dragged him out of harm's way. Chuck and Dunbar continued exchanging punches, and finally, the cavalry arrived. Ten responding officers came running around the block to assist. Chuck had his back turned to the main door, so it dumbfounded him for a moment as to why Dunbar stopped swinging at him and ran upstairs into his cell. Chuck wanted to go after him, but he had to get Perez off of Ben first. Plus, he heard that voice in his head. It was Gus saying, *Chuck, no fighting.*

Perez still had Ben in that tight chokehold on the floor. When the responding officers rushed in, Chuck yelled at some of them to go get Dunbar, who was hiding in his cell. Two officers, Sue Marlo and Kevin Chapman, ran up to the cell to get him. Sergeant Tonya Fisher, who had also responded to the scene, had a can of issued pepper spray with her. She immediately began spraying the chemical directly in Perez's face. With so many officers trying to free Ben in a small space, it was inevitable that some of them got a good dose of spray, too. Finally, Perez screamed, cried actual tears, and let Ben go.

Chuck and another officer, Chris Wayne, yanked Perez up off of Ben and onto his tip-toes. They threw Perez against a cement wall close by and put handcuffs on behind his back. Chuck coughed from the spray, spitting all of the phlegm right into Perez's face and hair. Tonya saw that Chuck appeared physically hurt, so she had another officer relieve him from escorting Perez any further.

Chuck, Sean, Dave, and Ben immediately went to the outside lobby to be taken to a nearby outside hospital for medical attention. Before Chuck reluctantly walked out of his block, he said, "See that some harm comes to that asshole, Chris."

Chuck and his fellow officers were driven to the hospital in a state car by officer Betty Mills. She was an older woman, close to retiring, who worked out in the lobby, and was very worried about their injuries. Ben had two black eyes while Dave had one. Chuck had a short-sleeved uniform shirt on, and he couldn't help but notice that his right bicep was not where it should be. He had shooting pain in his lower stomach, running down to his right leg, which he thought maybe could be his appendix.

After the injured officers checked in with the medical staff, they were brought to their separate beds for further evaluation. Chuck went in for x-rays and a CT scan right away and then returned to his room. Betty waited with Chuck while the other guys were being treated.

Twenty minutes passed and a very concerned-looking doctor came into Chuck's room. He said to Chuck, "Your x-rays and scans are back. Let's start with the arm. The x-rays show nothing. It looks as if you tore the bicep. We need to make sure there is no damage to the tendons, so I'll need an MRI of that later."

"Okay," Chuck responded.

"Now your stomach and leg pain... that's a bigger problem. Our pictures show that you have a good-sized hernia in the lower right quadrant. I am recommending surgery right away. I'd like to have it done today- it's that serious."

"A hernia?"

"You must have torn it from the strain of fighting with the inmates; it happens. There is a surgeon who can take care of this at the hospital in Brookfield in two hours."

"What will they do to fix it?"

"The surgeon makes a few small incisions, then slips a mesh material over the tear on the lining inside the stomach."

Chuck thought about it for a minute, while Betty urged that he needed to have it done.

"Okay, doc," said Chuck.

"We'll be taking you over to the other hospital in an ambulance. After the surgery, you will need someone to bring you home."

Chuck nodded.

After the doctor left the room, Betty told Chuck to give her the combination to his locker and she would take care of bringing his Jeep back to his house. Shortly after, Chuck got wheeled out of the rear entrance and placed in the back of an ambulance.

He couldn't believe it. Another surgery, over nothing. Over some crazy, nutjob inmate.

As the ambulance was driving, Chuck asked the EMT if his fellow officers were okay. She told Chuck that she had no information, so he text-messaged Ben to see what was up with him. Ben's text back was that he was more worried about Chuck and apologized for the incident. He also thanked Chuck profusely for helping him out of the situation.

Anytime, brother, Chuck texted back.

Chuck remembered Kelly wanted to get together after work. He texted her, saying he got injured at work and he was on the way to the hospital in Brookfield for an emergency hernia operation. He apologized that he wouldn't be able to see her. Chuck went back to talking to the EMT about his injuries, asking questions while looking at his phone constantly to see if she replied back. Nothing.

He called Stacey and told her what happened and that he would need a ride home afterwards. Stacey said she was leaving work immediately and she would also call their mother, but Chuck asked her not to; they could tell her later on.

The ambulance pulled into the emergency ramp and a nurse came out to greet them. They wheeled Chuck through a lobby and down hallways until they reached another private room. The nurse gave him a Johnny and asked him if he needed help with it.

"No, ma'am, I can handle it. Do I take everything off, even my underwear?"

"I'm afraid so. I'll bring you some socks, if you want."

"Yes, ma'am."

After a time, Stacey arrived and came into Chuck's room, with a look of concern. Chuck told her about everything that had happened at work, then they discussed him selling his house through Kelly. Stacey told Chuck about what a smart, ambitious woman she was, and he told her a little about his date, leaving out the part about sleeping with her. The nurse eventually came back with his socks and to hook up an IV to his arm.

Even with all Chuck had been through in life, two things scared the shit out of him: snakes and needles. The nurse looked for a vein. Chuck cringed at the thought of it piercing his skin.

"Still hate needles, big brother?" Stacey asked.

"You know it. Mmmm!" Chuck groaned as the nurse stuck the needle in, and she let him know the surgeon was coming to speak with him before the surgery.

Chuck kept looking at his phone. No Kelly. He wondered if he may have scared her off. Most women hated violence, and that was a big part of his job. That was one reason why he never dated much after Shandi. *Fuck, I probably blew it*, he thought. With his job came a lot of heartache. He saw it first hand with fellow employees and what they suffered outside of work. It paid decently but was hell on relationships.

The doctor came into the room and greeted Chuck and Stacey. He explained the procedure and what to expect afterwards. In a couple of weeks, Chuck would return to have stitches removed and he could not go back to work for at least six weeks, possibly longer. The doctor himself would have to approve his return to work. He explained that Chuck had a long road to recovery and he needed to take it seriously. Stacey told the doctor she would sit on Chuck if she had to and they all laughed.

The doctor left the room. Fifteen minutes later, a different nurse came in to wheel Chuck into surgery. She turned the knob on a thin tube going in Chuck's arm, pumping a light sedative through his bloodstream. In the actual operating room, the anesthesiologist would sedate him heavily enough for the operation.

Chuck began to feel loopy.

"See ya in the next life, sis!" he said as he was taken away.

"That's not nice to say in a hospital," said the nurse.

"Sorry, ma'am. Just a joke, I hope," he giggled.

There were several staff members in the operating room. Most were women, some holding notepads. The nurse explained to Chuck they were interns there to observe. He said to himself, *Oh, shit, it's like that. Here I am, all sprawled out, completely naked except my new hospital socks and there's a room full of pretty ladies.*

"Oh, wow, just like King Arthur!" Chuck said aloud.

"What was that?" asked the nurse.

"Ah, never mind," said Chuck. He was thinking of the classic movie *Excalibur* when, at the very end of the film, King Arthur had completed his gallant journey in life. He was rewarded, so to speak, by being taken aboard a ship full of beautiful, angel-like women who surrounded him as he departed for his ultimate destination.

The nurse turned the knob further, increasing the sleeping agent, and said, "Now, Chuck, count backwards from ten to one."

"Ten, nine, eight, sev….."

Chuck was out like a light. He felt as if he were traveling through a long, beautiful tunnel of clouds. He had experienced this in the past.

The first time he could recall it happening to him was when one late night, he and Shandi were on their way home from a late gig they had played in the city. They were driving down a winding, back road that was not very well lit. They came across two cars, partially in the woods, that had smashed into each other head-on. They were still smoking.

Chuck's Charger pulled up to the scene, and that's when he started to feel strange. If felt like there was this surrounding, comforting cloud tunnel all around him and Shandi, the wreckage in front of him being the only clear image.

One of the wrecked cars was a Beetle Bug convertible. The top was down and there were five lifeless teenagers in the vicinity of the car. It was a gruesome scene. One body was slumped over the passenger door. A girl was lying in the middle of the road. The other vehicle had four bodies inside it.

Chuck quickly got out of his car and checked the girl in the road's pulse, which was close to lifeless, and then dragged her off the road in case of any other oncoming cars. He then heard the boy hanging over the door moaning softly. Chuck told the boy to hang in there, that help was coming. He checked the rest of the kids inside the convertible for signs of life, while Shandi looked inside the other vehicle. She found them all dead.

Another car came down the road and pulled over to help. Shandi told the driver to go down the road where there was a gas station and call 911.

Chuck's dream state led him to another memory. He was walking through the tunnel again when he saw his father at the end of it. Gus looked good, maybe a few years younger than he had been when Chuck had last seen him in real life. He only had a few grays. He was slim, with a bright red buttoned-down shirt and crisp jeans. Gus had that famous gigantic smile on his face when he saw Chuck. They walked closer to one another.

"Chucky, take care of our land, son. Watch out for the bridge, look out for it!" he said, then he faded from Chuck's vision.

"Dad, I don't understand," Chuck called after him.

Chuck heard an old familiar sound, a song he purposely never listened to anymore.

"Sometime in the not so distant future I'm getting to reach for the sky/ But then if you're not willing or capable/ I'll put my pride aside for now, maybe/ Cross my heart and hope our love won't die/ I'm trying to find you to create all my dreams happen/ And that's why, babe."

It was Shandi, singing her song. She walked towards Chuck, dressed all in white, like before- jeans, sneakers with no socks, and a turtleneck. Her amazingly long, black, hair was pulled back. Shandi continued singing as she drifted closer. Chuck felt a warmth come over him in anticipation of her lips against his ear when she reached him.

"Dear presently I feel like I am past due/ I search high and low to find my pot of gold/ And that's why," she sweetly whispered in Chuck's ear, "Chuck… Chuck… Chucky, beware of those bearing gifts!"

Chuck woke up with his chest beating a hundred miles a minute, body drenched in sweat, and the first person he saw was Kelly sitting next to him. Her hair and makeup, as usual, were immaculately done. What he could vaguely make out at the moment was that she was wearing a red v-neck sweater with black dress pants and gold jewelry.

"Hey there, handsome," she said.

"Kelly… holy shit. Where am I?"

"You're in recovery. From surgery."

"Oh, yeah, I forgot. How long have I been out?"

"I think it must be about six hours now."

"Jesus, that's a long time," he said, still feeling pretty out of it and therefore braver with his words than usual. "I thought I scared you off."

"No way. You're the sweetest man I know. I was showing a house and I left my phone in my purse. I'm sorry."

"No, I just, you know… we just started dating, and me being a corrections officer, and you're so…"

"Stop being ridiculous. You're not getting rid of me, mister," she smiled at him.

"Where's my sister?" Chuck asked.

"She went to get a coffee. She'll be back."

Kelly gave Chuck a sip of water while they waited for the surgeon to come in and talk to him before he was discharged. The doctor said the procedure went well and reminded Chuck of everything they previously talked about.

Kelly helped Chuck put some sweatpants on that she had brought for him while Stacey waited outside the room. That's when Stacey figured out that their date must have gone better than Chuck had let on. Kelly ended up driving Chuck home from the hospital while Stacey followed them in her car.

Over a week had passed since Chuck's operation and he was taking it easy, sitting on his front porch and doodling on a yellow legal pad with the radio on low. It was a gorgeous, sunny day out. Chuck's mom and sister came over almost every day to visit, and Kelly was sleeping over every night when she got out of work. She mostly worked out of her office in town to be closer to him.

She had brought over a decent-size suitcase full of clothes. They were hanging in the closet and folded in piles all over the bedroom. Cosmetics were spread out in his bathroom like it was the dressing room of a Hollywood movie star. She sure looked like one to Chuck. He hadn't seen female things in his home in a very long time.

It was the middle of the day and Chuck was waiting for Jed to arrive on his front porch. He was coming to see him for the first time since the incident. Uncle Armond had just gone out for his daily walk with Rupert when Chuck heard a car coming down the road. Jed's car pulled into the driveway and he got out, smiling.

"Hey, buddy. Holy cow, not bad. It's beautiful out here. What a nice place," he said.

"Thanks, Jed." He got up to greet Jed. His arm was in a sling, but he could still use his hand.

"How's your arm doing?" Jed asked as he walked up onto the porch.

"Have a seat. My arm is fine. The bicep is healing on its own. No surgery needed, thank God."

"That's good."

"You want some coffee? I set it up right there for us."

"Oh thanks, great."

There was a small, round wooden table with a coffee thermos, cups, cream, and sugar on it. Jed poured himself a cup and said, "I'm sorry I wasn't there for you, Chuck."

"See what happens when you don't have my back?" Chuck joked.

"I know. I'm really sorry."

"No, don't worry about it."

They talked in detail about what happened that day, and Chuck explained to him how it all played out. Jed loved talking about the job. He was passionate about work, family, friends, politics, and religion. That's why Jed was perfect for the new job he was trying to get.

"So, how did the interview with El Smuck-o go?" Chuck asked, even though he already knew Jed had the job through Kelly.

Jed was reluctant to tell Chuck he got the position because he knew it was the end of their successful partnership at the prison.

"I got it," said Jed.

"Congrats, really, that's awesome."

"Thanks, Chuck."

"Now is your boss Chip Karrington or Nick Columbo?"

As he mentioned Columbo's name, Chuck rolled his eyes. Jed caught it and laughed. He knew something about his partner that most didn't. If Chuck hated you, he'd wish actual harm on you. The thing that amazed Jed was that when he did, most of the time something bad would somehow actually happen to the person, unrelated to any action of Chuck's.

"Nick's my boss. I'm his assistant, but I'm also supposed to have free rein to conduct my investigations with no interference from Nick or Chip. This program is a new crime commission to catch corrupt businesses, politicians, and law enforcement officers."

"Wow, that sounds pretty cool. When do you start?"

"In three weeks. I'm putting my notice in tomorrow. Yeah, it will be interesting, but you know I'll still be around and check-in with you all the time."

"I know that. I'll be fine."

"Yeah, well, I've been thinking about that. You know, maybe you can try for a retirement settlement with the Department due to your injuries. You don't need that place anymore. Looks like you're doing pretty good here."

"Funny you say that. This real estate agent, Kelly, I've been seeing... I met her at that campaign rally you brought me to."

"Oh, right, I remember."

"Well, she says she has a lawyer friend who might be able to get me seventy-five percent of my pay from the department. She's trying to talk me into it and I'm thinking about it pretty hard."

"Chuck, she's right. You should do it. And with your military pay, you should be in great shape."

"Yeah. And I have the rental money from my father's commercial building. Kelly says she has a buyer for my house here for a great price."

"What are you going to do with all that money?"

"The construction of the barn and stables starts next week, and the money I make on this place will pay for that."

"That's awesome, Chuck."

"Yeah. And I owe nothing on this house, so maybe I'll have money left over for horses… to pay ranch hands. When that all gets underway, that'll be another source of income."

"And your new house on that land is paid off also?"

"Yep, and because of the acreage, I get tax breaks and refunds on it."

"Great Caesar's Ghost! I'm jealous. We should switch places."

Chuck laughed.

"What are you writing on that little yellow pad? All your business plans?"

"Ah, no. Don't laugh. When I have the chance, I'm writing a book loosely based on all our adventures at work and some other stuff."

"No way! What made you want to do that?"

"Well, growing up, my father always talked about writing a book. He's gone now, so I thought maybe I'd give it a go."

"What's the title?"

"Kelly said it should be catchy and grab you, so the working title is *How Booze, Women, and Corrections Ruined My Life.*"

Jed laughed. "That is catchy, I like it. She sounds like a smart lady."

"So far, so good."

"What kind of stories are in the book so far?"

"Oh, I just started, but it's flowing out of me pretty good. You know Tonya, the Sergeant? You know how she speeds into work every morning and gets pulled over by the police all the time? There was that time when she didn't want to get another speeding ticket and she stabbed her leg with a pen so she'd be crying when the officer got to her window."

Jed started laughing again. "Oh yeah, I remember her telling us about that. What about the time CO Henderson threw a water balloon at the perimeter vehicle up from the security tower and hit the windshield and it shattered?"

"Jesus, I forgot about that one. Let me jot that down real quick," he said as they both laughed at the memory. "Hey, Kelly's staying over tonight and we might go to dinner. You want to join us?"

"Oh, I'm sorry, I can't. I have tickets to the Patriots game, but maybe another night."

"Oh yeah, some other time. And you can check out my new place. I'll be moving in there soon."

"Definitely," said Jed.

Kelly was working in her office in town when Chip walked in abruptly, as he often did.

"Hey, girl. Miss me?"

Kelly was sitting at her desk doing paperwork. "I just saw you last week."

Chip smiled. "I know, but you were with that tough-looking guy. Ah, Jed's buddy."

"Chuck Barreto."

"Not really your type. He doesn't look all that sophisticated."

"Why, Chip Karrington, you sound like you're jealous. And he's very smart and sophisticated because he's with me," she said, laughing.

"Touché, Miss Teixeira. Well, I came to discuss Gussy's Pitts. Have you made any progress? My donors have been up my ass over it."

"Funny you should say that. Chuck just inherited some of that land."

"What the... Damn girl, you work quickly."

"I try. But there's a problem. His brother and sister got a piece of it, too."

"Oh, boy. Can you find a way around this recent development?"

"I'm on it, Chip. I'm not a miracle worker, but I'm close to being one."

"I know you. You'll find a way."

"Well, let's not worry so much about this. For now, we have to get you across the finish line with your opponent. I hear it's looking good in the polls for you."

"Yeah, I feel good, but never trust the polls."

Chip tried getting comfortably close to Kelly like he always did, but she gently pushed him back, telling him she was smitten with Chuck and batted her eyelashes at him flirtatiously.

CHAPTER 17

CROSSROADS

A MONTH HAD gone by, and Chuck and Uncle Armond were completely moved into the new house. Kelly successfully sold Chuck's old house at a
stellar price, giving him more than enough money for the construction of
the barn and stables.

Chuck was out by the construction area watching Chad and his men
build the barn. Kelly's attorney friend also got Chuck's work to settle for
early retirement at seventy-three percent of his pay for the rest of his life.
He was officially retired and getting ready to be a rancher.

Rita was having a blast decorating and furnishing the new house. Uncle
Armond lived at the far end of the house and Rupert preferred to stay with
him when Kelly was there for some reason. He didn't take to her at all,
though Kelly was practically living with Chuck full time.

Kelly was going in a little late to work. She had just finished getting
dolled up and had made a decision to sneak Chuck's finished pages of his
book into her briefcase. He had left it in his top dresser drawer with his
t-shirts. She was going to photocopy the pages and have her friend, attorney Jeff Downing, send them out to a known book publisher as a surprise
for Chuck.

She had read his manuscript and thought it was superb, even though Chuck didn't agree. She wanted to make more and more aggressive moves to snare him for herself; she was even thinking of marriage for several different reasons.

Kelly got on Chuck's golf cart and drove herself out to where Chuck was observing construction. She pulled over by some of the workers, whose heads turned. A few of them called out, "Good morning, Miss Teixeira."

Kelly smiled at them. "Make sure this guy right here doesn't try to help you all."

"Oh, no ma'am."

Chuck smiled and walked over to Kelly and kissed her.

"I'm off to work, hon. I came for that sweet kiss and to remind you to get some things ready for our trip."

"Oh yeah, of course. Rhode Island, I'm excited," said Chuck. Chuck and Kelly were going to Rita and Gus's beach house for a long weekend alone. It would be Kelly's first time there with Chuck. Rita had talked them into going; she loved her beach house and wanted Kelly to see it.

"Me too. I get my handsome man all to myself."

"Hey, I'll ride back to the house with you. I have physical therapy for my arm today."

Chuck and Kelly rode back to the house, kissed goodbye again, and Chuck watched her drive away in the Corvette as she waved out the window. He noticed Kelly get on her cell phone as she got further down the road and assumed it was probably work-related.

Chuck went into the kitchen to have a quick coffee with Armond. He commented to Armond about how far they had come and how things seemed to come together. He wished Shandi could be there to see it come to fruition. It had been her dream, after all. Armond kindly changed the subject, reminding Chuck of the beautiful woman currently in his life before he left for his appointment.

Chuck fired up the Charger and increased the volume of the music to enjoy the drive to therapy.

Jed was getting settled in at his new office in the city. It was in an enormous brick building filled with attorneys and their staff members. It was a tad overwhelming, but Jed fit right in and everyone welcomed him with open arms. Chip was in a lot. He wanted Jed to help him promote his political agenda moving forward, and Jed was keen to prove himself as an asset. Nick Columbo assigned five of his aides who would all work under Jed- Alfred Ford, Abby Taylor, Chester May, Felix Donovan, and Harlan Lee, some of them being law students. Jed also had a private secretary, Lesly Fox. Nick told Jed to let him know if there was anything or anyone else he needed.

The investigators would bring in complaints of nefarious behavior to look into, and it was Jed's task to wade through it all and figure out what could be indictable. Nothing he had so far seemed big enough to help rid the city of corruption until Abby Taylor brought in something that caught his eye. Jed had Lesly call Abby into his office to inquire more about it.

"Hello, Abby, come on in. Sit down, please," Jed said as he motioned towards a chair. He then asked her about the dossier she wrote of a complaint by a couple that lived on the outskirts of the city.

"There is an older couple, Mr. Ferrari, who owned and lived in a small apartment building with a take-out pizza place on the first floor. It all burned down to the ground. Isaac and Rose McGovern alleged the fire was arson. A land developer offered to buy them out for twice as much as what the building was worth several times, but the couple kept turning them down. Several months later, the place went up in smoke. Fire investigators ruled out foul play. According to their report, it was electrical."

"I see. Did they sell yet?"

"No, but they're now thinking about it pretty seriously."

"Can I talk to the couple?"

"I'm sure. They're staying with their daughter. I'll give them a call."

"Great, thanks Abby. Nice work." After Abby left, Jed thought to himself, *Yes sir, I think I'm going to like this job a lot, so much more than being a corrections officer.*

Chuck pulled into the parking lot for physical therapy and walked into the small lobby where there was only one elevator. Chuck pressed the button and the door opened. He got on and pressed the number six. The doors slid open when he reached the floor. As Chuck walked off the elevator, a woman walked past him to get on and said, "Excuse me." When she got in, he noticed she had a very distinct sound to her voice. Chuck turned to see her.

God damnit, it was her!

Chuck's mystery woman from the rally and nightclub was staring straight at him and smiling as the metal doors slid closed. He was in total shock. He noticed she had her platinum blond hair pulled back and wore a black v-neck shirt with Def Leppard on it, tight blue jeans, and cowboy boots. And Shandi's face.

Chuck quickly looked for the door to the stairwell and carefully ran over to it, trying to avoid adding injury to his healing wounds. He used the railings for support and got down six flights as fast as he could under the circumstances. Chuck's heart was pounding. It was the closest he had come to her.

He made it to the bottom stairwell, out the exit door, back into the lobby, and out of the glass doors. He scanned the parking lot for her. In the rear of the lot, he saw what looked like a gray Pontiac Sunfire pulling out. The car was too far away for Chuck to get to on foot. He looked to see if he could get a visual of her inside the car, but the windows were slightly tinted. Chuck memorized the license plate number and made his way over to the Charger. He got inside and turned the ignition to pursue her. The car would not turn over. Chuck knew for the longest time his car starter was on the fritz, but of all the times for it to act up…

He had a hammer in the backseat to smack the starter with when this happened. The problem was that by the time he got under the car and turned over the engine, she'd be long gone. He grabbed a pen and wrote the plate number down.

A guy he used to see at the gym, Allan Miller, was an ex-cop who had a private detective agency. He had given Chuck his business card and advised him to contact him if he ever needed anything. Chuck found it tucked into the visor where had stashed it long ago and decided he'd give Allan a call.

Jed had just finished talking with Isaac and Rose McGovern at their daughter's residence about their apartment building and restaurant burning down. He felt awful for them. When he left, he took a ride over to the destroyed building to see it for himself. Abby was with him and they discussed the situation. When they arrived, Jed was even more saddened by it all.

"For what it's worth, Abby, I believe it could've been arson and would like to help them," said Jed.

"I know, me too. I'm getting some pushback on this case. Higher-ups are insisting it's just a coincidence."

"Who? Do you have anything yet on the developer that made them the offer?"

"A judge I ran into named Costanza and some clerks – and believe it or not, Nick – said basically I should drop this. They go by the name of The LoneStar Group."

"Hmm, that's odd for them to say. Anyway, who owns this group? Who are they affiliated with?"

"I'm still looking into it. They have a management office somewhere in the city. I'll track it down."

"Okay. Let's stay on this, Abby."

Chuck and Kelly pulled the Corvette into the Narragansett beach house driveway on a sunny afternoon. It was a small, raised ranch with a little yard located only a half-mile from the beautiful beach. There were five bedrooms and a medium-sized kitchen and living room. A deck projected from the back of the house.

"Dag-nabbit! This place is gorgeous, Chucky!"

Chuck felt a little guilty leaving home while Chad and his men worked overtime to get the barn finished up, but they needed this little getaway badly. Chuck and Kelly were having a whirlwind romance. She treated him like a king and loved taking charge. He was not used to that.

They put their luggage in a bedroom and Kelly gently pulled Chuck down with her onto the bed. They kissed and laughed.

"Be careful, young man. Don't want to hurt yourself."

After they got done fooling around and unpacking, they decided to walk down to the beach. Chuck loaded up a blanket, towels, chairs and an umbrella in a red wagon that was in the shed. They strolled along, holding hands. Heads were turning, checking out Chuck in his trunks and Kelly in her white bikini. They set up their blanket and umbrella on the sand and sat side by side in reclining beach chairs with their sunglasses on, staring out at the blue waves and then back at each other.

Chuck reached over and put his hand on Kelly's smooth, sexy leg. She smiled and blew him a kiss. After some time went by, Kelly suggested they go for a swim. They got up and Chuck again scooped up Kelly.

"Chuck!" she yelled playfully.

He felt a slight strain in his lower stomach and placed her safely back on her feet.

"You okay?" she asked.

"Yeah, I'm fine. Just not ready for that yet, I guess. I'm fine." He laughed.

"Okay. I'll race you to the water, old man!"

Kelly took off running and Chuck walked fast. She beat him there.

"C'mon, baby. The water is beautiful," she said as she waded through the ocean ahead of him. Chuck tried to catch up when he saw an enormous wave coming towards her.

"Kelly, the wave, look out!"

She looked upwards, and the wave crashed down and engulfed her. Kelly disappeared inside it. Chuck sloshed through the water to where it crashed and thankfully Kelly popped up out of the water and he grabbed her.

"You okay, Kell?"

She nodded, gasping for air.

Chuck noticed her top was completely off, so he put his hands over her naked breasts.

"My top... where's my top?"

Chuck saw it floating next to her. "Right here."

She swiftly grabbed it and put it back over her well-endowed chest as Chuck held her close to his body so no one could get a free peep show. They laughed hysterically, the threat of the previous moment over.

"See what happens when you run off without me?"

"I'll never do that again."

They played in the ocean a while longer and then went back to the blanket to dry off and sunbathe. Chuck woke up from a pleasurable nap and whispered in Kelly's ear that he was going to take a walk down to the pavilion to get something to eat. She told him she wanted a salad and a Tab soda.

"Don't talk to any strangers, handsome," she teased.

Once he was out of her sight, Kelly checked her phone for text messages. There was a text from Chip.

Any progress yet?

Kelly sent a text back. *Relax, it's under control. Talk to you later, sweetie.*

When Chuck reached the pavilion he called Chad who told Chuck not to worry about a thing; it was all coming along and he should enjoy himself. Chuck thanked Chad immensely and then checked in with Uncle Armond. He told Chuck everything was good at the house, so Chuck got his food order and made his way back to Kelly. When he got back to their blanket she was positioned with her back arched like an alley cat.

"Sorry, no Tab," said Chuck. "Got you a Diet Coke."

While they were relaxing, Kelly said nonchalantly, "So, mister big land-mogul man, are you considering selling your portion of Gussy's Pitts? Because ya know your girlfriend is one hell of a good licensed real-estate broker! I've had a lot of inquiries."

"Ah, I think we are all set on not selling for right now," Chuck answered awkwardly.

She smiled and batted her eyelashes at him. "I could make y'all super rich!"

He laughed. "I'll let you know if anything changes."

After their day at the beach, Chuck made reservations at the Coastal Restaurant on the waterfront for them. He put on a debonair black tuxedo and she a sparkling sapphire blue dress that fit her like a second skin. The restaurant resembled a castle and it impressed Kelly. It was a stunning replica of a 16th-century facade, made of real stone and featuring turrets, towers, and a small moat.

"Now this is my kind of place!" said Kelly.

"I figured," said Chuck, "and you can help me order because the menu is complicated, I'm sure."

"You've never been here?"

"No, but I've driven by it plenty of times."

They went inside and sat at the table Chuck had reserved outside on a raised rear patio overlooking the beach. Kelly thought wryly, *I'm training this man.*

They ordered a bottle of wine. She understood the French menu and knew Chuck had taken her there to impress her and suit her tastes.

They talked about Chuck's plans for the ranch.

"When we get back home, I've gotta put some ads in the local register for a few ranch hands to start out with, and most of all, an experienced foreman."

"Ya know, I came across a young lady who was looking for a house. She told me she was a former boss on a ranch somewhere out west before moving here. She might be interested."

He thought for a second. "Hmmm, you still have her number?"

"I think I can find it."

Chuck accepted, saying that would be great. Thanks to Kelly's connections, he would enter his sixth career in such a short time. She knew how to get things moving quickly somehow. Chuck thought his mother was aggressive, but Kelly's ambition was on a whole new level.

He would need all the help he could get to learn the business now that he was permanently retired from corrections. He had been a factory worker, an almost-rockstar, soldier, auto body tech, correctional officer, and now he would be a rancher. Chuck was becoming what his father warned him about when he was younger.

Gus would say, *Chucky, don't become like that guy.*

What guy, Dad?

A jack of all trades and master of none!

After dinner, they went inside the restaurant and danced the night away like they had on their first date, and the rest of the weekend went idyllically for them. Chuck didn't want to leave, but he was eager to see how the barn and stables were coming along. While they were packing to go back home, Kelly was busy on a phone call for work and Chuck got a text message from Allan Miller.

Hey, what's up, pal? Got your message- sorry I missed your call. What can I do for you?

Chuck responded, *Can I call you later this week? I'm away right now.*

No problem, take care.

Kelly had Chuck put the roof up on her car for the drive home. As they were driving, Kelly had a big, mysterious smirk on her face.

"Must have been a pretty good phone call," he mused.

Kelly snapped out of the strange smile. "Oh yeah, business."

Once they got out of Narragansett and on the highway, Chuck started messing with the radio stations to find a good song.

"Nice, The Eagles!" he said when he landed on something to his liking.

"Sing for me, handsome. I love how you sing," said Kelly.

"He was a hard-headed man/ He was brutally handsome, and she was terminally pretty/ She held him up, and he held her for ransom/ In the heart of the cold, cold city/ He had a nasty reputation as a cruel dude."

Kelly reached over and touched the back of his neck softly and said, "I love you, Chuck."

He stopped singing.

"What?" That was the first time she had said it.

"I'm madly in love with you!"

Chuck couldn't believe it.

"I love you, too. I really do," he said as she pulled the car over to the breakdown lane to give him a hug and kiss.

"Let's get married," Kelly said.

"Whoa, uh, maybe we should think about that one first."

"Well, you better get moving, cowboy. We could have a huge wedding right at the ranch. You think about it. I'm sorry I brought it up like this. It just popped out. I'm so crazy about you and I'd like the world to know."

"Whew, this is a surprise. I never thought a sophisticated, smart, gorgeous lady would want any type of life with me."

"Well, I do, mister. And I have one more surprise for you. Please don't be mad at me."

This frightened Chuck a bit. "What's that?"

"Promise?"

"Of course."

"I made a copy of your book and my friend, Jeff…"

Chuck's half-smile left his face. "Yeah?"

"Babe, I knew it was special when I read it. So Jeff faxed it to a well-known publisher in New York. They love it and they want to meet with you next weekend."

"You're messing with me, right?" Chuck said in disbelief.

"I'm not. I'm sorry. Are you mad at me?"

"I'm in shock. No, I don't think so."

Chuck was bewildered by what she did and couldn't believe someone of importance loved his book.

"Well, what do you think?"

Chuck looked at her seriously, fixing his face in pretend anger, and said, "What do I think? I think you and I...... are going to New York!"

Chuck burst out laughing, and Kelly squeezed his leg. Secretly, Chuck was most grateful for the turn of subject away from marriage. Because while he had been unprepared for the entire conversation, marriage was something even further from his mind than the book had been.

CHAPTER 18
I LOVE NEW YORK
JULY 2002

ABBY CAME INTO Jed's office to update him on the inquiries into The LoneStar Group.

"Hey, Ab. Anything new yet?"

"This group seems to be very elusive so far. But what they *are* is a commercially licensed broker firm, the technical wording for land developers."

"Are they in bed with the mob? Or any other type of corporate corruption?"

"Nothing on that, but what's bizarre is they might be a conglomerate. There is an office they may work out of in the SkyTower in the city."

"Great work, Abby. Stay on this."

Nick walked into the office as Abby left.

"Hey, buddy, how's everything going?" said Nick.

"It's going."

"How about you fill me and Chip in on everything today during lunch?"

Jed didn't want to go, but these were his bosses so he reluctantly agreed.

Chuck, Kelly, and the attorney, Jeff Downey, were driving to New York together to meet the publisher for Chuck's book. Jeff had rented a minivan and was graciously driving it. Kelly and Chuck sat romantically in the back together with her head on his shoulder as they held hands. She was very excited, but Chuck was wary. He asked Jeff how he knew the publisher. Jeff explained to Chuck that he knew people that knew people, and after so many conversations, he was eventually pointed to a publisher that came highly recommended. Jeff's answers seemed flighty to Chuck, but what did he know about these kinds of matters?

"Boy Kell, I feel bad about leaving, with Chad almost finishing up with the barn and stalls."

"Don't worry, Chucky. Chad's doing fine. Everything should be done in another week or two. It looks wonderful."

"Yeah, they're doing a great job."

"I haven't been on a real working ranch in a very long time."

"What do you mean?"

"Oh, well I grew up on one."

"What?" Chuck said in surprise.

"I grew up in Texas, as you know. Daddy owns a ranch. He's not just into oil."

Chuck was speechless. She was constantly full of surprises.

"Sorry, guys," Jeff interrupted. "Is it this road, Chuck?"

"Yep. That's the one, Jeff."

After a few hours of driving they turned into the street where his aunt Joanne lived. Not only was he going to meet the publisher, but it was also an opportunity for Chuck to visit his aunt and have Kelly meet her. He had not been to New York since Vovo's funeral. He never talked about his father or his grandmother's death with Kelly. He was sure she already knew through his mother, anyway. As the vehicle pulled into the driveway, Chuck's aunt came out of the back door to greet them.

In Woodrow, a black stretch limo pulled into the entrance of Gussy's Pitts followed by a Mercedes. An armed security guard dressed in a black suit got out and opened the rear door. A tall, thin, middle-aged and well-dressed man got out. He was cynical-looking like no other. Chip got out of the Mercedes and walked over to him.

"Mr. Kobol," said Chip.

The mysterious, well-guarded man raised his hairy right eyebrow at the politician.

"Silus... how can I help you?" asked Chip.

"Chip, you see all this open land with nothing on it?"

"I do see it. Yes, of course."

"Your biggest admirer, not just financially, is wondering why we are not breaking ground on all this virgin land. He has infinite plans for this place and cannot wait much longer. We have other powerful investors to worry about."

"Silus, the situation is under control. I have someone on the inside working hard on it."

"I hope so, Chip. You don't want us getting involved."

"No need. It's taken care of."

"OK then. We'll be in touch. Oh, and Chip, we'd like you to get that little nuisance you hired for your campaign boost to stop snooping in our business."

Silus got back into the limo and they left Chip alone, deep in thought. He grabbed his cell phone and began texting Kelly about getting her new boyfriend to sell Gussy's Pitts. She of course didn't respond because, unbeknownst to Chip, she was busy meeting Chuck's aunt.

Chip got back into his car thinking, *FUCK!*

The morning after they arrived, Chuck, Kelly, and Jeff had an early breakfast with Joanne and then walked to the station and took the train into Brooklyn. They were to meet a woman at Yorkshire Publishing Company named Linda Mansfield. Chuck was intrigued and curious; it was reminiscent of when he, Shandi, and the boys first met Bill Arkin.

They heard their stop announced over the train speaker, and as it came to a halt they all got off, looking worried. The station was run down and in an eerie-looking neighborhood.

They heard a loud voice calling, "Mr. Barreto! Mr. Barreto!"

A slender, young Asian man was holding up a sign with both hands as people who had stepped off the train walked by him. The bold black letters of the sign read Chuck's name. He looked at Kelly suspiciously.

She said with a smirk, "I swear, babe, I knew nothing about this."

They walked over to the man, and Chuck said, "I'm Mr. Barreto."

"Ah, nice to meet you, sir. My name is Jin. I'm here to drive you to meet with Mrs. Mansfield. The car is right this way."

Chuck thanked him and followed to an open area that led to a side road. Jin walked over to a gray Lincoln.

"The publishing company has cars for picking up guests," said Jin.

"Nice," said Kelly. "I guess Chuck is getting the special treatment here."

Jin smiled. "I guess so."

He opened the doors for them and Jeff sat up front with Chuck and Kelly in the back. As they were driving to their next destination, Chuck got a text. He opened up the phone.

Hey, Chuck, it's Al. Everything okay? You forget about me?

Chuck actually had completely forgotten to call him back when he came home from Rhode Island. He had been preoccupied with the book and the developments on the ranch.

"Everything okay?" asked Kelly as he quickly closed his cell phone.

"Uh, yeah, it's just Unc updating me about Chad and his crew."

"Everything is going well?"

Chuck smiled. "Yes, ma'am."

The Lincoln pulled right up to the curb of a grand-looking building that had pillars in the front.

"We're here. You can all go straight inside. The receptionist will show you where to go. I'll see you after your meeting."

They thanked Jin again and got out of the car. As they walked towards the front doors Kelly turned to Chuck and asked, "You excited?"

Chuck smiled at her. "I am, Kell."

When they got through the double doors, there was a large lobby with a desk in the middle of it where a young man greeted them immediately.

"Mr. Barreto?" asked the man. Chuck nodded and the man said, "Yes, welcome. Come right in and follow me. Mrs. Mansfield is expecting you."

The man led them to a small stairwell, they went up two flights, opened the door, and took a left turn and stopped at a glass office door. Embossed on the glass was the name "Linda Mansfield". They entered the office and standing behind a sleek, clean-lined desk facing a large rectangular window was an attractive older woman, maybe in her late fifties, with gray hair and wearing a conservative black suit. She turned as they entered her office and came around the desk.

"Welcome, everyone. It's so nice to meet you all. I'm Linda Mansfield, and let me guess," she said looking at Chuck, "you have to be Chuck."

"Yes, ma'am," Chuck replied.

Chuck introduced Kelly and Jeff to Linda. She had them sit down and asked her receptionist to bring in some coffee. While they were waiting, Linda complimented Chuck on his writing.

"Chuck, I've read it twice already. My editors here also concur and love what you've written. Where did you get all the ideas? Where did you learn to write?"

"I was out of work on an injury, a little restless, and it just started pouring out," said Chuck humbly. "I have no experience in writing, Mrs. Mansfield. It just came to me. I wasn't sure if it was even all that good."

"It's simply amazing. Why did you choose this publishing house?"

"My girlfriend here, Kelly, gave a copy of it to her attorney right here, Jeff."

Jeff interjected and explained to Linda how he found her. Linda then began telling them in more detail about her company and how it generally worked.

"Chuck, if you agree with the deal here, we will do all the promotion using your old status as a rockstar and your tour of duty to help sales."

Chuck didn't know what to say about that. He couldn't believe Kelly told them those private details that he had left out of the book. How did Kelly know about Panama? His mother must have told her when they worked together. Chuck was not used to this kind of strategy to get ahead. He and Kelly had their differences in achieving goals. Chuck was not crazy about the idea and Linda saw it in his face.

She assured him it was a smart move and said, "Your band had a hit song called 'You Matter to Me' that you wrote, correct?"

"Ah, I didn't write it. Our lead singer did."

"Sorry. But we can still find an angle to use there, and this book you wrote can be a tremendous success." Both Kelly and Jeff insisted it was strategic, even though he had a bad feeling about it.

Linda skillfully changed the subject and discussed Chuck having several obligations to promote the book with on-site personal signings. All travel, hotels, and food would be paid for by the company.

Linda pulled out the contract. She went over everything listed, point by point, and also held out a bank check for an initial twenty-five thousand dollars. Linda explained that it was a rare advance for a new author, but they really liked the manuscript. She discussed further profits if the book did well, and who knows- maybe it could be sold for television or a movie. Linda already had a second offer and contract on the table for a second book.

Jeff read the whole thing and said enthusiastically to Chuck, "This is a stellar deal. You shouldn't pass it up, Chuck."

"Well, darling, what do you think?" asked Kelly.

Chuck looked at Linda, bewildered, and said, "Where do I sign?"

You could feel the energy emanating from Kelly as Chuck signed the document.

Linda then explained that it would take some time for her team to edit and format the manuscript. She told him they would like to set up a photo-shoot to get a headshot for the inside jacket. Kelly suggested having it done at Chuck's ranch and Linda adored the idea. They unanimously agreed and Linda said she would send some photographers there for the shoot. After she finished going over some other details, Chuck asked to use the bathroom before they left for the train station.

As Chuck was in the bathroom alone, he sent Allan a text in reply.

Hey Allan, sorry, I got busy. You won't believe this. Now I'm tied up in New York. Long story. I promise to contact you when I get back. Thanks, Chuck

At the same time, Kelly was texting Chip.

Hey, Chip, I'm away right now. Don't worry, I got this. Trust me.

Chip swiftly texted her back. *Okay, sexy, maybe when you get back we can grab some dinner.*

Maybe, Senator :) Kelly responded.

On the train ride back to Joanne's house, Kelly was amped up. She had an idea. "Chuck, let's celebrate."

"Sure, where, at my aunt's?"

"Nope, how's about Vegas, baby? I've never been there. Have you?"

"No. When?"

"Let's fly from New York straight there. We can go for just a few days."

Jeff heard them and interjected. "Yeah, go. Let me know when you're coming back and I'll arrange a taxi to get you on the return."

"What about the ranch?"

"They can handle it. And Uncle Armond's there."

"Okay, why not."

Kelly jumped up and down and kissed Chuck all over his face as he blushed. He told Kelly that he was going to visit the 9/11 Memorial before they left and asked her if she wanted to join him. Kelly said she'd stay back to spend time with his aunt. She figured while he was off, she could multi-task and make their arrangements for Vegas.

After Chuck, Kelly, and Jeff got settled at Joanne's, Chuck hightailed it to the memorial. He had mourned the loss, but had always been in denial of his fathers fate; it was hard to imagine Gus had been inside one of the Towers as they fell.

Gus and Shandi should still be by his side today. *What a lousy deal*, Chuck thought. Even when things were going well for him, Chuck didn't feel as though he could ever really let go of the past.

Jed was in his office going over some of the expenditures that Nick was concerned about regarding his investigations when Abby knocked.

"Hey, Ab. What do you got?"

"You know the McGoverns?"

"Yes," he said, concerned.

"They want to back out of the complaint. They're taking the offer from The LoneStar Group."

"You're joking."

"I'm not."

"Why?"

"They wouldn't say why."

"Can you call them back? I'd like to meet with them again. Try to find out."

"I can do that."

"Thank you, Abby. Anything else?"

"That office I told you about in the SkyTower? I had Alfred track some of their people from there to another office in Richmond, Virginia. He made contact with an attorney from their organization named Silus Kobol."

Jed was intrigued. "Really?"

"Yes, and I think this may be a solid lead. Alfred is flying back in a week on a private flight with this lawyer, Kobol. So he might have some intel we could use."

Jed was now excited. "Okay, Abby, keep Alfred on this."

"I will, Jed. I'm picking him up at the airport personally on his return."

· · ·

Chuck and Kelly got off the plane in Vegas and flagged down a taxi to get to their hotel. The taxi driver helped them with their bags even though they had only brought what they packed for New York for this unplanned getaway. Kelly said that if they needed more clothes, they could get some more while there, though Chuck could always get by with very little.

The driver introduced himself as Bruce, then they headed for their hotel. Chuck and Kelly continued their ritual of sitting in the backseat together, snuggling and kissing. Bruce asked them if they were newlyweds. Chuck laughed a bit and answered no.

"Hey, if you see Robert Redford in the casino, I'm telling him you're all mine and I won't change my mind. Not even for ten million dollars!" Chuck said, making a wisecrack reference about the movie *Indecent Proposal*.

Kelly caught on quickly and laughed. "Bobby Redford has nothing on you, my sexpot cowboy! There's no amount he could get me for."

As they were driving along, they saw billboards advertising the entertainers performing in Vegas, like Cher, Marie and Donnie Osmond, Charo, and Wayne Newton.

Chuck pointed out Charo to Kelly. "Hey, Kell, remember her? She used to guest star on the old show, *Loveboat*."

Kelly gave him an odd look. "No, I don't think so."

Then Chuck saw all the Elvis impersonators' signage and grew visibly excited. Chuck was a huge fan.

"Give us some Elvis, baby," said Kelly.

Chuck began singing. "Wise men say/ Only fools rush in/ But I can't help falling in love with you/ Shall I stay/ Would it be a sin/ If I can't help falling in love with you."

"Hey, mister, that was pretty darn good," said Bruce.

"Thank you, thank you very much!" Chuck said, doing his best Elvis and they all laughed.

The taxi pulled up to the MGM Grand Hotel. They waited for some cars to leave so Bruce could get closer to the entranceway. Chuck couldn't believe his eyes.

"Holy shit. You gotta be kidding."

Kelly just smiled and kissed his cheek. The building looked like a huge pyramid, with waterfalls and statues everywhere. Once their taxi pulled up to the front, bellhops rushed over to the car to help them. Chuck kindly let them know they were all set and gave Bruce a nice tip. Bruce thanked them and wished them a good time in Vegas.

Chuck and Kelly walked through the enormous, marble lobby. He was still trying to take it all in. He carried both of their bags as they walked to the reception desk.

Kelly spoke to the woman behind the counter. "We have a reservation for 'Teixeira.'"

"Yes, ma'am." She handed Kelly a golden key and explained check-out times and other pertinent information and asked her if they needed help up to their room. Kelly declined. The woman pointed out the concierge, where they could find more information about restaurants, gambling, pools, and shows in their casino and on the Strip. Kelly thanked her again and they headed towards the gigantic elevators.

Once Chuck and Kelly got on, she hit the button for the top floor. Chuck couldn't believe she booked a penthouse; then again, he could. You could see Kelly was in her element whenever finer things were involved. She grabbed Chuck's hand and happily led him towards their room.

"Ahh, here we are," she said and inserted the gold key card into the slot. The green light on the doorknob clicked and the door popped slightly open.

They walked inside the room, and Chuck knew why the key looked like a small piece of gold. The room was humongous and open with a full bar and kitchen. Plush couches sat in front of a large television. There was an indoor jacuzzi, and what caught Chuck's eye was a round, king-size bed next to a glass wall overlooking the city lights of Vegas.

Chuck looked at Kelly in astonishment. "Did you pay for this, Kell?"

"I sure did, cowboy. My present to you because I'm so in love with you!"

"Kell, no. I can't let you pay for this."

"It's done, Chucky, accept it. I only want one thing from you."

Chuck was a little worried about what it could be she was about to say. "What?"

"That bed over there?"

"Yeah?"

"You make mad, passionate love to me tonight under the starlight!" she said as she batted her eyelashes at him.

Chuck relaxed. "Oh, you know it, girl!"

He picked her up carefully off her feet and brought her over to the bed, put her on it, and lowered himself over her. They began to kiss and laugh.

"Okay, big guy, let's get dressed, go to dinner, and walk around. I'd love to go dancing tonight, how about you?"

"You're on!"

"Okay and tomorrow after breakfast, maybe we can buy some clothes for me?"

"Sounds like a plan, Kell."

After Chuck finished getting dressed in their large, fancy bathroom, he came out and Kelly had already poured a Jack Daniels on ice for him from their bar.

"Here you go, big guy. Just relax while I try to get myself all gorgeous for you."

"I don't think you'll have any problems in that department."

"For you, it's easy. It takes a little work for us women," she said as she blew him a kiss and went into the bathroom with her suitcase.

Chuck started channel surfing on the killer television while sitting on the brown leather couch drinking his beverage. He came across the film *Tombstone* starring Kurt Russell and Val Kilmer and stopped changing the channels right there. He thought it was the perfect movie to occupy his time while he waited.

A half-hour went by. She was still getting ready, and he finished his drink. Chuck was already feeling good. He thought that was strange. It usually took him a few drinks to get a buzz going. Chuck made another one and yelled to Kelly to ask if she wanted one too. She did, so Chuck made her a martini as best he could.

Finally, the bathroom door opened. Chuck could smell her exotic perfume.

"Voila! Well?"

"Mamma mia. Oh my!" said Chuck.

Kelly had on a low-cut black dress that was tight in all the right places. She had put her hair up to show off her sculpted neckline and a black choker circled her tiny neck. Chuck thought, *Well, it will not be long before I beg her to come back to the room with me so I can carry out her earlier request.*

"Are you sure you didn't plan this brief trip all along?" he asked.

"No, silly. Come on, let's sit and finish our drinks before we head out for dinner."

Once they got to the restaurant downstairs, things got real hazy for Chuck.

He found himself in the long, white tunnel again with a soft cloud surrounding him. Like before when this happened, Chuck's clothes were suddenly all white as he traveled through it, the tunnel spinning around him. There was no one to greet him. No Shandi, no father. No one, period. He was literally alone. This had never happened before in this dream, if that was indeed what this was.

Far, far away, somewhere at the end of the tunnel, Chuck heard someone crying. He kept walking toward the sad, weeping sounds. As he got closer, he saw darkness at the very end of the clouded tunnel. He kept going forward until he reached its end. Chuck emerged somewhere unknown in the middle of darkness. His clothes had changed again, this time to dark jeans, a black t-shirt, and boots. He was outside surrounded by deteriorated streets with old, weathered apartment buildings on both sides. One building looked oddly familiar to him. It was a dark forest green.

Chuck walked over to the structure and stood before the front door. The tarnished knob was unlocked and he entered the building. The hallway inside was narrow, and Chuck started up a creaky, old wooden staircase until he reached another hallway.

He heard the crying again, only louder, and Chuck recognized the weeping sound.

It was Shandi.

Chuck walked more quickly down the hall until he reached a beat-up door covered in peeling paint. He again turned an unlocked knob and entered the room. The hardwood flooring had no shine and also appeared splintered and beaten. The apartment he entered was like a maze, but Chuck found he somehow knew his way around it. He walked through the kitchen and heard the faucet dripping. Then he continued through a dining room and a bedroom. A door adjoining the bedroom was ajar. The crying was coming from in there.

Chuck walked to the old, smoky-topaz stained door and gently pushed it open. Shandi was crying, curled-up in a ball on top of a small bed by a window. She was crying so very softly, and it was breaking Chuck's heart. He walked up to the bed, sat down beside her, and tenderly touched her head.

"Shandi, what's wrong?" he asked.

She looked up at him with tears in her deep blue eyes and a look of disappointment.

Chuck suddenly woke up in bed, startling himself, not knowing for a minute where he was or what had happened. He was sweaty and felt like shit. He felt as if he was going to throw up, or possibly die, and looked around to get his bearings. Chuck was lying in bed in their hotel room under the covers. He could feel Kelly's naked skin against his own.

Jesus, he thought, *what the fuck. We must have had one hell of a night.*

Chuck had blackouts before from drinking, but never where he didn't remember one solitary thing. He chalked it up as alcohol consumption gone horribly wrong. They were in Vegas after all, and he wasn't as young as he once was. His worry now was whether he had done anything dumb, but his guess was no because Kelly was still there. No doubt they made love, but he had no memory of it. Not only was he sick to his stomach from booze and complete memory loss, but also the haunting dream he just woken up from.

Chuck thought, *I gotta get up and get some water to hydrate so I can think more clearly.* Maybe when Kelly woke up she'd be able to shed some light on what went on. But then again, he was also worried that she might get upset if he told her he didn't remember anything. It was quite the dilemma.

Chuck slowly and painfully got out of bed, so as not to wake Kelly. He walked over to the sink with his head spinning and picked up a glass. He turned the cold water on, and guzzled one, two, three, four, five glasses down. Immediately, Chuck felt his body reacting positively to the refreshing H20 but still could not remember a damn thing.

Kelly heard the water running and began stretching her arms and legs in bed. She was moving around and purring like a happy kitten. Kelly opened her eyes and saw Chuck standing naked, drinking his water at the kitchen table and looking back at her. She smiled like she had the greatest night of her life. Chuck relaxed and thought, *Well, it couldn't have been that bad of an evening.*

"So nice to wake up next to my amazing, spectacular, sexy lover. And my hubby," she said as she smiled broadly.

"What?" Chuck replied. He put down his glass of water and he looked over at his left hand that was on the counter holding him up.

Holy shit.

There on his fourth finger was a ring.

"Nice, isn't it, hon!"

Chuck was getting dizzy all over again. He just kept thinking, *What the hell happened last night?*

Kelly energetically jumped out of the big round bed and joyfully ran up to her husband, wrapping her arms around him and kissing him.

"I'm so, so, so happy, Chucky. You've made me the happiest girl in the whole, wide world."

Boy, Chuck had one hell of a problem. How could he admit that he had a blackout and remembered absolutely nothing without hurting her feelings?

"So... you didn't mind getting married in Vegas, Kell?"

"I know it was maybe not traditional, rushing over to that little Elvis chapel on impulse, but you were not taking no for an answer last night. Given that and the fact I'm so crazy about you - and that I was also tipsy myself - I really, really wanted to. So I figured, okay, let's do it."

Chuck's head was still spinning. It just was so unlike him.

"What about our families? It might disappoint them that we eloped."

"I got us covered, babe. When we get back– and I mean as soon as we get home– we will plan a huge reception for all of our family and friends at the ranch. I'll take care of it all. The arrangements. The invites. Babe, I'll make sure to square it with your mom. I love her and want her to be included. Plus, I don't want my daddy being mad either, and you'll get to meet him, finally."

Chuck half-smiled at the overwhelming information, feeling even sicker to his stomach with each moment.

"We can afford a big reception?"

Kelly started laughing. "You're being silly again, my handsome hubby."

Chuck was confused again by her laughing at his question. "I am?"

"All that money you won last night in the casino?"

"I'm sorry, I'm a little tired and still hungover, hon. How much did I win again?"

"You won $50,000!"

Chuck's eyes grew wide. "Excuse me, Kell, I gotta sit down."

He looked for his underwear, found them on the floor next to the bed, put them on, and sat.

"You put $20,000 on red after being down $5,000. I thought you were going to lose all the money you earned on your book, but you okie-dokied the dealer on that table. The hotel comped our room for free to top it all off," Kelly said. She walked over to Chuck, sat next to him, and wrapped her arms around him again. "It's going to be a wonderful life, Chucky."

After the two of them got dressed for the day, they went down to the restaurant to have breakfast. Chuck drank his coffee and nibbled on a bacon strip. He couldn't help but stare at the intrusive new piece of jewelry on his ring finger. He was still in total disbelief and thinking, *I don't even like gambling.* Chuck would never sing an Elvis tune the same way after last night. Even though he was very skeptical, he decided his glass was half full. She was gorgeous, smart, ambitious, rich, confident, and seemed to be crazy for him.

They had agreed that she would go clothes shopping after breakfast and Chuck would check out the sights. He promised to do no more gambling while she shopped. In fact, Chuck told her he'd never gamble again. Even though he won big, he realized he could have lost it all being foolhardy.

He took the opportunity while he was alone to call Allan back. He asked him if he could find out who owned the gray Pontiac Sunfire. Chuck gave him the license plate number he had memorized. It was ironic that Chuck had just got married last night, and now he was asking a P.I. to find another woman. He knew he was nuts to do it, but he had to know. Allan told Chuck he'd be in touch in a few days.

Kelly was in a private changing room of a store called Tadashi Shoji when she dialed Chip's number.

"Hey. What's my girl doing? Are you back home?"

"I'm still away, Chip."

"Really? The Rockstar's on a roll, huh?"

"Well, you could say that."

"I'm a little jealous. I guess there's nothing yet on the land? I have to tell you, Kelly, these investors are serious individuals. I'm not sure how much longer I can hold them off."

"What's that supposed to mean, Chip?"

"Nothing, nothing. They just know how to motivate people to get their ends to justify their means."

"Well, never fear, darling, so do I. So. Do. I!"

"Meaning?" Chip asked.

"Meaning, you want results? Here goes. I'm in Vegas right now, and when I get home, I will make a deal with this LoneStar Group personally!"

"How?"

"Here's how, Chip. Chuck Barreto is now my husband!"

Chip started laughing. "What? You're kidding me."

"Not about something like this. So here's what you're going to do. Put me in touch with the main contact for The LoneStar Group. I want to meet with him or her."

"I don't even know who that person is, Kelly. I can possibly put you in contact with one of their higher-up liaisons. That's all I've ever met with in the past. Whoever's actually in charge seems to stay very well-insulated."

"Well, that will have to do. For now. Set up a meeting. Give me some time to get back first. We'll be having a big wedding reception at Chuck's ranch. I'll send you and Mellisa an invitation. And don't forget about our dinner date, Mr. Senator."

"But Mrs. Barreto, you're a married woman now."

"Marriage never seemed to stop you."

"Touché."

After she hung up with Chip, she called Jeff Downing.

"Hey, Kelly. How's Vegas?"

"Better than expected, sir. I'm now Chuck's wife!"

"Holy cow! That's great, Kelly. Congratulations."

"Thank you, Jeff. I want to start building on Gussy's Pitts without Chuck or his siblings finding out about it. I have a land developer who is on board."

"That will be extremely difficult, Kelly."

"But not impossible?"

"Maybe not. I'll get to work on it right away. If you break ground and they find out, you could have legal troubles."

"Maybe, maybe not. I just want to break ground. After that, I'm not too worried. I have another ace in the hole."

"Okay, Kelly. I'll move on some avenues A.S.A.P. and I'll talk to you soon."

Kelly hung her phone up and screamed, "WOOHOO!" Then she peeked over the stall door, a smile on her face, to see if anyone overheard her.

CHAPTER 19

VANISHED

ABBY WAS IN a small section of the airport in Connecticut where private planes landed. She got special access in the waiting area of the lobby because of her law enforcement status. She kept looking at her wristwatch while waiting for the plane that Alfred was on to land. Before he had boarded, he told Abby he had serious informants who would report on The LoneStar Group.

Alfred was flying back from Virginia with an attorney named Silus from the organization, so Abby assumed he must be the informant. She tried getting more intel from Alfred over the phone before he took off, but he said he couldn't say much until he got back. He told Abby not to worry; what he had was well worth the wait.

She was sitting next to a wall of windows overlooking the runway. Abby observed a large commercial plane being loaded with suitcases when a small private plane came in for a landing. She anxiously went over to a woman who was a member of the airport staff and politely asked her if the small plane coming in was Flight 370. The woman confirmed. Abby went back to the window to watch for Alfred getting off the plane.

A few minutes passed and a door opened on the pilot's side. A man came out and arranged a small set of steps for the passengers to exit.

A group of men got out and she counted them. Five men dressed in black suits. She could hear their muffled talking and laughing. They walked towards the lobby that Abby was watching from. She saw that none of the men were Alfred.

What the fuck is going on? Where is Alfred? Abby thought.

She rushed to the door where they were coming in to head them off. The door opened and the five men stepped inside; the pilot was lagging behind. Most of the men looked like bodybuilders or some sort of security types, except for a gauntly, cynical-looking man that stood out from the others.

Abby caught their attention. "Excuse me, gentlemen. Are any of you Silus?"

The tall, eerie man replied, "I'm Silus."

"Excuse me, sir, you were supposed to be on this flight with an associate of mine, Mr. Alfred Ford? I don't see him with you."

"I'm sorry, miss, we're the only ones on this flight. I never heard of the man you just mentioned."

"That's impossible. I got your name from Alfred. How did I know your name and flight?"

"I don't have a clue, miss. This must be some sort of misunderstanding. But I have pressing business, so I'm sorry but I must carry on. I hope you find your friend. Good day."

Silus and his companions remained quiet as they walked away from her. The pilot walked into the building and Abby frantically grabbed him.

"Excuse me, sir. I'm looking for my friend, Alfred Ford. He was supposed to be on your plane but did not get off with you."

"I'm sorry, ma'am. That name is not ringing a bell. The men that came in ahead of me were the only ones on that flight."

"What's your name, sir?"

"Vince, Vince McQueen."

"And you work for...?"

"Whoever hires me. If you'll excuse me, I have another flight to prepare for. I'm sure you'll find your friend. He probably took another flight."

Vince abruptly walked away. Abby stood in the lobby, bewildered for a moment, then ran back over to the podium and showed the woman working her law enforcement badge and asked to see the flight log of the passengers. It showed only five men and a pilot.

Abby took out her cell phone and called Alfred. His phone did not ring. It went straight to voicemail. Abby left Alfred an urgent message for him to call her back.

She then called Jed. He answered, "Hey Ab, you got our boy?"

"No, I don't. I'm worried." She explained what had just transpired. "It appears he never made it on the plane. Or they threw him off."

Abby was only half-joking about that comment.

"No, Ab, I'm sure he got held up somehow and maybe his cell phone died. Keep trying. Don't worry. I'm sure he's fine."

Kelly enthusiastically unlocked the door to her empty office in town. All of her employees had the day off and some of them would be helping out at the ranch for the big day. Jeff was standing behind her with his briefcase.He was the perfect partner and confidant for her. He'd go along with any venture she could conjure up to get ahead. If Kelly told Jeff she saw Bigfoot and wanted the rights to own the Sasquatch, he would assure her the copyrights.

"Come on in, Jeff. Grab a seat. We can't be long. I have to get back to the ranch for my reception," she said smiling. "I told Chuck you and I were working on putting together our special interests to form a united company. He, of course, could not care less about any of it."

They sat down and Jeff opened his case. He had prepared different sets of paperwork for them to go over. He made small talk about the reception and asked more about Vegas. She was evasive about how she and Chuck had decided to get married there. He asked her if she was keeping her apartment in the city.

"Of course I am. For those long nights when I'm making business deals for Kelly & Chuck's Enterprises, I can just stay there instead of driving back home," she said with a playful smirk on her face.

Jeff smirked. "I like the name of your new business. Chuck doesn't mind your name ahead of his?"

"He's happy on his little ranch. That's all he cares about."

Jeff changed the subject back to the matter at hand. "So, let's get to it. You will buy an existing subsidiary. When you buy it, you do it under

Chuck's name. When Chuck signs the paperwork for your new joint enterprise, you have him sign his Hancock on this document here. Hopefully, Chuck doesn't read it all because of the wordiness."

"Don't worry, he won't."

"Okay, so now if I'm correct, you want to partner up with The LoneStar Group instead of selling to them?"

Kelly smiled. "Correct you are!"

"You will start your own private company in addition to the one you begin with Chuck. For now, I named it the MoonRiver Foundation, unless you have any other name in mind that is not being used."

"No, that's fine, Jeff. Out of curiosity, where did you come up with that?"

"My wife made me watch this awful Audrey Hepburn movie last night, and that song was in it."

Kelly laughed. "Okay, gotcha. I understand completely. Chuck's a big movie buff and tries to get me to watch them. It's not my thing. Making lots of money is my thing!"

"I know we're short on time, so moving right along. With your joint company, you will funnel money over to the private company as needed. With the money in MoonRiver, you will buy out the management company that is in charge of this building we're in right now, owned by your husband and his siblings. MoonRiver will continue to send Chuck's sister and brother their rent checks with no interruptions. This keeps them none the wiser. Hopefully, they do not frequent this land when you eventually break ground with The LoneStar Group."

"Trust me, I work in this building a few days out of the week. They never come out here. Chuck's brother lives in Virginia and his sister is very busy. His mother has other properties and a beach house she's always tending to."

"You know you will need variances and will have to lower density to build without detection?"

"Right, I understand. For local zoning laws to protect property values, to act as waivers. And to use as a number of housing units given on the land." She smiled.

"I forgot who I was talking to, you know your stuff! Are you counting on LoneStar to help you with that?"

"It's a long game, Jeff, but you are brilliant in your assessment so far. That's why I keep you around!"

"LoneStar has their own office in The SkyTower."

"Really? I didn't know that."

"They don't advertise it. I had to do some snooping. If you get them to partner up, you can also use that office for the MoonRiver Foundation business dealings."

"Okay, that's a great idea. Now I just have to persuade LoneStar to join up with me to develop Gussy's Pitts. Chip Karrington is arranging a meeting for me with them."

"What happens when Chuck and his siblings do eventually find out, Kelly?"

"It won't matter. We'll all be filthy rich and Chuck's signature will be on all of this along with mine. But if things get ugly, I'll go into denial mode and say Chuck was in favor of it all from the ground up."

Jeff grinned slightly. "Okay, Kelly. You know best."

"Not to worry, Jeff. And if all else fails, I have an insurance policy."

Jeff didn't want to ask what she meant by that, so he gave her all the paperwork she needed to get Chuck to sign and congratulated her on the new marriage. She then handed him an envelope of money for his services and thanked him for everything before they left the office.

It was still fairly early in the morning when Jed arrived at Chuck's ranch. Chuck had told Jed to come early so he could show him around before all the guests arrived for the reception. The gate was already wide open, with a homemade sign off to the side of the entranceway that said, "Welcome to Our Roundup!" Over the gate was an oval, wooden plaque that read "Chuck's Homestead".

Jed drove slowly up the long driveway. Light posts were still under construction on both sides. Jed pulled up to the parking area in front of the house, and a hired valet dressed in a tuxedo came over to Jed and told him to drive further down a dirt road. Another valet by the barn directed him where to park. He got out of his car and looked around, amazed at it all.

"Good morning, sir. I'm Paige. Are you Jed?" asked the valet.

"Yes, I am."

"I am to take you to Mr. Barreto."

"Okay..." He was curious.

She walked him over to a white golf cart. They got on and Paige hit the accelerator. They started moving forward, away from the barn and house.

"Mr. Barreto has a shooting range out here. That's where we're going. He thought this would be an invigorating way for you to see some of the property."

"It's beautiful."

Paige nodded. "Yes sir, it is."

"You work for Chuck?"

"Ah, no, I'm a new agent under Kelly and I volunteered to help her when I found out she got married. I love working for her."

Jed thought she made a smart move by ingratiating herself with her new boss.

After driving for a few acres, they came to a large clearing. Jed could already hear gunfire as they approached. He saw Chuck with two other men, casually dressed for the upcoming occasion. Chuck turned and smiled, then walked towards Jed and Paige as they came to a full stop.

"Aaah, you made it, Jethro!"

"Great Caesar's Ghost, Chuck! Look at you! Looking good."

"You're not looking too shabby either, Mr. Assistant AG."

They both laughed and Chuck thanked Paige who then drove back to return to helping with guest arrivals. The two men with Chuck were his army buddies, Mike and Mitch. Chuck introduced them to Jed.

They had a few AR-15's and Glocks to play with. Chuck asked Jed if he wanted to give it a go.

"Don't mind if I do," said Jed.

Chuck had different paper silhouette targets set up on bales of hay and wooden stands. They were twenty yards back for the handguns and two hundred and fifty yards for the ARs. Jed picked up a Glock, took his time, and then fired away.

"Not bad, Jed," said Mike and then gestured towards Chuck. "How about this guy? He's been just watching the whole time me and Mitch have been working on these targets."

"Ah, me? Guys, I'm not that good anymore."

"Yeah, right!" said Mitch. He picked up one of the ARs and handed it to Chuck. "Prove you're not."

Chuck took hold of the weapon, loaded it, and charged her up. He aimed at the target furthest away, took a breath, and unloaded the weapon until the cartridge was empty.

Mike picked up a pair of binoculars from the plywood table, looked at Chuck's target, and said, "Mmmhmmm."

He then handed them to Jed. Jed looked at the target and saw every bullet hit on or around the bullseye.

Jed looked at Chuck. "Maybe you were in the wrong line of work?"

"Possibly, but I'm right where I wanna be now."

Chuck had a walkie-talkie in his back pocket that went off. It was Uncle Armond calling him from the house.

"Hey, what's up, Unc?" Chuck answered.

"Hey, Meathead, the band just arrived and Kelly and my sister are looking for you."

"Okay, I'm on my way back."

Mike and Mitch jumped on Chuck's four-wheeler, and Chuck loaded up another golf cart with the weapons and ammo. Jed rode with Chuck. As they were riding back, they caught up on recent events. Jed complimented Chuck on his ranch and congratulated him on getting married. Chuck asked Jed how everything was going with him and the new job.

"You know the land you inherited from your mother? Has anyone made you or your siblings an offer on that property?"

"I think there was an offer by a developer. It was Kelly who told me. I told her we're definitely not selling right now. Why?"

"You think sometime – when she's not busy, of course – you could ask her who it was for me?"

"Yeah, sure, not a problem. Everything okay?"

"Oh, yeah. Just working on some information for a case."

They pulled up to the house and Chuck's family was standing in the driveway as the band carried their equipment around to the backyard. Kelly and Rita had arranged an incredible setup for the event, especially in such a short amount of time. Wooden beams were brought in and hung with crystal chandeliers and flowers. One of Chad's John Deere tractors was also covered with flowers and lights. Glimmering sheer fabric of yellow and white was draped from beam to beam with little twinkle lights glistening. A beautiful horse carriage was decorated with yellow and white roses and an outdoor fireplace was lit creating a romantic mood.

Guests would sit at farmhouse tables with fruitwood chairs. They were set with China flanked by the shiniest silverware you had ever seen and crystal glasses. The centerpieces were jadeite crystal candle holders surrounded by a yellow and white rose wreath. Wine barrels were used for drinking stations or to be laden with plates of appetizers. Three portable wooden bars were available for the sizable crowd. They really had thought of every detail.

Kelly worked rather well with Rita because of their past partnership. Kelly had hired the caterers while Rita had arranged for a wooden dance floor to be brought in. The only part they didn't have a hand in was the selection of the band, who played mostly country music because they were hired by Kelly's father.

Chuck pulled the golf cart to a stop and got off.

Rita shouted, "Chucky!"

Chuck hugged her and then Stacey, and he clapped Gary on the shoulder. Stacey introduced her friend Candie who she had brought along, and he introduced his family to Jed, Mike, and Mitch. Uncle Armond came out of the house with Rupert and offered to put the guns and golf cart away.

Cars started pulling in and people were howling out their windows at Chuck. He graciously waved and smiled.

Kelly came out onto the front porch in a white dress with floral designs embroidered into the soft material. She wore white heels, her makeup was perfect as usual, and her soft silky red hair was pulled up into a ravishing bun.

"Hello everyone!" she said, smiling. "Chucky, darling, can I see you for one sec?"

Chuck excused himself and joined her inside the house. In the kitchen, Kelly gave him a kiss.

"What's up, pretty lady?"

Kelly had a bunch of paperwork laid out on the kitchen bar next to her briefcase. "Jeff drew up these contracts for our joint company, my love. I have to go into the office for an hour tomorrow for a sale. I just wrapped up, and I was going to bring this stuff with me if you don't mind signing it. If you want to take some time to read through it, we can do it another day."

Chuck, happy and distracted, saw no reason to put it off. "No, now is fine."

He signed next to all the x's on the dotted lines quickly, without knowing exactly what any of it was. Kelly, like a tiger shark, had picked this moment because she knew how predictable he was. She secretly got butterflies from the con job she just pulled on him.

Kelly kissed his cheek. "Hon, don't forget. Tomorrow morning you have that photoshoot here at the ranch with the publisher's photographers."

"Yes, yes, I remember. Afterwards I am meeting with a couple of new ranch hands, and you won't believe it, but Mike and Mitch are kind of working dead-end jobs, so they want to work here, too."

"Is that wise to have friends or family working for you?"

"Kell, these guys had my back in Panama. They'll have my back here."

"Okay, hon, just asking. You know best. It's your ranch. Don't forget that you also have someone coming for the supervisor position."

"Yeah. You said you knew someone?"

"Yes. Remember the woman I knew who was looking for a house? She's from Michigan, grew up on ranches, and was a foreman at a big one out there somewhere. We want someone competent, so your baby is an extraordinary success! You need someone who is very qualified to show you the ropes, and I know you'll pick it up quickly because of who you are as a man. I had Jeff do a background check on her for you, and she checked out with an A-plus."

"Wow. Thank Jeff for me. You know what time she's coming? And what's her name?"

"Around one, shortly after the photoshoot. And If I remember correctly, her name is Sandy."

"Okay, sounds good."

"And when I get home tomorrow, we have dinner with Daddy and his wife, and of course, your mom."

"Right, and are they staying with us?"

"They're going to stay in the city at my apartment."

"I see. I didn't know you had a stepmother."

"She's not. He has a new wife every few years. My Mom passed away when I was very young. Come on, let's get to our guests." She packed up the paperwork in her briefcase.

As Kelly walked into the bedroom, Chuck headed outside and ran into Stacey and Candie.

"Hey, Chucky, are you still looking for any ranch hands?"

"I am. I have only hired two so far."

"Candie was in the 4H Club with me when we were kids and she is very knowledgeable about horses."

He asked Candie a few questions about her experience and Stacey assured him that Candie would be a great hire.

Chuck said, "You're in, Candie."

Kelly finally came outside and they all walked to the backyard. By this time, many people had arrived. The tables had plates of Texas Trash Dip with Tostitos chips, meatballs in crescent rolls drizzled with marinara, stuffed mushrooms, barbecue sauce cocktail franks, and scallops wrapped in bacon. The cooks were grilling up all sorts of food on two gigantic grills, and the bartenders at the portable bars were already doling out drinks. And this was just to start off with. Kelly also had catering brought in from a high-end restaurant in the city.. There were shrimp cocktail shooters, watermelon cubes with balsamic vinegar, lobster and mashed potatoes, fresh cheese and herbs, seared tuna, sugar snap peas, and pot sticker dumplings.

Chuck thought it was probably best there was so much food as he watched one of the mobile bars pass by.

"What's that cost?" Chuck asked Kelly, gesturing towards it.

"Nothing. Open bar, courtesy of Daddy," she said.

Chuck had promised himself he wouldn't have a drop of alcohol for a long time after the Vegas trip. After all, if not for the blackout he had there, this party wouldn't even be happening. All of his friends were already coming up to him asking what he was drinking. Chuck had to keep turning them down and making excuses. He had been rock solid so far.

Chuck walked around introducing Kelly to people that hadn't met her before. She herself had no family coming aside from her father and his wife. He introduced his fellow officers from the prison. Chuck was so happy to see them again, especially Dave, who had also medically retired after the attack from a fractured eye socket. Chuck offered him a job on the ranch. He said he would think it over.

Some of Chuck's old bandmates showed up. It thrilled them that he was finally happy and could move on. Chuck couldn't bring himself to invite Shandi's parents, even though he remained in contact. Rita had called them to tell them the news and they too were happy for Chuck.

By the time Chuck and Kelly had made their rounds, the band was set up and had started playing. There were at least a hundred people mingling and eating. The basket of wedding envelopes was piling up.

Chip and Mellisa arrived and Kelly went right over to greet them. Rita, Stacey, and Chuck followed suit shortly after. They all asked Chip about his campaign, mentioning how everything seemed to be going well for him in the polls. Rita particularly enjoyed having a new political acquaintance.

"Chip, Mellisa, thank you so much for coming to my son and daughter-in-law's celebration."

"Thank you for inviting us. What a beautiful place Chuck has here."

Chuck thanked Chip and responded in kind that he had found a great hire in Jed.

"I love Jed and all the work he is doing for the Attorney General," said Chip.

Eventually, Rita and Stacey took Chip's wife away for a brief tour of the house, while Kelly and Chuck remained to talk to the next possible Senator. Uncle Armond joined them.

"Hello, Mr. Karrington. I'm Chuck's Uncle Armond," he said as he shook Chip's hand and then turned to Chuck. "I couldn't get the gun safe unlocked."

Chuck told him he'd get it and excused himself to go lock up the weapons. Armond asked Chip if he wanted anything at the bar or grill. Chip asked for a beer and Armond went to retrieve one.

When they were alone, Chip turned to Kelly. "Tomorrow at 9:00 AM, your office in town. You have a meeting with The LoneStar Group."

"Chip, you're an absolute doll. I could kiss you right now!"

Chip whispered, "Later. You owe me."

Armond came back with Chip's beer and Jed. Kelly formally thanked Chip for coming and then excused herself, a pep in her step. Uncle Armond went off to the grill for more food.

Jed and Chip started discussing business, Chip's chief goal being to lead Jed on a tangent to distract him from The LoneStar Group.

"Jed, you ever heard of a developer called Tewes? They're pretty big."

"I have. We checked them out, sir, from head to toe. They're pretty clean. By the book with everything they do. Everything they invest in, they put back twice as much into the communities."

"Hmm, I heard something different from a few constituents."

"I can take another look, but I think they're legit."

"Thanks, Jed. I appreciate it."

"No problem sir."

A slight commotion broke out. A car horn began honking repeatedly in the driveway and they went to see who it was. An extended white limo pulled in and Kelly went out front to greet her father and his wife.

A tall, lofty older man got out of the driver's door. He looked like an ancient football player. He opened the back door of the vehicle and out came another large, striking man wearing an enormous Stetson, a brown suit, and cowboy boots. Kelly's father looked like a cross between Lorne Greene and John Wayne. A much younger, attractive woman got out after him wearing a pink pants suit well-tailored for her figure. She had short, curly brown hair and looked close to Kelly's age. No wonder she didn't seem impressed with them being married.

The driver told Paige he would park the limo himself.

Kelly screamed, "Daddy!" and hugged him like she was still a little girl. She looked even tinier than she already was next to both of the big Texan men. Her father's wife gave her a begrudging, icy hug.

Chuck manned up and walked over to Kelly's father after they finished hugging and he extended his hand. "Mr. Teixeira, nice to finally meet you."

The big man grabbed Chuck's hand hard and pulled him in for a hug. "Chuck. Well, a man that can get my little girl to settle down can call me Vic, or as my friends call me, Big Tex!"

Chuck smiled. "Okay, Vic. Will do."

"And this here is my better half Cheryl Diandra."

She smiled broadly and gave Chuck a warm hug, very obviously unlike the one she gave her step-daughter. Kelly cringed watching Cheryl embrace her husband.

"Chuck, my new son-in-law, this here is my longtime associate, Mr. Chance Spangler."

The driver gave Chuck another hard gripped handshake and said, "To my friends, Chancey."

Chuck felt immediately comfortable with these loud, outgoing in-laws. "Okay, Chancey."

"Wowee shucks. This is some house y'all have here, Chuck. Very nice!"

"Thank you, Vic. We're getting there slowly."

"How many horses and cattle y'all have here?"

"Ah, no cattle here. It's going to be horses only, when I get some."

Vic looked at Cheryl and said, "Honeybuns, can I have that envelope?"

Cheryl pulled out a large, gold envelope and handed it to Kelly.

"Here ya go, darling, from us," said Vic. "That there should get y'all started on getting some horses. And my little Kelly Ann can help ya, Chuck, with that, even though it wasn't her thing, with the animals. When she was a youngin', she would rather come to work with me at my oil company than be with her sister on the ranch."

Chuck looked at Kelly, confused. She had never mentioned a sister.

"You have cattle on your ranch, Vic?" asked Chuck.

"Sure do. How many acres do you have here, son?"

"Just over ten."

"Ooooh no, Chuck, that's not a ranch. I have over three hundred acres on ours."

"Wow, and an oil company to Mr. Teixeria?" After Vic's comments about a sister and his ranch, Chuck was damn curious now.

"Yeah, my oil company. You heard of it? Texas Gold Perox!"

Chuck heard of it. *Holy shit*, he thought. *Who the hell did I marry? Why are there so many secrets?*

Vic had no qualms bragging about his empire, but Kelly had kept the details from Chuck. Maybe she thought it would just scare Chuck away.

Vic then looked at Kelly. "Where's my other daughter?"

"Oh, Daddy. Shalon? She fell in love with some guy and moved east towards the coast with him."

"Oh, hell, I wanted to see her too. Chucky, when she and my Kelly Ann were youngin's, boy, they gave me a run for my money! Seems like I was always bailing them two out of some mess!"

"And then some. And then some for sure!" said Chance.

Vic laughed aloud, boisterous and distinctly. Chuck enjoyed the ease with which he could laugh.

"Daddy, we weren't that bad," said Kelly.

Chance and Vic exchanged a knowing look. Chance bent over for a second to tie his shoe, and Chuck saw he was packing a piece, holstered under his jacket. Chuck also liked that. He thought, *These guys probably have one attached to their ankles, too.* Like the Texan adage: better to have them and not need them, than need them and not have them.

Kelly changed the topic and directed everyone to a table in the back-yard with the rest of the guests. Vic was so charismatic that everyone want-ed to listen to what he had to say. Chuck couldn't wait for his mother to meet this character; she would fit right in with him. But Rita was still off with Mellisa, showing her around.

Chance was more of the silent and observant type. Chuck caught on to that right off; he was the same himself due to being ex-military and having worked in corrections for so many years.

After they had settled in and introduced themselves, Vic grabbed Chuck by his arm and said, "We'll be right back, y'all. I'm gonna have a drink with my son-in-law. Miss Cheryl, your usual?"

"With a twist, Big Tex."

"You bet, honey bunny. Kelly Ann?"

"Oh, nothing right now, Daddy."

"Chance, a coffee?"

"You know it." Chance would never drink when he was the designated driver.

Chuck and Vic walked over to the bar.

"We'll have two whiskey sours, young man," said Vic to the bartender.

"Yes, sir."

Fuck, there goes my sobriety, thought Chuck. *How can I say no to my new father-in-law?*

"Bottoms up, son," he chuckled and patted Chuck hard on the back as he guzzled his drink. "Another, son?"

"Suuure," said Chuck reluctantly. He downed the second drink and thought, *I'll start my penance tomorrow.*

Just as Chuck finished his third drink, the lead singer of the band – thank the Lord – announced, "I'd like to have Kelly and Vic out on the dance floor for a father-daughter dance. Everyone gather around, please."

Applause erupted.

"Chuck, excuse me, son. We'll finish this later."

Chuck nodded with relief and Vic walked out to the middle of the dance floor with Kelly. They embraced for a slow dance, all eyes on them. The band played a Tim McGraw song, making guests tear up as they lis-tened.

"Gotta hold on easy as I let go/ Gonna tell how much I love you/ Though you think you already know/ I remember I thought you looked like an angel..." the lead singer crooned.

Rita, Gary, and Stacey found Chuck standing by the bar.

"Wow, who is that, Chuck? Is that Kelly's father?" asked Rita.

"That's him. He seems like a nice guy," replied Chuck.

Rita walked over to introduce herself to Cheryl while Chuck chatted with his siblings. While everyone was talking, Gary took the opportunity to ask Chuck and Stacey about Gussy's Pitts.

"Hey guys, the end of our agreement with mom will be coming up. What's the plan?"

"Ah, actually I'm in no rush to do anything at all with it for a while at least. There's no rush, Gary."

"Yeah, Gar, I'm with Stace on this. There's no rush. I love the land the way it is."

Gary's face held disappointment.

Chuck thought that maybe Lilly was putting pressure on him about it, so they could cash out. Chuck hoped that wasn't the case. It wouldn't be any of her business to do that to Gary. It was his inheritance.

Chuck's co-workers came over and insisted on buying him another drink. He was holding his own. For some reason, he was not reacting to alcohol the way he did in Vegas. Other than a slight buzz, he was in control.

After Kelly and her father danced for a second song, the band announced Chuck and his mother would come out onto the floor. Chuck joined Rita and they swayed to "Que, Sera, Sera", a song he hadn't heard since he was a child and his mother used to sing along to it. While they danced, a photographer circled them, capturing the moment.

"Wow, everything is going so beautifully, son," Rita said. "I only wish your father was here with us. I miss him."

"Me too, Mom. Me too."

After the dance ended, the band called Kelly back to the floor to dance with Chuck to everyone's applause. She looked graceful and beautiful as she walked out, first hugging Rita before putting her arms around Chuck. It was a slow country song, sung by one of the female members of the band.

"You know what, handsome?"

"What, gorgeous?"

"I love ya!"

He returned the sentiment, then gently inquired, "So, Kell, how come you never told me about having a sister?"

"Babe, it's no big deal, really. Shalon is not my actual sister. Her father was a foreman on my daddy's ranch. He was accidentally killed bringing in a herd. Shalon was only ten and he was raising her alone. They had no family and my father felt responsible, so he took her in with us."

"Oh, wow. That's incredible. I'm sorry for prying."

"No, I would too If I were you. I did tell you that Daddy was into oil when we first met," she said with a coy smirk.

"Yeahhh, that you did, but damn that's one of the biggest ones out there."

"It is. And almost all oil barons out there have their own ranches."

"Really? I did not know that."

"Yeppers, and Daddy is just considered average for Texans." She smiled at him again.

Chuck thought once again, *This woman is full of endless surprises.* When the band finished the song, the singer announced, "Here's one requested by the bride."

They began playing soft rock ballad chords on acoustic guitars. Chuck looked at Kelly in surprise. She smiled and said, "I had to have them play at least one KISS song for you, my hubby!"

Chuck smiled back. It definitely wouldn't be a boring marriage. He turned his attention to the song.

"I gotta tell you what I'm feeling inside/ I could lie to myself, but it's true/ There's no denying when I look in your eyes/ Girl I'm out of my head over you/ I lived so long believing all love is blind/ But everything about you is tellin' me this time/ It's forever, this time I know and there's no doubt in my mind."

The band encouraged the guests to join them on the dance floor.

"Babe, after this weekend with my daddy and your mom, you should go buy yourself a horse trailer."

"Hmm, I know we've come into some money, but should I really?"

"I peeked in my daddy's card to us. Trust me, we can, and you can use the trailer to buy and transport horses for this place and get the ranch going finally."

"Horses, too? How much did he give you?"

"Us, Chucky, us. $100,000," she said, batting her gorgeous eyelashes at him.

"Come on, stop joking around!"

"I never joke about money, sweetie."

Holy fuck, Chuck thought. *How did we get here so quickly?*

"Chuck, relax. It's nothing to Daddy. We have a glorious life ahead of us."

Chuck smiled. He was overwhelmed and deliriously happy. Their song ended. The band congratulated the newlyweds and announced that immediate family on both sides was needed for pictures. The singer asked all family members to meet Chuck and Kelly in front of the house.

As they walked out front, Chip and Mellisa came over to say goodbye and congratulate them again. Rita thanked them for attending and wished Chip luck with the election.

Chuck had a small wooden bridge built over a gorge, which was where they would be taking pictures. The photographer started with just Chuck and Kelly then continued the standard wedding lineup.

Chuck was excited to see his relatives from his dad's side; it had been a long time since any of them were in a picture together. They were staying at Rita's house for the weekend. Rita's older brother Richard had also made it to the event, and Chuck had talked him into staying at his house for the weekend, knowing that his mom would be cozy with his other relatives.

Uncle Richard didn't come around much; he seemed to prefer a more solitary life. Before Chuck had left for Panama, he had always wondered about Uncle Richard's quiet ways. After Panama, Chuck understood it better; it was important to him to try to make his uncle feel more at ease and at home.

Vic made a point to get a picture with just him and Chuck together. Rita was looking forward to getting to know him. He had embraced her son so openly, and in some ways, he reminded her of Gus. Ambitious, hardworking, outgoing, and friendly to everyone around him. She also knew from the past conversations with Kelly that she had lost her mother to cancer at a very young age. Loss was something else they had in common.

Chuck wanted to get a group photo with his friends as well, so after they finished with family, Uncle Armond went and retrieved most of them for Chuck. Except for Jed.

Chuck could see Jed from afar on his cell phone, stressed out about something. Whoever he was talking to, Chuck knew very well that Jed was upset; it was written all over his face.

Jed was talking to Abby, still trying to find out the whereabouts of Alfred.

"Abby, he's got to be somewhere. People don't just vanish like this," said Jed.

"His hotel room, according to the police, is clean as a whistle."

"I'm going to his apartment with the police. See if there's anything there. Do you have his address?"

"I can get it."

Chuck shouted to Jed and waved him over. "Jed, come on over for a picture!"

"I have to go, Ab. Please stay on this."

He hung up and walked over to Chuck.

"Everything okay, Jed?"

"Yeah, no worries. Just work stuff."

"Okay. I have to get a pic with my partner."

Jed forced a smile. "Of course."

After taking a couple of pictures with Jed, Chuck called over Mitch and Mike.

As they posed for a picture, Mike called out, "Stop your grinnin' and drop your linen!"

They all laughed, then went back to the party. It was a grand night for everyone except Jed. He reluctantly left shortly after.

CHAPTER 20
SILUS AND SAMANTHA
AUGUST - SEPTEMBER 2002

CHUCK GUZZLED DOWN a couple of Alka-Seltzers before going to bed in the hopes of not waking up in the morning with a hangover. He had another full-scheduled day ahead of him. Boy, being retired early from corrections hadn't freed up any time; Chuck was even busier than ever.

The next morning, he was lying in bed face down on a pillow, snoring and drooling on his arm, when Kelly gently put her fingers in his thick, messy hair. "Chucky, darling. Chucky? Time to get up."

"Huh?" Chuck groggily turned his head to the side and opened his eyes halfway.

As usual, Kelly was dressed to the hilt for work and smelled of exotic perfume. She kissed him and said, "I'm supposed to keep it a secret, so please act surprised tonight at dinner, Chucky."

"Okay, about what?"

"Your dad had some land in Portugal he held onto. I helped your mother sell it and she got close to a million dollars. She's splitting most of the money up between you, Gary, and Stacey!"

Chuck suddenly felt much more awake.

"WHAT?"

"You're just getting richer by the millisecond, hubby!"

"Kell, what the fuck. I can't believe it!"

"Have a delightful morning," she said as she gleefully kissed him again. "Don't forget you have your photoshoot for the book this morning, and the possible new ranch foreman is coming by to meet you."

She couldn't help telling him in advance, his good fortune was hers. Money excited her like nothing else. If she had to choose between love or money, money would win every time with Kelly.

Chuck was still thinking about the money and trying to come to grips with what he was just told. "Ah, yeah, right. You going in to work right now?"

"Yeah, I just have to finish a few things up. Then I'll be home, back in your loving arms. I won't be long." She blew him a kiss and left.

Rupert saw her leave and ran into the bedroom. He jumped up on the bed and started licking his master's face.

"Okay, okay, buddy. I'm getting up." Chuck pet Rupert on the head and slowly got out of bed. He walked down the hallway to the kitchen with his loyal friend tagging along. Uncle Armond and Uncle Richard were already up and at the breakfast bar having coffee.

"Hey, Meathead, I thought ranchers were up at the crack of dawn," said Uncle Armond.

Richard laughed at his brother's quip.

"Ho, ho, ho, Arm," said Chuck. "You're so funny I'm pissing my drawers. This rancher doesn't roll out 'til 8:00 AM."

"Coffee's on, nephew," said Uncle Richard.

"Thanks, Uncle Rich."

Chuck grabbed a cup and sat next to him. Rupert curled up on the floor nearby and Armond reached down to pet him.

"Good boy, Sir Rupert!" he said.

They all conversed and joked around while Chuck looked at the clock on the wall to see how much time he had until the photographer arrived. He thought, *Damn, more pictures today. It's like I'm a movie star or something.*

· · ·

Jed and Abby were at Alfred's apartment building in the city with two police officers and the landlord. He opened the door with the building keys for them to look around and search inside. It was a practical apartment: kitchen, living room, bathroom, and two bedrooms. The place was fairly neat, with the exception of some clothes lying around.

The landlord said he hadn't seen Alfred since before he left for Virginia. He stood in the living room as they poked around. They were coming up empty. Jed was examining notes and paperwork that had been left in the kitchen for a possible paper trail that would explain Alfred's absence. He looked at the items tacked to the fridge and bills on the kitchen table, but there didn't seem to be anything useful there.

Abby called Jed into the bedroom. Jed walked in with the officers and saw a gym bag off to the side of the bed. Inside there were some clothes, and on top of the clothes were a couple of zip-lock bags containing a white powder. Jed and Abby looked at one another in total disbelief.

Kelly had arrived at her office in town and Jeff was already there. They waited excitedly for the representative from The LoneStar Group to attempt to make a deal with them to develop the land in Gussy's Pitts. They negotiated their strategy, and Jeff tried again to warn Kelly about the consequences of Chuck finding out. Kelly gave Jeff all the paperwork Chuck had signed without reading the fine print.

"You are a brilliant woman, but this is not full proof," said Jeff.

"Don't worry, I have all the angles covered," she replied.

They heard a car pull into the lot. Jeff got up and looked out of the second-floor window towards the entranceway of the parking lot. A black limo had pulled in. The rest of the lot was mostly empty due to it being a weekend, and Kelly gave all her agents the day off for helping at the reception at the ranch.

"I believe they're here," said Jeff. He watched them get out of the vehicle and saw the driver and two other men dressed in black get out first. Then a very lanky, willowy man followed. "Yessiree, that's them."

He went back to his seat and sat down, trying not to let on how nervous he was to Kelly. She had made a pot of coffee which she began to pour when someone knocked on her office door. Kelly opened it and welcomed them all into her office.

The tall man approached Kelly and said, "Nice to finally meet you, Mrs. Barreto. I hear congratulations are in order on your marriage."

"Thank you, Mr...?"

"Silus Kobol, an associate of The LoneStar Group. As are my companions."

"Very nice to meet everyone. Please take a seat, and would anyone like a fresh cup of coffee?"

"That would be satisfactory," said Silus. "A lot of sugar and a lot of milk."

"No problem." She offered some to the other men, but they all declined.

As she was making Silus his cup, she couldn't help but think how odd and eerie-looking he was. He appeared to be seven feet tall and his hair was mostly dark and thick, though there were some grays showing through. He was so thin that he looked gaunt, and his most disturbing feature was that his irises were reddish like a rabbit. She also thought it was odd he did not introduce the other men by name.

Kelly handed him his coffee and sat down.

Silus began bluntly. "Mrs. Barreto, why is your husband not present for the meeting?"

Kelly composed herself for a verbal joust. "He wants me to be in charge of this project. He's home preparing to get our new ranch on its feet."

"Very well. You have a ranch?"

"We're working on it. Let's talk about Gussy's Pitts."

"Is your husband and his family ready to sell?"

"Not quite. We would like to develop the land ourselves, but need your help and connections to do so."

"So you are looking for a partnership?"

"Exactly."

"I'm still listening, Mrs. Barreto."

"I'll have my attorney, Mr. Downing, explain what we have in mind."

Jeff stood and leaned over the desk. He slowly and confidently began his pitch to Silus.

Chuck had just finished up the long, exhausting photoshoot. The photographers were very pleased with what they had taken and were loading up their van to leave for another assignment. Chuck thanked them and watched as the vehicle drove off the property.

His mind returned to the news Kelly gave him before she left for work. Chuck's brother and sister would also be at dinner that night. He knew Gary would be more than pleased and the topic of selling Gussy's Pitts would likely be dropped.

Chuck had a little time before the interview for the foreman job, so he pulled the Charger out of the garage to install a new starter that he had specially ordered. Thinking of how difficult it would be to completely get his hands clean for dinner, he decided to just wax her instead.

It was a beautiful, sunny day for detailing his baby. He drove her out and was waxing her slowly, enjoying the sun, when his cell phone rang.

"Dave!" answered Chuck. "Are you taking me up on the job?"

"Hey Chuck," he said laughing. "I had a great time last night."

"Yeah, it was awesome seeing everyone. What's going on?"

"I was wondering… would I be able to work part-time, see how it goes? I don't think I'm quite ready to do it full-time yet."

"Fuck yeah, that's perfect buddy."

"Nice, thanks. When do I start?"

"Ah, how 'bout in a week? Right now I'm working on hiring a foreman, getting a horse trailer, and, most importantly, horses."

"Okay, next week it is. Talk to you soon, bud."

Chuck went back to waxing his car and, damn, his cell phone went off again. He looked at the tiny screen. It was Allan Miller. Chuck had forgotten all about him.

"Allan, good morning!"

"Morning to you, Chuck. I'm calling back about that license plate number."

"Did you find anything out on it? Whose is it?" Chuck asked. He glanced up as he suddenly heard Def Leppard coming from the direction of the driveway, gradually growing louder.

"It's a leased car from the Jurkowski dealership in the city. Do you want me to see if I can pull some strings and find out who it is?"

Before Chuck could respond to Allan, he saw the Pontiac they were just speaking of pull into his driveway with the convertible top down. He couldn't believe his eyes. The mystery woman, with her platinum blond hair, sat in the driver's seat.

"Good work, Allan. Ah no, don't worry about doing that right now. I think I might have an idea whose lease it is. I'll give you a call if anything else comes up. Thanks so much for your help."

"Sure, no problem, buddy," said Allan, perplexed by Chuck's sudden disinterest.

The car pulled right up to the nose of Chuck's precious Charger and the engine turned off. Chuck stood in a trance.

The driver's door opened and the woman said, "Nice jacket."

"Jacket?" Chuck responded, in awe.

"Yeah. The astronaut jacket on your car seat," she said.

Chuck was having an issue snapping out of his stupor. She pointed inside his car. Chuck turned his head and saw the old jacket that he used to wear in the band draped over the car seat.

"Oh, yeah. The jacket. Thanks."

"I'm looking for a Chuck Barreto?" she said.

"Yeah, sorry. That's me," said Chuck, shaking his head and trying to get a grip. The woman walked over to him with a bounce in her step.

"I'm Samantha Dixon, applying for the foreman job here. Or forewoman, I suppose."

Even her hand felt like an exact match to Shandi's. It was absolutely perfect. As their hands connected, Chuck had a flashback to one time when he and Shandi were lying in bed together after making love. Chuck was cuddled tightly against her backside, running his fingers across her lovely curves while she purred at his touch.

"Excuse me, Mr. Barreto?" Samantha interrupted his reverie. "You okay?"

Chuck shook it off again. "Yeah, sorry again. Call me Chuck. I thought my wife said your name was Sandy. She must have mixed it up. Kelly gave me your resume. It all looks great."

"Thank you."

"Ah, what are you doing now for work?"

"I work for a temp agency, a lot of odd jobs."

"Kelly tells me you moved from Michigan? And you ran ranches out there?"

"Mmm, that's right."

"If you don't mind me..."

Samantha cut him off. "Why did I move out here? I have a girlfriend who lives here, and she talked me into coming here for a bit, so here I am."

Chuck couldn't help but stare at her intensely, looking for some flaw, but there were none at all. Her voice differed from Shandi's; where Shandi's had been raspy, Samantha's was soft. She also had a hint of the southern drawl. Samantha had those identical mesmerizing, deep blue eyes. It was uncanny. She didn't seem to mind that Chuck was looking at her the way he was.

Uncle Armond came outside with Uncle Richard and Rupert. The little guy needed his daily walk.

Samantha saw the pug right away and said, "Ahh, what a cutie pie! Can I?"

"Oh, yeah, of course," said Chuck.

Samantha walked over to Rupert and he took to her right away. She kneeled down to him and he excitedly jumped up on her, giving her friendly licks while she petted his fur.

"As you can see, animals tend to love me," said Samantha.

"I see that."

"How old is he?"

"Ah, he's an old man. About thirteen."

"Wow, he's pretty spry and chipper."

"He has Anglo-Saxon blood, like his Uncle," Uncle Armond said.

"Miss Dixon, the quiet one is my Uncle Richard. This here wiseguy is my Uncle Armond, a full time comedian on the ranch. That's why we keep him around."

Armond studied Samantha, then he looked at Chuck. Without words, he communicated that he noticed the resemblance. Uncle Richard took no notice at all; he had only met Shandi a few times.

Samantha finished greeting Rupert, who seemingly found his new best friend. She stood up and shook Armond's and Richard's hands. "Hi, I'm Samantha Dixon."

Uncle Armond kindly returned the hello, and Chuck told Armond that she would be working as their foreman. Chuck knew the second she got out of her car, he would hire her if she wanted it. He wondered what would his mother, brother, and sister would say when they saw her for the first time. Would they approve? The hell with it, he didn't care.

Chuck had to know more about her, even if curiosity killed the cat. What was the real harm in that? Even if Kelly caught on to her resemblance to Shandi, it was she who had recommended her, so he was covered on that end. Right off the bat, he felt an instant chemistry and comfort with her. Was it just because of her looks? He wasn't sure.

"Hey Chuck, why don't you give Samantha a ride on the golf cart and show her around the place?" Uncle Armond suggested.

"Good idea, Unc."

"That's what I'm here for, Meathead!"

Samantha laughed as Chuck led her over to the garage to get a golf cart. They rode off on their tour, talking about the business of getting the ranch up and running successfully. Like all the women in his life, she had amazing confidence and drive, though he could sense her motivation differed from Kelly's.

A month passed quickly. Kelly was working in the office at the SkyTower when Paige knocked on her door.

"Yes, come in," said Kelly.

"Mrs. Barreto?" said Paige as she entered. "Mr. Karrington is here."

Kelly's eyes brightened. "Oh, send him in, honey."

"Yes, Mrs. Barreto."

Chip walked in with a swagger. "Well, well, Mrs. Barreto, how do you do? And how's married life treating you?"

"I'm doing much better now that you have finally graced me with your dapper self. Thank you very much and married life couldn't be better," she said as she stood and gave him a pouty kiss on the lips. Chip had one arm behind his back. She assumed he had flowers for her. "Well, election night is only a month away, Mr. Senator. Are you nervous?"

"Yes, ma'am. You know how much I would hate to lose," he said sarcastically.

"You got this. I know you're going to destroy Lee."

Chip changed the subject. "Are you staying in the city tonight? Or does hubby want you home?"

"I could tell him I'm working late and stay over at my apartment. He doesn't mind if I do. He's so consumed with his little ranch right now. Why?"

"I have a surprise for you, and maybe a nightcap at your place would be nice."

"So, what's the surprise?"

"I'm personally here to deliver your variance for Gussy's Pitts." He brought his hidden hand out from behind his back and handed her rolled up papers tied with a red bow.

"Oh my God! I love you so much, Chip!" she squealed and kissed him all over his face. Chip drew himself away and walked towards the door.

"I'll see you at your apartment tonight. Ciao, baby!" he whispered.

Not far from Kelly, Jed was in his office in the city. He, though, was not doing quite so well. He also hated losing, and it felt like he was losing ground at every turn with obtaining enough evidence for indictments on The LoneStar Group.

Abby came into his office with more bad news.

"Jed, we still have no clue what happened to Alfred. There is an FBI agent meeting with us later today about his missing person's case. His name is Special Agent Jack Bufford."

Jed looked pissed off. "Any other bad news, Ab?"

"Unfortunately there is more bad than good," she replied. "First, Chester has put in his resignation with us."

"Why?"

"He just says for personal reasons."

"Okay. People do move on. What else?"

"The LoneStar Group is buying up old homes and businesses in the Brodey neighborhood of our fine city. That's on the west side."

"Why? That's a dump. What are they up to?"

"I don't know, but here's something curious. They got variances for a new player, The MoonRiver Foundation, and they're also sharing an office with them over at the SkyTower."

"Who owns MoonRiver?"

"Don't know, but I'm digging."

"What are the variances for?"

"I'm looking into that, too. Felix is out there now trying to get me everything on that."

There was a knock on Jed's office door. It opened and Nick Columbo appeared.

"Hey, Nick, come on in. Abby was just giving me some updates."

"Yeah, that's what I want to talk with you about. Abby, can you excuse us for a minute?"

"Absolutely, sir. I'll talk to you later, Jed."

After she left, Nick began. "Jed, I'll get right to it. The LoneStar Group... we should pull the plug on it."

"Nick, I'm close, trust me."

"You know I respect you, bud, but I hope you're not making this personal because of Alfred. He was into drugs and God knows what else."

Jed was not entirely convinced about that scenario.

"Okay. How's this?" said Nick. "Give it another month, but then we've got to move past this. One month, and then we move on if you have nothing substantial."

Jed reluctantly agreed.

Nick smiled. "Okay pal, and don't forget election night is coming soon."

He left. Jed sat with his mind spinning.

There was a man in an old ass Pinto station wagon at Chuck's homestead gate. The man reached out his window and pressed the button on the intercom to be let inside.

Uncle Armond's voice came through the speaker. "Hello?"

"Yes, hello, I'm John Cockney. I'm here to see Mr. Barreto for the landscaping job here."

"Oh yes, I'll buzz you in. Drive up to the house. I'll meet you outside."

The gate opened slowly and the Pinto drove up to the house. All those who worked there had a code to get in so that Armond wasn't spending his days manning the gate. People with means were already renting stalls for their horses; those folks had codes for the gate to get in as well.

Chuck was at the barn and stables with Samantha, the ranch hands, and twenty-eight horses. It was something else – invigorating, in fact – for everyone working there to see the ranch come to life first-hand.

Everyone on the ranch loved Samantha. She had an easy-going, friendly disposition. She was a superstar at her job and had a knack for helping the others learn, including Chuck. He quickly found out just how little he knew prior to embarking on this journey, but he was loving it. It was so much better than working inside a prison filled with miserable convicts.

Chuck had also hired Stacey's friend Candie, an all-star at working directly with the horses. She was a very hard worker and knew her shit; she really had the qualifications to be a foreman herself. Samantha adored her.

Then there were Chuck's buddies, Mitch, Mike, and Dave Loomis. Dave even ended up loving it so much that on some days, he would work a full day. Samantha helped Chuck hire Amy Potter, whose area of expertise was shoeing, and Andrew Norseman, who took care of the haying. Chuck was happy with the group he had pulled together.

The team alternated general duties every week so that everyone had a hand in the hay growing, cutting, bailing, horseshoeing, grain buying, and feeding. Samantha and Candie dealt with the veterinarians, cleaning horse stalls, riding the horses, and breaking them. As a favor to Chuck, Samantha took charge of the insurance for all the horses.

Samantha was getting ready to lead seasonal trail riding to bring in more revenue. She was also going to show Chuck how to breed their stock of horses. Once all of these avenues were in play, Chuck would need more ranch hands. He was planning on buying at least twenty more horses and hiring more employees once they were more situated.

Chuck and Dave were in the barn bailing hay, while most everyone else was outside or at the stable with the horses. Rupert was also outside, watching Samantha work with the horses she was walking. The dog loved following her around.

Chuck's walkie-talkie went off in his back pocket.

"Chuck, you there?" Uncle Armond called.

"Yeah, I'm here, Unc," Chuck responded.

"You have someone at the house for that landscaping job."

"Okay, thanks. I'm on my way."

Chuck told Dave and Sammy, as he'd become accustomed to calling her, that he'd be back. He jumped in the golf cart. Samantha checked him out as he drove away.

"Hey you!" Candie called to Samantha, snapping her fingers. She looked at Candie. "He's a hunk, yeah, Sam!"

Samantha laughed and waved her hand at her.

Chuck's cell phone rang as he headed back. It was Kelly.

"Hey, babe, how's it going?"

"Really, fantastic, sugar pie! How 'bout you?"

"I'll tell you, it's all coming together like a dream, Kell."

"Good, I'm glad. No one deserves this more than you. Hey listen, I was calling to see if you wouldn't mind me staying at the apartment tonight. I'm working late with a client in the city on a great property sale for us. If you want, you could come out here for the night, too."

"Ah, babe, I'm already exhausted and I have to be up real early tomorrow. Just do me a favor, text or call me when you're locked in safely."

Kelly was pleased that her predictions were yet again correct. "I will, Chucky. Hey, I love you. Don't work too hard. When I get home tomorrow I want some loving from my big, strong cowboy!"

Chuck laughed. "Okay, love you too."

Chuck did not have much experience with a committed relationship, no less a marriage, so infidelity never crossed his mind. He knew Kelly was a very committed businesswoman, and now that their original courtship was over, the mundanities of real life had to resume. It wasn't like that with Shandi, but nothing was like it was with Shandi. She was one in a million.

The golf cart pulled up to the driveway. He saw a scraggly-looking individual standing next to the rusted Pinto and Uncle Armond. He was not judging him; he thought maybe the guy just needed a break in life. Chuck knew what that was like. He gave the man a friendly greeting.

"Hello, I'm Chuck Barreto."

"Nice to meet you, sir. I'm John Cockney."

Chuck invited John into the house for a coffee. Before they got to talking about the job, Chuck asked him where he was from; he looked familiar somehow.

"Have we met before? Did you grow up here in Woodrow?"

"When I was young I went to the elementary school here, then my family moved us out to Connecticut. I couldn't find any work there, so two years ago I moved back here. Just been doing different jobs. Some landscaping here and there on the side."

"Oh. You just look so familiar. Well, John, when can you start?"

John's face lit up. "Really? I can start tomorrow, Mr. Barreto. The only thing is, like I said to your uncle, my lawnmower is in the shop right now."

"No worries, John. I have two brand new mowers you can use, as well as other equipment."

"Thank you so much, Mr. Barreto."

"You're welcome, John. Call me Chuck. I'll give you the code to get in the main gate and Armond will show you around . How's 8:00 AM tomorrow?"

"Yes, sir. Thank you very much."

Chuck left John in the excellent hands of his uncles and thought to himself again, *Yes sir, things are coming together*.

He rode back to the barn and spent the rest of the day working with his crew. Throughout the day, some of the renters came in and out to tend to their horses. After Chuck went home with Rupert, everyone else began to trickle out too, except for Candie and Samantha. A renter had another prospect for Samantha, and she also wanted to go over the inventory for horse feed before she left. She told Candie she was going back to the house to find Chuck before going home.

Samantha took one of the four-wheelers back. Since she started her job, she had not been inside the house. She knocked softly on the front door. There was no answer, so she knocked again. Still no answer. She slowly opened the screen door and went inside.

"Hello?" she called in a low voice.

Armond heard her. He was in the kitchen with Rupert. "Come on in, Samantha."

"Hi, Armond. I was just looking for Chuck."

Rupert ran up to her as he always did, and she knelt down to pet her little friend.

"Just down the hallway, first door on the left. He's down in the basement, Sam."

"Okay... he doesn't mind?"

"Don't worry. The Meathead won't mind."

She giggled and headed for the doorway. When she opened the door, she could hear music playing. It was a song by Don Felder.

"Drive it on up and let's cruise a while/ Leave 'em very far behind/ You can hedge your bet on a clean Corvette/ To get you there right on time/ Now if you're ready to dive into overdrive/ Baby the green lights are on/ It's like you're runnin' away on some high octane/ Every time she reached the boulevard/ Won't you take a ride, ride, ride/ On heavy metal/ It's the only way that you can travel."

When she reached the bottom step, she saw that the large basement contained evidence of Chuck's pastimes. The home gym had pulleys, pull-up bars, racks of dumbbells, benches, and cardio machines. On the other side were guitars, amplifiers, microphones, and a saxophone on a stand.

Chuck was working out on a flat bench. When he put down the weights, he looked over at her and got startled, which startled her too.

"I'm sorry, Chuck. I didn't mean to bother you," she said over the music.

Chuck jumped up and turned the volume down. "Oh no, you're not bothering me at all. You just caught me by surprise, that's all." He smiled.

"So, this is where you disappear to? This is a great space."

"Thanks. You like working out?"

"I love to. It's just I haven't found a good gym in this area yet."

"Sure you have. Right here."

"Here?"

"Yeah, why not? It's close and free and I insist. Consider it part of your employee benefits."

"What about the Mrs.? She won't mind?"

"Hell no. She's not the jealous type. Plus, she thinks you're a godsend here."

"I take it she doesn't work out?"

"Nope. I can't figure out how she stays so fit."

"Well.... Okay. Maybe tomorrow after work. I don't have any sweats with me."

"I got you covered. I'll run upstairs and you can borrow a pair of mine. There's a bathroom down here to change."

Samantha was wearing jeans, work boots, and a white ribbed tank top. Sometimes she wore classic rock t-shirts with cut-off jeans and cowboy boots. All the guys working on the ranch sure appreciated her attire.

"Oh, Chuck, wait. I forgot that I came to tell you about some inventory stuff and a new rental prospect for the stable."

"Okay, hold that thought. I'll be right down."

While he was gone, she walked around and checked out the instruments and equipment. A shelf full of old classic vinyl albums caught her eye. She flipped through some of them to learn more about Chuck's taste. About ten records in, she got to one she never heard of. It was the album Chuck and his band recorded. Samantha saw Shandi on the cover and her eyes widened in shock. She looked at it more intently until she heard Chuck coming down the stairs. Samantha quickly put it back and walked away from the shelf.

Chuck walked in and handed her a pair of gray sweats. "These should do."

"I thank you kindly," she said and gestured towards the saxophone. "You play all these instruments?"

"No, only the guitar, a long time ago. Why, do you play the sax?"

"No, I played the horn some in high school, but I wasn't very good."

"I'm sure you're being modest."

They began lifting weights. Her knowledge of lifting and form impressed Chuck; no wonder she was in great physical shape. As they took turns on different sets with the weights, they were secretly checking each other out. It was clear they had a physical attraction to one another, but they knew that was as far as it went. Chuck would not risk ruining his new marriage nor would Samantha put her job in danger. Chuck enjoyed her company. He invited her to stay for dinner, and she happily accepted.

In the apartment in the city, Kelly was ready for a romantic evening with Chip. She had candles lit and the fireplace going. Wine was poured in glasses and she had gotten some take out from a fancy restaurant. Kelly wore a sexy red nightgown. The doorbell rang and she opened it. Chip was holding a red rose for her. Kelly grabbed his necktie and pulled him inside the apartment.

CHAPTER 21
HOW BOOZE, WOMEN, AND CORRECTIONS RUINED MY LIFE
SEPTEMBER 2002

JED WAS MEETING Abby for an early lunch in a small cafe. The server came over and gave them both a refill on their coffees. They were discussing their next move on The LoneStar Group.

"Ab, I'm running out of time. Nick's going to pull the plug on this endeavor of ours. We're getting serious resistance and experiencing mishaps at every turn."

"We're close, Jed. I know it in my gut."

"So do I. That's why we're meeting this level of pushback. Every time we close in on them, this group finds a way to block us."

"Are you thinking what I am?"Abby asked.

"Yes, I think we have an internal issue."

"Someone in our department is leaking information to them."

"That's exactly right, Ab. And I'll speculate further. I don't believe for one second those drugs found in Alfred's place were his."

"Me either."

"Agent Bufford found nothing about Alfred having any drug connections. He's clean and missing without a trace."

"If we do have someone dirty working amongst us, who could it be?"

"I don't know, but from now on it's just you and me on this. Unless we are giving out false information to throw them off our trail."

"Even your secretary?"

"Everyone, Ab, everyone."

"So what's the next move?"

"I've hired a private detective to help us. I'm paying him out of my own pocket so no one finds out about it."

"Very shrewd, Mr. Ferrari," smiled Abby. "What's his name?"

"Allan Miller."

It was morning on Chuck's ranch and all of the ranch hands were gathered around the corral watching Samantha skillfully break in a young sport horse for a client. Mike, Amy, and the horse's owner were spectating from behind the fences. As they stood close to one another they whispered to each other. The client, Mrs. Santos, loved Chuck's ranch and all of the employees. She told Chuck she was bringing another horse in next week. The ranch was filling up nicely and becoming profitable. If it kept growing at this rate, they would need another barn.

Mike whispered in Chuck's ear, "Hey loverboy, I hear she's working out with you in the home gym after hours?"

"Ha ha, Mikey. It's not like that. We're just friends."

"Right. Friends with benefits?" Mike chuckled.

"You are more than welcome to join us after work."

"Only thing I'm lifting after work is 16 ounces!"

Everyone had their eyes glued to Samantha and the horse. The animal's name was Ranger. She spoke to him softly as they rode and trotted in circles. As Samantha was riding Ranger, he became suddenly disgruntled. The animal began tensing up and grunting. Samantha looked around and quickly discovered the reason. A golf cart came driving up from the main house. It was Kelly, with Uncle Armond driving.

"Chucky!" she yelled out to him.

Upon hearing her voice, Ranger began bucking wildly, trying to throw Samantha off of his back. Chuck and Mike jumped over the wooden fence to help her. She called out to Ranger to calm the beast down, but it was too late. Ranger bucked so hard Samantha lost her grip and flew off his back and into the air, landing in Chuck's arms. Mike lassoed the horse and pulled him in to get him under control.

Samantha looked at Chuck in utter disbelief.

"I gotcha, Sammy!" said Chuck.

"You do? Yes, oh, you do!" she replied, looking flushed. "Thank you."

He gently placed her feet back on the ground. "No problem."

Chuck turned around, surprised to see his wife pulling up on the cart. She had mysteriously come home midday, which was strange.

"Oh gosh, I'm so sorry. Did I cause all that fuss?" Kelly asked as she got down from the cart.

"It's all good!" Samantha answered. But it wasn't. She shot Kelly a look that said otherwise, and everyone there, including Chuck, picked up on it. Sensing the awkwardness, everyone else followed Mike into the barn with Ranger.

"Are you sure you're okay, Samantha?"

"I'm just fine, ma'am."

"What's going on, Kell?" Chuck interjected.

"I'm sorry, babe. I've been frantically trying to reach you."

"Sorry, uh, Sam was trying to break that horse. What's happening?"

"I've got phenomenal news. Your publisher called about the book."

"Yeah?"

"It's already a smash hit and in the top ten of the New York Times Best Sellers list!" she said as she jumped up and down and hugged Chuck. "You're famous, Chucky!"

"Wow, that's great, Kell."

He didn't know how to feel. He initially figured he'd only make a few bucks here and there for it, and that would be the end of his writing career.

"And that's not all!"

Chuck, Samantha, and Armond were intrigued.

"It's not?" Chuck asked.

"No, I have even bigger news!" Kelly raised her voice. "Linda has sold your manuscript to a producer in Hollywood. They want to make a mini-series on television."

"What? No way!"

Kelly jumped up and down again. "Yes way! Only one catch. You need to get on a plane immediately to meet the producer in Los Angeles and sign a deal with them in person."

"What deal?"

"Linda said you'll be attached to the project as a consultant executive producer for this. She says the money involved is significant."

"You're kidding me, right?"

"I'm not. It's true, Chucky."

"Why do I have to leave today?"

"I'm not sure. Linda said they wanted this deal closed yesterday. Babe, you have to strike when the iron's hot on opportunities of this magnitude. Linda is making all your flight arrangements, and she said the Hollywood execs will pay for everything else."

Chuck looked at his uncle and Samantha.

"Chuck, go," said Uncle Armond.

"He's right. You have to go. Don't worry about the ranch. We've got it covered," said Sam.

Chuck looked at his wife. "What about you, Kell? You coming with me if I go?"

"I can't this time. I'm closing two big deals this weekend. You know I would in a heartbeat if I could."

Chuck felt ambivalent about leaving. "What about Jeff? Don't I need him to represent me before I sign anything?"

"Jeff can't either. He's back at my office right now with clients, and they're waiting on me to get back. But you don't need to worry. Linda and her lawyer will be there to assist you," said Kelly, and then she looked at Sam. "Samantha! Would you mind going with Chuck? You have a good head on your shoulders and could make sure everything sounds legit. Maybe keep mister handsome here out of trouble."

"What about the ranch?" Sam asked.

"Candie can run things. She's fantastic, right?" suggested Kelly, always ready with an answer to a problem. "It will only be a couple of days. I'll call Linda and have her make arrangements for one more room and seat on the plane. Okay? It's settled!"

"I'd have to run home for clothes."

"I have a better idea. You look about the same size as me. Let's run to the house and you can borrow some of my things."

Samantha agreed, though still unsure.

"Great! Armond, can you take us back to the house?"

Samantha called Candie on her walkie-talkie to see if she was okay running things for a few days. She agreed.

On the ride back, they spotted John, the new landscaper, a ways away on a large riding lawn mower with his protective headphones on. They all waved at him and he waved back.

Once in the house, Kelly showed Samantha to the walk-in closet in the master bedroom. She told her to help herself to anything while she went downstairs to call Linda to make the extra arrangements.

Linda informed Kelly there was no problem and politely asked her to hurry Chuck up because they had a liaison waiting at the airport for them. Linda was taking a separate flight from New York and meeting them there. They had to be at a Connecticut airport in less than two hours to meet a private helicopter pilot who was flying them to Boston, then they were hopping on a direct flight to Los Angeles.

The idea of flying in a helicopter got Chuck excited; it had been his original dream to fly one in the military, a dream that had remained unfulfilled. Being a passenger might not be the same, but it would be the closest he'd ever gotten.

After they got Chuck's Jeep loaded for the trip, Kelly hugged and kissed Chuck goodbye, excitement radiating from her.

"Samantha, thank you for going with my man," Kelly said.

"You're welcome," she replied curtly. Rupert began barking at Samantha's feet. She petted him. "Be a good boy."

Uncle Armond wished them luck. "Go get 'em, Meathead!"

Chuck laughed. "Okay, Unc, take care of our ranch."

"No worries."

"Don't worry, Mr. Barreto. I'll take good care of everything," said Candie.

"I know you will. Thank you, Can. And please, call me Chuck."

After Chuck and Samantha drove down the driveway, Uncle Armond went back inside the house with Rupert and Candie headed back to the barn. When Kelly felt everyone was well out of earshot, she called Jeff on her cellphone.

"Hey, Kelly. I have the engineers here in your office waiting for you."

"Make them some coffee. I'm on my way back now." She hung up and smiled like she was getting away with the crime of the century.

Conversation flowed smoothly between Chuck and Samantha on the way to the airport. A staff member was waiting to let them through a back entrance out to a sectioned-off area of the runway. When they arrived, they saw an older-looking helicopter occupied by a restless man sitting in the pilot's seat. When the man spotted them walking towards him, he got out to greet them. He was a heavy-set, middle-aged Hispanic man with a friendly aura. Right off, Chuck could tell he was going to like him.

"Welcome, Mr. and Mrs. Barreto. My name is Junior. I'm looking forward to taking you wonderful folks to Boston today."

Samantha giggled and Chuck nudged her in the shoulder, causing her to giggle more. He shook Junior's hand, who helped them with their luggage and into the helicopter. They buckled up. Once Junior got his belt on, he began pressing buttons on the control panel while using the mic to confirm liftoff with air traffic control. He was permitted to take off.

"Here we go!" he said as the helicopter began to ascend.

Junior chatted amiably as they flew. Chuck had the sense that he'd also served in the military. Chuck and Samantha told him about the ranch and the flight they had to catch from Boston going to California because of the book Chuck wrote. Junior was inquisitive about it. Samantha looked somewhat worried that Junior was flying while talking so animatedly, but Chuck could see he was well-seasoned.

The conversation eventually turned to the military, and Junior shared that he had been in the Gulf War in Operation Desert Storm. He flew Apache helicopters and was in the second Battalion, 102 Aviation. Chuck had been right about that assumption. He told him that he had been in Panama, and that after he was injured, his unit wound up in that war, too.

They talked for a while about both wars, then Chuck told Junior he had applied to be a helicopter pilot in the army but didn't get it. Junior told Chuck that it was never too late and that he himself gave pilot lessons over at the Silver Lake Air Force base.

"Oh man, that base is only a few miles from my house. I know it very well," said Chuck.

"Here you go, papi," said Junior as he reached up into his visor and pulled out a card. "I'll even give you a discount because you're a brother and I like you."

Chuck was thrilled. "Really?"

"Yeah, of course. When you get back from Los Angeles, you call me. Of course, I want a free tour and ride on one of your horses," joked Junior.

"Thank you, man. You're on!"

"Hey, you guys like music?"

Samantha and Chuck looked at each other and smiled. "Hell yeah!"

"Okay, right on!" Junior turned a knob on the control panel and music spilled from the speakers.

"Proud drifters choose to stay/ They have lost their direction/ You keep the reason or you throw it all away/ Don't know what it means/ And you find yourself somewhere in between..."

Chuck and Samantha looked at one another and smiled, enjoying the movement of the flight and the company. Chuck found he had the strange urge to hold her hand and kiss her, but refrained. He wondered if she felt the same.

"You two look so in love. How long have you been married?"

"Oh, we're not."

Samantha giggled again. "We're just friends."

"Right," said Junior sarcastically.

The song continued. "Every heartbeat changes rhythm/ Feel that motion it draws you near/ Like a schoolboy studies a prism/ Look through the middle/ Do you see a view all too clear/ So easy to believe/ 'Til you find yourself somewhere in between."

By the end of the song, they could see the airport in Boston. Junior notified the air traffic control that they had arrived. He began setting the chopper down on the tarmac.

"Here we go," said Junior. He gently landed, and an airport employee came out to assist them. Chuck and Samantha collected their luggage and got ready to follow the man to the next destination. They said their goodbyes to Junior.

"Goodbye, Miss Samantha. Nice meeting you," said Junior as he shook her hand and then Chuck's. "Don't forget to call me, Hollywood."

"I won't, thank you."

They were led to the Delta Airlines check-in desk to get the two tickets that Linda had already arranged for them.

"Hmm, yes, Mr. Barreto. I have two first-class tickets here for you," said the clerk. She handed Chuck the tickets. He smiled at Samantha and whispered to her, "First class! Whew!"

Security was far more strict than it used to be. It reminded Chuck of the tragic loss of so many, including his father. Samantha took off her cowboy boots. Chuck could not help but notice how tiny her feet were, just like Shandi's. Oddly, he wished he could see them without socks to see how similar they were.

While they were waiting to board the plane, Samantha asked Chuck if he was going to call Junior for those flying lessons. He said he just might do that. She encouraged him to do so. Then the boarding personnel called for all first-class passengers to come on board.

They walked on energetically together. Chuck had definitely never flown first-class before. They shared a surprisingly good meal and some drinks. They enjoyed talking about everything they had in common, from music to working out to movies to horses. The only thing Samantha stayed away from discussing when Chuck asked her was family. Chuck sensed it right away, so he didn't push it. He figured maybe she had a tough upbringing, and when, or if, she was ever ready to open up about it, she would.

They were buzzed on champagne and Chuck couldn't believe how much he enjoyed her company. When Samantha asked Chuck about being in a rock band, he was also elusive and shied away from telling her because of what happened to Shandi. They talked about how they both loved working on the ranch with everyone. Eventually, the two of them fell asleep in their luxurious seats.

Chuck didn't know how long he had been sleeping, but he heard an announcement that they would land soon in L.A. The armrest between them had been pulled up, so nothing was separating them. Samantha's head rested gently on his right shoulder as she slept. He didn't want to wake her, so Chuck tried not to move. The plane hit a little turbulence when descending, which woke Sam up. She looked up at Chuck, startled, and moved her head from his shoulder.

"Oh, I'm sorry about that," she said.

"No, it's okay. Don't be," said Chuck.

CHUCK AND SAMANTHA had been back from LA for almost a week. It had been another tremendous success for Chuck. Not only was he making money from the book sales, but now he had another stream of income.

Chuck and Samantha had been given the royal treatment, with tours of the film studios and meals at fancy restaurants, all expenses paid. They even met Susan Collins, Richard Hatch, and William Shatner while on the tour. The stories they would have to tell when they got back...

When he, Samantha, and Linda met with an actual Hollywood producer, Kenneth Carlson, Chuck signed on to get his book made into a mini-series. Mr. Kenneth Carlson was very well known to Chuck, as he had created shows like *The Six Million Dollar Man* and *The Incredible Hulk*.

The producer under Mr. Carlson told Chuck if the mini-series did well enough, it could be picked up for prime-time. He said that an actor named Edward Albert might play Chuck's main character and his partner could be played by David Hasselhoff, if they could get him on such short notice. The series was going to be shot quickly; four months was their plan. One of the main assistant producers would call Chuck with updates on the filming of his manuscript, and that was enough to give him a nice paycheck as a consulting Executive Assistant Producer.

Dave was excited when Chuck told him everything because his character was in the book, which would likely mean he would have a character in the series. Dave kept busting Chuck about changing his name because in the book, it was Stew.

"Dude! Why did you name me Stew?" Dave would groan, and Chuck would just laugh at him.

Chuck was so happy to be back home from California and had already taken two helicopter lessons with Junior at the nearby military base. In exchange, he was just finishing up with taking him on his first horseback ride.

Chuck introduced Junior to Mike, Mitch, and Dave. They all got along great, especially Mitch and Mike, as they had the war in common. Junior was a big flirt with the ladies on the ranch, but they all knew he was a harmless teddy bear. Chuck had started calling him Ju Ju Bean, and Junior, of course, called Chuck "Hollywood".

Junior could fly almost any helicopter, but it scared him to death to ride a horse. Amy and Candie did an exceptional job calming Junior down when he was actually on one. After they returned the animals to the barn Samantha came over to say hello. Junior gave her an encompassing hug.

"Hey there, my little peach!" he said.

Samantha laughed. "How was your ride?"

"I don't think horses like me, Sammy."

"Oh that's nonsense. You keep on coming back. How's Chuck doing with his lessons?"

"Oh, let me tell you. Our boy here, he's a natural."

Chuck smiled. "Ah, he's just being nice, Sam."

"Oh no I'm not. He's going to be one of the greats at this. He'll be a pilot before you know it."

"Yada, yada, yada," Chuck brushed him off.

"Hey Chuck, do you mind if I run into town real quick? I have to make a payment in person on my car insurance. It's a little late, I forgot before we left," said Samantha.

"No, not at all, go ahead. We're good here."

"I should be back before our two new possible hires get here." They were hiring additional ranch hands due to how busy and prosperous the place was becoming. The ranch was the talk of the town.

Samantha said goodbye to Junior and walked off. It suddenly occurred to Chuck that her car was a lease. After getting to know her so well in the last few weeks, he had forgotten all about his former investigation.

When she was out of earshot Junior nudged Chuck in the shoulder and said, "Boy, she's crazy about you, Hollywood."

Chuck smirked back at him. "Nah, Ju Ju. We're just friends."

Junior looked at Chuck skeptically. "Right."

When Jed hired Allan Miller, he did not know that Chuck knew him as well. Jed got his number out of the phone book after hearing good things about him through the grapevine. Allan had set up a sting operation on The LoneStar Group for Jed. He had sent a staged proposal to The Moon-River Foundation to see where it led. They knew The LoneStar Group was in bed with this company somehow. They still had little information about who owned or ran MoonRiver.

Allan dropped off his phony proposal to their office in The SkyTower. He put the phony proposal in a long cardboard tube with red caps on both ends. The caps were on for a reason: he wanted to be able to get an easier visual on the object when someone came to retrieve it. After he had it dropped off, he waited patiently outside the elevators of the parking garage wearing dark sunglasses, smoking cigarette after cigarette. He hoped someone would come off one of the elevators with the tube in hand.

Several times he went to his car to sit and then went back to the elevators for another smoke. People kept getting on and coming off, but none of them were holding the tube, until finally a well-dressed woman got off one elevator with a medium-size leather bag of mail – and low and behold – the tube under one arm.

Allan watched her walk to a silver 1995 PT Cruiser convertible. She put her belongings in the car. He ran to his BMW and fired up the engine to follow her. Allan watched from afar, waiting for her to pull out of her parking space first. The cruiser backed out and he slowly pursued her. He followed her until she came to the ticket booth, handed the attendant a ticket, and the barrier was raised for her exit to the main road.

Allan didn't have a validation, so he speedily paid the man, telling him to keep the change. He was only a few cars behind her, which provided plenty of cover for him. She headed north onto the freeway to get out of the city; it was the only way in or out. Allan was damn curious where she was headed. He was dying to call Jed, but he wanted to stay focused on her. He stayed a good clip behind her car. So far she had not noticed she was being followed. After they passed several exits, he realized she was headed to Woodrow.

Allan carefully continued his journey, tailing her through town without her detecting his presence. He saw that she had turned the vehicle's left blinker on to pull into a large parking lot for an office building on the corner of Gussy's Pitts. Once he determined it was safe, he sped up and pulled in at the far end of the lot. He backed his vehicle into a spot so he'd be facing the building to observe which door the young lady was going to enter.

Allan was thrilled that he was making this kind of progress for Jed so rapidly. The mysterious girl got out of her car with her belongings and Allan's dummy cylinder, and she walked straight for the door leading up to The SilverBell Real Estate Company. He snatched his Nikon camera and snapped a few shots of her. Allan smiled to himself. *I'll be a son of a bitch, gotcha!*

He stayed and watched a bit longer. When he was about to leave, another vehicle pulled into the parking lot and parked right next to the PT Cruiser. It was a 1999 Pontiac Sunbird. Allan watched another woman get out of the car. *Wow, she is a vision with her cowboy boots and platinum blond hair,* he thought to himself. He snapped a few shots of her as well. The second woman also entered the door for The SilverBell.

Allan got a strange feeling after seeing her and that car. *Wait a goddamn minute.*

He reached in his shirt pocket, pulled out a little red notebook, and thumbed through the pages. Wouldn't you know it? The license plate was the same one that he had run for Chuck Barreto.

Allan didn't believe in coincidences.

There was a knock on Kelly's office door. She was busy going over her plans for Gussy's Pitts with Jeff.

"Yes, come in," said Kelly.

Paige opened the door. "Mrs. Barreto, I picked up all your mail at the office in the SkyTower." She held Allan's tube in her hands.

"Okay, great. Thank you, Paige. Just put everything down right there."

Paige put the mail on a chair and left the office. Seconds later there was another knock on the door.

"Mrs. Barreto, there's a young lady here to see you," said Kelly's secretary.

"Okay, Stephanie. Please send her in."

Kelly did not know who it was. She didn't have any appointments scheduled. Samantha Dixon walked in and Kelly's face paled.

"Jeff, do you mind giving me a few minutes?"

"Sure, no problem," said Jeff, having no clue who the woman was that just entered. He walked past Samantha and closed the door behind him.

"What in the hell do you think you're doing coming out to the corral like that when I'm on top of a horse trying to break him?" Samantha scolded.

Kelly's skin turned from pale to beat red. "What?"

"You know animals hate you, Kelly Ann!"

"Animals may hate me, but you still love me, right Shalon? Plus, you looked like you were enjoying yourself when my handsome hubby caught you in his big, muscular arms."

"Funny, I don't know if I love you. Better not let anyone overhear you calling me by that name."

"Speaking of that, are you crazy coming here like this in the broad daylight? What's wrong with you? Why aren't you at the ranch keeping Chucky-boy happy?"

"What am I doing here, my dearest sister? I'll tell you. What exactly are you up to with him? Christ, we're not kids anymore, Kell!"

"Shal, I'm not hurting him. Trust me, he'll be fine. I just need you to continue what you are doing, except for sleeping with him. Did you?"

"You have to ask? No, I wouldn't do that. But I just can't do this to him anymore. Whatever you're up to, it can't be good, and Chuck's going to get hurt in the end."

"Sounds like you're falling for him, Shalon."

"I'm not, believe me! He's just a sweet guy, Kell."

"Don't feel too sorry for him, Shal. He's still madly in love with a dead woman. That's the only reason he hired you."

"Thanks, I'm sure. By the way, your husband told me how you two ended up married. Did you drug him in Vegas?"

"What? I would never! How dare you!"

"He told me he had blacked out there, and I remember when we were younger and you used to mess with that old boyfriend's drinks."

"Yeah, yeah, I remember. But that's not what happened. Believe me, it was his idea to get married."

Samantha looked at her sister skeptically. "I don't know how much longer I can do this, Kelly."

"Look, Shalon. Since you brought up Vegas, who paid off all your gambling debts so Daddy wouldn't find out?"

"You."

"Who told me they would do anything to pay it back to me?"

"Me," Samantha sighed.

"Good girl. I promise you it's almost over, and no one is getting hurt on this one."

"I wish I knew exactly what you were up to, but then again I'm probably better off not knowing."

"I'm doing this for all of us, sis. I promise."

Jeff knocked on the door and Kelly told him he could come back in.

"Kell, the engineers and excavators just arrived."

"OK, Jeff, show them in."

Samantha glared at Kelly, then left to head back to the ranch.

Allan was still outside Kelly's office when he called Jed to give him an update.

"Allan, tell me you got something!" Jed answered.

"The decoy I sent to The MoonRiver office was a success. A young lady picked it up and drove it out of the city into Woodrow to The Silver Bell Realtor. I'm in the parking lot now, taking photos."

"Did you say The Silver Bell?"

"That's exactly right. Why?"

"That's Kelly Barreto's place. I sort of know her."

"Is she related to Chuck Barreto?"

"She's his wife. How do you know Chuck?"

"We used to work out at the same gym. And there's a strange coincidence here. Chuck hired me to look up a vehicle's license plate number. He was trying to find out who the woman was, and that very car and woman just pulled into this parking lot and went into the realtor's office. How do you know Chuck?"

"He's a good friend. We used to be partners at my last job."

"Small world!"

"Wow, you're not kidding. Anything else going on there?"

"Yep. A couple of well-dressed men walked in. Oh, wait a sec, Jed. The woman Chuck had me look into is coming out and getting back in her car. A couple of big trucks also just drove into Gussy's Pitts. One of them looked like an excavator."

"Did you find out who she is, the woman?"

"No, only that the car was being leased."

"Can you find out who's leasing it? And any background information on Kelly Barreto?"

"I can. You don't care about doing this without your buddy's knowledge?"

"I'll worry about that. You saw a construction truck drive into Gussy's Pitts just now?"

"Yep, and a regular vehicle too. A Ford Lincoln maybe."

"This whole situation is odd. That land is owned by Chuck and his siblings. He told me they had no plans for that property."

"Maybe they changed their minds."

"Yeah, anything is possible," said Jed.

They hung up and Allan decided to stick around the parking lot for a bit to observe while making some phone calls to see what else he could dig up.

TWO WEEKS LATER, Chuck's landscaper was deep into Chuck's land, mowing with his headphones on. He was watching Chuck and Samantha ride two new horses they had just broken in. John had a bizarre look on his face as they galloped by and waved to him.

Samantha was laughing and egging Chuck on to race the gorgeous beasts. She shouted, "Come on, Chuck, don't lose me!"

"Don't worry about me, girl, I won't. I'm gaining on you!" said Chuck as he trailed behind.

Their friendship had grown stronger every day. He couldn't wait to see her in the mornings. Samantha wanted to tell him everything she was keeping secret from him, but was afraid of the trifecta of losing him as a close friend, getting fired, and betraying her sister. The closer Samantha grew to Chuck, the more her deception pained her.

They led the horses into the stables after their robust ride. Mitch was working inside the barn. He poked his head out, laughing, and said, "Whoa, she beat ya again, Rockstar!"

"She cheats, Mitch," Chuck joked.

"Yeah right, mister. You wanna go again?"

"Ah, I gotta take a raincheck, Sammy."

"Why? You gotta hot date?"

"Nah, I have to sneak out of here early today. I'm meeting Junior for a flying lesson, then I have to get back home to get ready for the election reception I have to attend tonight."

"Ah, I see. When you gonna take me for a ride in the 'copter?"

"I'm a ways away from that, but you'll be the first."

"Don't look so thrilled about going to Karrington's event tonight," Mitch said.

"It's not really my thing, but duty calls. He's good friends with Kelly and my buddy Jed. I'll see you guys tomorrow."

Chuck jumped on the four-wheeler and headed towards the house. Before leaving to meet Junior, he grabbed his old NASA jacket off the driver's seat of the Charger. Junior got a kick out of it when Chuck wore it to lessons.

Jed was in his office working on a deposition for a smaller case when his cell phone rang. It was Abby. He flipped the device open. "Hey Ab, where are you?"

"Jed, can you get your ass down to our breakfast joint to meet me and Allan in an hour?"

"Yeah, why? What's going on?"

"It's better we talk in person for this. The shit is going to hit the fan!"

"I'm on my way."

Jed, Abby, and Allan had been meeting in secret because of their belief there was a mole somewhere in the department. He took it even further by leaving fake documentation around the office and openly having conversations full of false intelligence. Jed had suspected for a while that it was possible his secretary was in on the conspiracy and that she was getting her orders from a higher-up to spy on him.

Sometimes Jed had to laugh it off and say, *My Lord, I'm getting more and more like Chuck- paranoid!* When he and Chuck were partners, Jed always joked with Chuck about how he was overly suspicious and that everything was not a conspiracy. Now Jed thought maybe his buddy had the right idea all along.

He jumped out of his chair, grabbed his jacket and keys, and ran out of the office door. He told his secretary that he had to meet with a client and would return later. As he was sprinting down the hallway, Nick came out of his office.

"Jed! I need a word with you."

Jed turned, knowing that time had passed and Nick was going to pull the plug on The LoneStar Group investigation.

"I'm sorry, Nick. I'm so late for an appointment. Can I talk with you later?"

"When? We got the event tonight! Ah, don't worry, we'll talk soon for sure. I'll see you tonight, right?"

"Absolutely," said Jed and hurried away before he could be stopped again.

Chip Karrington's battle against incumbent Senator Byron Lee would soon be over. The polls were closing within minutes when Chuck and Kelly had arrived at the Sheraton. Did all roads lead back there?

Kelly had acquired a prestige parking voucher which she handed to the attendant in the garage. Chuck wore a black tuxedo. Kelly was stunning as usual in a black, gold-sparkled evening gown that accentuated her beautiful shape. No doubt she would turn heads.

Before they got out of the car, she ran her fingers through Chuck's hair. "Darling, you need a haircut, but I do love it like this. I'll show you how much I love it later tonight."

Chuck smiled at her flirtatious comment.

Once the car was parked, they made their way to the elevators and entered the place he recalled so well. She had her arm wrapped around his as they walked.

The ballroom was even more lively and full of energy than the time Chuck attended with Jed. Chuck remembered that this was also the place he first met Kelly and thought he got his first glimpse of Samantha. He never asked Samantha if that was her or why she had been at the political event.

The main hall was packed with attendees. There were large monitors set up for everyone to watch the numbers come in. Buffets and minibars were spread throughout.

Kelly stopped to talk with a group of people. After she had introduced Chuck, he went to get a coffee for himself and a drink for Kelly at the bar. She surely shined at events like this, but Chuck felt like an idiot poster boy. Even after his recent success, he hadn't fully accepted that this was a world to which he could belong.

Chuck was looking around at all the people, waiting for the drinks he had ordered, when he heard a familiar, obnoxious voice call out. It was Nick Columbo.

"Oooh, there he is! The cowboy, Stephen King, and a married man!"

Chuck turned around. *This asshole again.* At least he had approached by himself so Chuck was free and clear to give him a piece of his mind.

"Excuse me?" asked Chuck.

Nick had a shit-eating grin on his face. "Yeah, your book is becoming a movie and you got a gorgeous lady like Kelly to marry you. Congrats, all-star!"

"Actually, it's being made into a televised miniseries, shit for brains."

Chuck grinned back at him as he walked away. Nick stood there speechless in his wake, unsuccessfully trying to think of a quick comeback.

After Kelly talked with a few more groups of people, she and Chuck made their way over to Chip and Mellisa. They thanked Kelly and Chuck for coming and told them what a wonderful time they had at the ranch. Chip was growing on Chuck, and Chuck was beginning to think maybe Chip would actually be good for the state if he won.

Kelly was talking with Mellisa and Chuck was half-listening to everyone around him. A finger tapped him on the shoulder from behind. He turned, hoping it wasn't that irritable Columbo A-Hole again.

It was Jed. But he wasn't smiling. Chuck knew that look. Something was wrong.

"Hey, there you are. I was looking for you. I just saw your boss."

"Chuck, where's your phone? I've been calling and texting you."

Chuck looked perplexed. He searched for his phone in his pants pockets, pulled it out, and saw there were missed messages. He looked closer at the device and realized why he didn't hear it go off.

"Oh shit, sorry. I had it on silent."

"No, it's fine. But can I talk to you in private?"

"Yeah, sure," Chuck said, confused. He was curious what could possibly be so time-sensitive that he'd need to tell him in the middle of the event. He went over to Kelly and told her he'd be right back, that he had to talk to Jed privately. She greeted Jed and he assured her they wouldn't be too long. She gave Chuck a kiss, and Chuck and Jed headed out of the room.

Chuck didn't have a clue what was going on. He guessed that maybe it was something personal with Jed. They got over to the main elevators and Chuck spoke first. "You going to tell me where we're going, Jethro?"

He was trying to get him to lighten up a little, but that wasn't happening.

"I'm sorry about all this, Chuck. I can't tell you anything just yet. I have to show you."

Chuck became nervous when it suddenly occurred to him that maybe, just maybe, it had to do with Shandi's killer. After all, Jed was a member of law enforcement now.

"Okay, but why are we going to the parking garage?"

"We have to go for a quick ride somewhere. I promise you it shouldn't be too long, and if I'm wrong about everything, I'll apologize afterward. But I have a feeling it will be necessary."

Chuck felt the way he did when Shandi went missing. His stomach intuitively started to feel all knotted up and tense, and his heart beat faster. Once they arrived at Jed's car, he took out his cell phone and called someone.

"Abby, I found him. Can you and Allan meet us at the place right away?"

Jed then hung up, seemingly getting a confirmation. He got in his car with Chuck. They pulled out of the garage and headed towards the highway, away from the city.

"Chuck, I just want to say in advance that I'm really sorry I have to do it like this."

The friends sat inside the vehicle, an unusual, uncomfortable silence between them. Jed took an exit off the highway and Chuck's phone buzzed. It was Kelly, texting him.

Where are you, babe?

He texted her back. *Sorry, Kell, I won't be much longer.*

When he closed his phone, he realized Jed had turned off in Woodrow. He looked at Jed. "OK, I'm trying to be patient, but you got me thinking here!"

"Not much longer, Chuck. Promise."

Jed drove to the far side of town where Chuck seldom went these days, especially being so busy at the ranch. They arrived at the office building outside Gussy's Pitts where Kelly's office was located.

"We're going to my wife's office?" Chuck was completely confused.

"No, we're not," said Jed, not elaborating.

He drove them past the building and took a sharp left onto the dirt road into Gussy's Pitts.

"My father's land."

"I thought it was your land, with your brother and sister?"

"Yeah, well, you know what I mean."

Jed kept slowly driving until Chuck saw a yellow bulldozer parked behind some large mounds of dirt that had been obviously moved by the machine.

Chuck freaked out. "What the fuck is going on here? Who's fucking truck is that on my property?"

"I was afraid of this. You didn't know anything about it?"

"About what? What the hell is going on?"

"It's not good. Unfortunately, I've got a lot more to show you."

"How the hell did Kelly not see trucks driving in here like this, right past her office?"

Jed just looked at Chuck, waiting for him to connect the dots. After driving further into the land, Chuck observed additional spots where excavation had occurred. Then they came to Indians Leap where Chuck had smashed up the Charger. At the foot of the ridge, dead center in the middle, were two other parked vehicles with their headlights still on. Jed pulled his vehicle up alongside.

Abby and Allan Miller were standing together against one of the vehicles' trunks. Jed and Chuck got out of the car.

"This is my associate and investigator, Abby Taylor. She works with me at my office, and of course, you and Allan know each other," said Jed. Chuck skeptically shook Allan's hand and then Abby's. Each held a small leather briefcase.

"Are we all ready for a short climb?"

"Why do we have to climb up there, Jed? I think I'm getting the picture."

"Unfortunately, this is just a smidgen of it all. When we get up there, I think you'll understand a lot more."

"Let's get going then," Chuck said angrily.

Chuck had not climbed the landscape since that fateful night with his car. When they reached the very top, everyone but Chuck was out of breath. Allan and Abby were wheezing, and Jed gave them a few minutes to catch their breath before he continued revealing the truth.

"OK, Jed. Out with it," said Chuck impatiently.

"Chuck, look down the facade of Indians Leap, on this side of the city. What do you see?"

"I see big city lights."

"Yes, but directly below us on the other side of Indians Leap are all low-income apartment buildings and old homes and businesses. Do you remember that land developer I asked you about?"

"Vaguely. Kelly said some Star Group, I think, was interested."

"Yeah, The LoneStar Group."

"OK, yeah, I told her to let them know it's not for sale."

"That's what I needed to know. So, this group has been buying up all the land and businesses in the city alongside Indians Leap."

"I'm not sure what that has to do with me."

"Okay, here it comes… the tough stuff. Abby, can you take over from here?"

"Sure, so Mr. Barreto, ask yourself… why would this developer go out of their way to buy worthless land?"

"I'm clueless. Why?"

"If they got variances and tore down this beautiful obstruction we're standing on, they could build roads right through here. All that property down there would double, triple in price."

"They can't. This is not their land, and everything on this side of Indians Leap belongs to me, my sister, and brother."

"Well… they technically did." She pulled some forms out of her briefcase. "These forms I have are copies from a company that you co-own with your wife. Were you aware of this?"

Chuck looked at it quickly. "Yeah, she said it was a joint venture for us buying and selling homes."

"Okay, we are on the same page then. If you don't mind, when did you sign all these forms?"

"During our wedding reception. I remember signing a bunch of forms for that. Kelly told me that's what it was for."

"So you never really read any of this stuff?"

"No, not really. I just took her for her word. Why? Is anything wrong with it?"

"Not yet, but here's what she did. Do you know her attorney, Jeff Downey?" Chuck nodded and Abby continued. "They used this joint company to buy out the original company that took care of all your business rentals."

"Why would they do that?"

"Our guess... so your brother and sister continued getting their rent checks as usual and wouldn't be any the wiser about what they are up to on this land."

"And what are they up to on my land?"

"Here's where it gets tricky. Kelly also formed another company called The MoonRiver Foundation. Have you ever heard of it? Did she ever mention it to you?"

"Hell no, she did not."

"Well, your signature on the paperwork for that company says otherwise. Next time, read the fine print, Chuck."

"I hate to ask, but what is this MoonRiver company for?"

"Your wife is funneling money from your joint company into that one and using MoonRiver to build and develop on Gussy's Pitts."

"How? It's not hers!"

"It is according to this paperwork here that you blindly signed. In essence, you gave her permission. And that's not all. Her company shares an office in The SkyTower with The LoneStar Group. The same building, as you know, that her other office is in."

Chuck grew pale and looked like he might pass out.

"You alright, buddy?" Jed asked gently.

"Finish, Abby. I want to hear the rest."

Abby pointed at Detective Miller. "Allan's got more bad news."

"Your wife and The LoneStar Group – after they tunnel through Indians Leap or blow it up – plan on building a casino, hotels, and a golf course on this land. LoneStar doesn't own the land, Chuck, but they will own the buildings built on it. That makes you, Kelly, and your siblings all partners to a multimillion-dollar scheme whether or not you want it.

Chuck, I gotta tell you, Kelly is in way over her head. These are bad people- organized-crime bad. If they pull this off, your land will become a new freeway for their misdeeds. Woodrow and the surrounding communities will never be the same again."

"You can stop right there. I'm never going to let that happen! It all stops now!"

Jed recognized the anger in Chuck's face and knew he would stop at nothing to prevent what was underway. "We may need to get protection for you, Chuck. These people will not take this lightly. They already invested in all that land in the city."

"Fuck 'em. They don't scare me. Let 'em come. Is there anything else, Jed?" Jed still had a look on his face that Chuck knew well. "Jed, please. I want to know everything. We're partners!"

"Okay, buddy," said Jed reluctantly. "This is going to suck. Allan show him."

"Chuck, remember when you asked for that license plate number?"

"Yeah, you said it was a lease and then I found out myself who it belonged to. Her name is Samantha Dixon. She's the foreman on my ranch."

"Ahhh, maybe not. When I was looking into this case for Jed, I came across Samantha again. I saw her meeting with your wife, so I did some digging on her too. She actually does not lease the car she's driving."

"Who the hell does?"

"Your wife. And she leased it long before you met either of them. I dug some more. I had Kelly's senior high school yearbook overnighted when I saw them both together." Allan pulled the book out and flipped through the pages.

"Is this your wife?" Allan asked, pointing to Kelly's picture. Chuck nodded and Allan flipped to the section for Freshman. "Is this Samantha?"

Chuck's eyes widened. It was Samantha's picture, only under it was the name 'Shalon Dixon'. He was astonished. "Shalon! That's supposed to be Kelly's adopted sister. Why would they lie to me? Why?"

"I'm guessing, Chuck, she was brought into the game to keep you distracted. She looks a lot like Shandi, doesn't she?"

Jed interjected. "Easy, Allan."

"My apologies," said Allan.

Jed knew Chuck was getting close to his boiling point. "Chuck, maybe you should go stay somewhere else tonight. You know, away from Kelly, so you can think about all this. It's a lot to take in and who knows what she's capable of. She could accuse you of anything."

"Jed, I don't care! Nobody is doing anything to me anymore. Please take me back to the ranch. Right now! Just take me home!"

While Chuck got back into the car, Jed said goodbye to Abby and asked Allan if he could stick around and meet up after he dropped Chuck off at the ranch.

Chuck wore a look of defeat, a look he had often worn when he was about to embark on a path of self-destruction. Sometimes Jed wondered if there was a dark cloud following his buddy. He hadn't looked this depressed since they first met. Jed was extremely worried about the predicament his best friend was in and wanted to put some security measures in place. Even though Chuck wouldn't want protection, Jed was secretly going to make sure he had it anyway. He was going to pay out of his pocket to have Allan watch over him.

Jed didn't think it would be a good idea for him and Kelly to both spend the night at home, but Chuck assured him it was fine. Uncle Armond was there, too. They would be okay. Chuck hadn't said much about what was going on in his head, only that LoneStar would never set foot on his land again. Jed already knew this would set off a chain of events that wouldn't lead anywhere good.

As they drove back to the ranch, it started to rain, thunder, and lightning. When they arrived at the main gate, Chuck gave Jed the code to get in and told him to call him with any updates on the bamboozling bastards. Chuck got out of the car and Jed sadly watched him walk into the house before driving off the ranch.

When he got out to the main road, he called Allan to meet with him and Abby at a diner immediately to plan their next move in protecting Chuck from any harm.

Chuck was drenched from the short walk into the house. He slung his jacket over the kitchen barstool. Uncle Armond was in the living room with Rupert when he turned to say hello to him and Kelly. But there was no Kelly.

"Hey Meathead, where's your better half?" he asked. Armond saw right away that something was wrong with his nephew.

"Arm, can you do me a favor? Can you stay in your bedroom with Rupert tonight? I'd ask you to go to Mom's, but I don't want you driving in this. It's pretty bad out there."

"Yeah, sure... everything okay?"

"No. Nothing is okay! I'm going to have my first and last marital spat. No matter what you hear, please don't come out of the bedroom."

"Okay, I promise." Armond respectfully asked nothing else and took Rupert back to his bedroom.

Chuck debated whether or not to have a drink. Jack Daniels won the debate. He grabbed a full bottle and a glass, sat in the kitchen corner, and began his whiskey therapy. Kelly had messaged him a bunch of times. Since Chuck hadn't responded, she began calling and leaving voice messages. Chuck sent a text back to her. *I'm home. I got sick.*

Kelly's heart dropped to her toes, sensing that Chuck wasn't really sick. She excused herself from the group of people she was talking with and rushed to the parking garage to go home. While she drove back, Kelly repeatedly called Chuck, but he didn't answer. She had a feeling the jig was up, so she began rehearsing her story. Her typically over-confident demeanor was shaken. Until this moment, she didn't realize how much she truly cared for Chuck and wanted to get him to see things her way.

Kelly nervously drove through the rain. *I'll convince him*, she thought. *I always do.*

Chuck swilled his golden-brown whiskey and looked out the wide kitchen window. The storm overhead reminded him of an old Clint Eastwood western. Chuck's brain descended to a dark place. He saw Kelly's headlights pulling up to the house. The chimes went off on the grandfather clock Chuck had inherited from his grandparents. The stage was set.

Kelly got out of the car and ran up to the front porch with a sweater covering her head. She opened the front door and immediately began calling out for Chuck.

He startled her when he spoke hoarsely from the dark corner. "Over here. Did your boy win?"

"Oh, there you are, darling. I don't know, they were still counting votes when I left. Chuck, honey, you alright? You said you were sick."

He just stared at her through the dark. She could still see his green eyes and they had no love in them for her. Kelly went to turn on the lights.

"Leave them off!" Chuck snapped.

"Okay, hon. What's wrong?"

"You're what's wrong!"

"Me? What did I do?"

"What the *fuck* do you think you're doing on my father's land? I told you it wasn't for sale!"

Kelly started to shake. "Chuck, I wanted to surprise you. You're all going to be filthy rich."

"You mean Gary and Stacey? Oh, they are going to be surprised alright! I want you off my fucking ranch, right now! I pulled out your luggage. It's on the bed. Get your shit and get out."

"Chuck, honey, I'm sorry. Please, I don't want to leave," Kelly begged, tears falling down her cheeks.

"No, you're leaving right now!" Chuck yelled. Her apparent sadness didn't move him.

"Chuck, honey, this is my ranch too. My daddy gave us all that money to get started."

Chuck exploded. He stood up and swung his right arm across the kitchen table, causing everything on it to go flying. The whiskey bottle and glass went sailing and smashed against a wall, the ricochet cutting Chuck's right forearm.

"I'll cut you a check right now. I don't want your father's money! The LoneStar Group – and you – will stay the hell off my land!"

Blood began trickling from the cut onto the floor.

"Chuck, your arm!" she said and started walking towards him.

"Don't come near me!" He ripped the sleeve off his right arm and tied it around the wound.

"Chuck, this is crazy. Just let me explain."

"Are you going to explain that Samantha is really your sister? That she was hired by you to distract me?" Chuck screamed at the top of his lungs.

Kelly immediately stopped crying and looked shocked. *There goes my ace in the hole*, she thought. How did he find that out? Did her sister give her up? Samantha *had* been complaining about what she was doing to Chuck… but Kelly couldn't get bogged down with that issue at the moment. She had to quickly figure out a way to change Chuck's mind.

Chuck took Kelly's silence as an admission of guilt. "Kelly, I'm not going to ask again. Go pack and leave!"

Kelly started crying again and walked to the bedroom to gather her things. When she got to the front door with luggage in hand, she pleaded more with Chuck. "Please, Chuck, let me explain."

"Goodbye!" Chuck said, his voice full of wrath.

After she left, Uncle Armond came out of his room to help his nephew clean up the broken glass. He didn't say a word to Chuck about the argument. After hearing everything loud and clear, Armond's heart broke for him.

Chuck told his uncle to hold down the fort and left the house. He went outside in the pouring rain and packed his Jeep with shovels and wooden fencing.

Armond and Rupert watched Chuck take off into the rain. He looked down at the dog and said, "Oh boy, buddy."

Chuck didn't know how much more misfortune he could handle. It seemed like every time something began to go right, something horrible would happen to negate the good. He hadn't been in a dark place for some time now, but he was starting to feel that maybe the darkness would eventually devour him. The anger combined with the whiskey certainly fueled the downward spiral.

Up ahead, Chuck spotted the place where all the trouble started: the Boy Scout camp. Chuck veered off the main road, his tires crunching on the dirt and gravel. He drove around the old brick building and down a small path that he so had years ago run down on foot to his beloved Shandi. The Jeep bounced as Chuck sped over the bumps. He came to a clearing that had been burned into his memory. The wooden dock was ahead. Chuck stepped on the gas. For a second he thought of driving the vehicle right off of it, but he hit the brakes hard and stopped at the foot of the old planks.

The tires sank into the mud as Chuck shut off the ignition. He got out of the Jeep and walked out to the end of the dock. Chuck watched the rain hit the water and lost it. In his rage, he began to shout to the open air.

"Shandi, why? God damn you!" He fell to his knees and wept. He felt cursed.

A voice in Chuck's head told him to look out across the lake. On one of the docks on the other side of the lake, he saw a man wearing jeans and a scarlet red dress shirt standing and staring back at him. Chuck was startled. Chuck squinted, trying to make out who it was.

Yes, of course. It was his father.

"Dad! Dad!" Chuck shouted.

Gus just stood there and looked at Chuck the way he had when he was a boy facing something troubling in life. The stare would motivate his son to stand up and charge the problem head-on. Chuck cleared the rain and tears from his eyes to see his father more clearly, but he was gone. Even though he had vanished, Chuck felt invigorated. He instantly got up off his knees and stood up straight.

Okay, pops. I know what I must do.

Chuck got back in the Jeep and put it in four-wheel drive to get out of the mud. The vehicle climbed back up the narrow, hilly path out to the parking lot and then down the main road. He was on fire now.

Chuck headed towards Gussy's Pitts to put up a temporary roadblock to prevent anyone from getting on his land. Gus and Rita had never blocked the entranceway. They didn't mind the average person going in there to hike, ride, or have picnics. As far as they were concerned, everyone was welcome to enjoy nature's beauty. Chuck would let no one destroy that.

He sped down the back roads with unfettered determination and anger until he reached his inherited land's entrance. After shutting the Jeep off, Chuck pulled out all the wooden fencing and tools he had put in the tailgate. He began digging through the sludge in the pouring rain. He was digging his second hole when a car pulled in behind the Jeep and parked. Chuck was ready for anything. A large man got out of the car and walked towards him. It was Allan Miller.

"Jed told you to follow me, Allan?" Chuck asked.

"Hey, he's worried about you, Chuck. Plus the LoneStar boys can be rough."

"Allan, I'm fine, believe me. And I've got my buddy with me."

"What buddy?" Allan asked, not seeing anyone else.

Chuck turned and pulled up his soaked shirt. Allan saw a nine-millimeter gun holstered underneath. "I never leave home without it- just like my American Express!"

Alan laughed. "I should've known. Jed said you're a wild card. Well, anyway, let me give you a hand. I'm already drenched."

"Thanks. Here's a shovel."

As they dug, Allan kept gabbing, trying to cheer Chuck up. Allan told him that he knew firsthand marriage was tough; he himself had been through it three times.

"I'm certainly not implying, Chuck, that you're headed for the big D. But I know from my own experiences that it's not the end of the world, no matter the outcome. People get through it somehow," Allan said, while also realizing he wasn't helping Chuck's mood. He changed the subject. "So Chuck, what about the equipment already parked inside Gussy's Pitts?"

"That equipment is illegally on my land, so it's mine now."

Alan laughed. "I knew I always liked you."

"Thanks, Allan. I always liked you, too."

After they finished building the temporary barrier, Chuck shook the detective's hand. "Allan, I'm going to my mother's house now if you want to continue following me."

Alan laughed again. "No, I'll leave you alone for tonight."

They got back into their vehicles. Allan pulled away first. Chuck headed for his mother's house to tell her the bad news. He knew she was going to be upset after having willed all the land to Chuck and siblings. As he drove, he turned his radio up loud.

"You wake from a dream/ You step outside/ To find the world is changing/ Under your feet/ Somewhere in the past/ Is the world you knew/ Soon you'll find that freedom/ Is not so sweet/ I can't imagine why you'd throw it all away/ After everything, I've said to you today/ When you turn around to find there's/ No one then you finally realize what you've done/ In the night when no one there no one there at all."

Chuck grew emotional listening to the song, but it fit the mood.

As the track ended, Chuck pulled into his mother's driveway. He saw her lights still on in the living room. She liked to stay up late to watch talk shows. He used his key to get in. As Chuck walked in and quietly announced to his mother that it was just him, so as not to frighten her. Rita was pleasantly surprised to see him, even though it was unannounced and late at night.

"Hey, Mom. You're still up, I see."

"Yeah, I just finished watching the election results. I thought you were there with Kelly."

He stood in the poorly-lit kitchen as he talked to her so she would not see the wound on his arm. "I was, but I had to come to talk to you. How did Karrington do?"

"He won by a lot. He's on his way to the Senate. Now maybe we can get some things done for our state that align with our values and needs."

"Yes, that would be good."

"So, what's going on?" said Rita, sensing her son's hesitation to begin saying whatever it was he had to say.

Chuck explained everything to his mother in detail, sharing with her what Jed told him, from beginning to end. Rita was a tough old woman, and the news only put a fierce fire in her belly. She had helped build half the business in Woodrow with Gus. Rita was ready to do battle if necessary. Chuck's adrenaline grew again from her anger, but he could channel his energy into calming his mother.

"That little bitch! I can't believe she would double-cross our family like that! Chuck, I feel somewhat responsible. She knows me well and we've had so many past conversations about our family," she said, a light bulb suddenly coming on in Rita's head. "Oh my God, Chuck! It really is all my fault!"

"No it's not, Ma. Why would you think that?"

"I was working for Kelly on and off just to keep busy… I forgot, Chuck. I'm so very sorry."

"Forgot what?"

"I showed Kelly a picture of you and told her you were single."

"Yeah, so? You always do stuff like that."

"I know, but the picture of you also had Shandi in it. I told her that Shandi died. And here's the funny part. Kelly then told me she had a friend from high school that looked identical to Shandi. She must have been talking about her sister, Shalon. That bitch. She must have been scheming for some time. She's not getting away with this. I'm so sorry, Chuck. I had forgotten all about that. I should have picked up on it when I first met Samantha on the ranch."

"Ma, it's not your fault. It's all Kelly. She's the culprit here."

"Chuck, you remember that conversation we had before you bought your ranch? That thing you have, the negative anger and your positive side?

Those qualities are what give you the strength to fight back anything that tries to take you down. It's like that old TV show you and your father would watch when you were little."

"What show was that?"

" Ah, you know, Superman. And he got his strength from the sun."

"Wow, I'm impressed," he said. That cheered him up some. "So if that's true, what's my Kryptonite?"

"Your Kryptonite is no doubt women, just like the title of your book."

"Very funny, Ma, but it was Kelly who came up with that title."

"My point exactly."

"Good point. Listen, I was thinking of driving to the beach house tonight to get my head right. I'll be back in a day or two to take care of this mess."

"That's a great idea. But you're not alone in this. Do you mind if I fill your sister in and we find a good attorney to help us with this? Stacey works with a lot of lawyers that could help."

Chuck agreed to that.

"What about Samantha? Your hands-down going to have to fire her, and Candie could take over as foreman."

"Let me deal with her when I get back. She can't harm anything on the ranch. Armond and all my buddies are there. She won't try anything. That's even if she shows up there at all. I'm sure Kelly told her by now. Just promise me you won't do anything rash until I return, Ma."

"I promise. Have a safe ride and hurry back. We have some serious work ahead of us, Chuck."

CHAPTER 24

CHUCK VS. KELLY

CHUCK DROVE TO his parents' beach house in the middle of the stormy night with nothing but the clothes on his back. He felt like he did in the days when Shandi or his father vanished- stripped down. But he was a lot stronger these days, more ready to take on the challenge he had ahead of him. He decided the little drinking bender he just had was over. That's not how he was going to get through this. Chuck had proven himself in the world and built his own small legacy. He would not allow Kelly, a corrupt land developer, or anyone else to take it from him.

During his stay, he took long walks and jogs on the sand, relaxed watching the ocean, and drank nothing harder than coffee.

He had been texting his mother, Jed, Stacey, and Gary to make plans for when he got back to Woodrow. Chuck also texted Junior to let him know he couldn't make his flying lesson that weekend, but he gave him no specifics. The first night there, he got a text from Samantha.

Chuck, I'm sorry you had to find out about me like this. I'd love the opportunity to explain. I didn't know anything about Kelly's plans with your dad's land. If you want me gone, I understand completely.

Chuck didn't know what to think about her message. Half of him wanted to believe her. Samantha had a goodness about her that everyone recognized. It was hard to believe she would intentionally do something so low. He didn't return the text.

Chuck checked in with Uncle Armond and Candie a few more times to see how everything was going on the ranch. No one there knew anything about Kelly or Samantha except Armond. Chuck asked him to keep it a secret for the time being.

After a few days went by, Chuck was on his way home, prepared for the next fight of his life. He was going straight home to change and then he would meet his mother, sister, and Jed over at Gussy's Pitts. While Chuck was driving back, Gary called him and offered to fly out to help. He told his brother there was no need. He had everything under control and would keep him updated.

Chuck pulled into his homestead. Every time he came back from an extended stay elsewhere, he was reminded of how much he'd missed the place. Being on the ranch was like living a perpetual vacation to him.

It was still early in the day when he arrived, and Rita was already texting Chuck to let him know they were all waiting for him. He saw that Samantha's car was in the driveway. Chuck didn't have time for her at the moment. He ran into the house, said hello to Armond, and ran upstairs to throw on a suit, tie, and dress shoes.

When Chuck was rushing back out of the house, Armond noticed he was all dressed up. He was in the middle of devouring a large stack of thick and fluffy french toast with whipped cream marinated in syrup at the kitchen table.

"Whoa, where are you going?" he asked with his mouth still full.

"I gotta get the hell out of Dodge, Unc!" Chuck shouted over his shoulder, jokingly.

Armond looked at Rupert, who was watching him eat.

"Your Papa's so funny," he said to Rupert as he whined for Armond to share his breakfast.

Chuck hopped in the Jeep and flew to Gussy's Pitts with the radio blasting. He pulled into the parking lot at the corner of Gussy's Pitts. He noticed Kelly's Corvette was in the lot. Waiting outside for Chuck were Rita, Stacey, Jed, Abby, Allan, and a woman in her mid-thirties who wore a suit and held a briefcase. Her appearance portrayed that she meant business. He parked and walked over to them as they stood around the hood of Jed's car.

"Boy, oh boy! You clean up nice, especially after the other night," joked Allan.

Chuck laughed. "Thanks."

Chuck gave his mother and sister a hug and shook everyone else's hand. Rita introduced the woman in the suit to her son.

"Chuck, I want you to meet Miss Jessica Farnsworth."

He shook her hand as well and said hello.

Stacey had found Jessica through word of mouth at work. Jed had also heard of her being a barracuda in court, and so they both advised Chuck that she was the right fit. Jessica wasted no time at all. She opened up her briefcase, pulled out some paperwork, and put it on the hood of the car. Chuck signed the retainer agreement she had for him.

Jed suggested to everyone that he and Abby wait outside in the parking lot while everyone else went inside to confront Kelly about what she did. Jessica needed Allan to come inside as a witness. Stacey and Rita insisted on going in to support Chuck in addition to being joint owners.

They entered the lobby and approached the secretary who was flanked by Paige.

"Is Kelly in her office?" Rita asked Paige.

"Yes, ma'am."

"Tell her that her mother-in-law is here to see her!"

"OK, Mrs. Barreto."

Paige hurriedly went into Kelly's office where she sat with Jeff Downing. They were also currently discussing the situation.

"Yes, Paige? I'm a little busy right now."

"Your mother-in-law, your husband, and some other folks are out in the lobby here to see you."

Kelly's face paled. For once she felt unsure of what to do. "Uh, let them in, I guess."

Paige nodded and left the office. Kelly exchanged a glance with Jeff. Chuck and his family entered one at a time.

"Kelly Barreto?" said Allan.

"Yes," she said, appearing stunned.

Allan whipped out some paperwork and handed it to Kelly. "You are hereby served by the Commonwealth."

Kelly scanned it and looked up in disbelief. "Chuck, honey, what's this?"

"I'm divorcing you," Chuck said evenly and sternly.

"Chuck, sweetie, please don't do this."

Rita began to speak, but Jessica put her hand on her shoulder.

"I'm Chuck's attorney. The divorce proceedings will be in three weeks' time. Also in your hands are restraining orders to cease and desist all construction on your husband's land and to pause operations involving the MoonRiver Foundation until the conclusion of the hearing. If you agree right here and now, you can continue to conduct your business as a realtor, and your husband can run his ranch until we meet in court."

"Chuck, I don't understand. Why are you doing this?"

Rita exploded, unable to contain herself any longer. "You have some nerve, Kelly, to try and swindle my children's land right out from underneath them! We trusted you. How dare you do this to my son, to our family!"

"Rita, please, it's not how it looks. Let me explain. It's all a big misunderstanding," Kelly pleaded.

"No, it's no misunderstanding! We loved you like family and you got greedy, you lying, cheating bitch!" Stacey fumed.

"I wonder what else I'm going to find out about that you and Jeffrey have been up to behind my back," Chuck mused.

"Chuck, I swear I didn't do anything to hurt anyone. I love you."

"I'm sure you'd say anything right about now," retorted Chuck.

"You've got a real funny way of showing your love!" Stacey shouted.

"OK, Miss Farnsworth," Jeff interjected. "I'm Kelly's attorney and we will agree to the terms until the hearing."

"So, you're the one who assisted in doctoring up all these absurd companies to funnel monies from the Barreto family to join with The LoneStar Group?"

"I'm sorry, but any further discussion we have about the subject will have to take place in court."

"You will be sorry, Mr. Downing, that you've engaged in this illegal business. We are ordering LoneStar to remove all equipment from Gussy's Pitts or it will be impounded, effective today. The attorney general's office will also be serving them today with indictments for being on the land illegally. Have a nice day," Jessica concluded and left the office, the family following suit.

"You'd better not put one toe on that land again!" Rita said over her shoulder. Kelly started to respond, but Jeff shook his head at her.

Kelly was uncharacteristically feeling unsure about her future with Chuck and her plans with LoneStar. Jeff assured her once her husband cooled down a little, it would work out somehow. He told her every scenario in life was only temporary.

"What if he doesn't calm down?" Kelly questioned.

Jeff told her if that happened, he would use all the tools in the toolbox to protect her against Chuck and his family.

Jed and Abby were still in the parking lot, waiting to see how it went. Everyone except for Allan agreed to drive over to a nearby restaurant for lunch and a debrief. Before they left, Stacey pulled some "No Trespassing" signs out of her trunk to attach to the barriers Chuck and Allan had put up. Chuck nailed them in with Jed's help.

At the restaurant, they discussed their next steps while they ate and decided to regroup in a few days to talk about any further developments. As they said their goodbyes in the parking lot, Jessica assured Chuck, Rita, and Stacey the case would end up being a slam dunk. Jed told Chuck he'd be checking in with him daily to Rita's profuse thanks.

"Your son will always be my partner," said Jed.

Rita gave Jed and Abby each a big hug before they left. As Chuck was getting in his Jeep Rita hugged him, then grabbed him by the shoulders. "Now get that other nutjob off your ranch!"

It was early in the evening already when Chuck drove home. He was fairly sure everyone had gone home for the day, even Samantha. Although a lot was happening with his soon-to-be ex-wife, his current focus was on what to do about her. He was in the dark about how much she knew or was involved in the scheme. Why did she change her first name? Why lie about it? Could he ever trust her, period?

Chuck sensed she wasn't like Kelly in nature. He felt very close to Sam and not just because she looked identical to Shandi. She had a giving persona and asked nothing in return from others. She was the complete opposite of Kelly when it came to money; it wasn't what motivated her. Kelly was a dedicated capitalist and, on a level, Chuck understood and respected that. His father always said, "Money makes the world go 'round, Chuck." But there was a line Chuck wouldn't cross in order to achieve success; he wouldn't hurt others to get what he wanted.

Chuck also felt indebted to Samantha; if not for her, the ranch never would have fruitioned into what it had become. She shaped the whole place almost single-handedly. Samantha showed Chuck how to ride, manage horses, and the ins and outs of running a ranch. She trained almost all the people working there. If Chuck believed her – and that was a big if – Rita and Stacey would not be so easy to convince. When he summed it all up, it would be easier for him to wash his hands of her as well.

When Chuck pulled up to the main gate, his landscaper, John, was just leaving for the day.

"Hello, John," Chuck waved.

"Nice to see you back, Mr. Barreto," said John.

"Thank you. We'll see you tomorrow."

Chuck wondered what the staff would think when they eventually found out the whole truth about the separation from his wife. As Chuck pulled up to the house, he noticed Samantha's car was still there.

Just great. I was hoping to avoid this tonight. Well, I might as well get on with it and be done with her, too, Chuck thought.

He reluctantly got out of his Jeep and loosened up his tie. The last few days had reminded him of working the block with Jed when they had to put on their game faces for confrontations. They had reminded him of the days and nights in the jungle with his unit in Panama when they prepared to face potential guerilla warfare.

Chuck opened the front door and walked into the kitchen. He heard the television on in the living room. He looked over and Uncle Armond was on the couch munching on an enormous cinnamon bun with Rupert sitting by his side, whining for his share. The dog jumped off the couch and ran to his master to greet him.

Chuck bent down to pet him and said to Armond, "Wow. Nice dinner, Unc."

"This is my dessert. I just ate a Hungry Man TV dinner," Uncle Armond said through a mouthful.

"Nice, Arm, very nutritious!"

"Hey, I'm clearly a pillar of health."

Chuck laughed, then whispered, "Where's Samantha? Still at the barn?"

"Ah, no. She's downstairs working out."

*OK, here we g*o, Chuck thought, and started walking towards the basement door.

"You want me and Rupert to go to my bedroom?" asked Uncle Armond sarcastically.

"Thanks, Unc, but no. You guys are fine."

Rupert ran back to Armond to beg for food as Chuck headed to confront Samantha. As he walked down the basement stairs, he heard music playing. Usually it was classic rock that was playing, but this time he heard a song from the album that he, Shandi, and the boys had recorded. He could hear Samantha trying to sing along with Shandi's beautiful vocals. Chuck guessed she must have gone through his vinyl record collection down there sitting on the shelf and put it on the turntable.

"Observe the sky, it is crying/ Tears that never end/ The world seems to be passing on around me/ The absence of you hurts/ You so matter to me, that's why baby/ To me, you still matter/ That's what I have to get by it all/ Yes, you will always matter to me," Samantha sang with Shandi.

When Chuck turned the corner at the very bottom of the stairs, he grew enraged. Samantha wasn't working out. She was standing in front of a workout mirror and singing along to the record while looking at herself.

"What the hell do you think you're doing?" Chuck yelled.

She turned around, crying. "What? This is what you wanted! I could be her for you!"

Chuck angrily walked over to the stereo and hit the record arm across the record to stop the music. There was a *scratch* and then just the sound of the album turning. Chuck grabbed her arms firmly but gently and said to her, "That's not what I want, Sam."

"Well then what, Chuck? What?" Sam said, tears falling down her cheeks and into her mouth.

"You're so damn fucking clueless! I want *you*, Samantha! Not Shandi, not Kelly. *You*, Sam!" Chuck said, his face turning red and fighting back possible tears of his own.

Sam began crying more. In the excitement, her pinned-up hair came undone and flowed over her shoulders. Chuck put his hand behind her head; they could no longer fight it. He pulled her head forward so that their lips met. They began to kiss, with her tears of happiness wetting his face.

After a few minutes of embrace, their bodies were in agreement about what was to happen next. Chuck heard his father's voice in his head, *Two wrongs don't make it right, son!* He ignored the warning.

"Why don't we go to my place, Chuck?" Samantha whispered in his ear.

"I can't wait that long. Stay right here for a minute."

Chuck tip-toed up the stairs. He quietly opened up the hallway linen closet and grabbed some blankets. When downstairs Chuck grabbed Samantha's hand and led her outside through the bulkhead. They walked around the house to the garage and climbed onto the golf cart. Samantha sat practically sat draped across his lap as he drove toward the barn. Her mouth searched his face and neck, and he returned what he could while trying to keep his eyes on the road. He had secretly wanted to taste her lips since they met.

In their passion, Chuck wasn't paying attention as well as he should have and he almost drove the cart into a ravine.

"Watch out, Chuck!" Samantha cried. He rapidly turned the steering wheel and drove across the bridge going over the ravine. They looked at each other and laughed.

"Where are we going?" Samantha asked.

"Up in the hayloft. It's quiet and secluded. No one to bother us but the horses down below. Are you good with that?"

"What do you think?" she said as she kissed him.

He walked around the golf cart and met her, only to pick her up in his arms and carry her into the barn. He climbed the spiral staircase leading up to the loft.

As they were reaching the top a thought came to his mind. *Boy, was my mother right! Women are my Kryptonite.*

When they reached the top, he put her back on her feet and together they spread blankets over the hay.

"Hey... you're not doing this just to get back at Kelly, are you?" she asked timidly.

"That never crossed my mind, Sam. I've been in like with you since the first time I laid eyes on you. How about you? Are you trying to get even with your sister?"

"Get serious," she said and grabbed the tie hanging around his neck, pulling him back to her lips. Samantha pushed him down onto the blankets and climbed on top of him. She paused in kissing him and reached over to turn on a small radio that was sitting on a ledge. They undressed each other as the music played. The moonlight shone through a large triangular barn window.

"C'mon and hold me/ Just like you told me/ Then show me/ Why don't we steal away/ Why don't we steal away/ Into the night/ I know it ain't right/ Tease me, why don't you please me/ Then show me/ What you came here for..."

If Chuck wasn't a wolf, he sure made a good impression of being one; his hunger for her was insatiable. Samantha dug her fingers into Chuck's muscular back in pleasure, her body fitting his like a glove. They made animalistic love into the evening.

Samantha looked up over Chuck's shoulder, saw the deep blue night sky, and swore she could hear a choir of angels singing to her. Samantha moaned with unrelenting pleasure.

"You're killing me, Chuck! You're killing me!"

"You want me to stop?" he whispered to her.

"Don't ever stop, Chuck," she moaned. "Please, never!"

"OK, Sam, I never will. Never!"

Samantha couldn't believe her sister would have ever taken a chance on losing him. But that was Kelly. She always wanted more.

After they made love for what seemed like hours on end, Samantha got up to stretch her arms and legs. She walked over to the beautiful barn window in the moonlight, naked, with her back to Chuck. She looked over her shoulder as she stretched and saw Chuck smirking at her.

"What?" she asked.

"You know that in that moonlight, you have a gorgeous rump!" said Chuck.

"What did you say?" she laughed.

"You heard me."

Samantha giggled and joined him back on the blanket. They went for another long round of lovemaking. Once more, the radio played.

"Stranger in the mirror/ I was just somebody else/ Stoned into the/ Night so lost that I/ Didn't even know myself/ You came out/ Nowhere just in time/ One more minute I'd/ Have lost my mind/ There was something/ 'Bout the way you looked at me/ Shut the door on/ Everything I used to be/ I found myself in your arms/ Now I don't wanna/ Know a world without your love/ Nothing that you/ Could ever be in love, yeah/ You are the one, you are the one all along."

Afterwards, they lie holding each other, staring out into the beautiful night. Samantha's head rested on Chuck's chest.

"Chuck, your heart is beating a thousand times a minute."

"That's my Portuguese blood, Sammy."

She softly punched him in the chest.

"You better stop making fun of me, you," she said and then paused. "OK, confession time, Chuck. My real first name, as you found out, is not Samantha."

"I know, Shalon, but I like Sam better."

"I owed Kelly a big, big favor, so she asked me to come here and work on the ranch. That's all. Not to trick you, not to tempt you. Definitely not to sleep with you."

"Why?"

"I'm a lot of things, Chuck, but I'm not a liar. I don't know. She said to work here and get the place running properly for you, and to not tell you about us being sisters. I knew it was wrong, but at the time I didn't know you, and she swore to me that you weren't going to be harmed in any way. I knew nothing about your dad's land, I swear. I didn't even know you owned it."

"Why change your name?"

"I did that long before I met you. I got into serious gambling debt with a boyfriend. He left me after using me for my money. I had loan sharks trying to find me, so I changed my first name. Kelly stepped in and paid off my debts and got me set up out here. She leased me a car, found me an apartment. And then this job. I desperately didn't want Vic to find out about any of this, so I agreed to help Kelly in return.

I didn't want to do this once I got to know you. I went to her and told her I couldn't lie anymore when we got back from California. But Kelly insisted it wouldn't be for much longer, whatever she was up to. Then I could do whatever I wanted. As you know, my dear sister can be pretty persuasive."

"That she is," admitted Chuck.

"Trust me, now that I know what she's been up to, I won't let her touch your father's land or this ranch. If I have to, I'll go to Vic and he'll intervene for sure. Believe me, she doesn't want our father getting involved."

Chuck sat quietly, thinking about everything she had said.

"So where do we go from here, Chuck?"

"This is where. Sometime tomorrow, you go get some of your things to stay here at the ranch with me."

"Chuck, that might cause even more problems for you."

"Sam, things from here on out are going to get rough. Kelly got us involved with some bad men. I don't want to be worried about your safety, too. I have a spare room in the house. Please do me that favor?"

"Okay... but will you promise to visit me in the middle of the night?" she asked, smiling at him.

"That will be a requirement."

They smiled at each other and settled back into each other's arms, again getting lost in their passion.

It was morning at the ranch and Mike always got there early to start his day. He supposed it was part of being an ex-military man. He opened the big barn doors to get some saddles down from the hooks on the wall. Mike wanted to polish and inspect them thoroughly. Chuck and Samantha were still up in the loft sound asleep when they heard Mike rummaging around in the barn. They both quietly woke up, startled, and realized they overslept after being up most of the night.

Chuck laughed quietly and whispered, "Fuck, Sam, I think that's Mike down there!"

Samantha giggled. "C'mon, Chuck, get dressed."

They got dressed in a hurry and still looked slightly disheveled. Chuck tripped trying to get his pants on.

"Shit!" said Chuck.

Mike heard the stumble and was alarmed.

"Who's up there?" Mike yelled.

"It's me, Mike. I'm just straightening some stuff out up here."

"Oh. You're up early, Chuck."

"Yeah, couldn't sleep."

"Where's Sammy? I saw her car here already."

Samantha smiled at Chuck as he cringed. "I'm up here, helping Chuck."

Mike smirked to himself; he had suspected something would develop between them. They came down the spiral staircase. Chuck saw Mike's face and smirked back at him.

"We were just fixing up the loft."

"Right," Mike said.

"Oh, stop that, you big lug!" she said and hugged Mike as he raised his eyebrows at Chuck. Chuck just shook his head at him.

Samantha went to feed the horses while Chuck had a private word with Mike, then Chuck met Sam in the stables.

"When will you go get your things, Sam?"

"After work tonight, sound good?"

"I was wondering if you could go sometime this morning. Candie can hold the fort down."

"Sure."

"One more little favor. I'm going to have Mitch go with you once he gets here. I would, but I'm going to meet with my mother real quick. And probably Jed. Then I'll be back."

"Why do you want me to bring Mitch?"

"I have an uneasy feeling about this mess Kelly got me into. I'll feel better knowing you're not alone."

Chuck was afraid of losing her the way he lost Shandi, but he didn't want to tell her that. She agreed to let Mitch tag along with her.

It was still early when Jed walked down the hallway to his office. Nick caught his attention and asked him to come into his office for a minute. Jed had a feeling it would not be a friendly conversation. When they entered, Nick told Jed to sit down with a gloomy tone.

"You tried sending out indictments on that LoneStar Group? I stopped them from going through," said Nick, clearly irritated.

"You did? Why?" asked Jed.

"You didn't think to consult me first?"

"I was going to, but this was an emergency."

"There's no emergency here, Jed. These guys are in business with your pal Barreto and his wife, and she's divorcing him so their land project is frozen."

"No, that's not true. *He's* divorcing *her*, and LoneStar used Mrs. Barreto to try to obtain and destroy Indians Leap so they can develop all that land."

"Whatever the case, this office is not – and I repeat, *is not* – getting involved with your pal's marital dispute. End of story!" Nick chuckled. "I always knew that guy was a little tapped in the head."

"Excuse me?"

"Chip's going to D.C. in four weeks. I don't need a scandal, so I'm giving you a three-week suspension with pay."

"What? Are you kidding me?!" said Jed, furiously.

"No, I'm not. If you decide not to return, I'll understand. But if you do, nothing in your office will happen without me being notified first. So take the time off to think and retool."

Jed decided not to go any further and argue with him. Something already ticked him off enough. Jed agreed and left the building after getting some things out of his office.

Kelly was working from her office at The SkyTower. She wanted to stay out of town for a while; Paige was running things at the other office for now. She was banking on getting Chuck to miss her. He'd come running back to her and she'd get her way in the end. After that last ugly scene in town, she also wanted to avoid Rita and Stacey.

It was still early when Kelly's secretary came into her office to tell her The LoneStar Group gentlemen were in the lobby on an unannounced visit to see her over an urgent matter.

Kelly knew exactly what it was about.

She wished Jeff was with her, but he hadn't arrived yet. She signaled her secretary to show them in. Kelly immediately composed herself so that she would appear to be in control of a situation that she wasn't so sure she was in control of.

Silus and his typical entourage of men entered her office. Kelly got up, gave him a small smile, and shook his hand.

"Welcome, Mr. Kobol, so glad to see you again. What brings you here bright and early this morning?" she said, hoping how frightened she felt in her gut as she looked at this ominous man and his band of thugs didn't show on her face.

"We're not here for pleasantries, Mrs. Barreto. I'm here to find out why the construction has halted on Gussy's Pitts. Why are we not currently taking down Indians Leap?"

"Mr. Kobol, I assure you it's only a slight hiccup. I had a tiny disagreement with Chuck about something. We will be back to full speed in no time at all," Kelly assured him.

"Disagreement? Is that why your husband has filed for divorce? I'd call that a huge problem, not a hiccup!"

"Like I said, Mr. Kobol, it's not a problem ...."

Silus interrupted her. "We have many investors involved in this project. You signed contracts and we can't wait for your domestic problems to play out. Every minute creates a monetary deficit. You have one week to fix this," he threatened.

"I may need a little more time than that," Kelly said as she smoothed out her shirt.

"Sorry, Mrs. Barreto. One week. Good day. We'll be talking soon."

Silus and his men turned and left the office. Kelly's face was flushed. She slammed her fist on her desk in frustration.

It had been a long day for everyone except for Chuck and Samantha. They couldn't wait to be alone again to recreate the magic they had the night before. During the day, Samantha had successfully gone to her apartment with Mitch and brought back some belongings to stay at Chuck's ranch.

Uncle Armond was downstairs with Rupert pondering ordering takeout from a pizza joint in town. Chuck had only told Armond that Samantha was moving in the spare bedroom upstairs temporarily and that's all he knew. Armond would always ask his nephew if he wanted anything before he called food in, so he went upstairs to Chuck's bedroom and knocked on the door. There was no answer. Suddenly Samantha came out of the bathroom wet and wearing nothing but a bath towel.

"Oh, Sam," Uncle Armond said, slightly embarrassed. "I was looking for Chuck to see if you guys want any food. I'm ordering from Woodrow Pizza."

Chuck heard his uncle talking from where he was waiting in the spare room under the covers for her. Chuck yelled to him, "No thanks, Unc."

Armond always rolled with the punches. He turned around and went back downstairs without a comment.

Samantha went into the room and looked at Chuck, giggling. "You think he knows?"

"Oh yeah. Well, get over here, sexy lady," said Chuck.

She dropped her bath towel and jumped on top of him, kissing him vigorously. They seemed to have an endless amount of energy. After another marathon of mingling their bodies, they again lay exhausted.

"Oh! There goes that Portuguese blood again pumping through your heart for me," she said as her head rested on his chest.

"You're so damn cute, Sammy."

"You're not so bad yourself. So, how was your day?"

"Where to begin... Junior called me and gave me heck for skipping my helicopter lesson. I have to go tomorrow for sure."

"What are you learning?"

"How to land."

"Sounds like a lot of fun."

"It is. You wanna come?"

"Ah, maybe another time. It's too soon. How did it go with your mom?" Sam asked.

"Better than I expected. I think she's coming around to the idea that you would be on our side if Kelly decided to fight me in court. Don't get me wrong, she's still skeptical, but I think she'll be fine."

"You didn't tell her about us being together, together?"

"Hell no. Baby steps. Oh, you know my buddy Jed, from the prison? He works for the Attorney General?"

She nodded.

"He's the one who found out about your sister and The LoneStar Group trying to swindle me. He was suspended today and his office is not going after them any longer."

"What?!"

"Yeah, that's how powerful these guys are. That's why I sent Mitch with you."

"Don't worry, Chuck, I won't let Kelly go any further with this. I had Mitch drive me to her office today in town, but I guess she was in the city. I left her several messages."

Chuck kissed her on the cheek. "I got a fucked up phone call from my little brother. He's changed his tune about selling Gussy's Pitts. He thinks we should listen to LoneStar to see what their offer would be."

"What did you tell him?"

"I told him not a chance. My brother unfortunately doesn't care about what impact that would have on our town and all the surrounding ones. Gary and his girlfriend only have dollar signs rolling in their heads."

"Can he sell his portion?"

"Absolutely. But it's my portion that includes Indians Leap, which is the largest obstruction for building. I will never sell it to them. That rock stays right where it is while I'm alive! Sometimes it feels like it's almost a curse that we inherited this land."

"I have a feeling it will all work out," said Samantha.

"I hope so, Sam. Having a gorgeous woman lying naked with me is a good start."

Sam laughed and rolled her eyes. After a brief pause, she said, "Can I ask you something serious? Do you feel guilty about being with me like this?"

Chuck was silent for a moment, collecting his thoughts. "You know, it all happened so spontaneous-like, but now that I think on it all... yesterday when I was carrying you up to the loft, for a second I thought, I'm about to break my wedding vows that I don't even remember saying because I was blackout drunk." He pauses again. "So, for that second, I thought I'd be riddled with guilt during our lovemaking. But we made love and the guilt never came. And when Mike woke us up in the morning, I felt fantastic. Happy. Elated. How 'bout you?"

She smiled at him. "I never would've thought I'd do this to Kelly, but now that I did do it, I do not feel one bit bad about it either. She deceived us both - and that's not why I'm sleeping with you. I'm making love to you because I couldn't resist you any longer." She rolled back on top of Chuck. "Are you ready to go again?"

He gently put his hand on the back of her head and let his body give her an answer.

Chip Karrington was up working late on speeches for D.C. in his study when his wife came in to hand him the cordless phone.

"Chip, honey, you have a phone call," said Mellisa. She was used to getting phone calls at all hours due to Chip being a politician.

"OK, thanks hon." He took the phone from her. "Chip Karrington, here. Yes, what can I do for you, Mr. Kobol?"

CHAPTER 25

ONE WEEK LATER
OCTOBER 2002

IT WAS HIGH noon at Chuck's flourishing ranch. He had more horses coming in and almost fifty new clients. Chuck hired more ranch hands and gave everyone raises. There was an influx of clientele shelling out big money in order to take advantage of what the facility had to offer. His place was becoming the talk of the county. If it wasn't for Allan's men doing security checks on the grounds, Chuck would forget he was about to get a divorce and sue The LoneStar Group.

John was on a riding lawn mower mowing away. He had noticed a security guard walking the ranch on foot communicating with others on a walkie-talkie.

Samantha was out with clients riding horses, while Chuck, Dave, and a new hire were all working in the barn when Uncle Armond called Chuck on the walkie.

"Hey, Arm, what's up?"

"Ah, Chuck... the newly-elected Senator Chip Karrington is here at the main house. He wants to know if he could talk with you if you're not too busy."

Chuck couldn't believe Chip was at his house. He was damn curious as to why.

"Unc, ask the good Senator if he wouldn't mind meeting me out here at the barn."

"He said no problem."

"Could you drive him out here on one of the golf carts for me?"

"Will do," said Uncle Armond, and Chuck clipped the walkie back to his waistband.

"Fancy man's coming here, huh?" said Dave. "Speaking of fancy men, where's Mike been this week?"

"He said he had some personal things to take care of," said Chuck. "I didn't ask for specifics. He'll be back when he's back."

Chip's limousine was parked in the driveway and he was flanked by security, all paid for by the Commonwealth. He asked his men to wait by the limo. Armond got the golf cart for the Senator and they got in. As they drove towards the barn, Chip told Armond he was going to miss being in his state full-time.

Chuck heard the golf cart pulling up to the barn, so he went outside to greet Chip.

Chip got out, smiling. "Wow, Chuck, this place gets more beautiful every time I visit. It's the talk of the town and I can see why. You're doing really well here. Congratulations."

"Thank you, and congratulations on your victory as well," said Chuck. "This is quite a surprise visit, Mr. Karrington. What can I do for you today?"

"I'm leaving for D.C. soon, Chuck. I've come here today to ask you about your land on Gussy's Pitts. The development of that valley would bring in thousands of jobs and various other forms of prosperity for the folks of Woodrow. Just like what you've done here, only on a much bigger scale."

Chuck's friendly disposition changed quickly. Uncle Armond heard the turn in conversation and thought to himself, *I better stick around for this one.* Dave was attentively watching from inside the barn.

"Well, well, well!" Chuck said, angrily. "I was wondering when Lone-Star's cockroaches would come crawling out at me. I must admit, I never thought it would be you."

"I do not know LoneStar, Chuck. I only know a lot of folks could benefit from – "

Chuck cut him off. "Right, I'll speed this up for you, Senator. Get the hell off my ranch."

"I'm sorry, Chuck. I did not intend to come here and upset you. I'll leave now. If your Uncle wouldn't mind driving me back to the house..."

Chuck gave Chip a cold stare in response. The Senator got on the cart with Armond and then said to Chuck, "Just think about it is all I ask, Chuck."

"Yeah, you know what? Tell my soon-to-be ex-wife I said nice try," replied Chuck.

"I don't know what you're talking about. Anyway, have a nice day. Sorry to bother you."

Chuck continued to stare at him with hard, dead eyes as they drove away.

Jed and Allan met at the entrance of Gussy's Pitts, as they had been doing in secret, blatantly opposing Nick's direction to Jed.

"Jed, something terrible is going down," warned Allan.

"What do you mean?"

"Notice how they pulled out all their construction equipment off this land without one word or argument?"

"Yeah, and?"

"I've got really good informants out there, guys who have been snitching to me for years, and no one is talking about this. And I mean no one! It is highly unusual that I can't get even one person to talk."

"You got men on Chuck's ranch?"

"I've got one man there now and I'm headed back there as soon as I'm done here with you. I'll have two men working in shifts there starting today."

"OK, good. Let me cut you a check right now before you go."

"No Jed, you're all set. I'm officially on Chuck's payroll now."

"What? How did that happen?"

"He doesn't want you attached to this, especially with you being on suspension. He doesn't want there to be any paper trails leading back to you. In essence, he's concerned that a misstep will get you fired and we can't afford that. We need you in that office."

"Don't worry Allan, I have his back, even if I have to get fired over it."

"You guys really were partners in every sense of the word, huh?"
Jed's eyes were intense looking back at him. "Yup."

. . .

Kelly paced frantically in her apartment. She gave Jeff a call and vented to him. She went out onto her beautiful enclosed balcony overlooking the city where she first made love to Chuck.

"Jeff, sorry to call you so late, but I have an awful feeling about everything. LoneStar will not return any of my phone calls and they told me I only had a week to figure this out. That was yesterday."

"Kelly, that's all malarkey. Nonsense. That's how these types play."

"I don't know, Jeff. You weren't there with me."

"Kelly, I'll get a hold of them first thing tomorrow for you. I want you to relax, okay?"

After they hung up, Kelly's anxiety only heightened as she sipped a glass of wine and continued to pace around, thinking paranoid thoughts.

Chuck was in his kitchen packing items into a picnic basket while Armond and Rupert were contently in the living room watching television. His Uncle was engulfed in chewing vigorously on a box of Russell Stover chocolates as the TV played an old John Wayne movie.

"Whatcha watching, Unc?" asked Chuck.

"The Searchers," replied Armond.

"Nice. A classic."

"Where are you off to?"

"Oh... I gotta run to the barn to get something."

Armond knew better, but he kept quiet about his suspicions. Chuck took his basket and walked out the front door, calling over his shoulder, "Hold down the fort while I'm gone, Unc."

Armond just rolled his eyes and said to Rupert, "Meathead."

One of Allan's men was posted up outside.

"Sir, where are you going?" he asked.

Chuck lifted his shirt and showed him his gun. "I'm good. Please, go in the house and relax. I got this."

Chuck jumped on the four-wheeler and drove towards the barn, looking very enthusiastic to do so.

. . .

Kelly couldn't take it any longer, so she made a decision to break the silence and profess her undying love for Chuck, whether the depth of those feelings were entirely true or not. Convinced he was in some sort of danger and realizing that she did actually care about him, she'd beg him to take her back. She was going to tell him everything, and what a big mistake she had made in all she did.

Kelly desperately called Chuck's cell phone over and over. He didn't answer, so she left a couple of messages telling him to please, please call her. Then she tried the house phone, hoping someone would answer. Uncle Armond heard the ringing and leisurely hoisted himself off the couch, walked to the phone, and picked it up while still chewing on his chocolates.

"Hello," he garbled.

Kelly was so glad someone answered. "Uncle Armond! Please don't hang up. It's Kelly."

"Yes, Kelly?"

"Is Chuck there? It's really, really urgent I talk with him. Please."

Armond wanted to stay out of their marital dispute as much as possible, but he also didn't want to give her any specific information. So he lied. "He ran to the store."

Kelly's heart dropped to her toes. "He's not answering his cell phone."

Armond noticed Chuck's phone sitting right on the kitchen table.

"He forgot his phone in the kitchen. I'll tell him you called when he gets back."

"Is my sister there?"

"Ah no, I haven't seen her, Kelly."

"OK, thank you. Please, tell Chuck I wouldn't call if this wasn't super important."

"I'll tell him," said Armond. *I'll tell him, but that doesn't mean he's going to care*, he thought to himself.

Chuck carried the basket and a lamp as he walked up the spiral staircase to the hayloft. When he got to the top, Samantha was lying under some blankets waiting for him, soft music playing in the background.

"Hey, lover. Wherever have you been?" she asked.

"Missing you, Sam. Missing you all day long."

"But we've been together all day, working on the ranch."

"We haven't really been together. Not like this," he said. He began taking off his clothes while she watched.

"With you, it's like the first time, every time. I've never felt this before," she said.

Chuck climbed under the covers with her, eager to put what she had just said into action.

Kelly woke up the next morning with her cell phone ringing on the nightstand. She was groggy and hungover from the night before; too much wine and worrying about the LoneStar situation and her husband. She shakily grabbed her phone, hoping it was Chuck calling her back. To her disappointment, it was Jeff.

Disheartened, she answered. "Hello."

"Kelly, where are you? I'm at your office. We had a meeting, remember?"

Kelly looked around, searching for the clock. "What time is it?"

"10:30 AM. You okay?"

"Dagnabbit! I overslept and no, I'm not okay!"

"What's the matter?"

"Everything, Jeff. I'm miserable without him. I'm so done with it all! I'm getting dressed and going to the ranch right now."

"You think that's a good idea?"

"I don't care if it's a good idea."

"What about the office? What about our meeting?"

"The girls can handle things there while I'm gone. I'm upstairs in my apartment right now. I'll meet with you later today, Jeff, after I talk to Chuck."

"OK, I'll be here," Jeff sighed. "Just make sure you call me when you can. I have a recent development to tell you about. It's a good turn of events for you."

Kelly didn't care about any of it at the moment. "OK, Jeff, I'll see you later." She hung up the phone, then slowly crawled out of bed to get in the shower.

• • •

It was already a busy day. Chuck was in the kitchen with Detective Miller. Allan was filling him in on his ongoing theories about The LoneStar Group. Uncle Armond was in the laundry room with Rupert, and Samantha and Mitch had gone out of town to get supplies for the ranch. Mike was still away on personal business. John was out cutting grass on the far end of Chuck's homestead. Dave was at the barn tending to the horses that were still inside, and everyone else was out with clients and horses.

Chuck was still talking with Allan when his walkie-talkie went off. It was Dave.

"Hey dude, you there?" he said.

"Yeah. What's up, Dave?"

"I gotta leave the barn to help Candie and her client. They broke a horseshoe."

"Okay, Dave, take off. I'm on my way out to the barn right now. Where are they?"

"Down at acre 51." That particular acre was purposely named as a comical nod towards Dave's love for UFO phenomena.

Chuck put away the walkie, then asked Allan if he was staying at the house.

"No, I'll come with you, Chuck. I can do some security checks out there while you do your thing."

As they left the main house, Jed sent a text message to Chuck.

Hey bud, I'm on my way to your house for a visit.

Chuck sent a text back. *OK, I'll be at the barn with Allan. I'll leave a golf cart out in front of the garage for you.*

Chuck pulled the extra cart out for him, then he and Allan went to get on a four-wheeler when Chuck's cell phone rang. He pulled his phone from his pants pocket and made an ugly face at the incoming number. Chuck didn't answer it. He put the phone back in his pocket.

"Bill collector?" Allan joked.

"Worse. The soon-to-be ex."

Chuck started the machine up and they began driving to the barn. Allan remained vigilant as they rode, looking everywhere and anywhere for something amiss or out of place. Chuck's four-wheeler crossed the small wooden bridge and the barn was in sight when Allan shouted for Chuck to stop the vehicle for a minute.

"Everything alright, Allan?"

"Not sure. I thought I saw something on the west side of the tree line out there," he said. He got down, pulled out a small pair of binoculars from his fanny pack, and scanned the area in question slowly.

Chuck was impatient. "You see anything?"

Allan looked intently at the tree line before making a decision. "Nah, nothing. Maybe an animal. Deer or something."

When Chuck and Allan got closer to the barn, Allan said, "Let me off right here, compadre. I'm going to take a stroll over to that wood line."

"Here, why don't you just take the four-wheeler and I can walk to the barn."

"No, it's okay. I need the exercise. I'll check the area out then meet you back at the barn." Allan got off and walked slowly while scanning his surroundings with keen eyes. Chuck drove the four-wheeler inside the barn and shut the machine off.

Samantha and Mitch had just finished loading the trailer and bed of the pickup truck. Mitch was driving. When Samantha got in on the passenger side, she picked up the cell phone she had left on the seat. She saw she had a message.

"*Finally!*" she exclaimed. Mitch looked at her curiously. "It's my sister." She put the phone to her ear and listened to the message, then said to Mitch with panic in her voice, "Shit! Fuck! Mitch, how far are we from the ranch?"

"Maybe forty-five minutes or so?"

"Can you get us there quicker?"

"I'll step on it. Why, what's up?"

"Kelly is on her way to the ranch. I think she knows about me and Chuck being more than friends!"

"What? You're sleeping with the Rockstar?" Mitch feigned surprise.

"Mitch, please, not right now!"

He started up the truck. "We're on our way, Miss Dixon!" They sped out of the parking lot, rocks and pebbles flying from under the tires.

Jed pulled up to the corral on the golf cart and saw Allan walking towards the woods, across the way from the barn.

"Hey Allan, whatcha doing?" he yelled.

"Just doing a security check. Chuck's inside the barn."

Jed looked over at the doorway of the barn and sure enough, he saw his outline standing just inside with his back to him. Suddenly, a shot rang out from the treeline that Allan was walking towards. Jed saw his friend fall forward to the ground inside the barn as if he was watching in slow-motion. Jed could see the motionless body lying on the barn floor.

"I got this son of a bitch, Jed. You get Chuck!" Allan screamed to Jed as he ran the rest of the distance to the woods where the shot came from.

Jed ran, entering the barn with a fury, hoping and praying that Chuck was okay. Allan disappeared into the woods; for a big man, he could move fast. Only moments after Allan entered the treeline, three more loud gunshots were fired, but Jed could not help Allan, not now.

When he got inside the barn, he checked for a pulse and couldn't find one. There was nothing he could do. Chuck must have had his phone in his hand when he fell because it was lying on the ground nearby when it started to ring.

Kelly was still stuck in traffic in the city, so she tried Chuck's phone again. This time, Chuck's phone didn't go straight to voicemail. She was elated that he was actually answering.

"Chuck, honey, I'm so glad you picked up," she said in relief.

"No, I'm sorry, Kelly. This is Jed."

"Oh. Is Chuck there?"

"Kelly, I'm sorry but… Chuck's dead," said Jed mournfully.

Kelly felt like she was falling into a bottomless pit. "What? No. That's not possible."

"I'm sorry, I can't talk right now. I just saw him get shot in the back of the head inside the barn. I have to go." Jed hung up the phone.

ONE WEEK LATER

While Jed was dealing with an unthinkable situation and Allan's status was unknown, Rita was at home on the phone arguing with Gary. He had called Rita to tell her he had spoken to Jeff Downing the day before about what The LoneStar Group would be willing to pay him for his portion of Gussy's Pitts. Gary could only see green.

"Gary! How could you call that woman's office after what she did to your brother? And Chuck will never sell to them, never!"

"Ma, that's good for Chuck because he's already got money. He was a rockstar and a war hero. He gets a lifetime income from the military and his prison job. He's running the ranch and he just got a book deal. We're not in the same financial boat."

"Gary," Rita scolded. "So help me... shame on you! Shame on you for being jealous of him. I don't see your sister acting like this!"

"But Ma– "

"'But Ma' nothing! Your brother has enough to deal with right now with that horrible woman, not to mention that Chuck is right. If that land is developed and Indians Leap is demolished, the city's corruption can much more easily pour into the surrounding towns. And I know your brother. He will never allow that! You could do nice things with your portion of the land, Gary, other than selling. And by the way, don't you get a nice check every month from the office rentals, not to mention the money I recently gave you from Portugal?"

"Well, yeah, but…" Gary mumbled.

"Gary, I gave you kids that land because I felt your father wanted you to have it and do good with it."

"Why did you give Chuck the part of the land with Indians Leap on it?"

Rita grew angrier. "I don't have to justify my choices to you. Can't you just be thankful for what you have? Or is money all you care about now instead of this family?"

Jed was at the main house in the driveway with the local police and an ambulance. All the ranch hands were gathered around, many crying and holding each other. Everyone loved Chuck.

One of the police officers was keeping everyone away from the ambulance. Two covered bodies were being wheeled inside. The officer in charge

271

of the scene was Niel Reeves. He was now the Detective Lieutenant for the town of Woodrow.

"I never thought I'd be back at Chuck's place for something like this," Niel shook his head.

Allan had explained to Detective Reeves that the dead man lying next to them had shot and killed Chuck from the woods and how he gave chase. He had caught up to the assassin, so the man turned and fired a shot at Allan with his rifle, missing him. Allan then aimed his Glock and fired two shots, hitting the unknown man square in his chest. He was dead before he hit the ground. No one who worked on the ranch could identify the man. Jed and Allan hypothesized that it was probably a hit and they should discuss it further privately.

Uncle Armond and Rupert were sitting on the front steps, watching the whole spectacle go on. Armond's face was one of complete devastation. His expression did not improve when he saw Samantha and Mitch pulling into the driveway. Armond quickly got up and asked Candie to hold Rupert. She had a hard time keeping hold of him; he was barking and kept trying to pull away from her to get to the ambulance.

"What's going on?" Samantha asked Armond.

Armond looked back at her, tears streaming down his face. "Sam, there's been... it's Chuck.... Chuck's...dead."

Samantha ran towards the ambulance, screaming at the top of her lungs. Before Samantha could get to the rear of the ambulance to reach the stretcher, Jed leapt in front of her and stopped her. He picked her up as she flailed, his powerful arms completely wrapped around her body. She kicked and screamed and cried for the entire world to hear. Jed held her tight and whispered repeatedly that it was going to be okay.

An EMT, masked and wearing a blue cap and scrubs, took hold of the stretcher from inside the ambulance. The EMT on the outside grabbed the other side and together they hoisted it up into the vehicle. Samantha was still reeling and some of the other staff members tried to console her.

Mitch was in utter disbelief that his friend was gone. He had survived the guerillas in Panama, only to meet his demise like this? He stood alone next to the supply truck and began to cry.

Allan asked Detective Reeves if the other ambulance was coming for the perpetrator. They had called for two ambulances out of respect for Chuck; they didn't want the murderer's body in the same one as their friend.

"Yeah, the other one's coming, Al," said Niel. He shook his head. "God-damn, what a mess." He gave the ambulance driver the go ahead to leave and he would meet them at the coroner.

Jed joined Niel and Allan to discuss matters. Within minutes of the ambulance leaving the ranch, the second one pulled into the driveway. Detective Reeves directed the vehicle and his assisting officers handled the crowd. After the second ambulance left with the deceased killer, Niel turned to Jed.

"The ranch needs to be officially shut down for a proper investigation. A few necessary people can care for the horses," he said. "Who do I talk to about the ranch? Who's in charge now?"

Jed pointed his finger at a Stingray Corvette that was pulling into the driveway. "I guess she's in charge now. We'll have to talk to her."

"Who's that?"

"Chuck's estranged wife," said Jed.

Niel saw her get out of the car, a confused look on her face. They approached her to explain what had happened. Kelly's makeup ran down her face as she learned about the events that had unfolded. She was distracted and kept looking over at Samantha, who sat petting Rupert on the steps with the other employees. Kelly felt confused and disoriented by the situation.

"Who killed my husband? Who?"

"We don't know, but I do have some questions for you at a later time about your business dealings with The LoneStar Group."

Her demeanor changed. "Okay, sure. I have to talk to my sister."

Kelly excused herself and walked over to Samantha. She wanted to try and get her sister on the same page until she could figure out what to do next about the mess she may be in. "Shalon, can we talk?"

"Talk? Sure! Are you happy now?"

"Shal, please," Kelly pleaded and then addressed the others. "Can I have a second with my sister?"

They looked at Kelly and Samantha in bewilderment. Sister? They got up, confused, and gave them privacy.

"Shalon, I'm moving back to the ranch and I want you to stay here with me."

"Why?"

"Because I love you. Chuck loved you. He loved us both and it's safer here."

"It's not safe. Chuck died here! Was it your greed that got him killed?"

"Shal, I know there's nothing I can say right now but… everyone thinks it's wrong for me to be aggressive in business, just because I'm a woman. For men like our father, it's more than okay. But not for a woman."

"I've heard this spiel before. Save it! I'll stay for now because I don't want all these great people that work here to lose their jobs. They also loved him and what this ranch stands for. So I will stay until you find a replacement for me."

"Thank you, Shalon."

Jed walked over and interrupted their conversation. "Excuse me, Kelly, if it's okay with you. I'd like to take Samantha and Uncle Armond with me right now to identify the body properly. I know it's a lot to ask of you all right now."

"Are you up to that?" Kelly asked her.

"Yeah. I'll go. Chuck would've wanted people who truly cared about him to be there for him at a time like this," she said as she shot Kelly a look layered in meaning.

While Armond and Samantha got into Jed's car, Niel talked more with Kelly about what would happen with the ranch for the time being.

CHAPTER 26
R.I.P. CHUCK
OCTOBER 2002

JED WAS GETTING ready for Chuck's funeral. Earlier in the week, he received a phone call from Nick Columbo that he was reinstated early because of the FBI getting involved with Chuck's murder.

"How is it that you just happened to be at Barreto's ranch when he was shot?" asked Nick.

"Ah, I was bored from being on suspension, so I went to visit him and his horses," replied Jed.

"Horses? Right! Okay then. After your pal was taken to the coroner, who notified the FBI?"

"I don't have a clue, Nick. Someone called the FBI?"

"OK, Ferrari, you're back on duty for now," said Nick, clearly frustrated. "But I'll only warn you this one time: make no decisions without my knowledge or approval!"

Jed thanked him and Nick told Jed not to make anything personal this time around. He was to work by the book with the local authorities and the FBI Agent assigned to the case. Nick gave Jed the agent's name and contact number. It was none other than Jack Bufford, the same man who had also been in charge of Shandi's tragic unsolved murder and poor Alfred Ford's disappearance.

. . .

Vic and Cheryl, with Chance in tow, were staying at the ranch for a long weekend to attend the funeral. They knew nothing about the mess that Kelly was in with everyone or her separation from Chuck. Samantha let Kelly know as long as she did right by Chuck with the property, she wouldn't get Vic involved.

Vic, who couldn't imagine why anyone would kill Chuck, wanted to hire security for the ranch and his girls, but Kelly told him it wasn't necessary. When Kelly wouldn't listen, he tried to convince Samantha, but she brushed him off with noncommittal answers. Cheryl and Samantha got along pretty well during their stay, but Kelly barely acknowledged her as usual.

Gary had come home for his brother's funeral and was staying at Stacey's house. He and Rita talked no more about Gussy's Pitts after the argument they had over the phone the day Chuck met his demise. Everyone else was shattered over him being gone, but Gary was seemingly devoid of emotion. It was hard to tell how he was dealing with it all.

Rita and Stacey kept busy by obsessing over the details of the funeral arrangements and Kelly gave no resistance. She thought maybe giving them the reins could earn her some points, and she even agreed to let her husband be buried right next to Shandi and Gus. It would be a closed casket due to the damage caused by the bullet.

Armond went to Rita's house so that they could go to the services together. He now felt out of place at the ranch without his nephew. Rita was concerned about Armond, him having been so very close with her son. He was prideful and didn't like to share his emotions, but she knew he was having a tough time. Other than the current tragedy at hand, it seemed to Rita there was something else eating at her brother. She tried getting it out of him, but so far she hadn't been successful.

R.I.P. CHUCK

Kelly had to stay busy. She was washing some dishes in the sink when her cell phone began ringing. The screen read "UNKNOWN CALLER". She picked it up and ran upstairs to the bedroom to answer it.

"Hello?"

"Hello, Mrs. Barreto," said Silus. "My condolences on your husband's passing."

Kelly was speechless. She was furious and shocked that he would call her on the day of Chuck's funeral, but it wasn't her style to lose composure and start pointing the finger without proof. She was methodical in that way.

"What is it that you want?"

"I'll get to that. Hmm, your husband, it seems, died without a will. That makes you the sole owner of Indians Leap. Also, your attorney is in talks, I hear, with Mr. Barreto's brother about selling his piece of Gussy's Pitts. It's only a matter of time before the sister sells, too. Of course, it was an unfortunate accident for your husband, but with that, I'd say we're back in business."

"Accident? He was murdered!" Kelly raised her voice.

"Anyway, Mrs. Barreto, we will be talking soon. And again, sorry for your loss."

He hung up the phone and she stared vacantly at a wall mirror.

If you were driving through the town of Woodrow that day, it was empty and quiet, no sounds but the wind. A ghost town. It seemed there were cars for miles going into the town's burial grounds, all to escort Chuck to his final resting place.

Even though he hadn't been a Correctional Officer for a long time, there were about thirty officers in attendance, dressed in uniform. A special honor guard was sent from the Department that fired rifles into the air. Many of the officers came over to Jed and inquired about Chuck's last moments. Jed told them it was still an ongoing investigation and he wasn't allowed to discuss it.

Chuck's funeral and burial was equally as emotional as Shandi's had been. Her parents were there, sitting close to Rita, Stacey, Gary, and Armond. Chuck's former bandmates were also there; they couldn't believe that both he and Shandi had been murdered. Bob, once his very best friend, broke down crying as they all stood around his casket waiting for it to be lowered into the ground.

Junior was standing in the back, crying his own share of tears while Father Gosselin gave the eulogy. Stacey couldn't help but give dirty looks to Kelly, sitting in front and dressed all in black. She blamed Kelly for Chuck's death; if she hadn't gotten involved with LoneStar and made a deal without Chuck's knowledge, she was convinced none of it would have happened. The only person who didn't attend the funeral that was close to Chuck was Mike. He was still missing in action.

Father Gosselin finished up his speech, and the casket would be getting lowered into the ground within moments. Dave thought it was odd that Jed didn't say a few words and it kept gnawing at his thoughts.

Many people walked through and gave their condolences to Kelly and Chuck's family. Even Chip and Mellisa had shown up to pay their respects.

A most unexpected guest arrived in a long, black limo with tinted windows. A man got out and walked over to the casket. He was extremely tall and wore large sunglasses. When he got to Kelly, his presence startled her. It was Silus Kobol. He shook her hand and said, "So sorry for your loss, Mrs. Barreto." She said nothing in return and continued playing her part as the grieving widow.

While the burial was taking place, Allan and a junior trainee were parked in a position that allowed them a full visual of the service. They took pictures of people attending the funeral in hopes that whoever had Chuck taken out might be arrogant enough to actually show up.

While they worked the cameras, Allan's apprentice, Doug, asked him about the man he killed on Chuck's ranch. It had turned out that the shooter was an ex-convict from Chicago. The police later found his 1996 Buick GNX parked on the outskirts of the woods on the backside of the ranch, almost on the edge of the next town over. He must have walked miles through the woods to get into position for his shot at Chuck.

"His name was Karl Eiden. He had been in and out of jail for drugs, assault, robbery… the list goes on. The man had even once been suspected of murder, but it was never proven and he was never convicted. I know in my gut someone in The LoneStar Group hired this chump to kill Barreto. We just have to find the evidence."

"That's incredible you got the bastard, Allan."
He gave Doug a look and continued taking pictures.

As the attendees took one last look at Chuck's casket, Samantha grew upset. Seemingly unable to bear witness any longer, she stood and began to walk away. Jed immediately got up and followed her, then whispered something in her ear. They both then quietly left the preceding and walked towards his vehicle together.

Dave was standing in the crowd of heartbroken people and saw Jed leave. He wondered what the fuck he was doing leaving with Samantha in the middle of Chuck's burial.

Samantha got in the front passenger seat and Jed pulled out of the cemetery and onto the main road. They looked at each other and then kept completely silent during the drive. The silence was uncomfortable for them. He drove for a half-mile, then went through a set of lights and past a chain of restaurants before taking a right into a Holiday Inn parking lot. It was the only hotel in town. It was smaller than most but nice enough and built a few years back for visitors that didn't want to stay directly in the city.

Without breaking their silence, Jed and Samantha got out of the car and walked to the entrance of the hotel. They crossed the lobby, passed the desk attendant, and stepped into an elevator. Once the silver doors opened, they got inside and Jed pressed the button that said five, which was the top floor. The doors opened. Jed waited for Samantha to get out first, then they walked to the end of the hall, to the very last room on the right.

A man dressed in a dark gray suit was standing outside the door. He nodded at Jed and said, "Mr. Ferrari."

"Joel," Jed responded, and then Joel stood aside to let them pass. The door for the room opened slowly.

At the same moment in time, Chuck's casket was being lowered into the earth while bagpipes played. His family, friends, employees, and past co-workers cried resolutely.

Rita watched her son descend. While crying, she whispered to Stacey, "Though lovers be lost love shall not; And death shall have no dominion."

"What, Mom?" Stacey asked, confused.

"The inscription on Shandi's tombstone," she said and inclined her head towards the grave.

. . .

Samantha walked into the hotel room and saw the backside of a man that looked damn familiar. He was pacing the small room impatiently and bouncing a green tennis ball off the wall when he heard the door open. He turned his head to see who it was and smiled when he saw Samantha. She ran up to him, jumped up into his arms and wrapped her legs around him. Jed stood there after closing the door, and watched.

"I've missed you, Chuck," she said and kissed him.

CHAPTER 27
FLASHBACK
OCTOBER 2002

HOW WAS IT possible? How was Samantha hugging Chuck Barreto when he was just buried in the Woodrow Cemetery?

The day Chuck walked into the barn to check on the horses while Allan walked over to the treeline, he heard a noise behind him as he entered the door. From the shadows, a man walked behind Chuck, and Chuck turned around, surprised. He didn't recognize the man.

"Long time no see, Chucky!" he said sardonically. The man was on the tall side, and even in the darkened barn light, he looked old and haggard.

"Excuse me? Do I know you?" Chuck asked. He knew he wasn't a client or customer and quickly came to the conclusion that he could be someone sent from The LoneStar Group. The grungy-looking man was holding an old 357 Ruger handgun and it was pointed directly at Chuck.

"If you're going to ruin a man's life, Chucko, you should at least remember him!" the man half-smiled through rotted teeth, the gun still aimed.

Chuck was stealthily trying to reach his right hand behind his back to draw his hidden Glock while also engaging with the disturbed individual. "I'm sorry, sir, but you are...?"

"I want you to know who killed you, Chuck!" The man extended his arm as if preparing to shoot. "My name is L–"

Chuck tried to outdraw him, but his cell phone fell out of his pocket and he heard a loud *pop!* from outside the barn. The shabby man's head splattered. Chuck moved quickly to take cover as the man fell forward into the barn and onto the floor. He pulled out his Glock and ran out of the barn to see where the shot had been fired from. He thought maybe it had been Allan.

As Chuck took a step, Jed surprised him by knocking him to the ground for cover. As Jed lay on top of Chuck, he said to him, "Where'd you come from?"

"I told you I was on my way over," said Jed.

"Who's shooting at me?"

"I don't know. Allan went after him."

They heard three more shots come from the direction of the woods. "Fuck, we gotta see if Allan's alright," said Chuck.

"No, we stay here. I'll call him." Jed looked at the dead body. "Who's this guy?"

"I don't have a clue. He was about to tell me when he was shot. He was going to shoot me."

Jed got up and pointed at the gun. "That's the gun he had on you?"

Chuck stood. "Yep." His cell phone was still lying on the ground. It started to ring. Chuck picked it up.

"Who is it?"

Chuck made a face. "My wife."

Jed snatched the ringing phone out of his hands. "Follow my lead. We have to act fast."

Jed answered the phone and told Kelly that her husband was dead. At first, Chuck was confused, but then he realized Jed must have suddenly concocted a plan.

"What are you thinking?"

"I'm thinking someone in The LoneStar Group is trying to kill you, so let's let them think they did. They won't stop here if they've gone this far. They could go after anyone in your family next. Trust me, Chuck, this is how we'll catch them, but we have to move quickly."

Jed's own cell phone rang. It was Allan. "Oh thank God, Allan! OK, get to the barn ASAP. I have a plan."

Jed hung up his phone. "He's alright and he got the guy."

Chuck turned the dead man over onto his back and noticed he was wearing worn, ripped jeans and an old ass weathered, patched dark-green Army jacket. The place where the last name should be was blank.

"You know this guy?" asked Jed.

"Hard to tell with his face blown off, but I have a weird feeling I do. There was this bully way back in high school who had a jacket similar to this. I can't say for sure, though, if it could be him."

"Don't worry, we'll figure it out, buddy. C'mon, we have to get you hidden before I call an ambulance for these bodies."

From there, things got crazy. Some serious multitasking had to take place for Jed's plan to work. Jed talked to the Chief of Police about the situation with LoneStar and what had just transpired, and asked for him to send an ambulance with a detective. Jed explained to the Chief that he would need an extra set of EMT scrubs on the ambulance for Chuck to wear. Unaware that Jed was actually currently on suspension, his credentials as a District Attorney employee were enough to convince the Chief to go along with it.

Allan carried the would-be assassin from the woods to the barn. He threw him on the floor next to the other body.

"What about the integrity of the crime scene?" asked Chuck.

"Screw the crime scene. We know what happened. LoneStar wants you dead, out of the way."

Jed asked Allan to go out on the golf cart to keep an eye out for any employees returning to the barn with clients and hold them back so no one would see that Chuck was still alive. He then called the main house and told Uncle Armond to let the police and the ambulance in the main gate, urging him to remain at the house no matter what; he'd tell him as soon as possible what had happened.

Chuck felt conflicted about hurting the people he loved by faking his death, so Jed promised Chuck that once he was safe, he'd let Uncle Armond and Samantha in on what was going on, even though he thought it was a bad idea. It was the only way he could get Chuck to go along with his plan.

Jed didn't have much time to pull it all off. He drove back to the house and hooked up a small trailer from the garage onto the four-wheeler while Allan kept everyone away from the barn. He was figuring out the attachment to the trailer when Uncle Armond approached him, and at the same time, the ambulance pulled into the driveway. Then two cruisers pulled in with Niel Reeves and several other police officers.

Armond kept asking Jed what was going on and who was hurt.

"Armond, please, let me get the medics down to the barn area first. For your own safety and everyone else's, please help me and I promise to tell you more when I get back."

Armond was a patient and measured man. "OK, I will help, Jed. Is my nephew down at the barn?"

"I'll tell you more soon, Arm. And again I apologize for the way I have to do things right now."

Armond patientlly accepted Jed's answer.

Jed drove the four-wheeler with the trailer back to the barn with two EMTs and Detective Reeves accompanying him. He had the extra scrubs hidden underneath the seat. When they got back to the barn, Jed asked the three men to not say anything about Chuck being alive. He explained to them that Chuck's life was in danger and had Chuck quickly put the scrubs on over his clothing, the mask and hat on his head. He had to tie his hair up underneath the cap.

The EMTs placed the dead bodies onto the trailer and covered them. Niel called for two of his officers to come down to the barn via radio to search the area for any other accomplices. Jed, Niel, the EMTs, and the disguised Chuck drove the two dead bodies back to the main house where the ambulance was parked. Once that was done, Jed called Allan and told him it was all clear to bring everyone back to the house. One officer posted up at the barn as the ranch hands put the horses in their stables.

John was one of the first staff members to return to the barn. He was wide-eyed and concerned as he looked around. The police officer told him to move along, to bring his lawnmower to the house and wait there.

To keep anyone from recognizing Chuck, Jed had him wait inside the rear of the ambulance. When Chuck was pulling the unknown dead man's body up into the ambulance and he saw Samantha kicking, screaming, and crying, his eyes teared up under his mask. He wanted to take it off and tell her that it was all okay, that he was still alive. But he had to let it play out.

When someone is trying to kill you, your desire to stay alive is greater than ever. He had learned that in Panama. But this was his home, not a war-torn country. Chuck wondered, *How on God's earth could Kelly do this to me?*

After the ambulance left, Jed whispered to Allan for him to contact the FBI and tell them everything. It was his hope in doing so that if they got involved with Jed's boss, it would force Nick to take him off of suspension and put him back on the case. His hunch had ended up being dead on.

Once Kelly showed up on the ranch and she and Samantha talked, Jed had her and Armond go to the coroner's office with him. That's when he revealed to them that Chuck was alive and safe. Jed hid Chuck close by at the Holiday Inn. Uncle Armond and Samantha, full of relief upon learning of Chuck's resurrection, were more than happy to continue the charade as distraught mourners while they figured out how to take down LoneStar.

In the hotel room, Chuck turned to Jed, growing frustrated with the plan. "So how was my funeral?"

"Chuck, I'm sure this is all going to be over in just a few more days and then you can have your life back, I swear."

Chuck raised his voice. "You're not counting on the FBI, are you? Especially that idiot, Jack Bufford, who never found out who killed Shandi. No, I'm sorry, Jed. I don't have confidence in this plan. I agreed to stop LoneStar from tearing down Indians Leap and building on my property, but deceiving my family and friends like this..."

"If you go back out there, they'll try to kill you again, either you or someone you love, Chuck. Just give me two weeks at the most."

"Two weeks? I'm already going outta my mind in here like this. I feel like a damn inmate!"

"Listen, I'll work as fast as I can."

"Damnit, fine. Can you leave Sam here with me and have Allan come get her later tonight?"

"Sure buddy, no problem. Go easy, okay?"

Chuck rolled his eyes.

CHAPTER 28

CALLING DOWN THE THUNDER

A FEW DAYS after the funeral, the dust was settling and people close to Chuck were reluctantly coming to terms with him being gone. The ranch would soon reopen to the public. Regular clients were more than ready to resume their business at the ranch. Chuck's death didn't deter them from continuing on there. Rita was in constant contact with Samantha to check on how things were going. It killed Sam to talk with her, knowing her son was still alive and that she had to keep it from her.

Rita was on the phone with Jessica Farnsworth one morning. She was discussing what would happen to her son's estate with him not having a will. Jessica assured Rita that if Kelly decided to go ahead with building, she and LoneStar would have an uphill battle on their hands.

Chip was in his local office saying his goodbyes to the staff and packing boxes for D.C. when his manager came in with a look of urgency on her face.

"Hey Alicia, what's wrong?"

"We have to talk in private, Chip."

"OK, come in and close the door," he said, calm, cool, and collected as ever.

"What's going on?" asked Chip.

"The funeral you attended for that rancher? He might actually still be alive."

"What?" asked Chip, bewildered.

"It looks like it was all staged by Jed Ferarri, and he's trying to prepare a case to arrest members of The LoneStar Group. We have to get ahead of this, Chip." He stood and stared, blankly. Alicia waved her hands in front of his face. "Chip!"

"Alicia, I'm thinking. Do you know if there's a coroner's report on Barreto?"

"Way ahead of you. There isn't and he's already buried. That is big-time sketchy!"

Kelly was in her office in the city with Jeff, Jed, and Allan. She was unsure how to proceed and wanted out of the mess she was in with LoneStar, so she turned to them for help. She was expecting a phone call from Silus Kobol, which Jed and Allan would record.

"Kelly, you're doing the right thing here," said Jed. She looked scared, and for once, unsure.

"That's easy for you to say. It's not your life that's in danger," she retorted.

"As long as these guys think you're going to do their bidding, they won't touch you."

While they were talking, the office phone rang. It was listed as an unknown caller.

Allan pressed record. "OK, Mrs. Barreto, pick up the phone."

"Yes? Kelly Barreto here."

"Good morning, Mrs. Barreto," said Silus.

"Yes, good morning, Mr. Kobol. I have some good news."

"That's what I like to hear."

"I've already heard back from my husband's brother, Gary, and he's thinking seriously of selling. He's coming up with a price and will let me know in a few short days how much that is."

"Splendid news indeed. How about construction? When will it resume? We'd like to expedite tunneling through Indians Leap."

"I'd like to do some negotiating about that."

"Negotiating? You're alive, Mrs. Barreto, and Chuck's not. What can there be to negotiate at this point?"

"We'll discuss it tomorrow, Mr. Kobol, at the Villa Rose in the city at noon over lunch."

"There will be no further negotiations," said Silus.

"I'll see you tomorrow for lunch, Mr. Kobol. Good day, sir," she said with far more confidence than she felt and hung up.

"Let's just hope he shows. Kelly, tomorrow, meet us at the ranch and we'll wire you up. Undercover FBI agents will be throughout the restaurant. This is so important. You have to get him to admit to killing Chuck."

"How am I supposed to do that?" Kelly asked, exasperated.

"You know," Jeff interjected. "I don't blame Kelly for being nervous. You guys are putting her in some serious danger!"

"That's really helpful, Jeff," said Jed, growing upset. "Can everyone clear the room? I want to talk with Kelly alone."

Kelly nodded and Jeff and Allan left the office, closing the door behind them.

"Kelly, what I'm going to tell you now stays in this room, between us. More people could get killed if it gets out."

"OK, Jed, I promise. What is it?"

"If you pull this off, you could get back in good graces with your husband."

"Are you sick or something?"

"No... he's alive, Kelly. LoneStar killed someone else. They only think they killed Chuck."

Kelly's jaw dropped and tears pooled in her eyes.

"He's *alive*?" she whispered.

"The shot struck someone else who, ironically, was also trying to kill Chuck. We don't know who the man is yet because his face was blown off and he had no identification on him. We still can't figure out how the guy got on the ranch with the beefed up security."

"Do you realize how crazy this all sounds?"

"Crazy, but all true."

"Where is he? Can I see him?" she asked, hopefully.

"I have him in hiding, well and safe. After tomorrow's confession, I'll take you to him."

Kelly got up from behind her desk and hugged Jed. "I'll get Kobol to admit they did it. I will!"

Jed knew that by telling her the truth about Chuck, he had taken a calculated risk. He just hoped it paid off.

Uncle Armond was in the kitchen at the ranch. He had just finished setting up Chuck's old police scanner so he could listen to it during the day; he was a little paranoid after all that had happened recently.

Mitch came into the house to get something to drink. "Hey Arm, I see you have the police scanner working."

"Yeah, it's working pretty good now."

"You hear from Chuck?" Mitch asked quietly. The last time Chuck was alone with Samantha, he told her to tell Mitch everything so he'd be more vigilant. Chuck was worried about protecting her, and he wanted someone he trusted to be aware.

"No, nothing."

"OK, just checking." He finished his drink of water. "I gotta get back to the barn to help Sam. I'll talk to you later."

Mitch walked out on the front porch and was surprised to run into John.

"Oh, John. Sorry, didn't see you there."

"Yeah, it's hot out today. I just came over here to cool off for a bit."

"OK, see ya later."

John nodded.

Chuck lies impatiently in a king-size bed in the hotel room, throwing his tennis ball off the ceiling. The agent outside the door had previously suggested to Chuck that maybe he shouldn't make so much noise and draw attention to himself; the cold stare he got back was response enough. He felt like he was utterly losing his mind being stuck in there.

There was a knock on the door, then someone said, "Chuck, I'm coming in."

The door clicked and slowly opened, and FBI Agent Jack Bufford's head poked through. "Chuck, it's me, Jack."

Chuck motioned for him to come in. He walked in as Chuck got off the bed to greet him. "Anything new going on?"

"Actually, yes. You might want to sit back down for this one."

"I'm good, Jack. Just tell me."

"The man who had you at gunpoint in your barn... we now know who he is. Or rather, who he was."

Chuck's eyes lit up. "Who?"

"Your instincts were correct, Chuck. You did know him, apparently. His name was Leroy Stick. He went to highschool with you."

"Goddamnit, I knew it! I fuckin' knew it! What the hell was he doing on my ranch?"

"Chuck, you really should sit down for this."

"No, just get on with it."

"We went back to the ballistics and fibers that were collected when Shandi was murdered," Jack said and then paused. The room began to spin and Chuck felt like he was going to pass out. "The gun he had pointed at you was an exact match. It was the same weapon that killed Shandi. The fibers on Leroy's jacket were also an exact match to those we found on Shandi. We finally caught her killer, Chuck."

Chuck backed up slowly and sunk onto the bed.

"You okay, Chuck? Did this man have a grudge against you or Shandi?"

"All this fucking time, it was right under my nose," he growled. "He dated Shandi briefly when we were just teenagers and she broke up with him. She and I started going out right after."

"Jesus. Chuck, I'm so sorry."

"Jack, how the hell did Stick get on my ranch?"

"I have agents dissecting Stick's life right now. I will do my best to find out."

Chuck wiped the sweat off his head. "All this goddamn time! Now I finally know the truth, and I can't even tell anyone about it. Shandi's poor parents."

"We will, Chuck. LoneStar...their days are coming to an end. Your wife is wearing a wire to a meeting tomorrow and with any luck, we should have enough on them after that."

"Are you guys sure she'll come through?"

"Jed seems to think so."

CALLING DOWN THE THUNDER

. . .

Jed pulled into the parking lot of the Holiday Inn to see Chuck and tell him the news about Kelly personally. He also had to tell him he would have to be moved to another location for the time being. As Jed got out of the car, his cell phone rang. He looked to see who was calling and sighed.

"Hello, Nick. I was just getting ready to call you," said Jed.

"You were? For?"

"To tell you about tomorrow. We're putting a wire on Kelly. I think we got LoneStar. She's having lunch with the head guy at the Villa Rose."

"Great. You're the man of the hour, Jed. Oh, and Kelly must be ecstatic that her husband's not dead. If you told her," Nick said sarcastically.

Jed momentarily lost his ability to speak. He had avoided telling Nick and knew it was the final nail in his coffin.

"Nothing to say, Jed? The great Ferarri is speechless!" Nick taunted.

Jed cleared his throat. "Ah, Nick, I was going to-"

His boss cut him off. "Going to nothing, Jed. I warned you! I had to find out from Jack Bufford that you guys have Barreto hidden in a freakin' hotel room. If you get your man tomorrow – whether you do or fucking don't! – I don't care. After tomorrow, no matter the outcome, I want your resignation. End. Of. Story!"

Jed expected the consequences. "OK, you will have it, Nick."

Nick hung up without another word. He was sitting in his car in a dark parking garage, looking out the front windshield. He slammed his hands on the steering wheel and yelled, "FUCK!"

Uncle Armond was at the kitchen table putting together a John Wayne puzzle and eating some saltwater taffy with Rupert by his side, listening intently to all the police calls coming through the scanner. The dog stared at Armond and whined.

Armond looked down at him. "You can't eat this, Rupert. It'll make you sick."

Rupert barked at him.

"Oh, shush!"

The house phone rang. It was Rita.

"Hello. What's up, Mitzy?" he said, calling her by her childhood nickname. "Oh, everything is quiet here. Samantha is out at the barn. She said the Chief would call us in a few days to let customers back on the ranch."

Armond was dying to tell his sister that her son was alive and safe, but he knew he was sworn to secrecy.

Kelly was nervous and excited for the following day. All she had to do was wear a wire and get Silus to admit to having Chuck murdered, and then she would get to be with her husband. She was leaving work early to head back to the ranch; her girls were in charge for the rest of the day.

Kelly was getting off the elevator in the parking garage when a voice called her from behind a cement pillar. It startled her and she jumped.

She squinted and saw who it was. "Nick, you scared me. What are you doing here?"

"Jed Ferrari sent me. It's urgent you come with me now, Kelly. You're in danger, The LoneStar Group... they know everything!"

She looked frightened out of her wits. "Everything?!"

"They do. C'mon, honey, I'm going to bring you to Chuck right now."

"We're going to see Chuck?" Kelly asked, distracted.

"Yes, we are, Kell. I'm sorry about all the deception, but you don't need to worry any longer. LoneStar will be behind bars by tomorrow."

Kelly ran to Nick and put her hand on his shoulder. "Thank you so much, Nick."

He led her to his car and they got in.

Chuck and Jack were enthralled with something on the television, when there was a knock on the door. "Chuck, it's me, Jed."

"Hey, what's up guys? What are you watching?"

"You better check this shit out! Your boy is dimming us *out!*" said Chuck.

"What?" Jed turned to the TV to see Senator Chip Karrington in the middle of a public speech.

"I took all kinds of contributions for my campaign. The LoneStar Group was one of many. I was absolutely unaware of them being under any criminal investigation or the possibility that they had been involved in any criminal activity. The organization, of course, deserves its day in court before judgment is passed by any of us. They may, or may not, be exonerated. Whatever the outcome is, I, Chip Karrington ...."

Chuck went over to the TV and shut it off.

"Why did you shut it off?"

"I've heard enough, Jethro!" said Chuck angrily. "Someone in your department tipped Karrington off, so he's getting ahead of your investigation. Which means so is LoneStar. They will never show up tomorrow at that restaurant 'cause of that jackoff trying to save his own ass!"

"You don't know that, Chuck."

"The hell I don't!"

"You're clearly aggravated over more than just this. What else is bothering you?"

"What else," Chuck sneered. "Did Jack tell you about Leroy Stick?"

Jed lowered his head. "Yes, I'm sorry Chuck."

"Jed, you buried the man that murdered my Shandi right fucking next to her and my father!"

"Chuck, we didn't know that at the time. Please, just calm down."

"I fucking know that, Jed! I'm not stupid!" Chuck screamed at him with misplaced ire. He took the tennis ball and whipped it across the room causing it to ricochet from object to object. Jack and Jed ducked so they didn't get hit with it. When the ball stopped bouncing, Jed began to speak again when his cell phone rang. He pulled it out of his pocket and answered a call labeled 'PRIVATE CALLER'.

"Hello?"

"Mr. Ferrari?"

"Yes," said Jed.

"Please, put Mr. Barreto on the phone," the unknown voice said smoothly.

Jed was flustered and confused. "Who is this?"

"Never mind that."

Chuck snatched the phone from Jed's hand. "This is Barreto. What can I do for you, fucker?"

"There's nothing you can do for me, Mr. Barreto, but there's something you can do for yourself."

"Oh yeah, what?"

"Can you see the parking lot from that stuffy little room you're in right now?"

"Nope," said Chuck, growing impatient.

"If you tell Mr. Ferrari or the agent in your room what I'm about to tell you, you can say goodbye to your wife and Miss Dixon. And from what I hear, your track record is lousy when it comes to keeping your love interests alive. Do you hear me now?"

"I hear you loud and clear," Chuck said through clenched teeth.

Jed tried to ask what the caller was saying, but Chuck motioned for him to stop talking and be still.

"There is a black vehicle right in the middle of the parking lot. In the vehicle is your wife and Miss Samantha Dixon. It's very simple, Chuck. You find a way to get out here without the men in the room with you. Once you're out here, get into the car with me and these fine ladies. Once we get a ways down the road, I will let them out of the vehicle. Then you and I will leave to have a frank discussion. You're the one we want, not them. But if you don't get down here in two minutes, we will blow them up in this parking lot. Chuck, are you with me so far?"

Chuck's throat was dry. "Yes, I'm with you."

"Absolutely marvelous. The timer begins now."

Chuck dropped the phone on the bed.

"What's going on?" Jed exclaimed.

Suddenly, Chuck swung at Jed, hitting his friend square in the jaw. Chuck then jumped up and kicked Bufford in the stomach and bolted for the door.

Jack yelled to the man outside the door. "Stop him!"

But Chuck was too fast. He ran down the hallway until he reached the emergency exit. Chuck took two, three steps at a time, running all the way down to the bottom. He could hear someone chasing after him, but he refused to turn and see who it could be. He kept running.

Chuck could hear Jed behind him screaming, "Chuck! Chuck, stop!"

He ran out the double glass doors into the parking lot, stopped for a split second looking for the black van, and sped towards it once he had it in his sights.

"Kelly! Sam! Get out of there!" he yelled.

Chuck was about ten feet away from the vehicle when it blew. Was it luck that Jed played college football? He tackled Chuck just in the nick of time, and both men went flying into the air, landing to the left of the fiery scene.

Uncle Armond was sitting at the kitchen table, still working on his puzzle when he heard the local dispatcher say over the police scanner that there was some sort of explosion at the Holiday Inn. He almost choked on the Kit-Kat he was eating. He quickly found his walkie talkie and called for Mitch who was working somewhere on the ranch.

"Mitch, come in. Mitch, come in," called Armond.

"Yeah, what's up Arm?"

"Something bad just happened where you-know-who is! You and Samantha get back to the main house, quickly!"

"Okay, Arm, she's over in the barn. We'll be there shortly."

Chuck was still disoriented from the impact of the blast. There was fire everywhere, and it felt like Jed was jumping on Chuck's back. He suddenly became more alert and screamed at Jed, "Get off me, Jed! You 're not my type!"

"Shut up, you idiot, you're on fire!" said Jed, still trying to put out the flames by flicking Chuck's shirt.

"I know that," Chuck said with a smirk.

"No, your shirt is actually on fire!"

Chuck finally realized what he was getting at. He was wearing a heavy flannel shirt over his t-shirt. "Oh, fuck!" he yelled, then hastily took off the smoldering shirt and threw it on the ground.

On the right side of the parking lot, there was an old abandoned building that used to be a dry cleaner. Coming from that direction, bullets began ricocheting around Chuck and Jed. Jack Bufford and his partner Joel Cruz ran outside from the hotel lobby and immediately returned gunfire. Jack yelled at Chuck and Jed to stay low. Jed grabbed Chuck and pulled him behind a large cement planter in the middle of the parking lot.

"Stay down!" Jed yelled, and then they both joined the agents in returning gunfire. As Jed shot his weapon, he said to Chuck, "Boy, these guys must really want you dead!"

"You ain't kidding," said Chuck.

"Get Chuck into the lobby," Jack yelled to Jed. "We'll cover you!"

"OK, buddy," said Jed to Chuck, "on three. Stay behind me and crouch down when you run. Ready?"

Chuck nodded, his adrenaline in overdrive.

Jed counted down, then they sprinted while Jack and Joel turned up the gunfire on the enemy. Jed and Chuck made it into the lobby and ran over to a wall closest to the main door. They sat down against it to catch their breath. They could hear Jack, Joel, and the gunmen still firing their weapons at each other rapidly.

Jed looked at Chuck, soot smeared on his face, and said, "What did they say to you? What made you punch me and run out there like that?"

Chuck was still breathing heavily. "The caller said to me that Samantha and Kelly were in that van, and if I didn't get out there right away without you, they were going to be killed."

"Oh... Look, Chuck, that was undoubtedly a setup. I'm sure no one was in the vehicle."

"Let's see if you're right."

Chuck pulled out a small cell phone from his pants pocket. He opened an unread message that was sent to him.

"What does it say?" asked Jed.

Chuck finished typing something and then said to Jed, "Samantha is still on the ranch. She started texting me when she and Uncle Armond heard on the police scanner that there was an explosion at this hotel."

"What are you texting her back?"

"To stay put at the ranch with Mitch. He's watching her for me."

"Allan's there too, right?"

"Yeah, somewhere, making rounds on the perimeter."

"Where did you get the burner?"

"Samantha gave it to me on her last visit with me. Sorry, Jed, you know I trust you, but not the people you work for. So I took precautions."

The gunfire ceased and Jack Bufford ran into the lobby, sweating profusely.

"Where's Joel?" asked Jed.

"He's in pursuit of the shooters."

"There was more than one?"

"Afraid so."

"Did you get a plate number from the vehicle?"

"No, they got the jump on us. These guys are good," said Jack.

The local police were on their way; you could hear the sirens not too far off. The hotel manager was still hiding behind the desk at reception. Jack shouted to him it was safe to come out. Jed explained to Jack why Chuck had run out of the hotel room.

Jack smiled and looked at Chuck. "Chuck, you ever think of joining the FBI? Let me know. That was smooth, what you did to me and Jed."

"We can joke around later. We still don't know if Kelly is alright. I have to call her now," said Jed. He called her office and the secretary answered. "Is Kelly Barreto there?" He listened intently, then hung up. "She left the office early to go home."

"Well, Kelly's not back at the ranch because I would think Sam would have mentioned that to me."

"Maybe she stopped at a store or something?" Jed questioned. "I'll try her cell phone."

"That's okay. I got this." Chuck used his burner phone to dial a number. "Mike! Is Kelly safe?"

Chuck listened to Mike's answer as Jed and Jack exchanged a glance. "Hold on," he said into the phone, then looked at Jed and Jack. "The Lone-Star Group has kidnapped Kelly. They've taken her to a mansion on Prospect Street in Longmeadow."

"What mansion?" asked Jed.

Chuck listened to Mike some more and then repeated back, "Meadows Manor."

"I know it well. It's on the far side of the city," said Jed.

"That's going to take an eternity!"

"No it won't. I know some back roads to get us there faster."

"Fellas, I can get a chopper over there right away with a tactical team. Chuck, tell your friend to stay hidden outside the grounds until the cavalry arrives," said Jack.

"Did you get all that, Mike?" A moment later he hung up and said, "OK, Jack. Mike will stand by. Let's go."

"Jed, please don't go inside the estate until I have agents there. And sorry, but Chuck must remain outside the property. He is a civilian," said Jack.

Jed tilted his head to the side and gave Jack a look.

"Chuck, I need your word," said Jack.

"Yeah, yeah, yeah, let's go already," said Chuck, and that was as much cooperation as he was going to offer.

They ran out of the hotel doors to their separate vehicles- Jack in his sedan and Chuck in Jed's car. As they pulled out of the parking lot, Jed reached up and put a siren light on the roof.

Just then, Detective Reeves pulled his responding vehicle up alongside Jed's, an additional five cruisers and a fire truck piled behind him.

Jed poked his head out the window to say something to Niel Reeves, but the police detective cut him off. "I should've known you two were involved in this. What happened here?"

Niel observed that half the parking lot was still burning. Two more fire trucks arrived with their sirens on. They came in behind the cruiser, honking their horns loudly to get into the smoking parking lot.

"Niel, I'll have to fill you in later. We're on our way to another serious emergency," Jed yelled.

"It's always an emergency with you two!"

"Come on, Jed," said Chuck impatiently. "Let's get moving!"

Jed squealed out of the parking lot, with Jack following behind.

"Chuck, what made you think of having Mike follow Kelly?" Jed asked as they sped toward the mansion.

"The minute you told me everything about her and LoneStar, I knew she was likely in over her head. I wasn't going to lose another woman in my life, even if she did fuck me over."

Inside Meadows Manor, Kelly sat on an Artemis sectional sofa in a large living room by an oversized, ornate fireplace with her hands tied behind her back. She felt on the verge of a breakdown, wondering how she had ended up in this mess. Down a hall near the kitchen was Silus Kobol and four of his well-dressed bodyguards. Mr. Kobol was pacing back and forth, waiting to hear from the men that had been sent to the Holiday Inn to take out Chuck.

Nick Columbo suddenly came barreling into the kitchen from the outside patio. He had been on the phone and was now clearly in a panicked state. "Barreto's alive. They screwed it up!"

"Mmmm, I was afraid of that. How unfortunate," said Silus calmly.

"My days as Attorney General are over. We've gotta get out of here right now."

"Why's that?"

"They know we're here, in this house. They're on their way right now! You guys are going to have to set me up on one of those tropical islands that was promised to me if this all went sour. I can send for my wife when it's safe," said Nick.

"The extra money we advanced you... some went towards renting this house for us in your name?"

"Yes and that's why I'm done for. Please, Silus, let's go. We don't have a second to waste."

"Then that's it, Nick, You've done an exemplary job for us. You were a great Huckleberry," said Silus cynically.

"A what?"

"Insurance, Nick! Our insurance policy."

Mr. Kobol pointed his finger at the bodyguard closest to him, then pointed directly at the Attorney General. Without hesitation, the bodyguard pulled out his gun and directed it at Nick. *Pop, pop!* Two bullets entered Nick's portly stomach. He grabbed his bleeding abdomen, the gun still smoking.

He plummeted to the floor and cried, "Why?"

"This is a dog-eat-dog world," Silus said coldly. "Come, gentlemen, it's time for us to go."

As they walked past a petrified Kelly, one henchman said, "What about her, Mr. Kobol?"

"Leave her," Silus said. He looked directly at her, piercing her with his sinister eyes. "We'll meet again, Mrs. Barreto. I'm sure of it."

Kelly gasped as they left, her eyes watering in relief. Silus just had Nick shot, but he left her alive for another day.

Silus and his men jumped into the limo and drove down the driveway to exit the estate. Something suddenly alerted the driver. "Mr. Kobol, we got company. A helicopter is coming in behind us."

"Well, we can't have that," said Silus. "Stop and take care of it."

The driver put the vehicle in park. Two of Kobol's men got out with AR-15's and commenced firing the weapons at the helicopter in pursuit.

The chopper pilot shouted at the agent sitting next to him, "They're firing on us!"

Bullets hit the helicopter blades, then went through the windshield hitting the pilot in his right arm. The man screamed in pain. "I'm hit! I have to take her down!"

The helicopter wobbled and descended slowly towards the backyard of the mansion.

"That's the money shot, gentlemen. Let's get out of here," said Silus. The limo headed for the entrance and took a hard right towards the highway.

Mike, hiding across the main road, witnessed the helicopter make its emergency landing behind the house and saw Kobol's limo leaving. He called Chuck to give him the license plate number. Jed told Chuck to tell Mike to stay put and not follow the limo; he would call in the plate number right now to have it flagged and pursued.

"What if Kelly's in the car?" said Chuck.

"They won't get far. It's over, Chuck," said Jed.

Chuck bit the inside of his cheek, trying to keep it together. He just wanted to get to the mansion and to find Kelly there, alive. What she had done seemed unforgivable, but with her life in danger, he realized he still cared for her - maybe even loved her.

CHAPTER 29

DAY OF THE RECKONING
OCTOBER 2002

JACK BUFFORD HAD fallen behind in traffic when trying to follow Jed's slick maneuvers through back roads. As Jed approached Meadows Mansion, Mike came running over to the car window.

"A shitload of law enforcement just rolled in there, guys!" he said.

"Get in the car, Mike," said Jed. He got in the back seat and Jed sped down the driveway until they reached the end, where officers swarmed like ants. They got out of the car and Jed pulled out his badge so their access wouldn't be questioned. Chuck looked pretty roughed-up from the explosion they just came from.

He started yelling at the first police officer he saw. "Is there a woman in the house?!"

Jed showed him his credentials.

"Yeah, she's inside being seen. She's doing okay," said the officer.

Chuck was relieved and took off inside. Jed and Mike followed him.

"Kelly?" Chuck called. "Kelly!"

"Sir, she's in the next room," said a nearby officer as he gestured to it.

Chuck entered the room and saw his wife sitting on a couch drinking water. She saw him and her eyes immediately sparkled like bright, shiny diamonds.

"Chuck!" she exclaimed and put the water down. They ran to one another until the space between them closed and they embraced. Kelly kissed Chuck on the lips and he returned it.

"I love you, Chuck!" Kelly blurted. "Don't give up on us. I'll never ever do anything to hurt you again. And besides, you saved my life. The Chinese have a saying, you know."

"Oh yeah, what's that?" asked Chuck.

"Once you've saved a person's life, you're responsible for it forever."

He smirked slightly and pulled away from her. "Damn you, Kelly Ann. I gotta sort out my feelings first, I just can't...."

Jed interrupted by calling Chuck's name from another room. He followed the voice into the kitchen and found that Nick Columbo was on the floor, bleeding out. Other officers and agents were gathered around him. Jed knelt to talk with him. Chuck knew it all along; Nick was no good.

"Nick, who's behind all this? Who did this to you?" questioned Jed.

The Attorney General looked up, the light fading from his eyes, and saw Chuck standing over him with a smug look on his face. Nick looked back at Jed.

"Jed, his name is Thorn. He's everywhere. Chuck here is as good as dead!" Nick tried to smile, and then he was gone. No one in the room attempted to resuscitate him; nothing was worse than someone sworn to uphold the law gone dirty.

Jed looked up at Chuck, and upon seeing his expression, gave Chuck a disapproving look. "This is not funny."

"Looks like you're in charge now, Jethro!" said Chuck. Chuck's expression turned to one of humility and determination. "Whoever this Thorn guy is, make no mistake. He's going to be my new pet project!"

Jack finally made it to the mansion and walked into the kitchen. They had found the limo abandoned at a rest stop on the highway. They must have transferred to another vehicle. Jack still assured them the FBI would not let them get away. Jack changed the subject and asked Jed and Chuck to walk outside on the patio with him.

"Chuck, I'm going to need you to remain calm. There's another situation, and it is already under control as we speak," he began.

"What situation, Jack?" asked Chuck.

Kelly and Mike joined them on the patio.

"There's been a new and interesting development in the investigation into Leroy Stick. We now know how he got on your ranch without detection."

Chuck's eyes widened. "How?"

"Chuck, as I said, the situation is being handled as we speak."

"Give it to me straight, Jack. How did he get on the ranch?"

"Leroy had a younger brother, Jonathan Stick. When they were kids, they had gotten in some trouble for robbing a Burger King in Woodrow. The boys were separated from their parents and each other. Leroy was sent to a residential program for boys, and Jonathan was adopted by a family, the Cockneys."

Chuck's head started to spin again. How many surprises could one man take?

"Shit! I knew I recognized him. John Cockney, my landscaper, is Leroy Stick's brother."

"My God," Kelly whispered, her face turning an impossible shade paler. "Shalon's on the ranch with him right now!"

Jack tried to reassure them. "I've already called it in. The local police are on their way now to arrest him. Everyone can relax."

But it wasn't in Chuck's nature to relax. He looked out onto the backyard and saw the helicopter pilot on the ground being treated for his gunshot wound. Past the injured man sat the helicopter, and standing next to it was an angelic, smiling man wearing a bright red dress shirt and jeans. He blinked and the vision of his father disappeared.

Chuck jumped over the patio balcony and yelled, "Mike, take care of Kelly."

Jed instinctively followed him, jumping over the balcony as well. He stumbled, but recovered quickly, and gave chase.

"Chuck, where are you going?" Jed yelled ahead of him.

"Home!" he yelled back as he ran straight for the chopper.

As Chuck ran by the wounded pilot and the agent kneeling beside him, the agent yelled, "Hey! Where do you think you're going?"

Jed flashed his badge as he ran by. "Emergency situation!"

"You can't take that helicopter!" said the agent, incredulous.

"Call my office!" shouted Jed as he continued to run to catch up with Chuck.

Chuck jumped into the pilot's seat while Jed climbed into the passenger's seat.

Kelly looked at Mike. "Is he crazy?"

"Kelly, Chuck is one dynamic individual!"

"How fast can you get back to the ranch?" she asked.

"Let's go," he answered and they rushed out of the house.

"Wait, Mrs. Barreto, I have a few questions for you!" called Jack.

"I'll be at the ranch!"

At the ranch, Uncle Armond, Mitch, and Samantha were in the kitchen, listening to the police scanner and waiting by the phone to hear news from Chuck. The three of them were so absorbed in listening that they didn't hear someone enter the house. It startled them when a voice said, "Armond."

Uncle Armond turned around. "Oh, hey John, sorry. We didn't hear you come in. Are you done for today?"

"Well, about that... I have to give my immediate resignation. I have some family issues to tend to."

They were all taken aback at his sudden news. "Oh John, I'm so sorry. Is there anything we can do?" said Samantha.

"Ah, no, but thank you," he said as he turned towards the door.

"Well, John, I'm sure it would be alright with Chuck if you took a leave of absence. No need to quit."

Before John could respond to her, a loud, clear call came through the scanner.

"Dispatch to cars 54 and 51: proceed to Chuck Barreto's homestead. We have an APB for a John Cockney, the landscaper. Proceed with caution as he may be armed and dangerous. Do you copy?"

Armond, Mitch, and Samantha looked at John with mouths agape.

"Ah, shit," said John. He pulled out a gun from underneath the front of his shirt and pointed it at Mitch.

"Whoa, John, it's –"

"Shut up, Mitch! Armond, you got any rope or duct tape in here?"

"Yeah," said Armond. Rupert started barking viciously at John.

"Shut that mutt up!" John yelled at Sam. She took Rupert and held him close to her chest.

. . .

Jed put on a headset so he could talk to Chuck while they flew. He was scared out of his wits, hoping to God that Chuck really knew what he was doing. "Chuck, please stop. Just call Samantha first."

Chuck turned the ignition and the blades were spinning. "You got your milk money?"

"My what?" yelled Jed over the thrum of the blades.

"Ah, never mind," said Chuck.

"You can't do this. If we live, this is illegal on so many levels."

"When did that ever stop me? You can get out. I can go solo on this one."

Jed looked him in the eye. "Not a chance. We're still partners, right?"

Chuck nodded and winked. "Always. Hang tight to your britches. We're going for a ride!"

The helicopter lifted off the ground, swaying side to side. The FBI agent broke off from helping the injured pilot, and he and Jack Bufford went running after the chopper, screaming at Chuck to stop.

"Chuck, you sure you can fly this thing?" asked Jed.

"Nope!"

"What do you mean, no? What about landing?"

"Junior was getting ready to give me that lesson, but then I had to go into hiding. Don't worry, I'll improvise."

Jed's forehead was beaded with sweat. "What if you can't figure it out?"

"Put your head between your legs and kiss your ass goodbye," said Chuck.

The helicopter rose higher and higher, and the nose of the machine awkwardly dipped towards the ground. Jed began yelling at Chuck in a panicked state, "Uhh, Chuck... Chuck! We're going to crash!"

"No worries, Jethro," Chuck replied, calmly. "I just push this doohickey and this gizmo over here and..." Suddenly, the chopper straightened out. Chuck hit the throttle and off they went.

Jed held on tight.

At the ranch, things were heating up. When the first two police cruisers pulled in, they couldn't get close because John came out onto the front porch with his left arm around Samantha's neck, using her as a shield. He fired off a warning shot. The officer in the first vehicle stopped far enough back to not further agitate John, but close enough to see the house. They called in shots fired and for the dispatcher to send more backup.

The Chief approved the call for help from some of the surrounding towns because most of the local police force was still at the Holiday Inn. Niel Reeves also heard the call as he was still investigating the crime scene Jed and Jack left behind. He decided to break off from it to get to Chuck's ranch; his intuition told him it was linked.

One of the police officers at the ranch took out a bullhorn to try and talk John down. He could see that John still had a gun pointed at Samantha's head. He shouted through the horn, "What do you want, Mr. Cockney? Let the girl go. No one needs to get hurt."

"I want Chuck Barreto here or she dies!" screamed John.

The officer looked at his partner, confused. "Chuck Barreto? He's dead!"

Allan Miller had been hiding behind an oak tree to the left of the house, trying to get a good line of sight of John's head, but Samantha kept getting in the way. Cockney pulled her back and they went inside the house. Uncle Armond and Mitch were duct-taped in the spare room down the hall. Their wrists and legs were wrapped and they were lying on the floor. Rupert was also with them, crying and licking Armond's face.

"Rupert, stop! Stop, boy!" said Uncle Armond.

"Arm, I'm going to move my legs close to your hands. I have a buck knife wedged in my right boot. See if you can get your hand in there and pull it out," said Mitch as he squirmed on the floor.

Samantha looked out the kitchen window, feeling scared and trapped. Cockney knew one thing for sure- he wasn't going to prison. He had it in his mind, it was do or die. A light bulb came on in his puny brain.

"Give me your fucking phone!" John said to Sam. She pointed to it sitting on the kitchen table. "Pick it up and unlock it right now. Right now!" She unlocked it, her hands shaking, and handed it to him. John looked at the content on the phone and pointed the gun at her head. "Don't fucking move!"

John opened up a text message and smiled. "I knew he was still alive. Guess what? We're going to give your boyfriend a call!"

. . .

Chuck and Jed were well on their way to the ranch, and Chuck was getting more anxious about Samantha's safety. An alarm went off inside the helicopter and Jed, normally so tranquil, was anything but.

"Chuck, what's wrong? We're going to die!" said Jed.

Chuck took control of the throttle again and moved it until the sound went away. "Sorry, had to level her out."

"Sorry? Great Caesar's ghost! Lord help us!"

Chuck snickered. "Jed, I don't think I've ever seen you this way. Oh, look- there's an FM radio. Let's see if I can get my station."

"Music? Are you kidding me right now?"

"Music helps me focus."

Jed slapped his hand away. "I'll do it. What station do you want? You need to concentrate on flying!"

"Rock 102," said Chuck. Jed found the station. Chuck smiled, turned the volume up, and hit the throttle to increase their speed.

"Hey, little sister, what have you done/ Hey little sister, who's the only one/ Hey, little sister, who's your Superman/ Hey, little sister, who's the one you want/ Hey, little sister, shotgun/ It's a nice day to start again/ It's a nice day for a white wedding/ It's a nice day to start again."

Chuck said to Jed over the loud music and engine noise, "Look down there, Jethro."

"What is it?"

"My land, Indians Leap!"

Jed could not have cared less in the moment. He had bigger things on his mind, like staying alive. "Great!" he said sarcastically.

"Hey little sister, who is it you're with/ Hey little sister, what's your voice and wish?/ Hey little sister, shotgun (Oh yeah)..."

Chuck's singing along to the song was interrupted when he felt his cell phone vibrating in his pants pocket. He pulled it out and turned the radio volume down to answer.

"Hey Sam!" he said excitedly, relieved that she was still safe. But it wasn't her voice he heard.

"Sorry, Chucko! It's not your little Shandi look-alike," John sneered.

Chuck's fear was being realized. "John?"

"Boy, are you one dumb fuck. All this time I have been working for you, and you never recognized me!"

" John, I–"

"Shut up and listen," said John menacingly. "You killed my brother and then you fucks covered it up!" John raised his voice. "What'd you do with him?"

"John, I didn't kill Leroy. I don't even know what you're talking ab– "

John interrupted again. "Barreto, you better get here quick or your little girlfriend is dead! Do you hear me?"

"John, if you touch a single blond hair, I'll kill you!"

Chuck hung up and threw the phone over his shoulder. Jed didn't say a word. He knew the look on Chuck's face so well. When he was furious with an inmate, Chuck would take out one of his handy rubber bands to put his long hair into a ponytail before a skirmish. Yeah, that was the look he had right now. Jed wanted to talk him down a little so he wouldn't do anything rash that would get either one of them hurt before they could even attempt a rescue.

"Hey, buddy, she's going to be alright," said Jed.

"Jed, do me a favor, hold on to this stick for a second and don't move it."

"That's not a good idea."

"Just hold on to it, please. Or I'll let it go anyway."

Jed nervously took over the control and Chuck reached into his pants pocket to pull out a rubber band. He quickly tied his hair up and took the control back from Jed.

Jed couldn't help but laugh. "Old habits die hard, huh?"

Chuck didn't respond. He had sunk deeper into his thoughts. Nothing was going to distract him.

He was filled with mixed emotions when he thought about Kelly and Samantha, both because of what they had put him through and how he felt towards them. A part of him still loved Kelly, but he was also madly in love with Samantha. Chuck was relieved that Kelly was safe, but sick to his stomach with worry about Sam. He thought to himself, *Why is it so hard to keep the women I love safe?*

Jed brought him back to the present as he pointed ahead of them. "Chuck, the ranch!"

"I see it. I'm going to put her down right over there in that clearing," Chuck said, motioning at a spot on the grass fairly close to the main house. They could see about twenty police cruisers clustered at the main entrance.

Jed eased up as he felt the helicopter near the ground; Chuck landed her with more confidence than he had originally let on. Either he had been joking earlier with Jed about his ability, or he was so focused that he figured it out naturally. The chopper landed without difficulty and Jed let out a temporary breath of relief. Now they had to worry about the next problem.

Chuck turned off the helicopter. The engine began winding down and the blades slowly came to a halt. Chuck and Jed were sitting in silence when John Cockney came walking out of the house, his left arm again around Samantha and the right holding a gun to her head.

Chuck saw red with Sam in John's grip as his hostage. He walked out into the middle of the field with her between the police and the helicopter. John could see Chuck sitting in the pilot's seat.

"Wow, Chuck. You're a pilot now, too? Don't you just do it all. Well, you, your girlfriend, and I are all going to take a ride in it together," said John. Chuck didn't respond. "Did you fucking hear me?"

Chuck looked at Jed. "You got my back?"

"You have to ask?"

"OK, be ready." Chuck got out of the helicopter and started to slowly walk towards Samantha and John.

Inside, Mitch and Uncle Armond had managed to free themselves with the pocket knife and made their way to the front door. Mitch couldn't find his gun; John had taken it from him before he tied them up.

Chuck was cautiously walking when he heard Allan whisper to him from behind the tree. "Chuck, don't! He's crazy!"

The police officers waited, watching the scene play out. They couldn't fire on John as long as he had a weapon on Samantha. Jed waited in the helicopter with his hand on his gun, ready for action.

"Stop right there, asshole!" John yelled at Chuck. "Not one step further!"

Chuck paused thirty-five yards away, then took a few more steps forward as he held his arms open wide across the open air as if he was ready to sacrifice himself, "I'm tired of people trying to kill me and the ones I love, John! On this day, it all ends!"

Uncle Armond opened the screen door and yelled at his nephew, "No, Chuck, no!"

He had forgotten about Rupert, who bolted out of the door and ran straight at John to attack him. He, too, wanted to protect Sam. John panicked, took the gun from Samantha's head, and fired a shot at Rupert, missing him. Chuck seized the moment and pulled out the glock that was wedged in the waistline of his jeans. He was so fast when he drew his weapon, no one noticed at first.

There was a loud *POP!* and John let go of Samantha, falling backwards onto the ground. Sam looked at John and saw a wound in the middle of his beady eyes. Rupert jumped up onto Samantha, kissing her. Chuck ran to her and embraced her. Samantha cried happy tears.

"I gotcha. You're okay, Sam. It's over. I'm never leaving you again!" said Chuck as he kissed the top of her head.

"What happens now?" she said as she leaned slightly away from him.

"Now? Now, Sammy, we live happily ever after!"

"You know what?"

"What?"

"I'm crazy about you!"

"I know!" Chuck said as he smiled. Sam laughed and gave him a small jab in the chest.

Chuck looked over at John's body where Jed and Allan were checking his pulse.

"Well?" he asked.

"I think he'll be joining his boneheaded brother in hell," said Allan.

Reeves and other officers ran over to the scene. Uncle Armond and Mitch came over, too.

"Hey, Meathead. Way to go!" Uncle Armond clapped him on the back.

Chuck smiled at him. "Thanks, Unc." Dave was standing in the crowd of people, watching next to Candie, when he said to her, "I fucking knew Jed was up to something! The dude was alive all along!"

Chuck and Samantha turned their attention back to each other, seemingly unaware of everyone else. Jed cleared his throat to draw Chuck's attention. He stopped kissing Sam and looked at his partner. Jed gestured for Chuck to look further behind him where Kelly stood next to Mike. She watched Chuck and her sister embracing, brokenhearted.

"I have to find a way to get him back, Mike," she said, her lips trembling. "I can't do this right now. Can you take me back to my apartment?"

Mike nodded.

Chuck looked over at Jed, as if waiting for Jed to tell him what to do next.

"I can't help you out on this one, partner," said Jed.

Chuck was in turmoil over his dilemma. He puts his thoughts on hold when Niel Reeves yelled, "Hey, you two!"

Jed and Chuck looked at Niel.

"Yeah, I'm talking to you two idiots. Do you think you can stay out of trouble for the rest of the day, or do I need to lock you both up?"

"Ah, Detective, do us all a favor and lock them up. Please!" joked Uncle Armond and they all laughed, releasing some of the tension of the day.

Suddenly, the helicopter radio kicked back on, playing loudly.

"Never settle for less than gold/
You're the best that the world will know/
No one'd ever guess how far you'd go/
You're the greatest, the greatest that ever was/
You're a star, you really are/
You're the one shining bright from all the rest in the dark/
A champion with nerves of stone/
You trained for this since the day you were born/
Full of pain, full of sweat, full of tears/
But never giving up or giving in to fear/
A quick prayer for the ones you love/
Props to the Gods as they watch from above/
Your enemies line up for miles/
You crush them all with your hope and a smile/
When you win, put your fists in the air/
Your fans cheer you on while your victims stare/
So go all the way/
And they will scream your name/
You're the greatest, the greatest that ever was/
Your legend will never die/
You'll never quit till the finish line/
Find your strength, feel alive/
Find your power deep inside/
Live forever, never die/
You're the best that the world will know."

EPILOG
NOVEMBER 2002

A DOOR OPENS to a darkened room. A man is sitting at an antique, golden oak desk alone in the room. The mysterious man behind the desk has suave thick, gray hair. He's a distinguished gentleman, in his early fifties, wearing bifocal glasses. A lamp provides just enough light so that he can see *The Washington Post*. He reaches behind him and grabs a long wand attached to the Venetian blinds. He twists the rod just enough to let a small amount of sunlight into the room.

"Come in, Silus. It's been three weeks. You finally made it back safely, I see," said the man.

"Yes, sir. We had to use Senator Karrington's yacht to get out of the harbor undetected."

"Well, that's the least he could do for us."

"We lost our inside man. The Attorney General is dead and we are off course in this battle against Barreto and Jed Ferrari."

"That's unfortunate. Are we going to lose the war against these two interesting individuals?"

"No, sir, of course not."

"Good. Why are you still standing here? No one sleeps until these two pestilences have been disposed of permanently."

"Yes, Mr. Thorn."

Silus turns and closes the door as he leaves the shadowy room.

ACKNOWLEDGEMENTS

TO MY COVER artist, Lou Tulik, who believed in this project and worked tirelessly to bring the images of my characters to stunning visual life. Thanks for your patience, Lou.

Thank you to Palmetto Publishing, Nicole, Kristin, Erin for the magnificent job on this book and helping me make this dream come true for me.

To my Editor-in-Chief, Briana Buffone: without you, there's no possible way I could have achieved this or gotten this far. A genius extraordinaire with words, structure, development, and more. You turned my words and ideas into something special, making the world of Chuck a reality. I hope to work with you on future books.

I searched for an editor for months after finishing my first draft, frustrated with not knowing who to trust or where to turn when my friend and partner's wife, Maryellen, found the perfect person for me to work with. So, a big, grateful thanks to you.

To Gary's Asylum Fitness and his wonderful staff, and Bill and Paulo's Family chiropractors, for keeping me fit and pain-free :)

To all my brothers and sisters throughout my career who have had my back and I theirs. What a ride!

My good friend Junior, "Landon, hey Landon- join the expedition!"

Many thanks to my good Uncle Armond #2, who spent decades with me laughing, joking, and talking about classic films; his charm, the inspiration for a character in this novel.

A thanks to my aunt Ellie who gave me valuable advice on writing my book early on when I was unsure how to proceed with this endeavor.

I'd like to thank my siblings, Gary and Stacey, along with my daughters, Paige, Candie, Alicia, and Jess. Oh, my beautiful family!

A thanks to my Mom who brought me into the world, raised me on Fonix, taught me right from wrong, and so much more. Thanks, Mom!

A raised wineglass to my lovely lady and wife, Cheryl Ann, who's been on this great journey with me for over a decade and will be for many more to come.

And finally, to my longtime friend and partner, Teddy Beriau. A commodity that can't be bought or sold, and the adventure continues!

ABOUT THE AUTHOR

BORN IN 1967, I was brought up by two hard-working entrepreneurs. My parents raised me in a world of opportunity, and I witnessed firsthand the legacy built around us. Growing up in the '70s was a special time for us kids: being in rock bands, playing sports, and driving fast muscle cars.

After high school, I worked on airplanes- yes it's true! In the early nineties, I decided to go to college for law enforcement. While raising a family, I worked as a part-time police officer, in a lock-up for juveniles, and then eventually went on to work for over two decades as a corrections officer.

Now, finally, as I prepare for retirement, I decided to write a fictional, epic story to entertain the masses. Currently, I am working on a sequel to this novel and am excited to continue to write about these characters. I hope it pays appropriate tribute to the types of novels I myself have enjoyed and that all will love this read!

CPSIA information can be obtained
at www.ICGtesting.com
Printed in the USA
BVHW071500310522
638503BV00013B/692